PRAISE FOR

THE HOUSE ON PRIMROSE POND

"An intricate story full of family mysteries, heart, and hope. Every time I closed this book I couldn't wait to open it again."

—Amy Sue Nathan, author of *The Good Neighbor* and *The Glass Wives*

"Prepare to be beguiled. *The House on Primrose Pond* proves that the past—warmest memories to darkest secrets—can be the key to unlock the lost treasures of the present. McDonough writes of the heart's ability to love beyond betrayal, death, and all of history's storytelling."

—Sarah McCoy, *New York Times* and international bestselling author of *The Mapmaker's Children*

"Filled with characters as beautifully drawn as their New England setting, *The House on Primrose Pond* offers a fascinating and tender journey of a recently widowed woman who returns to the landscape of her youth for comfort, only to face a family mystery that may turn her already topsy-turvy world upside down even further. Atmospheric and deeply romantic, McDonough's latest is exactly the sort of novel I long to lose myself in."

—Erika Marks, author of *The Guest House* and *It Comes in Waves*

continued . . .

Written by today's freshest new talents and selected by New American Library, NAL Accent novels touch on subjects close to a woman's heart, from friendship to family to finding our place in the world. The Conversation Guides included in each book are intended to enrich the individual reading experience, as well as encourage us to explore these topics together—because books, and life, are meant for sharing.

Visit us online at penguin.com.

"Pulls you into the charm of small-town New England where Susannah Gilbert is a single mom trying to start again while she handles it all. Filled with secrets, history, gossip, friendships, and sexy romance—pour yourself a cup of cocoa and get lost and found again on Primrose Pond!"   —Marci Nault, author of *The Lake House*

"How well do we really know our own histories or those of the people we love? In a blazingly original novel, McDonough uncovers the mysteries of marriage, connection—and possible murder—and the tug of the past on the present. A gorgeous, sweeping read with a gloriously beating heart."

—Caroline Leavitt, *New York Times* bestselling author of *Is This Tomorrow* and *Pictures of You*

"A beautifully written story about loss, the power of family ties, and finding love in places you'd least expect. Once caught in the emotional currents of her story, you'll not be released until the last, satisfying page."   —Kellie Coates Gilbert, author of *A Woman of Fortune*

"An unforgettable story of love and redemption, and finding your way back to what matters most, this perfect combination of mystery, history, and romance will keep you guessing until the very last page, and then regretting that you've reached the end."

—Roberta Gately, author of *Lipstick in Afghanistan*

"Totally engaging . . . a well-crafted and compelling read."

—Daphne Kalotay, author of *Russian Winter* and *Sight Reading*

"At times heartbreaking yet full of hope, *The House on Primrose Pond* is a deeply moving portrait of grief, healing, and how the past often carries the secrets that can make us feel whole again."

—Natalia Sylvester, author of *Chasing the Sun*

ALSO BY YONA ZELDIS McDONOUGH

You Were Meant for Me
Two of a Kind
A Wedding in Great Neck

THE
HOUSE
ON
PRIMROSE
POND

Yona Zeldis McDonough

NAL
ACCENT

FIC
McDONOUGH

NAL ACCENT

Published by New American Library,
an imprint of Penguin Random House LLC
375 Hudson Street, New York, New York 10014

This book is an original publication of New American Library.

First Printing, February 2016

Copyright © Yona Zeldis McDonough, 2016
Conversation Guide copyright © Penguin Random House, 2016
Cover photographs: house © Alberto Biscaro/Masterfile; windows © Øyvind Markussen/plainpicture/
NTB scanpix; trees © Marco Maccarini/E+/Getty Images; couple © Maridav/Shutterstock Images; lake
and sky © Andrew Mayovskyy/Shutterstock Images

For more information about Penguin Random House, visit penguin.com.

Names: McDonough, Yona Zeldis.
Title: The house on Primrose Pond/Yona Zeldis McDonough.
Description: New York City: New American Library, [2016]
Identifiers: LCCN 2015035957 | ISBN 9780451475381 (softcover)
Subjects: LCSH: Women novelists—Fiction. | Family secrets—Fiction. |
Domestic fiction. | BISAC: FICTION/Contemporary Women. | FICTION/Family Life.
| FICTION/Psychological.
Classification: LCC PS3613.C39 H68 2016 | DDC 813/.6—dc23
LC record available at https://protect-us.mimecast.com/s/pVWoB6C881MgIe

LIBRARY OF CONGRESS CATALOGING-IN-PUBLICATION DATA:

Printed in the United States of America
10 9 8 7 6 5 4 3 2 1

Designed by Kelly Lipovich

Penguin
Random
House

For Kenneth Silver,
who taught me that history really is a narrative

THE
HOUSE
ON
PRIMROSE
POND

PROLOGUE

It's two p.m. on a freakishly warm afternoon in January. Susannah Gilmore reluctantly looks up from her laptop. Standing in the doorway of her home office is her husband, Charlie. "Have you seen what it's doing outside?" he asks. She nods, attention drifting back to the screen. "It's sixty-nine degrees."

"The January thaw, right?" She's read about this someplace, though she can't recall where.

"Whatever. We should take advantage of it, though. Let's go for a bike ride before the kids get home."

"I wish I could." She turns to him. At six foot three, he's lanky and lean. Ginger hair, great smile, and, under his shirt, a constellation of freckles dotting his shoulders and upper back. Forty-three, yet still so boyish. "But I've got a deadline."

"One afternoon is not going to make or break you. Not even an afternoon. An hour and a half, max. Carpe diem and all that."

She smiles at him. "I really can't. But you go."

"It'll be more fun with you."

"Next time," she says. "I promise."

He sighs and Susannah turns back to her work. But Charlie remains standing in the doorway.

"What?" she says, trying to conceal her impatience.

"Are you sure?"

She hesitates. But the chapter, the deadline, the meal she'll need to prepare in a few hours—the perpetually revolving domestic wheel keeps her rooted to her chair.

"All right." He sounds a bit deflated but finally heads toward the stairs. Susannah barely registers his leaving. She wants to get back to the novel she's writing, a novel in which a minor English noblewoman has become ensnared in a dangerous court intrigue. Tapping on her keypad, Susannah follows Lady Whitmore along vast, tapestry-lined corridors and up curving flights of steep stone steps. Now Lady Whitmore enters the bedchamber of the young and essentially powerless queen and closes the heavy oak door behind her. Will she be able to help the sovereign outsmart the cunning noblemen who want her out of the way, making room for an even more pliant pawn?

Sometime after three o'clock, Susannah registers her son Jack's arrival home, and a short time later, her daughter Cally's. Leaving Lady Whitmore, Susannah switches off the computer and goes downstairs. Time to start dinner.

As the sky darkens—despite the warmth, it *is* still winter, and dusk comes early—she moves around the narrow but cozy kitchen of her Park Slope brownstone, getting the meal together.

Charlie built this room almost single-handedly when they moved in nearly twenty years ago. The wood for the countertops was reclaimed from the bar of an old Irish pub that was going out of business; the floor tile was a manufacturer's overstock that he'd bought for next to nothing. That was so like Charlie—he could see possibilities in the most unlikely of places, and he was a consummate craftsman, able to turn his vision into a reality.

Susannah checks the clock on the stove. Charlie said an hour and a half and it's been more than three hours. He must have gotten sidetracked. She pictures him peddling up the hill on his green bicycle, exertion making his cheeks glow pink. He'll be all excited about his outing, and eager to tell her where he's been, what he's seen. He really *is* a big kid. Four days a week, he teaches illustration at the School of Visual Arts in Manhattan; on Fridays, he works at home. His current project is a picture book about intergalactic travel, and the preliminary drawings of the spacecraft—sleek and silvery blue—are pinned up around his studio.

She likes having him home on a day when the children are not here; sometimes she fixes them a special lunch or sometimes they go upstairs for what Charlie loves best: daytime sex. "I'm an artist," he always said. "And for an artist, there's no light like daylight."

As Susannah bastes the chicken, she feels a small tug of guilt. Maybe she *should* have gone with him today. She'll make it up to him, she decides. She'll work extra hard this week and next Friday she'll take the whole day off. She'll bring him breakfast in bed and then climb back in with him. He'll like that. So will she.

"Where's Dad?" Cally walks into the kitchen and begins setting the table.

"He went for a bike ride; he should be home soon." It's almost six o'clock, the time they usually eat dinner. The roast chicken is ready and Susannah debates whether to keep it in the oven or take it out; does she want it dry or does she want it cold?

"He's on Dad time," Cally says. But she's smiling. They all know Charlie is dreamy and easily distracted: by the sight of a splashy sunset that tinges the clouds with gold, by an old buddy who wants him to stop by for a beer, by a picture he just has to take with his iPhone. Jack, who has just walked in, goes over to the cutlery drawer and is now handing silverware to his sister; they are a good team. "Well, I hope he gets here soon. I'm starved."

"Me too." Cally straightens a place mat.

"He will," says Susannah, though she is pricked by annoyance. She takes the chicken out of the oven. Cold is fixable. Dry is not. Both Cally and Jack have washed their hands and are sitting down, waiting. Everything is ready; everyone is here. Except her husband. She picks up her phone, and as she could have predicted, the call goes straight to voice mail; Charlie routinely turns off the ringer on his phone. But it is now four hours since he left. Couldn't he have at least called to say he was going to be late? "Where the hell is he?" She does not actually mean to say this aloud.

"Don't curse at Daddy!" Cally scolds.

"I'm not cursing at him." Susannah is instantly contrite. "I'm just . . . cursing."

"Well, you shouldn't!"

"You're right, sweet pea. He probably stopped to get something." Charlie is apt to do that—tulips for the table, or an extravagant dessert. "Remember last week when he brought home that salted-caramel pie?"

"Don't even talk about pie!" says Jack.

Then the bell rings. Oh, good—Charlie's home. Obviously he forgot his keys—he does that a lot—and she hurries to let him in. But instead of Charlie, apologizing profusely, leaning down to kiss her, pressing his offering into her arms, she finds two police officers standing at the door. One has a blond crew cut showing from under his blue hat; the other is a dark-skinned woman. "Mrs. Miller?" She flashes her badge. "May we come in?" Susannah tenses but steps aside. "Your husband, Charles—"

"My husband isn't Charles. He's Charlie." Susannah seizes on their mistake; whatever they think their mission here is, they have gotten it all wrong. And she isn't Mrs. Miller anyway. She kept Gilmore, her maiden name, the one her grandfather Isaac Goldblatt decided would help him move more easily through the world.

"There's been an accident. It was in Queens and—"

"What kind of accident?" Susannah is aware that Cally and Jack are standing close behind her.

"Bicycle." The word is delivered by the young blond officer. "Your husband was thrown off. He sustained a serious head injury."

"Queens? What would he be doing in Queens?" Charlie barely knows where Queens is; they joke about this occasionally. But the words "head injury" send her panicked glance over to the row of hooks by the door. Suspended from one of them is the expensive, glitter-flecked helmet she bought Charlie for his last birthday, the one he swears up and down that he'll wear—and then almost never does.

The two officers look at each other, and in that look Susannah knows everything. She will not let herself believe it; still, her gaze is pulled almost magnetically back to the helmet. Charlie thinks it is an encumbrance; he wears it only when she reminds him. But today she didn't remind him. Today she'd been busy and wanted to get back to work.

"I think maybe you should sit down," says the female cop.

There is a sickening numbness gathering around her, a horrible, this-can't-be-real feeling that she desperately wants to swat away. But Susannah allows herself to be led to the table. Cally and Jack silently follow. "How bad is he?"

The officer shakes her head. "I'm sorry. The injury was fatal. By the time the ambulance got there, he was already gone." There is a pause before she adds, in a low voice, "We'll need you to identify the body."

Jack starts sobbing. Cally emits a single, strangled sound. But Susannah cannot speak. Identify the body? *Charlie's* body? It's just not possible. He was standing there, in her office, mere hours ago. *It'll be more fun with you,* he had said. Why hadn't she gone with him? *Why?*

Jack is crying noisily but Cally marches over to the row of hooks, takes down the helmet, and thrusts it in front of her mother. "He wasn't wearing it."

"No," says Susannah. "He wasn't." The helmet has a reinforced safety strap and an impervious, mocking gleam. She turns her head away so she doesn't have to see it anymore.

"You didn't remind him." There is recrimination in her words. Also, a cold, adult-sounding fury. "It's your fault. You let Daddy get killed!" And with that, she bolts from the room. The officers stand with their heads bowed, and Jack continues to sob. Susannah cannot move, and the sounds of Jack's continued weeping, the blond officer's abashed cough, recede. All she can hear, in a relentless, repetitive loop, are her husband's last words: *Are you sure?*

ONE

One year later

They were driving on I-95 and had just crossed the state line into New Hampshire when the snow started falling. Hitting the windshield like cats' paws, the fat white flakes seemed to outpace the wipers, which had a wonky, syncopated rhythm—*click, click CLACK, click CLICK, clack.* The sound was mildly alarming and Susannah knew she had better get them looked at—soon.

The snow was pretty, picturesque even, the kind of snowfall that made her want to curl up under a blanket and get comfy with a cup of cocoa and a Jane Austen novel. Or a shot of bourbon and a rerun of *Law & Order: Special Victims Unit.* But Susannah was not at home, where she could choose her opiates: chocolate or alcohol, nineteenth-century literature or twenty-first-century crime drama. No, it was New Year's Day and she was on the road with her two fatherless children, heading toward Eastwood, New

Hampshire, and a house she had not been to in more than twenty years. They had already been on the road for over four hours and had another hour to go. Which, with this weather, might very well turn out to be more.

"Do you think it will be snowing when we get to Eastwood?" said Jack.

"I'm not sure," Susannah said. The small town where they were headed was midway between coastal Portsmouth and the state capital in Concord; she had not heard a local weather report.

"I hope it snows, like, ten inches," he said. "Then we can build a fort. Dad used to build the best forts . . ."

"Well, Dad is dead." This zinger was delivered by Cally, who at sixteen had cornered the market on snark.

"I know Dad is dead," Jack said. He turned to look out the window, where the snow kept falling from a numb gray sky. "Lavender is the state flower of New Hampshire," he said. "The state bird is the purple finch. Of the thirteen original colonies, New Hampshire was the first to declare its independence from England—six months before the Declaration of Independence was signed."

"What are you talking about?" Cally asked.

He showed her his phone. "I'm on the New Hampshire Fun Facts Web site. Want to hear more?"

"There's nothing fun about them," said Cally. "Could you please stop?"

"The first potato planted in the United States was at Londonderry Common Field in 1719. Alan Bartlett Shepard, Jr., the first American to travel in space, was from East Derry, New Hampshire. The New Hampshire state motto is *Live free or die*."

"I said stop!" Cally punched his arm and Jack fell silent.

"Cally!" Susannah abruptly pulled over to the highway's shoulder, causing a volley of honks from the cars behind her. "Are you okay?" she asked Jack.

"I'm okay." He rubbed the place where Cally had hit him.

"I can't believe you punched him," Susannah said to her daughter.

Cally was silent, but her expression—blazing, furious, accusatory—said it all. Looking at it, Susannah felt her anger drain away, leaving her utterly defeated.

Cally really thought her mother was partially responsible for her father's death and that their move to New Hampshire was something she had designed specifically as a way to ruin her life. Susannah understood her daughter's need to lay blame. The alternative—that the world was an unpredictable place in which random and terrible things could and did happen—was too scary. "There's no need to attack your brother," she said more quietly.

"Fine. Whatever." Cally put in her earbuds and retreated to the cocoon of her iPhone.

Susannah waited for a break in the stream of cars to get back to the road. "Go on—read me more fun facts about New Hampshire," she said to Jack.

"That's okay. Maybe they're not as much fun as I thought."

"Please?" she wheedled, but Jack didn't respond. Sometimes that ever present affability of his could be a problem. Sometimes he was *too* easy, too willing to give in.

Then Cally asked, for what might have been the tenth—or hundredth—time: "Why do we have to move up here in the middle of *winter*? Why couldn't we have at least waited until school let out?"

"Because the buyers for the house were offering all cash, Cally." Susannah tried to keep her tone even; she'd explained this before. "Do you realize what that means? No waiting for a bank to approve a mortgage or not. Just all the money—ours. And in the bank for the future. Your future."

"My future in the woods," muttered Cally. "Big whoop."

They continued along I-95 without speaking for a while, the snow on the car piling up faster and faster and the road getting icier and icier. Susannah had to slow down; at this rate they wouldn't be there until after dark, a panic-inducing thought since she did not know if she could find the house at night, even with the GPS. Then she noticed that the needle on the fuel gauge was low; she'd have to stop for gas. Another delay. As soon as she saw the Shell sign, she eased the minivan onto the exit ramp, pulled up to the gas pump—maybe someone could have a look at those wipers—and gave the kids each a ten-dollar bill to use at the convenience store.

"Can I buy a Heineken?" Cally said.

"You'd drink beer in the car? With Mom right there?" Jack was incredulous.

"I was making a joke." Cally's contempt was obvious.

"Go," Susannah ordered. "Before I take back my offer."

The gas station attendant made some minor adjustments to the wipers—"I'd have those checked out when you get home, ma'am"— and filled the tank. Cally and Jack emerged from the store, and they were on the road again in minutes. Jack had bought an outsized bag of licorice and some chips; he was alternating between them. Cally had bought no food, only a couple of fashion magazines. She had already been plotting out a life as a hip, urban-inspired designer. But she was convinced her plan would be thwarted by a move to Eastwood, New Hampshire, a place, she took great care to inform Susannah, where there would be no street fashion, *because there were no streets.*

The traffic thinned out and, to Susannah's great relief, the snow began to taper off. As Cally pored over the glossy, bright pages, Jack settled into one of his marathon naps; he might sleep until they got there. Susannah actually shared Cally's distaste for the Granite State; she had no desire to sell her Park Slope brownstone and move. But without Charlie, she had to concede that selling the house—whose value had increased astronomically in the years they'd lived there—made a lot of financial sense. Charlie's ninety-year-old father lived in a retirement community in Florida; he could not be of much help. Her own parents had died, within a year of each other, when Jack was a baby, and they had left her the mortgage-free house in Eastwood. Apart from a single summer when she was a teenager, Susannah had never actually lived in it, though; it had always been rented out to a series of tenants.

All that was about to change; the last tenants had moved out two weeks ago and Susannah and her children were about to move in. Living was much cheaper in New Hampshire and state taxes were nonexistent, which meant that Charlie's modest pension and life insurance policy, along with her even more modest income as a writer of historical fiction for Out of the Past Press would go much further.

It was almost five o'clock when they drove into town. Nothing looked familiar at first. She peered out the window, trying her best to make out the row of small brick buildings that made up the main street. A darkened storefront with a big window kindled a memory. That was the ice cream shop where she had gone with Trevor Bailey. Trevor had been her sort-of boyfriend the only summer she'd spent here. They would often drive into town and sit in front of that shop with their cones. He always ordered the same flavor—coffee—which used to irritate her; didn't he ever want to try anything new?

As she slowed the car, she saw the shop no longer sold ice cream, but frozen yogurt. Sign of the times. She kept driving. The drugstore where she'd bought Tampax and tubes of Bain de Soleil tanning lotion—with a mere SPF 8 back then—was now some kind of exercise studio, and the office of the *Eastwood Journal*, the local paper where her mother had once worked, was now a store that appeared to sell healing crystals and scented candles. There was a pizza place, open, and she stopped in quickly to get a pie. The kids munched on their slices in the dark, but her own oily, congealed wedge sat untouched beside her.

As Susannah turned off the main street, the road started to look more recognizable; there was a huge old oak tree she remembered, and soon she came to a three-story house, mint green clapboard, with black shutters and a sloping garden off to one side and a meadow with a barn on the other. Another landmark.

The minivan rounded a curve and then there was a turn down a pocked and bumpy dirt road, now covered with packed snow and chunks of ice. The road had been plowed, but badly; she was glad she'd thought to have snow tires put on the minivan before the trip. At the very end of the road was the house on Primrose Pond.

Dark brown, two finished stories with an open attic room under the shingled roof. There was a screened-in porch on the pond side, not visible from the road. God, it looked so small. Dreary too. Why had she ever thought it would be a good idea to come up here in the dead of winter? That all-cash offer had blinded her to every other consideration. But she couldn't share any of this with her kids; she felt compelled to be a cheerleader for the new life she'd dragged them into. She pulled up, and Cally jumped out of the car even before Susannah had switched off the ignition.

"Where are you going?" Cally ignored her and kept walking. As Susannah and Jack unloaded the minivan, Cally rapidly circled the house once, twice, a third time. Susannah, digging in her purse for the keys, let it go. The lights downstairs were off and she silently upbraided Mabel Dunfee, who'd been hired to clean after the tenants left, for not remembering to leave them on as she'd asked.

The door creaked slightly; it would need to be oiled. Or something. Susannah and Jack went inside with their bags; the movers would be here with the rest of their things tomorrow. Cally, who had reappeared, followed behind. Susannah didn't even realize how uncomfortable her daughter's pacing had made her until she'd stopped.

"The kitchen is so big," Jack said. "Bigger than our kitchen in Brooklyn."

"But it's a dump." Cally looked around with palpable distaste. "No dishwasher. That fridge—it's ancient. And look at the sink— does it even have running water?"

"Of course there's running water." Susannah walked over and turned on the tap. After a gurgle and some spurting sounds, some brownish liquid trickled out. Linnie Ashcroft, the Realtor who had been in charge of renting the place, hadn't mentioned this. Neither had Mabel Dunfee. Yet another thing Susannah would have to deal with. Jack walked over to the fridge and opened the door. Even though he was just thirteen, that legendary teenage-boy appetite had started to kick in. "Look—there's food. Where did it come from?"

"Mrs. Dunfee, I suppose." Susannah walked over to inspect. A dozen eggs, a stick of butter, milk, bacon, orange juice, and a loaf of bread. She closed the refrigerator door, making a mental note to reimburse Mabel when she saw her next.

"Mom, I'm still hungry," said Jack.

"There's not a whole lot here, but I can make some toast." She looked over at Cally. "You too?" Cally shook her head and wandered off, presumably to inspect the rest of the house. Susannah moved around the kitchen. As Jack had pointed out, it was certainly big.

But she didn't like the table, and the chairs were even worse. Well, her own things would be arriving soon and the room would look better then.

She took out the bread and butter, then rooted around the cupboards until she found a bottle of cinnamon sugar. Decidedly crusty around the rim, but still serviceable. She'd make the kids a snack and they would feel better. And if they felt better, she would feel better too. What was the line? A Jewish mother was only as happy as her least happy child. And despite the name that obscured her origins, Susannah was a Jewish mother.

The toaster had four slots; she adjusted the dial and filled them all. But just as she pressed the lever down, the kitchen—and all the rest of the rooms on that floor—went suddenly, totally black.

TWO

"Mom?" Jack's panicked voice cut through the darkness. "What happened?"

"I must have blown a fuse; maybe it was the toaster." Susannah fumbled around with the cord and managed to unplug the damn thing.

"What's going on?" Cally had come into the kitchen, her irritation obvious.

"Mom blew a fuse," Jack reported.

"Oh, great," said Cally.

"It's not a big deal." But Susannah did not know where the circuit breakers were, and finding them was not going to be fun.

"Maybe there's a flashlight," Jack said.

"Flashlight! Of course!" Susannah smiled in the dark. That was Jack all over. Don't bitch about the problem; find a solution. She began opening cupboards and drawers, her eyes gradually adjusting. And under the sink was a high-powered flashlight; to her relief, its batteries were intact. "Now we're cooking!" she said. Then, looking at the unplugged toaster, she added, "Well, not exactly cooking . . ." Using the beam of the flashlight, she managed to butter several slices of bread and sprinkle them with cinnamon sugar. Standing in the darkened room, she crammed a slice into her mouth; she had not eaten any of the pizza and was now ravenous.

Once she was sated, Susannah could focus on the circuit breakers. Maybe she and Jack could look for them. He was hunkered down in the living room, gobbling a slice of bread in front of the fireplace. The fireplace! Of course. Why hadn't she thought of it sooner? There were logs stacked neatly on the hearth, and another trip to the kitchen yielded a box of matches. Pretty soon she had a decent little blaze going, and the primal warmth exerted by the dancing flames lured even supercilious Cally back into the circle. For the next few minutes, they all sat gazing at the popping logs as they polished off the rest of the bread.

"That was delicious." Jack burped. "Sorry!"

"I hope we're not going to have to live in the dark all winter. It's like the Stone Ages in here." Cally, who had not eaten any of the bread, was pressing her fingertips to the sugar-dusted plate and licking them.

"Of course not." Susannah's tone sounded sharper than she'd intended. But things were difficult enough, and Cally's unending bad attitude only made them worse. "Why don't you get your jackets?" she said in a gentler tone. "I want to show you something." There was still that circuit breaker she had to find, but she needed to do this first.

They tossed their balled-up napkins into the fire, got their jackets, and followed her out onto the screened-in porch. She knew that beyond the winter storm window was the silent, black expanse of Primrose Pond. "What are we looking at?" asked Cally. "I don't see anything."

"Primrose Pond," Susannah said. She had good memories of this pond, but Cally was right: it was barely visible. It would be different in the summer. She had to keep telling herself that. Though, at this moment, the summer seemed a long way off. "Once it gets warm enough, we can swim," she said. "And boat too—there's a rowboat and a canoe on the property."

"Can we water-ski?" Jack asked.

"If we meet someone with a motorboat," Susannah said. Jack seemed satisfied and Cally didn't have any other negative comments to make, which in Susannah's view constituted a small miracle. They went back inside to the glowing embers of the fire. Susannah added another log and watched the flames leap up again. It felt so strange being back here; she hadn't anticipated that.

"Are there, like, snakes or eels in there? What about leeches? Aidan Shenk went to a camp on a lake and he said it was crawling with leeches." Jack abhorred all creatures slippery or slithery.

"No snakes, no eels," Susannah said firmly. "And no leeches."

"Good. If there are leeches, I'm not going in."

"You're not going in now anyway," Cally pointed out. "It's January." And then, more quietly, "Moron."

Jack looked whipped. Susannah could only guess what he was feeling. Those two had been so close for so long; now they seemed to be spinning in wholly different orbits. Instead of bringing them closer, their father's death seemed to have splintered the bond.

"Your sister is tired and cranky," she said. "She doesn't want to be here and she's taking it out on you. It's not fair and it's not nice and I am counting on her to *cut it out right now.*" She was looking at Jack but speaking to Cally. And it seemed to have an effect—sort of.

"Sorry." She stood there with her fists clenched, firelight playing across her sullen face.

"It's okay. I know you didn't mean it." Too-easy Jack, always the peacemaker, never the grudge holder.

Susannah stood up. "I'm going to try to find the circuit breakers. Anyone want to help?" Cally remained by the fire, but Jack, eager puppy that he was, followed along. They bumped and bumbled in the dark, the flashlight illuminating a bright but narrow path through the living and dining rooms. Susannah shone the beam into the kitchen, and there, near the side door, was a metal panel with a ring in its center. When she pulled the ring, the panel opened to reveal the circuit breakers, all their switches in a row—except one. She was just about to flip it so that it would be in line with the others when Jack put his hand on her wrist. "Don't!"

"Why not?"

"You have to flip it down first. Then back up." In the flashlight's bright pool, he demonstrated. Immediately, the lights returned.

"How did you know to do that?" Susannah was impressed.

"Dad showed me," he said.

The phrase hung there for a few seconds. Susannah could just imagine it—Charlie, Mr. Fix-It, explaining how the circuit breakers worked, Jack nodding seriously, taking it all in—and her eyes welled. But all she said was, "You saved the day. Or night." Jack smiled. His deep-set brown eyes and long lashes (how he hated them, thinking they made him look like a girl) came from her, but she had not passed on her small, neat chin or her sun-loving olive skin and dark brown hair. Jack had lighter hair and his father's freckles. And his smile—tremulous and heartbreaking—was pure Charlie.

Cally came into the room. "I want to go to bed."

"Let's all go up," said Susannah. "The movers will be here first thing." She headed up and they followed. At least things were ready for them up here. Susannah helped Cally settle in the bedroom with the rose-sprigged wallpaper and brass bed where she had stayed that long-ago summer. Jack took the room that had been her mother's study—her father had been relegated to the porch—and Susannah decamped to the largest bedroom, the one where her parents had slept.

Alone for the first time in hours, she felt herself sagging under the weight of the day she'd just spent and the knowledge that the next day would be no easier. But she had gotten them here safely, hadn't she? They were okay. Sort of. She walked over to the window. Through the parted curtains, she could see the pond, illuminated by the cool, silvery light of a winter moon.

Susannah had been seventeen when her mother announced she wanted to spend the summer in New Hampshire. Yes, she had known about the house, but her parents had always kept it rented out and neither one had ever expressed any interest in going there. So everything had been brand-new for her, the pond most of all. She was raised a Jersey girl; her experience of water meant pounding surf and a seemingly unending shoreline.

By contrast, this finite, tranquil body of water had seemed dull. But gradually she grew to appreciate it. Instead of waves, there were subtle ripples or eddies. Instead of stinging salt, there was liquid so pure she could have bathed in it. There were frogs and toads that lived at its perimeters, silvery minnows that rose to its surface in search of bread. Loons swam and hunted in the pond and geese used the wooden rafts to congregate. The ocean, with its potentially treacherous tides and mercurial changes, was exciting, but not to be trusted. The pond, in comparison, laid all its secrets bare.

Susannah got into the bed that Mabel had made up with flannel sheets and a down quilt. Yet, as tired as she was, she found she could not sleep. The energy of the house, or the spirits of the people who'd lived here—her parents; the younger, innocent version of herself—were too present, too noisy even. The internal clamor was keeping her awake.

That had been a strange, intense summer. Her mother had been even more moody than usual, crying a lot, or awash in a kind of manic joy; her normally even-tempered father had seemed preoccupied and, at times, morose. Swimming in the clear, cool water of the pond, Susannah was relieved to escape the drama of whatever her parents were going through; the pond had been her refuge. She hoped it would still be true, and that she hadn't made a huge mistake in uprooting her kids and dragging them up here.

Yanking back the covers, she got out of bed and padded down the hall. Quietly, she opened the door to Cally's room. Her daughter was on her side, curled in on herself; even in sleep she was guarded. The magazines she'd bought earlier were splayed on the floor. Susannah knew that she was largely indifferent to the features and bodies of the models who cavorted across the pages; instead, she was mentally ripping apart the garments, trying to understand their inner architecture, the scaffolding that held them together. Cally's face had lost its habitual scowl, the one she'd assumed when Charlie was killed and that had not faded since. Her red hair was fanned out on the pillow around her. Susannah had the urge to kiss that smooth, untroubled forehead but did not want to run the risk of waking her, so she stepped out and closed the door behind her.

When she went to check on Jack, she found him flat on his back, arms stretched out and one leg hanging off the bed. His clarinet case was propped in a corner; he would not trust it to the movers. Susannah stood there listening to the light rasp of his snoring. He slept like his father—with complete abandon.

. . .

Susannah and Charlie had met when she was sixteen and he was eighteen; they had both been working at a summer camp in the Poconos. There had been no romance between them, but they'd become instant best friends and spent hours dissecting everyone at the camp, from the director to the littlest kids. They remained friends too, and would get together a few times a year in Philly. It wasn't until they had graduated from college—she from Vassar, he from Bard—and were trying to make their way in New York that things between them changed.

Charlie had a job doing merchandise display for Macy's and Susannah worked at a small educational publisher where she typed, filed, answered phones, and obsessed about an on-again-off-again romance she was having with an older, and tantalizingly elusive, coworker. She had a standing once-a-month date with Charlie when they caught up on each other's lives.

One of these dates took place at a noodle shop they favored in the East Village, where, over tiny cups of sake, Susannah was lamenting her romantic situation—yet again. Charlie listened for a time, nodding or offering the occasional comment. But after about fifteen minutes, he put down his cup, leaned across the table, and took both her hands in his. "Forget that guy," he said. "He doesn't appreciate you and he doesn't deserve you. *I'm* the guy who loves you. The guy you're going to marry." Then he kissed her. Susannah's eyes did not close, but opened very wide. This was Charlie, her familiar, adorable, loyal best friend forever. But the kiss—it was totally brand-new and more wonderful than she could have imagined.

They had a giddy dating spree—so much lost time to make up

for—and within a year they were married. Charlie retained his boyish charm even through marriage, two kids, the ups and downs of their respective careers, a couple of health scares, the deaths of parents and, in his case, an older brother. And now he was gone.

After a few seconds, the memories subsided, and Susannah stood, breathing hard, in the hallway. Then she trudged back to bed, where she prayed she could salvage at least a couple of hours from what promised to be a ruined minefield of sleep.

THREE

A scant few hours later, Susannah was jolted awake by the insistent chime of the doorbell. Hastily grabbing the flannel bathrobe that had been Charlie's—try as she might, she could no longer detect his scent in the soft plaid folds—she flew down the stairs to find a young bearded guy in a ski cap and down vest. Behind him, a huge red truck with the word SCHLEPPERS emblazoned across the side hulked like some enormous animal.

"Morning," he said. "We'll start moving it in whenever you're ready."

Damn. She'd overslept. Now the movers were here, the kids were still asleep, and she hadn't showered, dressed, or had so much as a sip of coffee. "Come on in." She stepped back to give him access. "I'll just run up and throw something on." When she returned, dressed but still frazzled, a few boxes had already been unloaded and carried into the house.

"You're sure you're going to have room for everything?" He seemed doubtful.

The room was already furnished in an amiable if generic fashion—a beige sofa and two matching chairs around the fireplace, faux Navajo rug on the floor, various end tables topped with various lamps and vases. Susannah did not remember any of this stuff; it looked like it had been purchased from a catalog, and all on the same day. Sometime after that summer they'd spent here, her mother had come through and taken almost everything of theirs out, replacing it with these characterless pieces.

"Most of this stuff downstairs is going. And upstairs there's a lot less." The bedrooms, sparsely furnished as they were, contained pieces Susannah did remember, like the brass bed and the maple four-poster in her parents' room.

Ski Cap looked around. "Do you need any help getting rid of it? I know some people in Brooklyn who were flooded a couple of months ago and lost most of their furniture. We could load anything you can't use back onto the truck and take it down to them." Susannah had planned to call the Salvation Army to cart off what she did not want, but he was saving her a step. And she was glad the stuff would go to people who could really use it. "Sounds good to me."

Ski Cap smiled and inclined his head; his big beard touched his down-clad chest. For the next several hours, the crew unloaded furniture and lugged boxes. Cally and Jack emerged from their respective rooms; Susannah just hoped Cally could keep it together while the movers were here, and so far she was getting her wish.

When everything was in the house, Ski Cap, whose name was Sean, asked the guys to take all the beige-and-bland pieces out and to set up Susannah's own eclectic assortment of furniture— the wing chair covered with a gaudily patterned curtain panel from the 1940s; the midcentury sofa and coffee table, the latter shaped like a kidney bean—in the newly emptied space.

"It looks good." Jack settled into the sofa.

"Not exactly good," said Cally. "But better."

"We'll make it ours," Susannah said. "You'll see." She tipped the movers generously and stood waving in the open doorway as the Schleppers truck rumbled off.

Once they had gone, Susannah turned and went back into the house. From the living room she could see the porch, and beyond that the pond. It had been such a big part of her life that summer. Except when it rained, she was in that water every single morning, wading out until she was waist deep and then diving in. Then she would swim a steady path along a shoreline that was ringed in pines and birches, past the same eight or ten houses and back again. She passed several wooden floats tethered to weights below the surface, warped, weathered things coated in slime and moss. She had liked to stop at each of them in turn, hoisting herself onto the surface and plunging cleanly back into the water again. During these long swims, she almost never saw another soul. The people who lived there year-round had no kids, and she never mingled much with the people who came for only a week or two. The pond had seemed hers, and hers alone.

After her solitary morning swims, Susannah would spend the day hanging out with the crew of kids she'd met, like Trevor Bailey. Sometimes they went boating, but mostly they lolled on the floats or the pebbly strip fronting the water. Susannah's place within the group was not well established, which was why she'd so quickly paired off with Trevor: he was her ticket in. He was nice enough, but she secretly found him dull, and his hand on her thigh or under her shirt—overtures she had rejected—elicited no response in her at all. He'd had a brother, though. Corbin. Now he was interesting, but he was three years older, a gap that at the time had seemed enormous.

A small crash brought her back to the present and she went hurrying in the direction of the sound. "What broke?" she asked, standing in the kitchen.

"I dropped a glass," Jack said. "Sorry, Mom."

"No biggie," she said, hunting for a broom and dustpan. There was still so much to do; taking the contents of one life and fitting it into a new vessel was not going to be easy. Susannah helped Jack with the broken glass, lifting the jagged bits from the floor. Then she went upstairs to begin unpacking some of the boxes that now lined her bedroom.

The first box contained summer clothes. She wouldn't need them for a while. Same with all her sandals, the round hat box containing her straw panama, and her two black bathing suits. Unlike her Brooklyn home, this house had an attic—the perfect place to store her out-of-season wardrobe. She mounted the flight of bare wooden boards that were concealed behind a door adjacent to the bathroom. When she pulled the cord dangling from the ceiling, a single bulb lit the room.

The attic was a pretty raw space: wide-plank floors, a pair of windows at one end, and a circular window at the other. Exposed beams bisected the ceiling. There were three large boxes stacked against one wall and an old iron bed on the other. Also a harp with several shot strings—one of her father's crazy finds that summer— and, sitting alongside the boxes, a black Singer sewing machine that Susannah did not recognize but may have belonged to her mother.

Depositing the clothing on the bed, she walked over and put her hand on its dusty surface. Cally had been asking for a sewing machine. Then she turned to the boxes, whose contents were unknown to her. When her mother died, she had just given birth to Jack and she couldn't deal with the house; her father had died the year before, and so her mother's best friend, Linda Jacobsmeyer, had kindly packed up whatever personal effects had been left and brought them up here.

The first box was crammed with yards and yards of fabric. All of it was old.

Had it belonged to her mother? She had no idea. She found spools of trimming tucked between the folds—velvet and satin ribbon, lace, and rickrack. There was a bag filled with embroidered appliqués, another bag of buttons, and still another of beads. The more she pawed through the box, the more puzzled she became. As far as Susannah knew, Claire had never used anything here. But Cally would *love* this stuff, and Susannah badly wanted to find something about this house, and the life they would be leading in it, for Cally to love.

She turned to the next box. Inside it she found papers belonging to her father; he'd been an economics professor, first at the University of New Hampshire and later at Rutgers, in New Jersey. There were also a few small oil paintings, mostly of the pond, house, and the surrounding woods. Susannah remembered how her father had had a sudden urge to try his hand at painting that summer, and she'd driven with him to an art supply store in Concord to pick out materials. "Your mother always says I have no appreciation of the arts. But I'm going to surprise her!" He'd kept his project hidden at first, clearly hoping to surprise and delight her. That was how it had been between them: her quiet, bookish father perpetually amazed that he'd captured—and married—his beautiful bird of paradise. It seemed like he'd always been trying to appease and charm her, a process of wooing that never ended. What she had seen in him Susannah had never really known.

She took the paintings out and laid them on the floor like a patchwork quilt. The last one was not a landscape, but a portrait of her mother, painted from a photograph of her as a young woman. The photo was in the family album; Susannah had seen it many times. Her mother had indeed been surprised by her father's artistic output. She'd exclaimed over the paintings of the house and pond, praising the colors and the composition. But when she saw the portrait, she'd seemed upset.

"Something's off about the expression," she had said. "I look dazed. Or terrified."

"I don't know what you're talking about," her father said. "I used a beautiful photograph of a beautiful woman. That's what I saw. That's what I painted. Or tried to."

Nothing more was said, but the painting went up to the attic and, as far as Susannah knew, her father had never painted again. *Nice try, Dad*, she had thought at the time. *Too bad it didn't work out.*

The last box was heavy and, when opened, looked to contain books, mostly on economics, with a few biographies and historical books in the mix. But here was an anomaly: *The Collected Poems of W. B. Yeats*. Had this belonged to her father? She doubted it. And when she turned to the flyleaf, it was her mother's name she saw there. So Claire read Yeats? Who knew? And from the look of this tattered volume, with its loosened spine and torn cover, she had read him often.

Susannah brought the book over to the bed and moved the clothes aside so she could sit. Here were poems her mother had wanted to single out, tiny penciled checkmarks near the titles. Occasionally a word or phrase was lightly underlined. In one instance, three exclamation marks stood at attention in the margin.

Not only had Claire read Yeats, she had clearly been engaged by what she read. Susannah turned another page and a piece of paper, folded in thirds, slipped out of the book and into her lap. She opened it. There was no date and no signature, only these lines:

> *I know it's crazy, I know it's wrong, I know we shouldn't. You don't want to hurt him and I don't want to hurt her. But, Claire, you are "my lovely lizard/my lively writher" and I can no more give you up than cut out my own hot, beating heart. Please "say yes."*

Susannah read the note over several times without fully understanding it. Or rather, she understood it, but only in the most literal way. This was a love letter, and although it was clearly written to her mother, it was not from her father; she knew his careful, tidy penmanship as well as she'd known his patient, perpetually resigned face. So these bold, looping lines had been written by someone else. Who? There was passion in them. And guilt. *I know it's crazy, I know it's wrong, I know we shouldn't.* Could her mother have had a lover? An *affair*? If so, when? And if it had happened during her parents' marriage, had her father known? Oh God. Oh. God.

She remained on the bed for several minutes and then abruptly got up. She stacked the paintings in a neat pile, repacked the box of fabric and trimmings, and pushed it, along with the other boxes, back against the wall. The only thing she took was the Yeats, and the note, which she tucked between its pages once more. Then she pulled the cord dangling from the ceiling and went back down the stairs.

FOUR

All the while that she was cracking the eggs and frying the bacon, Susannah thought about the note. Even though she had read it only a few times, the words were fairly pulsating—tiny, hot points of light—in her mind. *Lovely lizard/lively writher.* That came from Theodore Roethke, a poet she had studied in a modern poetry course. *I don't want to hurt her.* So he was married too. *Please say yes.* Yes to what? Loving him back? Leaving her husband? Clearly that had not happened.

"Jack, Cally!" she called. "Come and get it!" Susannah's own farmhouse table and set of ladder-back chairs had been moved in and the room was beginning to assume her imprint.

The note was now in an empty shoe box on the shelf of a closet, safe for the time being. She couldn't just leave it there, though, with the mystery unsolved. She wished she could drop everything and go immediately back to those boxes in the attic. Maybe there were more notes—or other clues—inside them.

Instead, while Jack and Cally cleaned up the kitchen, she drove to a nearby supermarket. Densely packed snow lined the sides of the road, and snow, mostly white but sometimes gray, covered the ground, trees, and roofs of the houses. Susannah wasn't used to seeing such an accumulation; in New York, streets were plowed in a matter of hours, and snow was a vestigial, not dominant, feature of the winter landscape. She would have to get used to it.

After driving fourteen miles—yes, she was counting—she parked in the nearly empty parking lot of a Hannaford market, got her cart, and began to cruise the aisles. Back in Brooklyn, Charlie had done the bulk of their grocery shopping; he actually enjoyed the task. Once in a while he made questionable choices, like the six outsized boxes of Lucky Charms he had brought home, gleefully explaining that they were on sale. "But the kids don't even eat Lucky Charms," she'd said.

"These are for me," he'd answered.

Mostly he did a good job of it, though, and she was glad to be spared the crowded stores and long lines. But here in New Hampshire, the terrain was clearly different. The parking lot should have been the clue, because the aisles were nearly empty too, almost spookily so. Where was everyone? Also, the cart was so large, it was hard to maneuver, and as she moved from baked goods to frozen foods, she felt like she was battling with it. And when she crashed into a large display of stacked soup cans, sending tomato bisque and split pea rolling all over the aisles, she knew that the cart had won.

"Are you all right?" The store manager, a young man with slicked-back hair and very ruddy cheeks, came hurrying over.

"I'm so sorry." Mortified, Susannah knelt and began gathering cans; the cans, like the cart, were thwarting her and began to roll toward the dairy case at the back of the store. God, but she wanted to get out of there and back to the familiar cramped aisles of Brooklyn!

"Don't even worry about it," said the manager. He helped her up, and when he discovered that her cart's wheels were malfunctioning, he brought over another cart and helped her transfer her groceries into it.

Back at the house, she got a pot of chili going for dinner. That had been one of Charlie's favorite dishes and she had not made it since he died. With the voices of the kids floating down to the kitchen—*Did you find a box marked 'Sewing Stuff'? Where did Mom put all the towels?*—she wept silently as she diced the celery and the onions.

The loss had been brutal at first. She cried constantly, trying her best to hide it from the kids. That sharp, raw edge had softened, though, and she was able to get through first days, then weeks without crying. But the move had opened the wound; in leaving the old house, she was forced to say good-bye to Charlie all over again.

Once the chili was simmering, she rinsed her face in the kitchen sink and blotted the mixture of tears and tap water with a paper towel. The voices upstairs had been replaced by the sound of music; Jack had clearly taken his clarinet out of its case and was practicing. He wasn't the most technically proficient player, but he was certainly a passionate one. "He really feels the music," his clarinet teacher back in Brooklyn had said. Jack had been happy to find out that his new middle school had a band and a jazz ensemble; he'd be able to try out for both.

He was playing an arrangement of "Somewhere Over the Rainbow," and the familiar tune traveled down to where Susannah stood. Even though the melody was simple and not quite confident, it seemed to contain a message just for her: *You'll get through this,* warbled the plaintive notes. *You'll survive and they will too.* She made her way up the stairs toward the music. Jack's door was open, and she could see the concentration on his face, his hands carefully placed on the instrument, body inclined slightly back. If he saw her, he did not register it, and she moved by the room without saying anything.

The door to Cally's room was closed. Susannah stood in front of it. She wanted to go up to the attic; she'd been itching to do it all day. And it now occurred to her that she even had a pretext: the box of fabric and the sewing machine, both of which she wanted to show Cally. Jack was lost in his music; if Cally showed an interest in the fabric, Susannah would have a little time to do some more poking around. "Cally?" Susannah knocked tentatively on the door.

"What is it?" She sounded guarded, but not antagonistic.

"There's something I want to show you. Something that you'll like."

A silence, and then the door opened. Cally had shot up recently, was now taller than her mother. Charlie's genes. She was slender like her father too, and had his wide-set green eyes, his red hair, and the smattering of freckles he'd had as a boy. Today Cally wore cut-off overalls on top of a boldly striped sweater and patterned tights; on her feet were red Keds high-tops, not too practical a choice for snowy, icy Eastwood. Susannah added *Boots for Cally* to her mental to-do list.

"Tell me what it is."

"It's better if I show you." Susannah gestured for Cally to follow her. "Look," she said when they had entered the attic room. "I found this sewing machine." Cally immediately went over to inspect. Susannah watched as she ran her hands over the machine's graceful black lines and touched the gold lettering.

"It's beautiful," Cally said at last. "But I didn't know Grandma sewed."

"Neither did I," Susannah said. "In fact, I'm not even sure it was hers."

"Well, I don't care who it belonged to—I'm just glad it's here, because I love it."

Just hearing the word "love" emanate from Cally's mouth made Susannah inordinately happy. "Wait," she said. "There's more." And she brought Cally over to the box, where, as she had hoped, Cally began eagerly pulling things out. "Look at this paisley!" she said, clutching it to her chest. "And these brocades—Vivienne Tam uses fabric like this." She looked up at her mother. "Can I have it, Mom? Can I, please?"

"Of course," Susannah said. "It's all for you." She and Cally made several trips to bring all the fabric, trimming, and the sewing machine to Cally's room. Jack was still playing the clarinet now but had switched to something jazzier; maybe a swing tune? The chili, which Susannah could smell, had another hour to go. "I'm going back up to the attic," said Susannah. She waited, almost expecting to be challenged.

"Sure," said Cally. "Whatever."

And with that, Susannah turned and tried not to bolt up the stairs. The winter afternoon was quickly fading and she pulled the chain for the light. There was the box with her father's books; she would start there. She began taking them out, methodically flipping through the pages, and stacking them neatly on the floor near the window. When the stack grew too high, she began another. It was not likely her mother would have left a personal note in a treatise on economics, but at the moment these boxes, and their contents, were the only source of information she had.

When the first box was emptied of books, Susannah saw something wadded up at the bottom. More fabric? She pulled it out and gave it a shake. It was a two-piece dress with a black-and-white tweed skirt, and an ivory satin bodice and black velvet collar. The matching cropped jacket was black velvet with tweed cuffs. Badly wrinkled, it held a whiff of mildew. Susannah had never seen it before. Had it belonged to her mother and, if so, how and why did it end up with these books?

She shook the dress out and laid it on the bed, unsure of what she wanted to do with it. The sky outside the window had grown dark and it was time to go downstairs; the chili would be almost ready by now. Not one of the books had yielded anything else. But she had not gone through the entire volume of Yeats, which was on the bed next to the dress. Susannah picked it up and began flipping through it. Were there more poems her mother had marked?

"What are you doing?"

Startled, Susannah looked up to see Jack standing there. She'd been so absorbed, she had not heard him on the stairs. "Nothing really." Why did she feel so guilty? She couldn't be accused of snooping—her parents were dead.

"So then what are you looking at?" He came closer.

"A book. It belonged to your grandmother."

"Can I see?"

Susannah hesitated. What if he found something else, something even more revealing or incriminating, that she had not yet seen? But to deny him would make it seem as if she was hiding something. She handed him the book, hoping her trepidation did not show.

"Just some poems." He flipped through the pages. "She liked these?"

"She must have. It's practically falling apart. And she made all kinds of notes inside."

"And what's that?" He pointed to the dress.

"I think that was hers too."

"What do you mean, 'She must have' and 'I think'?" Jack handed her back the book. "Don't you know?"

"Not exactly." She paused. "No."

"But she was your *mom*. How could you not know what she liked? Or what she wore?"

Because right now I'm not sure I even know who she was. But all she said was, "I'm getting hungry. How about you?"

"I'm starved."

"Let's go downstairs." Relieved that the direction of the conversation had shifted, Susannah got up and moved toward the stairs.

"You're making chili," Jack said as they descended. It sounded like a challenge.

"You like my chili."

"So did Dad," he muttered.

"I know, sweetheart. I know." They had reached the landing and she extended her arm to draw him close. He remained there briefly, head pressed against her shoulder before he pulled away. Then he was off, paces ahead of her and down the next flight of stairs in a clatter. She followed more slowly. The book and the dress were still up in the attic; she would go up later to retrieve them. But when she did, she would be more careful. If she didn't understand the connection between the clues she was amassing, how in the world was she going to explain it to her kids?

FIVE

"Can you *please* stand over there?" Cally said. "I don't want anyone to see you." It was seven forty-five the next morning, and she and Jack were waiting for the school bus; Susannah had walked down the snow-packed road to wait with them.

"No one will see me," Susannah said. "You don't have to worry."

"I don't understand why you even need to be here."

"Your brother asked me to come."

"Big baby," Cally muttered, and moved another two steps away.

Susannah put her hand on Jack's shoulder, but he did not respond to the taunt. "It's the first day of the new semester; it's not too likely anyone is going to be paying attention to me."

"Whatever." Cally shifted her weight a couple of times and shoved her hands deeper into her pockets.

"Are you cold?" Susannah had to ask.

"No, Mom. I'm not cold." Cally still would not look her way. "Just like I wasn't cold the last time you asked, and the time before that."

Susannah was hurt. Also worried that Cally's feet, in the thin canvas sneakers, were in fact freezing. Susannah had shown her the L.L.Bean boots, but her daughter had rejected them, asking instead if she could order a pair of purple Doc Martens sporting a sheen as lustrous and dark as an eggplant.

"No one at school will be wearing boots like that," Susannah had pointed out.

"Exactly."

Susannah knew better than to argue. Did she really care about which boots Cally chose? She did not. But what she did care about was her daughter fitting in and making friends in her new school, and in her mind the boots posed an impediment to that goal.

"My new boots are great," Jack volunteered, looking down at his feet. "Super warm."

"I'm glad." Susannah touched his cheek, knowing that not only would he allow it, he would welcome it. He had always been a cuddly kid; Cally never had.

The bus finally chugged up the road, larger than life and twice as yellow.

"It's here!" Jack sounded excited and clambered up the stairs, clarinet case bumping against his thigh. Cally followed more slowly and Susannah hung back, trying to stay out of sight. Then the door wheezed shut and the bus lumbered on. There was a momentary sense of deflation as they left; the empty house faced her, along with numerous still unpacked boxes. The gray sky overhead didn't improve her mood. Nor did the cold—it was probably ten degrees.

The last time she had settled in somewhere, it had been with Charlie. They'd bought their brownstone during a market down-turn, but it was still a serious fixer-upper, and Susannah had felt daunted by the enormity of the work they faced: the broken lino-leum that covered every room except, inexplicably, the kitchen; the woodwork calcified by layers of paint; the decades of neglect

that shrouded the house like a fog. But Charlie had been relent-
lessly upbeat about it all, and kept going on about the "great bones"
and "untapped potential."

One day, shortly after they had moved in, she thought she
couldn't stand being in that dilapidated old house one second
longer and went out for a walk. When she came back, she found
bunches of tulips stuffed into large plastic drinking cups set all
throughout the rooms.

"What's the occasion?" she asked.

"I wanted to cheer you up." He looked at her hopefully, and
Susannah melted; she knew that he wanted her to see what he
saw, feel what he felt.

"It worked." She held out her arms.

Today there would be no Charlie when she got back to the
house on the pond, and the work of turning it into a home would
fall almost entirely to her.

She was just thinking about baking cookies—that would be
a nice treat for the kids this afternoon—when she spied the
horse. Its head was sticking way out of its stall, and it seemed to
be stretching the thick column of its neck in her direction. The
barn that housed this animal was in a meadow adjacent to the
pale green house with the shutters. A fence surrounded both land
and building, but the gate was wide open. Surely that was a mistake.

Susannah stopped, intending simply to close the gate and continue on her way. But the horse uttered a low, insistent neigh,
almost as if he was calling to her, and so she crunched across the
snow-covered meadow to get closer. Once she reached him, she
extended her hand, palm flat and upturned; Cally, who had ridden
for a few years, had taught her to do this. Immediately, the horse
nuzzled her open palm, looking for a treat. His coat was a glossy

chestnut brown; his long face was dappled with white markings. She rooted around her pocket, not thinking she would find anything.

But wait—there was a peppermint candy cane, left over from some Christmastime offering at a store or the bank. Susannah vaguely recalled that horses liked peppermints and she offered it to him. The horse peeled back his upper lip, revealing his large stained teeth; the candy cane was gone in one decisive crunch. Then he turned his head to fix her with his steady black stare.

She wished she had another candy cane, but since she didn't she stroked the horse's face. The upper part of his head felt taut and solid, but the area around his nostrils—which were nearly as big as her fists—was plush and covered with tiny, tickly hairs. She stretched her arms way up so she could scratch the spot between his ears; he bobbed his head, almost as if nodding. She gave him a final pat before plodding back across the meadow and closing the gate on her way out.

Her encounter with the horse had cheered her a bit, and once back inside she worked efficiently and quickly at the unpacking. Around two o'clock, she stopped to bake the cookies; along with butter, eggs, sugar, and flour, she'd tossed a bag of chocolate chips into her cart the day before. By the time the kids walked in, the cookies were just cooling on the table.

"Smells good," said Jack, who took one in each hand as Susannah went to the fridge for milk.

But Cally bypassed her offering and went straight up to her room. "How was your day?" Susannah called after her.

"Fine." There was a pause and then the sound of the door closing, quietly but with a pointed emphasis.

Susannah knew better than to press. To counter her disappointment, she sat down at the table with Jack, who had eaten both the cookies and was now working on a third. "How about you?" she asked.

"It was good, Mom! The kids were really friendly. They wanted to hear all about what it was like to live in New York City. There's this gigantic field where we'll get to play volleyball and stuff in the spring. I'm going to try out for the school band on Friday and I met this really nice girl named Gilda Mooney on the bus—she lives in a house right across the pond and she invited me to a party . . ."

"Sounds like a good day." Susannah let his enthusiasm soften the rough edge of her hurt about Cally.

"It was, Mom. It really was." He took a long drink of milk. "I didn't want to tell you, but I was kind of worried about it. Now I'm not."

She got up from the table, deposited a kiss on his rather shaggy head—he really needed a haircut; where would they find a barber around here?—and returned to her unpacking. The living room was looking pretty good—furniture in place, a rug covering the floor. But over in a corner of the living room were several framed posters; they were leaning against the wall, not hanging on it.

The largest of the lot showed the stylized prow of a ship slicing through the water. **TO NEW YORK** ran the sans serif type across the top; **HAMBURG-AMERICAN LINE** was printed along the bottom. There were others too, advertising skiing in the Alps, a sparkling Italian wine, candy, a racing bike—that one was very hard to look at—films first seen sixty years ago. As an illustrator, Charlie had appreciated the quality of their draftsmanship, their sophisticated graphics. They had hung on the walls of his studio, interspersed with some of his own drawings and other pieces of ephemera he'd never bothered to frame but had tacked up with pushpins in an ever evolving arrangement. The posters had monetary value, but they represented almost two decades of Charlie's collecting, and Susannah had been unable to part with a single one.

They should be hanging, she decided. Right here, in these rooms where they would be seen every day. But she did not have a hammer or nails. Somehow these essential items had gone missing from the toolbox; they had probably been left behind and were still buried somewhere in the basement of what had been her home. Well, she could fix that.

"Jack?" she called out. He was still in the kitchen, texting. "I have to run an errand."

A pause. "When are you coming back?"

"Soon." She had already started gathering her parka and her bag. If she could find a hammer and a box of nails before dinner, she could hang the posters tonight; tomorrow morning, this little bit of Charlie would be there to greet her. And she needed a shovel: she had looked around but had not found one.

Driving down the road, Susannah wondered whether Bailey's Home, Garden, and Lawn was still in business. That would be the closest place. Was either Trevor or Corbin—and hadn't there been a sister too?—still in the area? She didn't know, but she had not made any attempt to keep up with any of them after that summer.

The store was on the edge of town, or at least that's what she vaguely recalled; she'd gone there with Trevor once or twice. Susannah drove to the corner where she'd remembered the store. It was gone, replaced by the Sunny Skies Day Care Center. She felt oddly disappointed and supposed she would just have to drive back toward Concord, to the Home Depot that was on Route 4. Bailey's was just one more mom-and-pop establishment that had succumbed to the might of the chain store.

But instead of turning right at the light, she turned left. She was still finding her way here and taking a detour down an unfamiliar street was a good way to become oriented. The street sloped down rather sharply. On one side was a narrow house whose dark green paint was peeling in great spiral strips; on the other, a rambling white house that appeared to be empty. Clearly this was the less tony part of town.

When she got to the bottom of the street, Susannah first saw a small parking lot and then, to her surprise, a low-rise building with the sign **BAILEY'S HOME, GARDEN, AND LAWN—ESTABLISHED 1957** out front. So it was still in business; it had just moved. She got out of the car and walked into the store. A small silver bell announced her arrival; cute. A fortyish black woman with elegant cheekbones, mahogany lip gloss, and a very friendly manner was at the counter; she asked if Susannah needed help. The place was well stocked and seemed busy enough for a weekday afternoon in January; clearly Bailey's was holding its own against the onslaught of the big-box stores. And then, surrounded by the snowblowers, deicing agents, and several boxes of marked-down Christmas lights, Susannah found herself face-to-face with Trevor's older brother, Corbin Bailey.

Her first thought was, *He hasn't changed.* Her next thought was, *Oh, yes, he has, and he's better looking than ever.* He'd filled out some, seemingly all lean, hard muscle. His hair was shorter, and threaded with a few filaments of silver; they made his electric blue eyes seem even more dazzling. God, how could she even be thinking this way?

"Are you finding everything all right?" In his red apron with the words **BAILEY'S—SINCE 1957** emblazoned across the front, he was all business.

Susannah glanced down at her list. Clearly he did not remember her. She wasn't sure if she felt relieved or disappointed. Corbin was patiently standing there, pencil stub behind his ear, waiting for her reply. It was only when she looked back up at him that his expression changed and she saw the recognition settle in. "You were Trevor's girl," he said.

"No, Susannah Gilmore," she said. She had never been Trevor's girl, not really.

"Of course," he said without missing a beat. "Nice to see you back in town."

Susannah bought the things she'd come for, was told to "have a very nice day," and left the store.

There had been an evening that summer when they had all gathered down by the water and were sharing lobster rolls and French fries from Gilly's Lobster Shack. Corbin had showed up with a couple of six-packs. He yanked the cans from their plastic holders and began passing them around. Not wanting to appear prissy, Susannah had taken a few tentative sips. She did not like the taste but she certainly liked Corbin. He wasn't quite as tall as his younger brother, but while Trevor was kind of gangly, Corbin was compactly built and deeply tanned besides; in addition to helping his dad at the store, he had a summer job working as a lifeguard at Wallis Sands. With his startling blue eyes and black hair, he was the sexiest boy she had ever seen; she wished she had been dating him, and not Trevor. When the evening wound down, she managed to fall into step with him as they all walked up the embankment toward the house. "You're new," he said. "I've never seen you around before."

"My parents used to live here but they moved away when I was a baby. We're just back for summer."

He said nothing but stopped and brushed a bit of hair from her face; even now, standing in the gray, snow-pocked parking lot, Susannah could remember how the slightest grazing of his fingertips against her skin had electrified her in a way that all of Trevor's earnest pawing had not.

A week or so later, her father had been painting the floor of the porch and run out of paint, so Susannah had gone down to pick up a gallon. Corbin had been there and he'd waited on her.

"Here you go, Trevor's girl," he said, adding a couple of wooden stirrers to the bag that held the paint.

"It's Susannah," she said. "Susannah Gilmore."

"Right." His eyes held hers for a few charged seconds. "I'll remember that."

"Susannah!" The sound of her name made her turn. There was Corbin, the present-day, still sexier-than-life Corbin, walking across the parking lot carrying a bag in one hand, a shovel in the other. "Here." He handed it to her. "You forgot something."

No, she wanted to say. *I haven't forgotten a thing.*

SIX

Susannah was sitting at her desk in her bedroom, laptop open and ready. There were only three rooms up here—not enough for her to claim a separate study, but that was all right. And since she had put the desk in front of the window—it fit so nicely, as if it had been made for the spot—she was able to look out at Primrose Pond while she worked.

Except she wasn't working. Not exactly. Not, if she cared to be honest with herself, at all. She got up from the desk and began to run in place. Outside the window, the frozen layer of ice on the pond glittered in the January sun; she kept her eyes on the brightness as she pumped her arms. After several minutes of stationary running, she switched to jumping jacks. The pond continued to glitter. When she'd hit thirty, she sat down, mildly winded, but no more inclined to work than she had been ten minutes earlier. *Coffee,* she thought, even though she had had a cup earlier that morning, and went downstairs to make it.

Susannah's novels were always set in Europe, and always about women. She dabbled in different centuries, and apart from the occasional queen or empress, she tended to stick to minor royalty. Archduchess Gisela of Austria and Duchess Marie Gabrielle of Bavaria were two of her more recent subjects—she had studied German at Vassar—and she'd also written on Margaret, Countess of Pembroke and Maria Cristina Pia Anna Isabella Natalia Elisa di Borbone delle Due Sicilie, more commonly known as Maria Cristina of the Two Sicilies, for which she'd had to take a crash course in Italian.

She had stumbled into her métier by chance. After the small educational publisher was swallowed up by a bigger company and she lost her job, she answered an ad for an editorial/administrative assistant at Out of the Past Press. She was good at the work, and often made editorial suggestions that pleased her boss, Tasha Clurman, enormously. Once, during a long and drawn-out rewrite, Tasha had said in exasperation, "I wish you'd take a stab at this chapter! I think you'd do a better job." Susannah took the chapter home to work on it; the result was so good that she'd been asked to start writing the novels instead of editing them.

For years Susannah had enjoyed her work, the detective-like uncovering of the factual elements, the artful embroidering of the fictional ones. She was not a biographer, so she did not have to adhere as closely to the facts, but the facts were the scaffolding. She started with primary source material where and when she could get it—letters, journals, firsthand accounts. Some of the items had major historical import, but others were more personal, like the itemized list of the garments in the trousseau of a duchess on the eve of her wedding; another list, just a year later, of the members of court who'd attended that same duchess's funeral when she died of childbed fever.

Once she had a feel for whatever primary material there was,

Susannah could move on to secondary sources. Often, since the subjects she chose were not the most well known, there might not be too many of these. Still, she diligently hunted down what she could and added those later interpretations to her file. It was only when she'd built this edifice of names, dates, places, and events that she could begin to shape the material. A life made coherent and comprehensible, even through the long lens of time.

Her publisher was happy with her output and had her on a schedule of one book every eighteen months. Readers populated her Facebook page and left enthusiastic comments on her blog. She had a decent following on Twitter, and by many people's standards, including her own, she was a modest success in a highly circumscribed category. Except that, lately, something had soured inside her, making the act of writing seem stale, repetitive, and flat-out dull. Was it just the aftermath of Charlie's death that had taken the savor out of everything? Could be. But she suspected there was more to it than that. With mug of coffee in hand, she mounted the stairs, determined to try again.

The darkened computer screen bloomed when she touched the keypad. Her editor had suggested Jane Seymour, the third wife of Henry VIII, who had borne him a son and then conveniently expired before he had time to grow bored with her. Jane was one of his least famous wives; there had been others with more dramatic—and gory—endings that tended to fascinate. Susannah had agreed to write the novel and began the research. She consulted books and Internet sources, and looked for the usual letters and diaries—documents that would give her an insight into character and motivation as well as a feel for the period. But as she probed and read, she found herself increasingly drawn to Jane's immediate predecessor, Anne Boleyn.

Anne was intelligent and well educated; she spoke French and was known as an accomplished archer and horsewoman. Singular and captivating, she had straight dark hair, a long neck, and a double nail on the pinkie of one hand. She designed trailing sleeves that she had her dressmaker execute, turning her perceived flaw into a fashion trope—Cally would have approved. Anne—who refused to sleep with Henry without a ring and a crown—in holding out got them both. Henry had his marriage to his first wife, Catherine of Aragon, annulled and wed Anne in a secret, private ceremony. The commoner had succeeded in becoming a queen.

But Anne's triumph was short-lived. She bore a girl and then a stillborn boy. Henry's perpetually lustful eye began wandering. Infuriated that he had moved heaven and earth to marry yet another woman who could not bear him a son, Henry decided he needed to get rid of her. No long, drawn-out, messy divorce this time, though. He accused her of sleeping with several of her favorite courtiers, including her own brother. On a beautiful day in May, she was beheaded at the age of thirty-three. But it was Elizabeth, Anne's daughter Elizabeth, and not Jane's son, who ruled England with acumen and grace for fifty or so years.

Staring at the screen, Susannah realized that Anne was so much more interesting than Jane, whom she had aptly called "a whey-faced bitch." She did not want to write a novel about Jane. Anne's ghost would have haunted her for the rest of her days. Unfortunately, Out of the Past Press had published a novel about Anne only two years before; it was called *Brief, Gaudy Hour* and it was quite good. Two years was not long enough in historical fiction land to occasion another book from the same publisher. If Susannah wanted her turn with Anne, she would have to wait.

She stood up, leaving the barely touched coffee to cool on her desk. Before she could change directions, she'd have to come up with someone better, someone so interesting and irresistible that dull-as-days-old-porridge Jane wouldn't matter anymore. It would have been easy to troll the Internet, looking for other ideas, other possibilities. But she had an urge to get out and explore her new surroundings. There was a library in town, wasn't there? And libraries had librarians. Susannah loved librarians and considered them pillars of civilization; it was time she met the one in Eastwood. And on the way home, she could stop at the supermarket and the hardware store, taking care of three errands in a single trip.

She drove the short distance to the town center. In daylight, she could better see the neat houses—saltbox, Cape Cod, a Georgian or two—that dotted the streets and the big trees that framed and embraced them. There was a main street lined with shops and anchored by a pair of churches—one Catholic, the other Presbyterian—that culminated in a small town square. The square was surrounded by an iron fence, and in its center stood a gazebo. Beyond that was a big open field, frozen over now, but she remembered it was used for kids' baseball and soccer games in warmer months.

The Eastwood library, which she found easily enough, was a modest, two-story brick building with three slate steps leading up to a dark green door on which a Christmas wreath still hung. Susannah parked and went in. Fiction was housed on the right side of the circulation desk and biography on the other; a children's area, designated by a colorful checkerboard rug, made up the entire back of the space. There was a bank of computers near the fiction area, but the multipaned windows, oak shelves, and green-shaded lighting fixtures all looked as if they had not been changed in more than fifty years. The librarian, a small, plump wren of a woman with cropped silver hair and big tortoiseshell glasses, looked up immediately. "Can I help you?"

"I hope so," Susannah said. "I'm looking for something but I don't quite know what it is."

"Is there a particular area you're interested in?"

Susannah explained her purpose: writer, historical fiction, in search of a female subject, possibly with a local slant.

"We have a local history section upstairs." The librarian came out from behind the desk and gestured for Susannah to follow. "It's not as big as the one in Portsmouth, but it's surprisingly good for a library this size. There was a pair of Harvard professors, both in American history, who had a summer place in Eastwood, and they left their entire personal collection to us. Such a nice couple." She led Susannah to a wooden card catalog whose drawers had worn brass pulls. Susannah must have looked surprised, because she added, "We're still raising the money to have the collection digitized; for now, we have to make do with this."

"I don't mind." Susannah opened a random drawer. Cards handprinted in blue ink hinted at possible scenarios, intriguing new characters, the tight coil of a well-crafted plot. "I don't mind at all."

"Good. I'm downstairs if you need me."

For the next hour, Susannah riffled through the drawers in search of something or someone that would get her tail wagging. She read about a nineteenth-century landscape painter in Maine who went off to live with the Eskimos in Alaska for a time, and a wealthy thread factory owner's daughter in Massachusetts who organized her father's workers into a union; both were interesting, neither was riveting. Weak winter light played across the library table and her stomach rumbled; she hadn't eaten much breakfast and it was past the time for lunch. Soon the kids would be home, dropped off by the school bus that stopped down the road from the house. Although they both had keys, she still wanted to be there when they got back. Especially Jack. He still got panicky if he didn't find her at home. She would return to the library tomorrow.

Just as she was gathering her laptop and getting ready to go, she spied a book, face out, in a section marked "Portsmouth." It was called *Hanging Ruth Blay: An Eighteenth-Century New Hampshire Tragedy.* Susannah plucked it from the shelf and began to read. Within minutes, she was drawn into the story of the thirty-one-year-old schoolteacher who, in December 1768, climbed the steps to the gallows that had been erected on the high ground of what was now Portsmouth's old South Cemetery. Blay had had a child out of wedlock and maintained the infant was stillborn. Though she was suspected of murder, the crime she was convicted of was concealment of the baby, which, shockingly, carried the death penalty. There had been several appeals, two stays of execution, but no pardon; she was condemned to die by hanging, the last woman to be executed in the state.

Susannah closed the book. If she'd had the time, she would have read the whole thing right here—it wasn't all that long. But she could check it out and finish it at home. Downstairs, she realized she did not yet have a library card and she began to complete the form taken from a stack on the counter. As she printed the information, the librarian looked at the book. "Oh, Ruth Blay. What a sad story. But fascinating. And an important part of our local history, even if not the most exemplary one."

"You're familiar with the book?"

"And the author. Carolyn Marvin has been up to Eastwood to do a library talk. We had a packed house that night."

"I can see why." Susannah handed her the form.

"Gilmore?" The librarian looked up. "Are you by any chance related to Claire Gilmore?"

"She was my mother. She died a few years ago."

"I'm so sorry to hear that."

"Did you know her well? She hadn't lived here in some time." Susannah's mind darted immediately to the note, now tucked in the shoe box along with the volume of Yeats. Could this librarian know anything about it? It didn't seem too likely, but then, finding a love letter written to her mother while she was married didn't seem too likely either.

"I remember, though. She came in here a couple of times a week. That was all before the Internet and Amazon; libraries were more of a hub back then, especially in a place like this."

"I know what you mean." Susannah took the card the librarian had just issued her. "She was a big reader, and she always belonged to one book club or another."

"There was a club that met right here in the library. They'd focus on novels—Russian for a while, then English, and then American. Maybe German too . . . I can remember her checking out *The Magic Mountain* and *Buddenbrooks*. And at some point, she left off with the novels and wanted only poetry."

"Really?" Susannah thought of the well-thumbed volume of Yeats.

"Wordsworth, Keats, Shelley, Byron. But she told me she was drawn to some of the more modern poets too: Yeats, Auden, Roethke. I asked if she was joining a poetry-themed book group and she said no—it was because of the Poet's Corner."

"Poet's Corner?"

"At the paper. The *Eastwood Journal*. She was the arts and culture editor, and somehow she got the idea that the arts page should publish poetry. So she wanted to familiarize herself with 'the canon,' as she called it. She would be reading submissions and selecting them for publication; she wanted to feel like she was qualified. I admired her for it; I really did."

Susannah was silent, processing all this new information. She had known about her mother's job at the paper; Claire had spoken of it often and with great animation. But she had talked about profiles they ran, or the film, theater, and art reviews. Had she ever mentioned poetry? If so, it couldn't have been often, because Susannah didn't remember it.

The librarian had placed the checked-out book about Ruth Blay on the desk and was now typing something on the keyboard of her computer. Susannah picked it up and extended her hand. "Thank you for all your help . . ."

"Janet," said the librarian. "Janet Durbin." She shook Susannah's hand. "If I can be of any further assistance, please let me know."

"I will." Susannah returned to the car and put the book on the seat beside her. Ruth Blay's story was fascinating, distinctive, tragic— all qualities that might make it a suitable basis for a novel. A novel that she would write, right here, so close to the very place where it had happened. She decided she liked the connection, loose as it was. Although her circumstances were not at all like Ruth's, she did feel exiled here in New Hampshire. And she was husbandless too.

This, she saw, might be an idea worth further investigation. She could read the rest of the Marvin book, and do a little more research too. And she could think about it—she definitely needed to let the notion settle and percolate. God knew she would have plenty of time, buried as she was in the sticks and the snow. *You wanted to come here,* she told herself. *You chose this.* But if Charlie were here, she would have chosen none of it.

Traffic was light on the way back to the house. Whatever she decided about pursuing the Blay story, she was glad she had gone to the library. Janet's revelations about her mother made her even more curious about the note she'd found. Meeting her had been a lucky coincidence; she had known Claire and she might have known other people who knew her as well. Susannah was pretty sure the newspaper had folded—so many local papers had—but maybe there were still people around who had worked on it. Same for members of the book club. And hadn't her mother belonged to an amateur acting group here as well as in New Jersey? There were several possibilities she could pursue.

But when she arrived at the Hannaford market, she sat frozen behind the wheel for a few seconds. What was she *doing*? All her digging might well lead to some deeply upsetting revelations; this wasn't like writing a historical novel, teasing out the backstory and then speculating on the motivations of characters long dead— and with no connection to her besides. This was about her own mother, her father—and ultimately about herself.

She made her way through the wide, empty—yet again!— supermarket aisles, filling the cart up with groceries. More snow was predicted and the driving might be iffy; best to stock up now. As she filled the cart—apples, oranges, a pineapple, a wedge of cheddar—her anxiety dissipated. Shopping for food calmed her; she was fulfilling a basic, essential function. It was likely that she was going to uncover something about her family that she wished she had not known. But standing in the cookie aisle—the bright, cheery packages calling out to be bought, consumed, enjoyed— she understood that the novelist in her would win out.

That wasn't the whole reason, though. Her mother had always been the elusive presence in her life. Loving but often distracted, easily moved to anger—at her father, seldom at her—or disappoint- ment or sorrow. Her father had been the rock, the one who read to her at bedtime, helped with her homework, took her to the zoo, taught her to ride a bicycle. As she peddled toward him, first hesi- tantly and then with growing confidence, she saw his slow smile widen, a perfect mirror of her own.

"I'm doing it, Daddy," she'd called out.

"You certainly are." And he'd waved his arm in a slow arc of approval that seemed to enfold her, and her brand-new accomplishment, in its airy embrace. She had known her father through and through. She could rely on him. Her mother had been less predictable and more of a mystery. Now she was beginning to understand why. She couldn't go back to the time before she'd found the note; what was known couldn't be unknown. She had to move forward, into the uncertain territory she was trying to map. It meant exposing what had been hidden and revealing what had been unsaid.

Susannah paid for the groceries and wheeled them across the parking lot to the car. When she arrived back at the house, she sat there for a moment, staring at it, before she went in. Houses had lives and houses kept secrets. She'd already stumbled upon one of them. If she kept up her search, what else might she find?

SEVEN

The sky above Primrose Pond that morning was a pallid, anemic gray, but the temperature hovered in the thirties—practically balmy given how cold it had been—so Susannah was taking advantage of the slight spike to get some much needed exercise. It was just under four miles all the way around—a bracing but not impossible walk. The path was uneven and there were some slippery patches along the way, but it was navigable, especially if she took careful steps over the ice. Fallen pine needles provided some natural traction, and someone had been out here with a bag of gravel; bits of it were strewn on the ground, like Gretel's bread crumbs in the fairy tale.

The pond and its environs looked better in daylight: bare tangles of dark branches, white birches striated with slender slashes of brown, the occasional burst of hard red berries that stood out against the wan winter landscape. The gloom that had been with her since she first saw the house again was dissipating a little; she breathed deeply, in and out, in and out.

Soon she came to a house, covered in cedar shingles, that she remembered. She and her friends had canoed the pond many times that summer, mostly during the day, but once at night. There had been a party at that house—the parents of the girl who lived in it were away—and of course there had been drinking and the predictable pairing off of various couples.

That was the night Trevor Bailey had stuck his hand under her shirt; when she rebuffed him, the two of them sat, in wretched, awkward silence, as everyone else made out in the darkened living room. Corbin had not been there, but he had shown up later, as the party was winding down. She thought she saw him staring at her, though she might have just imagined it. She hadn't seen him again since that meeting in the hardware store, but she'd learned that he'd come back home at some point to help out with the business when his father had suddenly become sick, and he'd stayed on. Not sure that she wanted to see him again so soon—the rush of adolescent feelings and memories he'd unleashed were disconcerting— she had deliberately stayed away from the store. But Eastwood was a small place and she knew she'd run into him again one way or another.

As Susannah rounded the next curve in the path, she saw both a tall woman and a dog, off leash, approaching. The woman's coat— black, with an asymmetrical cut and oversized buttons—was a marked contrast to the down coats that absolutely everyone wore up here. A soft white knit hat framed the woman's deeply lined but still lovely face, and a black-and-white scarf in a bold abstract pattern looped around her neck.

"Hello!" The woman, who up close appeared even taller—was she five-ten or -eleven?—raised her hand; the leather glove she wore was a bright teal blue. "You must be Susannah Gilmore." She extended the other gloved hand to shake.

"I am." Susannah thought her own puffy mitten seemed faintly ridiculous and she pulled it off so she could take the woman's hand.

"Alice Renfew. I live in the green house around the bend from yours. We're neighbors."

"With the barn, right? I met your horse."

"Jester?"

"Is that his name? Anyway, I saw the gate open, went to close it, and then couldn't resist going over to pet him."

"I'm glad you did. He can get lonely out there."

Susannah studied Alice's face—there was something familiar about it. "I remember you now," she said. Alice had been married to a man they had called Dr. Dave; he was the town's pediatrician. She and her husband were well liked. Trevor had told her about their Fourth of July party, with its long tables piled with barbecued chicken, potato salad, and strawberry shortcake, and the lavish fireworks display the doctor set off at night. Everybody in town was invited. But they hadn't had the party the summer that Susannah spent there; she would have remembered it.

"And I remember you. Claire and Warren Gilmore's daughter, right?"

"Yes. Though they're both gone now."

"I'm sorry," said Alice. "And about your husband. Such a terrible thing."

How had she known that? But Susannah just said, "It was."

"I think you'll find Eastwood a comforting place to be," Alice said. "I know I did. My husband's been gone over twenty years now, but when he died the community just wrapped its arms around me and took me in."

"That's because you'd lived here a long time," said Susannah.

"You have roots here too. You'll see them blossom."

Susannah did not entirely believe her, but rather than seem

contrary to her neighbor, she allowed her attention to be diverted by the black standard poodle that had been patiently standing at Alice's side all this time. "Is she friendly?" she asked as she reached out her hand for the dog to sniff.

"Friendly and more well mannered than most people you'll meet. Also sharp as the proverbial tack."

At the sound of her mistress's voice, the dog turned and wagged her tail, but not before giving Susannah's hand an experimental little lick. "She's a beauty."

"Hear that, Emma?" Alice said. "You have a new admirer."

They said good-bye and Susannah stood for a moment watching the two forms recede. Ever since her discovery of that note, she was on a mission to find out as much about her parents as she could. Next week she was going to have lunch with Janet Durbin, the librarian; Janet had very kindly offered to put her in touch with a couple of people from the newspaper, and she'd even provided a list of the book club members that she had found stuck in an old notebook. Now here was Alice Renfew, who said that she knew her parents too; maybe she could be another source.

Susannah kept going. Farther on was a pair of houses, one yellow, the other white, both sealed up pretty tightly. Not all the houses on the pond were winterized. Over on this side, the bare bushes had given way to dense clusters of pine trees against whose deep green nettles the birches glowed white. A rustling in the trees attracted Susannah's attention; in the next second, a small grayish brown rabbit darted by. She'd have to tell Jack.

She began to feel warm inside her recently purchased down coat. And her feet were toasty and warm too, thanks to those L.L.Bean boots she'd ordered for Cally; instead of sending them back, Susannah decided to keep them for herself. At least Cally had boots now; Susannah had agreed to the purple Doc Martens.

She didn't really oppose her daughter's choice; she'd been letting Cally pick out her own clothes since she was three. But she fretted that the oddball boots would make Cally even more of an outsider at a school where she seemed determined not to fit in.

Now she had reached the halfway point and could see her own house from across the pond. There was a girl in one of these houses Jack had been talking about nonstop; her name was Gilda Mooney. Golden Gilda with her skein of blond hair and her dimpled smile. It was all so sweet, her son's first infatuation, and Charlie would never know a thing about it. Susannah's eyes filled, but she used her mittened hand to brush the tears away and kept going. She wished that Cally could acclimate as easily as Jack seemed to be doing, but that was not happening. Instead, she said virtually nothing about her days at school and spent her free time in her room, the sewing machine making its steady whirring sound from behind her closed door. But when Susannah asked what she was sewing, Cally became evasive, as she was about pretty much everything.

Back at home, Susannah opened a can of lentil soup, added a few oyster crackers, and brought the steaming mug upstairs to her desk. The idea of pursuing Blay as her next subject had been steadily growing on her; now she decided she was ready to test it out in the form of a proposal. She had read Martin's book quickly and then ordered a copy so she could mark it up with comments and questions of her own.

As she sipped the soup, Susannah began to put together a timeline of the events surrounding Blay's life and death. Her notes were accumulating, and she started a loose synopsis of the plot as she saw it unspooling. The grim trajectory made Susannah feel indignant all over again. What had it been like, stealing away and giving birth for the first time alone and in a strange place? Where were the mother, the sisters, aunts, cousins, and friends who could have soothed and helped her? What happened to the man who got Ruth pregnant? If Ruth's crime was punishable by death, why had he remained unscathed? The facts of the story, scant as they were, did not reveal the motivations of these people. It would be up to her to create them.

The doorbell rang and she went downstairs to answer it. Maybe it was a delivery; she was expecting a package. But instead it was the woman she had met on the path, Alice Renfew. The black poodle stood quietly beside her. "I hope I'm not disturbing you," said Alice. "We're kind of informal around here."

"No, not at all; please come in." This wasn't entirely true, but Susannah did not want to be rude to a neighbor, especially one who might become a friend. "Let's sit in the kitchen. I can make tea. Or coffee."

"Coffee would be nice." Alice sat down and placed a round gold tin on the table. "I brought these for you. A little housewarming gift."

"Thank you." Inside the tin and nestled in pink tissue paper were shortbread crescents dusted with powdered sugar. Susannah was touched. Maybe Alice really *would* become a friend; this was certainly a friendly offering.

"Try one."

Susannah bit into a cookie. "Scrumptious. Did you make them?"

"I did. I like to bake."

Susannah finished the cookie and reached for another. "These are so good you could sell them."

Alice smiled. "Actually, I did. I had a little bakery in town. It was called Lady Alice's. Shortbread was one of my most popular items."

"Really?"

"Oh, yes. It was years ago. I enjoyed it for a time—and then I didn't. Besides, it was too hard to manage along with all my domestic responsibilities." Susannah didn't say anything and Alice continued. "Things were different when I was young. I went to Smith at a time when everyone believed in the 'ring before spring.' We enjoyed our classes, but our main interest was to marry well. And when I did, I believed that my husband's needs always came first."

"Did you mind?" Susannah hoped she was not being intrusive, but Alice had introduced the topic.

"No, not really. Dave and I were very happy. And he allowed me a lot of latitude. The bakery wasn't the only thing I tried. I had a dress shop for a time too—I stocked it with things I made and ready-made clothes. Accessories too, like hats and scarves I ordered from Boston or New York. I think your mother may have bought something from me once. But that didn't do well here in Eastwood, so I had to close. And then there was my charity work, and being on the board of the library, and the civic council. I guess you could say I was a bit of a dilettante."

"No, maybe you were a Renaissance woman—someone with many talents."

"That's a nice way to look at it."

Susannah got up so she could prepare the coffee; when she was through, she brought the brimming mugs to the table.

Alice added milk and sugar; she'd taken a few sips when the bell rang again. A certain something flickered across Alice's face. Expectation? Hope? The bell sounded again and Susannah headed for the door.

"Sorry, I forgot my key." Jack stood there, shrugging the straps of his backpack from his shoulders.

"Jack, come and meet our neighbor, Alice Renfew," said Susannah. Whatever she'd seen on Alice's face a moment ago was gone.

"Hello, Jack," said Alice. "I hope you like shortbread." She nudged the tin in his direction.

He took a cookie and began to eat. "Wow, this is awesome. You made these?"

"I did." Alice was clearly pleased.

"You should get the recipe, Mom." He hauled the gallon container of milk from the fridge and poured a glass. Then he noticed the poodle, which had been curled up near Alice's feet. "Cool dog. Can I pet her?"

"Her name is Emma and she would love that," said Alice. Emma lifted her head at the sound of Alice's voice. Jack stroked the puff of dark fur above the poodle's eyes. The poodle blinked and then her long, elegant tongue unfurled to lick his wrist.

"I think she likes me," said Jack.

"I think so too. She has impeccable taste." Alice stood up. "I don't want to take up any more of your time."

"Thank you so much for stopping by," Susannah said.

"And for the cookies," added Jack. He was onto his second and a third was in his hand.

When Alice had gone, Susannah left Jack to watch TV for a while; the kid needed to unwind before he tackled his homework. And even though she would need to get dinner going soon, she still wanted to look over today's notes before she started. Alice's visit had interrupted her, but sometimes an interruption turned out to be useful, because it enabled her to see things more clearly when she got back to work.

The plot outline was her working tool; it would be fleshed out with scenes, conversations, and descriptions. She would turn these elements into the sample pages that would, she hoped, convince Tasha that Ruth's was a tale worth telling. But she still wasn't ready to start writing; she hadn't heard the voice yet. And voice was always what started her on her way, her cue to begin.

At first the voice was elusive, emanating as it did from another century—a whisper from behind a damask wall hanging or a velvet drape. Soon the voice grew louder. *Listen to me,* it said. *Tell my story.* Then Susannah began seeing images that embodied the voice: a woman in a crimson stomacher, seated at an inlaid escritoire where she was composing a letter; a different woman standing in front of a cheval glass as a maid laboriously tightened the laces of her corset.

Susannah had not heard Ruth Blay's voice, not yet. She was close, though; she could sense it. What if she used a first-person narration, telling the story in Ruth's own voice? Then the book would have to end with her death, and Susannah had a feeling the story was bigger, and needed more space around it, more context. Third person would give her some distance but would also sacrifice the immediacy—and the impending horror.

The winter sky was darkening outside the window as Susannah considered the shadowy but haunting figure of Betsey Pettingill, the child who had found the infant's body in the barn. How would she have felt, knowing that she had played such a pivotal, albeit unwitting, role in this story? When did she fully understand what she had done? She was sure Betsey would have felt responsible for what happened to Ruth. Implicated in her hanging. And most obvious of all: she would have felt guilty, the weight of Ruth's death sitting like a massive stone in her heart for the next one hundred years.

Susannah thought of her last exchange with Charlie: the bicycle ride she had not taken, the helmet she had not reminded him to wear. The guilt for those two crimes—of omission, not commission, but what did it matter when he was dead, dead, dead?—had sliced a psychic wound inside her, a wound that would never heal. Had it been like that for Betsey too? At that moment, Susannah felt she would give anything to know.

EIGHT

The clarity Susannah had felt that night had vanished by the next morning. She woke with a dull, throbbing headache, and all the strands of her story-in-the-making were a tangled mess in her mind. After downing a pair of Tylenol tablets, she made coffee, hoping the combination would banish her headache and jumpstart her writing. But it did not do the trick. When the headache faded, she was left with a jittery, restless energy that propelled her from her desk to pacing around her room. When she was in a state like this, she yearned for some physical activity; even cleaning the house would work. Yes, that was a good idea. She'd do a deep clean of this room, setting the stage for her own creative process.

First she changed the sheets and made the bed with military precision. Next she gathered the various articles of clothing strewn around and put them away. She'd dust, and vacuum too. And what about those windows? Already she was feeling better—more centered. But when she went to hang her black pants in the closet, her attention was diverted by the sight of the two-piece dress, the one she'd found in the attic. Just back from the dry cleaners, the dress was still wrapped in the transparent plastic through which Susannah could see the fitted jacket with its velvet collar and shiny jet buttons. The dress was demure, yet elegant. She had never seen her mother wear it; could Susannah even be sure it was hers?

On the shelf above the rod where the dress was hung was the box with the book and the letter. Was there anything else here in the house? She'd combed the attic carefully, and she had brought down the portrait of her mother and set it on the dresser, propped against the wall. But what about the other rooms, like the bedroom? Her parents had slept in this room; maybe it too held some clues.

Suddenly, cleaning the bedroom seemed beside the point and instead she began systematically going through the deep dresser drawers and the more shallow drawers in the night tables that flanked the queen-sized bed. Nothing of interest in any of these places. And the same was true of the bedroom closet.

By now she was frustrated—two plans derailed. And she was hungry—she hadn't had anything besides the coffee. She would have breakfast. But downstairs, the living room felt chilly and unwelcoming. What if she made a little fire? The basket where she kept the logs was empty, so she pulled on her parka, went outside, and crossed the snow-covered patch of ground that led to the woodshed. The small, peeling structure—she'd need to have it painted this spring—stood a few yards from the house, and she yanked on the stubborn door for several seconds before it yielded. She stepped inside.

Two narrow windows set high in the walls let in a weak wash

of light, and Susannah pulled a few of the logs off the top and set them near the door. Spiders scurried away and a dark shape darted by—maybe a mouse. Then she noticed something pink that was shoved down between the wall and the logs stacked against it.

Curious, she got closer. The pink shape resolved itself into a faded floral pattern that included some other colors, mauve and lilac, as well. It seemed to be made of fabric. She had to climb over the logs to get at it, but even when she pulled hard it would not come free. She began moving the logs away, and despite the cold, she grew warm from the exertion. She also scratched her wrist, and a long stripe of blood rose to her skin. Damn.

But finally she had moved enough of the logs away to retrieve what turned out to be a makeup case. The zipper was rusty and stuck, but after a little effort Susannah was able to get it open. Inside, she found a lipstick in her mother's signature shade—Revlon's Fire and Ice—a bottle of nail polish whose contents had solidified to a dark mottled mass, and, most puzzling of all, a bunch of yellowed newspaper clippings. When she opened them up, she saw that they were poems. Janet Durbin had mentioned that the Poet's Corner had been one of her mother's pet projects; maybe these poems had something to do with that.

The light inside the shed was not conducive to reading, so she stuffed the poems back in the case and then balanced it on top of the logs so she could carry everything back to the house. She dumped the logs in the basket. The fire and her breakfast could wait; she wanted to read the poems now. One described a pond in summer: "hidden places / hidden spaces / iridescent green, with algae traces." Was this Primrose Pond? There was one about an owl and another about some loons. Then she came upon one entitled "Say Yes."

The pale blue flowers on your dress
So small, so shy
Did they say yes?

I heard your voice
I watched you dance
I made you mine with just a glance
Though I would never dare to press
Still I hoped you would say yes.

Your lilting laugh
Your sidelong glance
I held you when you came to prance.
We spun and twirled; no more, no less
And yet it seemed you might say yes.

Your ink black curls cascading down
Your doelike eyes, so warm, so brown
Your easy smile, so wide and free
All these, did they say yes to me?

It was signed, as they all were, by someone called I. N. Vayne. That was a nom de plume if there ever was one. Susannah read the poem over several times. In her youth, her mother had had a head of rather unruly black hair, a tangle of ringlets and corkscrew curls that she would gather up into a loose ponytail or messy top-knot. Sometimes she let her hair down, though; her father always called it "Claire's dark cloud" and told her how pretty she looked. In the portrait he painted, Claire's hair was down. She also had large brown eyes; these too were visible in the portrait. Was it possible that the woman in the poem was Susannah's mother? That

the poet had written it to and for her? If so, he would have been
courting her openly, right there on the page, for everyone to see.

There was one last poem in the batch. She smoothed it out so
she could read it.

MORNING LOVE

The dawn came gently
first gray, then rose
I turned, beheld you:
a somnolent pose.

The slope of your shoulder
the curve of your breast
so beautiful but when
would you reveal the rest?

Then your eyes flew open
and joy was mine
we kissed, we arched
O joy sublime!

Who cares about the dawn,
be it gray or bright,
when you are here, my love,
my soul's own delight?

If "Say Yes" had posed a question, then "Morning Love" cele-
brated the answer. The lover's query had been fulfilled and he'd
claimed his beloved, in clear, emphatic language. Only this was
no poetry class, no academic dissection of lines written by and to

people she did not and would not ever know; if her suspicions were correct, in the first the poet was asking her mother to yield to his desire, and in the second he expressed his exultation that she had.

Suddenly, Susannah felt sick. This was more than the leftover discomfort with a parent's sexuality—way more. If she understood the sequence of the poems correctly, she was watching a stranger woo her mother away from her father, away from them and into another life. It was as if someone had grabbed a corner of the rug that represented her childhood and yanked it cleanly out from under her. Bang, she went. Down on the cold, hard floor. *Oh God,* she said softly to herself. *Oh dear God.*

The scratch on her wrist, ignored and now an elegant brush-stroke of blood, had started to throb. She brought the poems and the makeup case to her room. Then she went into the bathroom to wash her wrist and apply a coat of Neosporin. How had the makeup bag ended up in the woodshed? Had her mother hidden it there? Possibly. Claire had suffered from Alzheimer's, and in the early stages, before she had been diagnosed, Susannah remembered episodes of hoarding and related behaviors: a stockpile of pastries, rotting and attracting ants, found under her bed, wads of cash stuffed into cereal boxes or the toaster. So it was conceivable that she'd put her makeup bag in the woodshed, but the timing wasn't right—her illness began years later. Unless she had come back here, alone, without telling Susannah. Yet another secret she had kept from her daughter?

Susannah picked up the phone to call Mabel Dunfee. But no one answered and she had to leave a message. The headache returned, full force, and now she was feeling the kind of chill that was often the prelude to getting the flu. Why was the house so damn cold, anyway? She made a fire and sat eating a bowl of granola in front of it.

Better. That was much better. And when she had finished the granola and washed out the bowl and spoon, she returned to the fire and settled down on the couch to watch it for a few minutes. Instead, she dozed for what must have been an hour, her sleep punctuated by dreams in which she was back in the woodshed, pawing through the logs, only the logs somehow became animate and began to wriggle and writhe. The pulsating mass of them was quite horrible and she bolted awake, relieved that the only logs she could see were the ones in the fireplace, burning steadily and cleanly. The phone rang and she went into the kitchen to answer it. Mabel Dunfee was on the other end of the line.

"Thanks for calling me back," she said. "I just had a couple of questions I wanted to ask you about my mother."

"Your mother?" Mabel sounded confused.

"I know it seems strange," said Susannah. "But since I've moved back here, I've been finding things of hers tucked into the oddest places."

"I thought all her personal effects were in the attic," Mabel said. "That's what Ms. Jacobsmeyer told me."

"Yes, I did find some of her things there. My father's too. But I've also found things in other places, like the woodshed, and somehow I don't think it was the tenants who put them there. Do you?"

"No. Your mother must have done it when she was back here."

"My mother was here?" Susannah's voice was sharp. "When?"

"I thought you knew." Mabel sounded apologetic. "Linnie Ashcroft told me she'd come to town once. It was in between tenants. Mr. Gilmore didn't come with her. Some boy from the university drove her up. Linnie said that they stayed overnight at that nice B and B on the pond—Meadow Flower Farm. She also said that your mother seemed a little . . . confused."

"I see." The dream image of the dark squirming logs filled her head again.

"Maybe I should have mentioned it when you came back," Mabel said. "But it's been so many years and, to be honest, I forgot all about it. Anyway, your poor mother's long gone now."

"Long gone," Susannah repeated. But in her mind it seemed as if Claire was very much alive and present. And that, like one of the characters in Susannah's novels, she was desperately trying to make her voice heard.

NINE

From the front porch of her house, Alice watched the girl as she came up the road. She had stepped outside to deposit a neatly tied bundle of newspapers by the door; the next time she drove into town, she'd bring them to the recycling center.

Alice had seen her a couple of times, hair as bright as a flame against all the white and gray of the surrounding landscape. And she knew who she was too. Her erstwhile neighbors, the Gilmores, had a daughter, Susannah, who'd moved back into the house with her two children. Claire and Warren were, Alice recalled, a pleasant, if mismatched, couple, Claire all light and shimmer—how could *she*, of all unlikely people, have succumbed to dementia?— the husband, Warren, gentle but earthbound, a plodding soul. That he'd ever managed to win her was an unsolved mystery.

A week or so ago, Alice had gone to visit Susannah hoping she might meet the girl. It had not happened, but Alice knew there would be other opportunities. And look—here she was again. The girl walked—or trudged, really—with her head down. She did not look happy. In fact, she looked downright glum, which was just the way she'd looked the two other times Alice had spied her. Something was weighing on her, poor dear. It was a pity too, what with those looks: tall, slim, nice posture. And the hair, of course. The hair that was a veritable gift from God. Everyone always went on and on about blondes; Alice had been blond as a child, and even though her hair had darkened somewhat, the skillful handiwork of her colorist had allowed her to maintain the illusion for years. But to her eye, red was the far more interesting color, so commanding and improbable.

Then the girl did an unexpected thing. She stopped, ducked under the fence, and walked across the snowy meadow to the barn. She must have seen Jester. When the weather wasn't too cold, Alice opened the top of the stall to give him a little light and air.

The girl walked right up to him but did not attempt to touch him right away, as people tended to do. Instead, she waited, letting Jester take her measure. Only then did she extend her hand to rub the place between his nostrils. Jester exhaled mightily. How had she known this was his favorite place?

Alice stepped off the porch and began to walk across the snow. She wasn't wearing boots and her feet felt the cold instantly. Still, she did not want this moment—or this girl—to slip away. Redheaded, brooding, and with an instinct for horses, she seemed unusual, and Alice wanted to get to know her.

"Do you ride?" Alice called out.

"Excuse me?" The girl turned. There were a few freckles on her nose and upper cheeks; otherwise, her skin was very pale.

"Horses. Do you ride horses?"

"I used to," said the girl. "When I was younger."

Younger? thought Alice. *Why, you're younger than springtime.*

Younger than the newest buds. But all she said was, "You seem to know how to handle him."

"I love horses. I went to an equestrian camp for a few summers. I always wanted a horse of my own, but my parents said no." She continued to stroke Jester's muzzle.

"You lived in the city," Alice said. "That wouldn't have been practical."

"How did you know that?" The girl didn't seem alarmed, only curious.

"I've lived in this house, and this town, for years and years. So I hear all the local goings-on. I know that you, your mother, and—what is it, brother? sister?—moved here from New York City."

"That's right. My mom, my little brother, and me. I'm Calista." She stopped stroking the horse and extended her hand. "Calista Miller."

"Alice Renfew." She took the hand, thinking that the girl had been very well brought up; this pleased her somehow. "Calista is such a lovely name. From the Greek, meaning, 'She who is most beautiful.'"

"You know all about me!" Calista seemed to like this.

"Well, I know the myth. There was a nymph, daughter of the Arcadian king Lycaon. Zeus fell in love with her, and so Hera, who was jealous, transformed her into a she-bear. Zeus felt sorry for her, so he placed her high in the sky, among the constellations."

"Wow," said Calista. "You really do know everything."

"Maybe not everything." Alice smiled. "But I took a Greek and Roman mythology course in college. And did know your grandparents."

"Really?"

"Oh, yes. They were my neighbors."

"They died when I was little; I don't remember them."

"I remember them quite well. I'll have to tell you all about them."

Jester emitted an impatient snort. "Oh, he's cross that we're not paying attention to him," said Alice, and Calista began stroking him again. "Would you like to ride him sometime?"

"Could I really?"

"If it's all right with your mother, yes. And we'd have to get you a helmet."

Calista suddenly looked very grave. "I'd never ride without a helmet," she said. "Never."

Alice noted her reaction but did not remark on it. The wind began to pick up and she had to acknowledge that, while she was enjoying herself immensely, her feet were almost numb. She'd better go back into the house. "Come and visit sometime," she said to Calista. "I'd love to have you over."

"Thanks," Calista said. The wind whipped that hair of hers around her face. "I'd like that."

Alice went back inside and made herself a cup of tea. She was glad to have met her new neighbor. She'd already met the girl's mother, and she vaguely remembered that she'd been up here one summer; it must have been before Dave died. But she'd never felt any particular connection or rapport. Whereas with Calista it was different.

There was a box of thin chocolate wafers in the cupboard and she took them out. Dave would have liked this girl, she decided. Dave would have liked her very much. Years ago, when they were newly married, she and Dave had tried to have children, but it had not happened for them. Month after disappointing month, thinking, *Yes, maybe this time; I'm two days late, now three,* only to have all that hope literally bleed right out of her. Alice knew that the disappointment ground away at him too. Back in those days they didn't do much testing, not at all like now, when everyone was poked, prodded, and analyzed to death. So it was never entirely clear where the fault lay; Alice was not sure she even wanted to know.

She finished the tea, rinsed out the cup, and put the cookies away. It was too early for dinner and she felt restless in this blue, not quite evening hour. Emma seemed to pick up on her mood; she tilted her head inquisitively and looked at her mistress. Alice got up. It might have been too early for her evening meal, but it was not too early for Emma's. She prepared the dog's food and set it on the floor. Emma ate, as she did everything, with great delicacy, and when she was through, she nudged the bowl with her snout, her signal to ask for a biscuit. Alice gave it to her, then went to the door to let her out into the yard.

While Emma was outside, Alice took a couple of carrots from the crisper, her coat from its hook, and a flashlight. Then she joined Emma in the yard. Emma trotted up and followed her beyond the fence and across the meadow. Alice rarely visited Jester at night, but Calista's interest earlier in the day urged her toward him, as if she could recapture some of the hopeful anticipation she'd felt at their meeting by returning to where it had taken place.

Alice unlocked the latch on the barn door and let herself inside, using the flashlight until she located the pull chain that illuminated the stalls. Jester whinnied and Alice produced a carrot from her pocket, which she fed him. It was cold out here, but Alice didn't want to go back into the house yet.

There had been an afternoon back in the late 1960s when Alice was in the office filling in for Dave's receptionist, who was out sick. A girl of about seventeen came in. She had very close-set eyes and an unfortunate beak of a nose but her luxuriant mane of red hair—even gathered into its girlish ponytail, it was something to see—must have turned heads everywhere.

"Hello, Mrs. Renfew." The girl's voice was just above a whisper. "Do you remember me?" Alice looked carefully. "Lucy," said the girl. "Lucy Delvaux."

"Lucy!" said Alice. "Of course!" She remembered the child as one of three or four in a large, noisy family that never paid its bills on time. Dave continued to treat the children anyway. "I haven't seen you in ages—you're practically all grown up now."

"We moved," Lucy said. "To Kittery."

Kittery was just over the Piscataqua River, in Maine. "Well, it's nice to see you again. What brings you here?"

"I wanted to see Dr. Dave." The ponytail seemed to quiver. "I don't have an appointment but I was hoping—that is, I thought—"

"I see," said Alice. And she did. There was some kind of trouble; she could sense it. "He's with someone now, but if you wait here just a little while, I'll squeeze you in."

Lucy sat down to wait and Alice went back to her filing. Every now and then she would cast a surreptitious glance at Lucy; the girl sat with a copy of *Life* magazine open on her lap but she did not turn a single page. Tears shone on her cheeks.

When the boisterous but darling Harris twins had emerged from the examining room, Dave ushered Lucy inside and closed the door. Alice had a feeling she knew what the story would be. And over dinner that night, Dave confirmed her hunch.

"Knocked up," he said succinctly over a plate of roast chicken, mashed potatoes, and brussels sprouts. "By a sailor, no less. He was stationed at the base." The naval base was midway between Portsmouth and Kittery; they passed it often. "But he's long gone, shipped out along with the fake last name he gave her."

"Oh, dear," said Alice. "Does her family know?"

"Not yet." He speared a sprout. "I offered to tell them, though."

"Can she—you know . . . ?"

"Have an abortion?" Dave never did like to mince words.

"Well, yes." Alice knew that what she proposed was illegal. But she also knew Dave didn't think it ought to be and that he would know where to send the girl if necessary.

"Too late for that. I'd say she's almost five months along."

"Five months!" Alice dropped the roll she'd been buttering. "I would never have known."

"Neither did she." He was fiddling with his fork now.

"She came to me for help; she didn't know where to turn. So I had an idea. An idea that I hope you'll like . . ."

"What is it?" But she knew even before he said it.

"I told Lucy she could come live with us. Her family could invent some reason for her absence. You'd take care of her and Jed Cooke says he could deliver her down at the hospital; he'll keep it very quiet." Jed was an obstetrician who practiced in Portsmouth; Dave had known him for years. "Jed's brother's a lawyer; he could draft the adoption papers. All legal and aboveboard, of course. I told Lucy we'd give her money for college and she could enroll next fall." Dave's fork had taken on a life of its own, circling, jabbing, jutting, poking. "You haven't said a word." Dave looked at her anxiously. "Won't you please say something?"

"You darling man!" She rushed from her seat to embrace him.

Jester finished the carrot and pawed the dirt impatiently until Alice produced another. Her hands were cold and she balled them into her pockets. Emma looked up and then placed her head down again. Clearly they weren't going anywhere.

. . .

Lucy had moved in the very next day. The long, snowy winter kept her inside a lot, which was just fine; she had no desire to run into anyone she knew. She was a good-natured girl, insistent upon helping Alice around the house, and grateful for her place in it. Those close-set eyes of hers? They shone with intelligence and feeling. That nose? Why, it was aquiline, not beaky: strong, proud, and beautiful. Alice taught her to knit, and together they churned out tiny garments and cozy blankets for the baby, all in yellow and white, since in those days no one knew what the sex would be. They grew close enough for Alice to feel she could ask about the baby's father. "He was a good dancer," Lucy said. "And he always brought me flowers when he came to pick me up."

"How long did you know him?" Alice was aware this was a delicate question.

Lucy concentrated on a sleeve. "Not very long," she said finally. "About ten days. But we went out together every night while he was stationed here, and by the last night I felt like I could trust him. He said he loved me; I believed him. And when he got us a room so we could be alone for a little while, I wasn't afraid to go with him."

"He didn't . . . force you, did he?"

Lucy shook her head, and her glorious red ponytail whipped from side to side. "Oh, no! I wanted to." The girl's face was suffused with pink.

"There's nothing for you to be ashamed of," Alice said gently. "You believed this young man when he said he loved you, and I'm guessing you felt like you loved him back. If there's anyone who should be ashamed, it's him. He's the one who ran away."

"I never thought of it that way before," said Lucy.

Alice waited, the sound of their needles clicking companionably as they worked. "You could have made an effort to find him, you know. It wouldn't have been impossible."

"Why?" Lucy asked. "To force him to marry me? That's not what I wanted."

"He should at least have been made aware of what he'd done and not left you to deal with it all on your own."

"I suppose." Lucy lifted up the sweater; it was nearly done. "But since you and Dr. Dave took me in, everything's all right now—even my mom thinks so. I'll have the baby; you'll adopt it. I can go to college in the fall, just like you said. No one will ever have to know."

"No one," Alice said. "It will be our secret." And it would. The baby would have so many more advantages than if she or he grew up with Lucy—two stable, loving parents, a spacious and beautiful home, an opportunity to attend the best schools and camps, access to lessons of all kinds—maybe they ought to get a piano, just in case?—exposure to a different class of people, regular trips abroad. She, not Lucy, would be the child's true mother. The accident of its birth would be nothing more than an obscure footnote.

Finally, the cold won out. Alice reached out to touch the horse's muzzle, but he shook his head and turned away; he was pouting because there wasn't going to be a final carrot. She checked the buckle on the heavy lined blanket that was strapped around his middle. Just before she turned to go, Alice noticed something in the straw. She knelt and retrieved a glove made of fluffy sky blue angora. It belonged to the girl, she realized. Calista. She must have dropped it.

Back in the house, Alice placed the glove on the kitchen table and ran hot water over her hands to warm them. She supposed she ought to eat some dinner, but she had no appetite and decided not to bother.

Sometimes preparing a single meal was just more trouble than it was worth. She could always have a snack later if she felt hungry.

Lucy's labor started on a Sunday morning in March. Alice helped her into the car and Dave drove them all to the hospital in Portsmouth. Jed Cooke had already been telephoned; he was waiting for them. Alice and Dave didn't go into the delivery room—that was another thing that wasn't done back then—but they sat together, hands clasped, in the waiting area. The morning turned to afternoon and the afternoon to evening. Dave wanted to get something to eat, but Alice would not budge, so he went to the cafeteria and brought her back a wedge of pie and a cup of coffee; she was too keyed up to touch either.

It was dark when Jed Cooke emerged from the delivery room. There was blood on his scrubs and his face shone with sweat, but he'd taken off his mask and he was smiling. "A seven-pound baby boy," he said. "He's perfect."

Alice rose from the bench as if she'd been drawn up by the top of her head with a string. "Can I see him?" she asked. "Please?"

"Let the nurse clean him up first."

Alice paced while she waited, looking out the window onto Lincoln Avenue. And then finally she and Dave were allowed into the room where Lucy was propped up on pillows, holding the swaddled baby against her chest. Above the white cloth, his eyes were slate blue and his brows, barely visible, were arched and achingly delicate. The tufts of hair on his head were a brilliant coppery red—just like his mother's.

"Oh," said Alice. "May I hold him?"

Lucy nodded and gave the baby to Alice. How easily her arms accommodated his weight; how naturally he seemed to fit against her. But if she felt an instant connection, the baby did not. He twisted and squirmed, his head turning back in his mother's direction.

"Maybe he needs to—you know . . ." Lucy pointed to the front of her green hospital gown, on which two wet patches were visible.

"Of course." Alice returned the baby to Lucy; instantly she felt bereft.

"The nurse said I should do it just for a couple days. It will be good for him, you know? There's special stuff in there that can help him grow."

Alice looked at Dave, who nodded. "Colostrum," he said. "Very healthy. We can get him onto the formula in a day or two."

"All right," said Alice. But, healthy or not, she didn't like the idea.

The next day, when Jed Cooke's brother Ronald showed up with the paperwork, Lucy would not sign. Nursing the infant, she had succumbed to the curve of his cheek, the flutter of his red-gold lashes as he drifted off to sleep. Her mother had come round to see her in the hospital and she too fell under the baby's spell; she was going to help raise him while Lucy lived at home and went to community college part-time. "I'm so sorry," she told Alice. "I know how much you were counting on having him."

No, you don't, Alice thought. But said, "I understand. He's yours, after all. It's hard to give him up."

"Not hard," Lucy said, gazing down at the baby she held. "Impossible."

Alice went into the pink living room with its profusion of cushions, tassels, and fringe, and sat down on the couch. Emma was right behind her. That redheaded boy of Lucy's? He'd be a man now, in his mid-forties, quite possibly married and with children of his own. If they'd been fortunate enough to keep him, she and

Dave might have been grandparents, and she'd have grandchildren filling her house. Instead, there was only Emma.

But now she had new neighbors. Neighbors who might become friends. And there was Calista. What was she doing now? Homework? Or was she texting or playing some inscrutable game on her phone, the way all the young people did these days?

Alice went back into the kitchen. The sky blue glove was still on the table; it seemed to be reaching out to her. She looked over at the clock: ten thirty, too late to return the glove now. But tomorrow afternoon, sometime after the school bus swung by, would be perfect. Alice went to the stairs and called Emma to follow. Delivering that glove to its red-haired owner would be a very neighborly thing to do; Alice had always prided herself on being an especially good neighbor.

TEN

The Yankee Crockpot, the restaurant Janet Durbin had chosen, was right in the center of Exeter, just a short distance away from the entrance to the venerable boarding school. Susannah parked her car and walked past the entrance, catching a glimpse of the well-maintained building and grounds; even in the dead of winter, the place exuded a subtle air of privilege.

When Susannah walked through the door, she saw that Janet was already at the table. Along with her were the two she had invited to this lunch. Damn. Susannah wished she'd gotten here sooner; it would have given her more time to prepare herself. Even though she'd wanted this meeting, the actual fact of it was more awkward than she had imagined. It was possible one of these men had been her mother's lover and had written that impassioned note to her. One of them had wanted her to leave her family— leave *Susannah*—to be with him.

Todd, the now retired editor of the newspaper and the elder of the two, half rose in his seat and took her hand in both of his.

"You look so much like Claire," he said. "You could have been sisters." He seemed to be about eighty, with wisps of white surrounding the pink dome of his skull. His eyebrows were thick, and surprisingly dark, a sharp contrast to his hair.

"No, she doesn't." George Martin spoke before Susannah had a chance to respond. "You're a very attractive woman. But Claire was one of a kind." George was a fellow actor in Claire's theater group who taught drama at the high school.

"I've never thought I looked like her either," Susannah said.

"Well, *I* see the resemblance." Todd reached for the breadbasket. "Clear as day."

"People see what they want to see," said George. He was looking at the menu, so Susannah could not read his expression. She guessed he was in his late fifties, so he would have been younger than her mother, with straight gray-brown hair that he tied in a ponytail; he wore a stretched-out cable-knit sweater over a blue denim shirt. She couldn't imagine him as her mother's lover; he seemed too subdued, too quiet. *Too much like Dad,* flashed through her mind. Any lover of her mother's would have been more like her—mercurial, sporadically brilliant, charismatic.

The waiter appeared to take their order; at Janet's suggestion, Susannah ordered the chicken potpie. "It's one of the best things on the menu," she said.

Susannah still used a black leather-bound Moleskine for taking notes, and she pulled it from her purse along with a pen. She had to move aside the cobalt blue napkin—it matched the tablecloth and the heavy, faceted water glasses—to make room. "I'm hoping to write something about my mother, so I'd love to have any recollections you could share."

"She was a wonderful woman." Todd tore open a roll, which he buttered lavishly. "So bright. So engaged. Very organized and detail oriented too. I adored working with her."

"She loved her job," Janet said. "She said so all the time."

"I was sorry when she left us," said Todd. "I told her I'd be glad to give her a recommendation. But she never contacted me about it."

Susannah hastily jotted down what Todd had said. "She didn't get another job when we moved to New Jersey. She got involved with my school and was active in the PTA. Local theater too. And she was always in one book group or another."

"I told her she was spreading herself too thin." Apart from "hello," this was the first thing George said, and as an opening gambit it seemed just a shade hostile. "She was good at so many things but she never honed or perfected any of them. She should have harnessed her talent better." His expression was disapproving.

Susannah bent over her notebook, glad to have an excuse not to look at him.

Was this a man her mother would have been drawn to? Loved? Todd seemed more likely a choice. Then the food arrived and so her note taking was suspended.

"Susannah is doing some research about Ruth Blay," said Janet. "She's been in the library several times now, delving into our collection."

"It's a good one." Susannah pricked the crust of the potpie with her fork and a wisp of steam escaped. "And you've been so helpful, Janet."

"Have you been to the New Hampshire State Archives, in Concord? That's where a lot of material is kept."

"Not yet. I'm still trying to map out how I want to handle the story first."

"A worthy goal." He helped himself to another roll. "Lovely Claire

Gilmore, with her black curls, her big eyes, and tiny hands . . ." He looked at George. "I don't happen to agree with you, old man. Not at all. Claire wasn't spreading herself thin. In her case, one skill enhanced the others, you know? Her theatrical talents made her a good reader, and being a good reader made her a good editor. And her knowledge in so many areas was also a help; a cultural editor needs to have a feel for culture at large, and that's exactly what Claire had."

Susannah opened her notebook again and scribbled furiously; Todd called her mother "lovely" and had mentioned her "big eyes" and "tiny hands." Weren't these the observations of a lover? And like the poet, he mentioned Claire's dark curly hair. Could he have written the note? It was extremely uncomfortable for her to imagine this—and he seemed to feel no guilt in her presence, no remorse or awkwardness at all—so she pushed the feelings away. She had committed herself to this quest; she wasn't going to abandon it now.

"You're missing the point," said George, almost angrily. "Yes, she was multitalented. But she couldn't commit to any one thing and as a result she just squandered herself." He threw his hands out in an exasperated gesture and hit Susannah's water glass, which tipped over, wetting her notebook. Quickly, she snatched it from the table. George seemed agitated, even angry. Why?

"I'm so sorry." He stood and began blotting the table with his napkin. A waitress hurried over with more napkins, these for George's pants, which had also gotten wet. When they sat down again, Susannah put her notebook in her lap, just to be safe. "So we were talking about Claire," said George.

"And Todd thinks you were being a bit harsh," Janet added. "I happen to agree."

"Am I? I don't think so. She was once offered a role in a play in New York City. But she wouldn't take it because she didn't want to be away from her job at the paper. It was a small part. Off-off-Broadway. But still—New York City."

"Was that the reason?" asked Janet. "I thought it was because she didn't want to leave Warren, even briefly. She said she didn't know how he'd manage without her."

Susannah could not imagine her mother saying that. Warren was the one who catered to her. They both did, really. She had loved her mother but felt a little afraid of her at times. Her temper. Her moods. When Susannah was about twelve, her mother had uncharacteristically surprised her with tickets to see the New York City Ballet perform at Lincoln Center. *The Firebird* was on the program and Susannah had been riveted by the scarlet-clad ballerina, her every movement and gesture an expression of anguish. How she loathed her captivity. And how desperately she wanted to be free. And sitting there in the dark, with the Stravinsky music swelling around her like a storm, Susannah remembered having the sudden, alarming thought that her mother was a bit like that bird. She loved her daughter and her husband, but there was always something of the wild thing about her—something that resisted taming or domestication. Susannah had never said this to anyone, not to her mother—who adored the performance and at the intermission bought them each a glass of champagne, Susannah's first, to celebrate—and certainly not her father. Anyway, she had no words for what it was that she felt; it was just a current of feeling, an inchoate knowledge that was all the more terrifying for being inadmissible.

"—I vaguely remember that," Todd was saying. "Whatever the reason, she wanted to stay right here in town."

"Claire happened to agree with my assessment," George said quietly. "I discussed it with her—more than once."

"What do you mean?" asked Todd.

"Sometimes Claire got a little melancholy, a little blue," George said. "We were friends and she'd come to me for advice. And when I told her what I thought, she agreed with me. 'I want so many things,' she said. 'It's too hard to pick just one.'"

"Well, she never said anything like that to me." Todd stuffed the last bit of the roll into his mouth. "And the idea that Claire was *melancholy*, as you so quaintly put it, is ridiculous. I never knew a woman with a sunnier disposition." He seemed to be challenging George.

"A person can have many sides, many facets." George did not take the bait. "She might have shown me one face and you another."

Susannah looked at the two men sitting across from her. George seemed to know her mother well, and presented himself as her confidant. Maybe she'd been wrong in dismissing him as a possibility. Maybe he was more complex and challenging than she thought—qualities that would have attracted Claire. In any case, there was still evidence to suggest that either might have been her mother's lover. Evidence, but no actual proof.

The appearance of the waiter to clear their plates and leave the dessert menus was a brief distraction. And even though she was quite full from the potpie, she ordered dessert—apple crumble—so that the lunch would continue for a while.

The conversation turned to other things—there was a paper mill in a nearby town whose potentially hazardous waste was threatening to contaminate Primrose Pond; a town hall meeting had been scheduled to discuss it. A new restaurant was opening in Eastwood and another was closing; a big storm was predicted for the area this coming weekend. Everyone hoped it would veer off in another direction. Then the desserts were brought to the table and they all began to eat.

Susannah listened and nodded, but she wasn't really paying attention. Pushing her crumble around on her plate with her fork, she was still trying to connect first Todd and then George as the author of that note. But what if neither of them had written it? Then Janet turned to her and said, "Harry Snady."

"Excuse me?"

"Harry Snady. He was the director of the theater company. Why didn't I think of him sooner?"

"Of course. He'd be the perfect person to talk to," said Todd. "He was her biggest fan, onstage and off."

"That's true," said George. "He knew her as well as anyone. Maybe better. I heard he's over in Maine now, though," said George, "and that his health is bad." He'd ordered butterscotch pudding and was putting careful little spoonfuls into his mouth.

"Do you have a phone number for him?" Susannah discreetly pushed her plate away; she was done with the crumble.

"I don't, actually. But I'm sure you could find him without too much trouble."

The check came and the two men gallantly insisted on paying Susannah's portion of it. "It's the least we can do," said George.

"Our homage to Claire. She left us too soon." He stood and put on his coat.

"In more ways than one. So many people missed her when she left town." Janet had gotten up too. "After she died, some of the ladies from the various book clubs even established a little fund in her name."

"Really?" said Susannah. She must have made a deep impression on them. "To be used for what?"

"Keeping the poetry collection fresh and current. That Poet's Corner was so important to her and they all knew it."

"Ah, the Poet's Corner," said Todd. "I remember when she came into my office to pitch the column to me. I was reluctant at first. Poetry in a local paper? But she was so passionate. A real zealot. I decided to give it a try, and you know what? It was extremely popular with our readers. And we even won an award in arts coverage because of it."

"I had no idea . . ." said Susannah. But why would she? Apart from Linda, who had cleaned out the house, she had not attempted to contact anyone in Eastwood when her mother died. And she had lost touch with Linda too.

"I remember the Poet's Corner!" said Janet. "And wasn't there some mystery poet she used to publish?"

"That's right," said Todd. "She ran a bunch of his poems—of course I wasn't even sure it was a him, but that's what I surmised at the time—without ever knowing his name. He used a nom de plume."

"Was it I. N. Vayne?" asked Susannah. Maybe the "mystery poet" whose work appeared in the newspaper was also the author of the poems she'd found. I. N. Vayne certainly sounded like a pen name. And those poems could have been snipped from the *Eastwood Journal*.

Janet and George shrugged, but Todd seemed to be thinking it over. "That could have been it," he said finally. "But I'm not sure." He moved toward the door. "I think Claire enjoyed the mystery. She was quite tickled that someone would go to the trouble of writing poems, sending them into the paper, yet keep his or her identity hidden."

What if his identity had been revealed? Susannah thought. And once it had, he'd become her mother's lover.

ELEVEN

They all said good-bye in front of the Yankee Crockpot; the sun was slipping quickly from the sky as Susannah drove back home. She was no nearer to establishing the identity of the note's writer than she had been two hours earlier. If either George or Todd really had had an affair with her mother, would they have been so willing to meet with her? Wouldn't they have felt too guilty? Though George had seemed defensive and at moments hostile; maybe that was a sign? Still, Todd was the one who commented on Claire's appearance. And then there was Harry Snady; Susannah decided she would try to call him right now.

The house was empty when she got home. Jack had texted her to say he'd be at Gilda's and her dad would drive him back later. Cally had mentioned she would be at the school library, though working on what exactly she hadn't said. Susannah noticed a fluorescent green flyer had been slipped under the front door. She'd deal with it later. Right now, she was intent on tracking down Harry Snady; maybe he was the man she needed to find.

Maine directory information was able to give her phone numbers for three people named Harry Snady. The first had been disconnected. The second was picked up by someone with a slightly Southern drawl to his voice. He sounded quite young and said he'd never heard of her mother. When she tried the third number, in Eliot, Maine, a woman answered.

"I'd like to speak to Harry Snady, please. My name is Susannah Gilmore and I believe he knew my mother."

"How did you get this number?" The woman's hostility bristled, immediate and tangible.

"From directory information," Susannah said. "But I got his name through Janet Durbin. She's the librarian in Eastwood and she said that—"

"I don't care who she is," the woman said. "Harry is *not* available. And I'd appreciate if you didn't call here anymore."

"I don't understand," said Susannah. "Janet said he knew her quite well. I don't mean to trouble you, but it would mean so much to me if I could—"

"The answer is no. And please—don't call again." She hung up, her voice replaced by the bland buzz of the dial tone.

Susannah had no idea what to make of this. Was that his wife? Daughter? And why had she been so rude? She was disappointed that she had not reached him; his inaccessibility made her even more anxious to talk to him. But there was nothing she could do about it now, and so she picked up the flyer.

PRIMROSE POND RESIDENTS TAKE NOTE!

The Wingate Paper factory, in Wingate, New Hampshire, has been secretly dumping significant amounts of dyes too close to our pond. Wingate claims the dyes are biodegradable, but we have reason to believe they are not being truthful, and if they are allowed to continue unchecked, our pond will soon be saturated with unhealthy levels of dye. Do you want to keep these potentially hazardous dyes out of our water? Do you want to preserve the pond we all know and love? If so, please come to this very important meeting. Since Town Hall had some storm damage and is currently being renovated, we will meet at the Eastwood Library on Tuesday, February 1. We need to let the folks at Wingate know we stand together on this and that we won't let Primrose Pond become the unofficial dumping ground for their industrial waste!

—Corbin Bailey,
Head of the Save Our Pond Committee

This was what they had been talking about over lunch; the flyer made it sound even more important, if not urgent. She took it into the kitchen and fastened it to the fridge with a magnet. February 1 was a little over a week away; even though she had only recently gotten to town, she cared about the pond enough to attend. And she had to admit, if only to herself, that Corbin Bailey's involvement made it even more intriguing to her. So he'd become something of an activist in the area; who would have guessed? But then, it seemed there might be many things about Corbin that Susannah had yet to discover.

The sound of a car door slamming out front sent Susannah over to the window. There was Cally, getting out of a banged-up little car; Susannah peered out, trying to get a look at the driver, but all she saw was a shock of dark hair with skunklike stripes running through it. Then Cally was inside. She was wearing the purple boots and a fuzzy zebra-print coat she had recently acquired. "Hi." She didn't look at Susannah but headed right for the stairs.

"Hello, honey." Susannah was on maternal alert. Why wouldn't Cally look at her? And was she *weaving* a little? Could she be drunk at four o'clock on a weekday afternoon? Taking the stairs quickly, she went to Cally's room and knocked on her door.

"What?" said Cally.

"May I come in?"

"Why?"

"Why?" echoed Susannah. "Because I haven't seen you all day and I want to talk to you." She didn't wait for permission but just opened the door.

Cally was on the bed, her boots kicked off and lying nearby. Her laptop was open and she was peering intently into the screen. Susannah approached. As she suspected, the distinctive whiff of alcohol was emanating from her daughter. She sat down on the bed and Cally jumped slightly.

"Mom, I'm trying to do my homework." She still would not look at Susannah.

"While you're drunk?"

"Who says I'm drunk?" Cally's head snapped up now, and in her eyes was what Susannah now thought of as *the look*—a mixture of blame, anger, and contempt—that just undid her every time.

"I do. I saw the way you were walking. Also, you reek."

"I am not drunk," Cally insisted. "And I do not reek. I had a couple of beers; is that a crime?"

"Actually, it is," said Susannah. "You're underage in this state and every other state in the country too."

"Oh, come on, Mom. Just because we're in New England, you're going to go all Puritanical on me?"

"Yes, I am!" Susannah got up from the bed and in an attempt to calm herself—it would be way better to have this conversation if she could demonstrate some measure of self-control—walked to the window. This room did not face the pond, but the snow-covered woods on the other side of the house. They looked mysterious and, at this moment, a little scary.

"What are you going to do? Ground me?"

Susannah turned to face her. Cally had the upper hand and she knew it. Susannah thought of the beat-up car and its skunk-haired driver. She was the only person even approximating a friend that Cally seemed to have here and, as such, Susannah recognized her importance. She did not want to ground her daughter; she wanted her to find her place and fit in. "Who was that who drove you home?" she asked, switching gears.

"Megan."

"Is she a friend from school?"

"Not exactly. She graduated already and she works in town."

"Then she must be at least eighteen." This so-called friend was looking less attractive by the minute.

"So?"

"So? She's older, she's not in college, and clearly she drinks—she doesn't seem like a good influence, Cally. Not a good influence at all."

"Oh? So who's a good influence in Mudport? The dumb jocks at school? The trampy girls with their boobs on display? Or how about the rest of the mindless, soul-zapped sheep that populate the hallways? Are they good influences, Mom? Are they?" Her voice had scaled up considerably and by the end of her tirade she was practically shouting.

Susannah did not know how to respond. She felt that she was losing her purchase as this girl's parent. Glancing around the room, she desperately searched for something—anything—that would restore her sense of authority. Her gaze settled randomly on the Doc Martens; there was something stuck to the bottom of one; it looked like hay. Bending down, Susannah detected the distinct odor of horse manure. Where had Cally *been*? "What's on your boot?" she asked.

"What are you talking about?"

Instead of replying, Susannah picked up the boot to examine the bottom more closely. Sure enough, there was manure caked around the sole; it had acted as glue for the bits of hay. "This."

Cally leaned over to look. "Oh, that. It must be from Jester."

"Jester?"

"He's a horse. He lives in a barn behind that green house. The one Alice lives in. She owns him and she said I could see him whenever I want. So that's what I've been doing. And in the spring, I'm going to get to ride him."

"You've met Alice Renfew?"

"Do you know her? She's really great. I like her so much."

"So you've been visiting Alice Renfew and getting to know her horse?"

Cally's anger of a few minutes before was gone, replaced now with a kind of mild, almost indulgent exasperation. "Yes, Mom. I just explained all this." And when Susannah didn't say anything, she added, "Can I get back to my homework now? I've got a history paper that's due tomorrow."

"Okay." Susannah left the room and closed the door behind her. The conversation had certainly taken a weird turn; Cally had gone from surly to smiling in a matter of minutes.

Worse, Susannah had just been dismissed by a slightly intoxicated teenager—and had not offered a single word of protest.

TWELVE

As soon as Alice got Emma into the car, the dog began trembling. They were on their way to see Dr. D'Arco, who had very kindly agreed to squeeze her into the schedule, even though she did not have an appointment. Emma's slight wheezing, which had started yesterday, had gotten worse overnight and Alice was worried. Dr. D'Arco was as deft and gentle as any vet in the state; he had two chocolate brown standard poodles of his own, and he really knew the breed. Yet whenever they drove to Epsom, this was how Emma reacted. "It's all right," she told the dog. "Everything is all right." And despite the frigid day, she cracked the window so Emma could angle her long, tapering snout toward the opening and inhale the enticing smells of the world.

Once they'd reached the vet's office—a small white house just off the main road—Emma hung back, reluctant to come out even when Alice offered her a biscuit. Finally Alice had to reach and nudge the dog from her seat; with an offended glance at her mistress, Emma jumped down. The wheeze intensified.

Corinne, who functioned as both receptionist and groomer, looked up when they came in. "Someone's all congested," she said.

"It does sound pretty bad," said Alice. "Like she's struggling for breath."

"Poor girl." Corinne patted Emma's shaggy head. "Dr. D'Arco will make it all better."

"I hope so," said Alice. Emma was eight, not a young dog. Who knew what that wheeze might signify?

"You just let him do his job. And if she's up to it afterward, I'll bathe and cut her."

"Thank you, Corinne." She started moving toward the door and Emma tried to follow.

"She'll be fine." Corinne took the leash and held it firmly. "You can go and we'll call you."

Alice turned away; she did not want to see the mute appeal that would undoubtedly be visible in Emma's eyes. Then she left the office, got back in the car, and drove off. What if Emma had some serious condition? The wheezing might indicate a heart problem. Alice's own heart accelerated at the thought. Even though she knew it was likely that she would outlive the dog, the thought of losing her now felt close to unbearable.

She was grateful she had errands to do. If she stayed at home, she'd have nothing to distract her. After she'd been driving for a few minutes, the windshield grew speckled with moisture. Rain. Or, more accurately, sleet. She turned the wipers on and slowed down; the road already felt slippery. When she pulled into the parking lot behind Bailey's hardware store, she saw that it was almost empty. Yet as soon as she'd gone inside and put the six-pack of lightbulbs in her cart, she ran into someone she knew: Janet Durbin.

"Good to see you!" Alice said. "Today the library opens at one o'clock, right?"

"Right. Winter hours." Janet was buying birdseed, duct tape, and a fat roll of insulation.

"How is that working out?" Alice was on the board of the library, so these details were important to her.

"It's fine. It might be smart to cut back even more; that way, we'll have more money in the budget in July and August."

"Attendance is always up then; all those summer people from Boston and New York."

"I was hoping we could implement more evening hours in the summer," Janet said. "I'd love to expand the author talks. And maybe add another book club. We have one that meets on Thursday afternoons, but I think we could use one at night too."

"There's a board meeting later this month," said Alice. "I'll bring it up." She put a package of sponges in her cart. Though she could have bought them at the supermarket, she liked to patronize Bailey's; all three of the Bailey children had been patients of Dave's back in the day.

She had already turned away when Janet added, "Have you met your new neighbor, Susannah Gilmore?"

Alice swiveled back around. So Janet knew Susannah? Interesting. "Yes, actually. I've run into her on the pond."

"Very nice woman. I told her I knew her parents."

"Yes, I knew them too. At least, I knew the mother. Her father was less . . . outgoing."

"Did you know that Susannah writes historical novels and is working on one about Ruth Blay?"

"Ruth Blay . . . I've heard the name but can't remember in what context."

"She was the last woman hanged in the state of New Hampshire. People said she killed her baby, but that was never proved."

"And they hanged her anyway?"

"For concealment of an illegitimate child. That was a capital offense too."

"Gruesome." Alice wondered what drew Susannah to such a grim topic. Surely there were more uplifting events about which she could have written.

"Extremely." Janet, who, it had to be said, was more than a little overweight, unzipped her jacket. Well, the store was quite toasty and people with more meat on their bones were apt to feel it more keenly. "But history is filled with gruesome chapters and it's important that they get told. I'm eager to see what she does with it; I said I'd help her in any way I could."

"And I'm sure you will, Janet. The library—and the town—are lucky to have you." Privately, she thought Janet a bit dogged and unimaginative, but she did admire her work ethic and her devotion to her job.

Alice continued down the aisle, plucking an item here and there for her basket. Down at the far end of the store and talking on a cell phone stood Corbin Bailey. He wore a red apron over his jeans and sweater; red was a good color for him. Only men with a certain confidence could wear red well. Corbin was one of them.

Corbin must have finished his call, because he put the phone in the apron pocket. "How are you, Mrs. Renfew?" He smiled as he came toward her. "Finding everything you need today?"

"Yes, I'm finding everything," she said. "But please call me Alice," she said.

"Alice." His smile widened. "Old habits die hard. I'll always think of you as the doctor's wife."

"It's how I think of myself, even after all this time."

"Your late husband—he was a great guy. He had a real way with kids."

"He did, didn't he?" *Too bad he never had any of his own.*

"We've got a sale on all holiday items—seventy-five percent off. That includes wreathes, ornaments, artificial trees—"

"I would never, ever have an artificial tree," she said. "Would you?"

"I suppose not, though I haven't put up a tree since my mother died. But there are plenty of people who like them just the same. They get the feeling of Christmas without all the hassle."

"Sometimes the hassle, as you call it, is a key part of the pleasure. Anyway, I miss your mother. Since she died, that local history club died with her." *That* was where she'd heard Ruth Blay's name—from Millicent Bailey; she'd just pieced it together.

"Maybe someone will start it up again. I kind of hope they do."

"What about Susannah Gilmore?"

"What about her?"

Did something in his face change, or was Alice imagining it? That was part of why she had wanted to stop in here today, wasn't it? Whether she'd admitted it to herself or not, she'd come to gather information about Susannah, because Susannah was Calista's mother.

"She's my new neighbor and she's been looking into our local history. Janet Durbin was telling me about her latest project. She wants to write about Ruth Blay." Even though just a few minutes ago she could not even recall where she'd heard the name or why, now she spoke it with great authority, as if she was familiar with the story.

"My mother was interested in Ruth Blay," Corbin said. "There was a library talk with the author of some book about her. My mother was very excited and insisted on having everyone over for a luncheon afterward. She prepared for days."

"Yes, I remember that now." And she did. "But I didn't end up going; Dave and I had a trip planned or something." She studied Corbin's face for clues. "Anyway, you might want to get to know her."

"I'm sure I'll bump into her at the store or in town."

Alice wondered if they had met already, but before she could ask, his phone rang. He gave her an apologetic smile as he answered it. Alice took her purchases to the register, where Tiffany, the soigné cashier, rang them up.

The sleet was coming down a little harder now and it was slow going on the road. Without Emma, the house felt empty and even mournful; she called Corinne, but Dr. D'Arco was in with Emma now. "I'll call you as soon as we have something concrete to report," said Corrine.

Alice tried to suppress her anxiety, but she was restless and ate her slice of toasted cheese standing up. Then she made a cup of tea that she drank so quickly she scalded her tongue. She put her coat back on and, ignoring the stinging needles of sleet, got into the car. Had she been going anywhere else, she might have postponed her trip and endured the gloomy emptiness. But she was on her way to see Evangeline Toms, and she did not want to disappoint her.

Evangeline lived at the other end of town in a three-story gray clapboard house with eyebrow dormers and three disintegrating stone steps that led up to the weathered front door. It was too big for a single occupant, but Evangeline was adamant about staying put. Alice was part of a local network of women who brought meals to shut-ins like Evangeline. It was worthy work, but altruism was not the only reason Alice spent a day bustling about her kitchen preparing a stew or casserole, baking a loaf of date nut bread or a coffee cake to bring with her. One of her best friends had died in the fall and two others had had their fill of New

Hampshire winters and moved away. She was lonely, and cantankerous though Evangeline was, she helped fill the void.

"Hello?" Alice let herself in. "Evangeline?" She didn't hear anything and the silence felt ominous.

"I'm in here. Where else would I be?" Evangeline's cranky voice called back.

Relieved, Alice left the parcels of food—today it was baked chicken with saffron rice, string beans, and coconut pudding—on the table and walked into the living room. It was dim and crowded, not only with lamps, crystal pitchers, silver candlesticks, and other bric-a-brac, but also with newspapers, stacks of mail, and shopping bags that held nothing but more folded or crumpled shopping bags. And it smelled bad. Terrible, in fact.

There, in a worn brocade chair and seemingly oblivious to the odor, sat Evangeline. Her white hair was pinned haphazardly on her head and she wore a nubby shawl over what appeared to be a Red Sox sweatshirt. Diamonds glittered on her earlobes. Alice knew that those earrings had been a gift from Evangeline's father more than seventy years ago; she planned to be buried in them.

"Maybe your daughter would like them," Alice had ventured. "Or your granddaughter." Evangeline's family did not visit often, but, still, they were her flesh and blood.

"No, it will just *kill* them to see them go into the ground. I only wish I could see their faces as they watch the casket being lowered; they'll mourn these earrings more than they'll mourn me."

"I hardly think that's likely," said Alice, surprised by Evangeline's vehemence.

"Oh, no? That's because you don't know them!" She gave Alice an appraising look. "You never had children, did you?"

"No." Alice tried to keep her voice neutral.

"You're lucky." Her fingers crept to the earrings. "Ungrateful, selfish . . ." she muttered. Then her voice got louder. "Screw them all!"

Alice had been shocked by this comment, but as she began to know Evangeline better, she understood such remarks for what they were: a solitary old woman's bravado.

"What did you bring me today?" Evangeline now asked.

"Chicken with rice."

"I hate rice," Evangeline said.

"Then you don't have to eat it. But I put saffron in it—that gives it a little kick."

"Saffron!" snorted Evangeline. There was a silence during which Alice wished she could tidy up; it really was a sty in here. But she knew better than to attempt it. "That's what they use in Indian food, right? I went to an Indian restaurant in Boston once. I liked it."

"Then you might enjoy the rice. Give it a try." Alice went back to the kitchen to heat a plate of food in the microwave. The microwave had come from Bailey's; Corbin had donated it, and several others, to Alice's network of helpers. Apart from the microwave, everything else in the kitchen was either deteriorating or in wretched taste, like the avocado green appliances and the curtains appliquéd with hideous green and orange flowers. Evangeline had no talent for decorating and clearly never had, but it wasn't for lack of resources. Alice happened to know that she was well provided for, though it was true she had squandered a lot of her money in the state's Indian casinos; everyone knew she'd been a gambler.

Evangeline ate heartily, and even asked for a second helping of the rice. Then Alice set up a Scrabble board on a card table— the only surface in the room not completely covered or buried— and they began their weekly game.

Evangeline was still an adept player, and when she placed a

seven-letter word, "acquits," on a triple-word-score square, racking up a whopping ninety points, she clapped her small, gnarled hands. "I may be old, but I haven't lost my touch."

"No, you haven't." Alice made her own modest play.

"Dick and I used to play all the time. He was the only one who could beat me."

"Then he must have been one brilliant player." Dick was Evangeline's husband; he had died many years earlier.

"He was . . ." She rearranged her letters in their wooden holder. "I still talk to him. Sometimes I even think he answers." When Alice did not reply, she added, "Do you talk to your dead husband too?"

"I suppose I do," said Alice, selecting her next batch of letters. "Though not out loud."

"Out loud or in your head, it's all the same. The relationship doesn't end just because someone dies. And the older you get, the more appealing the dead become. They're the only ones who understand you."

"You have a point." Alice had found herself mentally conversing not just with Dave, but with her long dead parents and more recently deceased friends too. Unlike Evangeline, though, she resisted the pull. She still had plenty to say to the living.

Then Evangeline abruptly dumped all her letters back in the box cover.

"What are you doing?" asked Alice.

"I'm so far ahead you'll never catch up. Why drag it out?"

"I suppose you're right." Alice collapsed the board and sent all the tiles back into the box. Then she helped Evangeline to the bathroom, and afterward got her settled in front of the small flat-screen television that had been her own gift. She covered her knees with a throw made of some awful synthetic stuff and handed the older woman the remote.

"Thank you," said Evangeline. Her mood had mellowed considerably since Alice had come in. "I've got everything I need. I'm fine."

"Good," said Alice. "I'll be back soon." Next time, she'd bring her a decent blanket and sneak that horrid thing she was wrapped in out with the trash. And maybe she'd manage to get a window open here—air out the place.

"I know you will," said Evangeline. "You're a widow. Widows have too much time on their hands." Alice said nothing. Even sated with food and nourished by company, Evangeline was not *that* mellow; she still had to deliver her parting shot.

It was dark when Alice stepped outside. Her phone rang just as she reached her car. "Everything's fine," said Corinne. "She has a slight chest infection, but it's mild; it's good you brought her in so soon. Dr. D'Arco's prescribing an antibiotic for five days and . . ."

Alice did not even hear the rest. Emma was all right. Emma was *fine*. She realized she felt a little shaky and had to brace herself against the roof of the car. Had Corinne's news been different—well, she really didn't know what she would have done. When she felt steady enough to drive, she got in.

The sleet had tapered off but the temperature had dropped, so that the road was slippery with a glasslike sheen of ice. But at the end of the trip, there was the ordinarily demure Emma bounding across the office to greet her. "Hello!" She knelt so Emma, freshly washed, combed, and fluffed like a show dog, could lick her cheek. The tears that welled suddenly were the sweet tears of relief. Grief had been averted, pushed down the road. At least for now. Alice put the bottle of Emma's medicine in her purse and paid the bill.

Twenty minutes later, she was walking up the path to the house, Emma right beside her. She had left herself some of the same chicken and rice dish she'd brought to Evangeline, so she would eat that for dinner. Only now that it was over could she allow herself to feel the stress and strain of the day. She felt worn out and looked forward to a quiet evening, with either the Georges Simenon novel she was reading or a program on television.

But there was a surprise waiting by her front door: a tall, slim figure in a fluffy black-and-white-striped coat. Calista! "Is something wrong? Have you been locked out of your house?" The fatigue she'd felt just moments earlier had vanished, replaced by equal parts worry—was the girl all right?—and delight—how good it was to see her.

"No, nothing like that." A strand of red hair had escaped Calista's black beret, vivid against her pale cheek. "I hope you don't mind that I'm here. I just needed to talk and you seemed like someone I could talk to. I mean, there's my mom but I don't want—I mean—"

"Why don't you come in? Have you eaten?" Calista shook her head. "Neither have I. Let's have a bite together, shall we? And you can tell me all about it." Hand on Calista's elbow, Alice ushered her inside, where she would feed her the chicken, the fragrant rice. And didn't she have a baguette in the freezer? And some crisp gingersnaps she had baked, to go with the coconut pudding? While they ate, they would talk. Naturally, she was someone Calista could confide in. She would listen, say all the right things, in exactly the right tone of voice. "You can tell me anything, you know. Anything at all."

THIRTEEN

Immersed in the steaming water, Susannah leaned her head back, closed her eyes, and willed herself to relax—as if will had any part in relaxing. It had been a day of small irritations: the washing machine had gone on strike, the cable guy had failed to show up, and some raccoons had overturned the trash barrels, gnawed through the black plastic bags, and merrily strewn garbage all around the side of the house. Her efforts to reach Harry Snady had been futile. She could have written, but she thought her letter would be intercepted. That woman was not letting her guard down for a second.

And even on a day that had not been peppered with such annoyances, Susannah would still feel as if she was camping out in the house rather than living here. There were unpacked boxes and various items she wanted—her stapler, her heather gray cashmere shawl, her set of nesting Fire-King mixing bowls, a collection of sea glass that spanned three decades—had not yet surfaced. She'd been so busy she'd hardly had a chance to talk to any of the friends she'd left behind—not the tight-knit Park Slope circle of women she'd met and bonded with when her kids were babies, or the friends who stretched back even farther than that, from her publishing job and college.

The water was beginning to cool, so she turned on the tap, filling the tub nearly to the brim. It was a massive old thing, claw-footed, with a sinuous porcelain lip that extended several inches over the sides. The tub was not original to the house; it was one of her father's salvage yard finds that summer they all spent here. Her mother was the one who took baths, so the tub had in effect been a gift to her. But when it was lugged, with much effort and cursing, up the stairs and installed, Claire's reaction had been chilly at best and rude at worst; Warren had looked so hurt.

Susannah was no closer to unraveling the mystery of her mother's secret or the reason for her own preoccupation with it—and she knew it was a preoccupation. She had achieved not a resolution but an uneasy stalemate with her daughter, and her new novel's point of view continued to bedevil her. And then, as she lay immobile in the tub, looking up at the ceiling with its faint tracery of old leaks, it came to her: the elusive voice she'd been praying that she'd hear. But it was not Ruth's voice she heard. It was Betsey's.

She immediately stood up and pulled the plug; the water began to drain in a voluble gurgle. Then she wrapped herself in a terry robe and hurried to her room. Everything else could be put on hold, but this—this could not wait. Betsey was the key. No, not the key. The frame. Susannah could tell the story from Betsey's point of view, in the first person—that would give the events the immediacy she wanted. Betsey's narration would provide a sense of context and history. Betsey had lived to the age of 105; she had plenty of time to reflect on what had happened. And she could be a mouthpiece for the years following Ruth's death. Adopting her point of view would allow Susannah to explore the themes of guilt and responsibility, regret and remorse. These were universal themes; they would crack the story open and make it widely appealing. It certainly appealed to *her*.

Although it was past eleven o'clock and she had not planned to do any more work this evening, Susannah sat down at her desk and turned on the computer. She should have been reading or watching television—activities that would calm, not stimulate her. But inspiration of this kind was mercurial; now that it had come to her, she wasn't about to let it go. She didn't have to strain anymore to hear the voice she had been waiting for. It had finally started talking to her. All she had to do was listen.

Salisbury, New Hampshire, 1828

I am an old woman now. My face is lined, my hair is white, and my joints are stiff. But although my body is giving out, bit by treacherous bit, my mind is still as sharp as ever. I was born in 1763, more than sixty years ago. So much has happened since then. To the world. To me. Yet I can still name the trees outside my door and the birds that find sanctuary in them. I remember hymns learned in girlhood. Prayers too. The birth dates of my children—I had many—and of their children. I recall days that waxed full with joy, and others picked clean by despair.

But there is one day, June 14, 1768, that stands out even clearer than all the rest. I remember it like it was painted on the limpid glass of my mind only minutes ago. I will remember that day until the moment I die, and am facing the final judgment before our Creator and Lord. And that may not be so far off; none of us knows when our Maker will call us home. Only last week, as I stepped out the kitchen door, my foot slipped on a wet leaf plastered to the stone, and down I went in a heap. I was alone in the house; I could not get up and I could have been there for hours had not a neighbor chanced by to help me rise again. I was fine, with only a bruise or two to show for my clumsiness. But the incident reminded me of how truly fragile I am. How fragile we all are. And that the time given to us is not unending, but finite. How much of mine is left I do not know.

So it is for that reason that I want to unburden myself now, and tell the tale that has haunted me for decades. I tell it now because I need to relieve myself of its heavy weight, but also because I wish to share it with future generations. I have been a modest and quiet woman, not one to seek attention or stir up discord. Yet I have seen many wrongs perpetrated against those of my sex. I could not right them in my lifetime, but I believe that if I bear witness to the past, my words may serve to change the hearts and minds of those who come after me.

This is a harsh story. A cruel one. And it ends in tragedy. I had a pivotal role in those harrowing events. But even though I set it all in motion, it was not my fault. For I was so young then—as young then as I am old now. Too young to understand the implications of my actions. Too young to predict or comprehend their dire consequences. But I am getting ahead of myself, and telling it out of order.

I will start at the beginning. First I must offer my fervent thanks to my mother, God rest her soul, who insisted that I be taught to read and write. Reading and writing were gifts denied to her, and so she was all the more determined that I should have them. And what gifts they were! Once I learned to read, I never stopped. The Bible was my first primer, and I read its stories again and again. Later, the glorious plays of the bard

William Shakespeare. Novels by Master Henry Fielding, and Miss Jane Austen, bound in wine-dark leather and shipped all the way from England. That weighty tome by Master Richardson, Clarissa, *that took me more than a year to complete. The poems of Anne Bradstreet, a wife and mother whose ability to express herself I admired and at times envied. All these words have worked their way into my soul and it was my mother who gave them to me. Because of her gentle tutelage I am now able to take up my quill and draw forth the past with no more than the nib of my pen and a bottle of ink.*

To tell this tale, I rely heavily on my memory, which, as I have said, is excellent, as well as a diary I kept as a younger woman. Years ago, I adopted the habit of setting down my thoughts and feelings because the very act of writing seemed to put the world in some kind of comprehensible order; I emerged from this task restored and refreshed, as if newly baptized. I never showed these writings to anyone, so their existence is entirely secret. But this document I write now is quite different. I am writing it to be read; I want to blare my truth to the world, and hear it resound and echo back at me. Then maybe I will find some peace; Lord knows it has eluded me thus far.

It was June, a halcyon month in New Hampshire. Neither stiflingly hot nor oppressively damp, it was perfect, with days that were long, fair, and golden. But that particular day it was warmer than usual, the kind of day when you would want to slip off your shoes and hitch up your petticoats to wade in a stream. My uncle Benjamin and I were on our way to the frontier town of Salisbury, New Hampshire. Along the way, we would stop at the Curriers' farm. I was riding on a pillion behind him, the horse a dainty little dappled mare with a quick trot and a habit of rearing her head back and shaking it from side to side that made him very cross. But he was too softhearted to use a crop and merely scolded her for her bad behavior.

The woods we passed through were very green and still; I remember the branches of the trees hung so low that Uncle Benjamin had to stop frequently to push or even cut them out of the way. We saw a cluster of blueberry bushes circling a small pond and we stopped there too. "We'll bring the Curriers some berries," Uncle Benjamin said, and we put them in my apron, which Uncle Benjamin tied closed and gave to me to carry when we continued on our way.

When we finally arrived, we were hot, hungry, and thirsty. I gave Mrs. Currier the berries we'd gathered and she brought me inside for a cool drink and a thick slice of bread with butter and molasses. We would be having dinner, but that would not be until later. Mr. Currier showed Uncle Benjamin where the horse could have a drink; she too was hot and thirsty.

After I had rested for a little while, Mrs. Currier asked me if I'd like to join the other children who were playing outside, and I said, "Yes, ma'am, I'd like that very much," the way I'd been taught. So she took me back outside and down into the flower-dotted meadow, where I saw two boys and three girls, all running and laughing. "Patience and Sarah! Please come now!" And when they did, she introduced me; they were her daughters. Sarah was seven, two years older than me, and Patience was a big girl of twelve—nearly grown. Then the other children came over: James, Will, and Margaret, who was called Peggs.

"Betsey is our guest and I know you'll all play nicely together, won't you?"

"Yes, Mother," said Patience. She was older than any of the others and seemed to be in charge.

Mrs. Currier went back up to the house and James ran over and touched my arm. "Tag!" he called. "You're it." Then he dashed off and so did everyone else. I ran after them, giggling and shrieking. Finally, I caught up with Peggs and tagged her on the shoulder. Now it was my turn to run from her. We played at tag for a time, and then hide and seek and then leapfrog. Peggs and I picked daisies and clover; Patience and Sarah wove them into garlands. It was all great fun.

But the afternoon sun was strong and high and after a while we grew too hot to be outside anymore. "Let's go into the barn," said James. The barn did not belong to the Curriers, but to Mr. Clough and his wife, Olive. Patience said we were allowed to play inside.

"Maybe we'll find buried treasure," added Will.

"Not likely," Patience said. "But the ginger cat who lives in the hayloft had kittens; they're so small and they have the bluest eyes."

So we all trooped into the barn, which was cool and pleasant after the heat of the day. It smelled of fresh hay and of something more pungent, the different animals that lived there. I saw an old horse, a couple of cows, and a large spotted sow.

"Let's find the kittens," said Sarah. She went off to see, and Peggs and Patience went with her. I stayed behind.

"I still think there's buried treasure in here," said Will. "Gold pieces. Or silver."

I didn't really believe him, but I ambled around, pretending to look. But there was nothing so very interesting down there after all. I decided to join the girls and walked toward the ladder that led to the hayloft. That's when I noticed the loose floorboards—three or maybe four. They intrigued me and I *stopped to inspect them more closely. Maybe Will was right and there were gold pieces hidden underneath. Wouldn't that be marvelous? And if I were the one to uncover them, that would be the most marvelous of all.*

So without saying anything to any of the others, I knelt beside one of the boards. It was very worn and stained with mold; it was also so loose that I could pry it up easily with my hands. I got a splinter, but it was a small one. I pulled it out by myself and I didn't even cry. I was too eager to see what was under there. But instead of the winking treasure I anticipated, I saw only a bit of wadded-up white cloth. How disappointing. I thought it was a rag, so I gave it a tug. It did not move.

"What are you doing?"

I looked up and there was Will, with James right beside him.

"These floorboards are loose," I said. "And there's something under them. But it doesn't look like treasure."

"Let me see." Will elbowed me aside. "It could be part of a sack and the gold pieces could be wrapped up inside."

"That's right!" said James. "They could."

"Let's pull up the rest of the loose boards," I said. "Then we'll know."

The boys agreed and we all set to pulling. Surely we would find something wondrous inside the bundle once we had unwrapped it—bright coins of gold or silver, shiny necklaces heavy with colored stones.

This is the part of the story that replays over and over in my mind. I can still see it all so clearly. The late afternoon light streaming through the open barn door, the horse dipping his head to eat, the eager voices of Peggs, Patience, and Sarah, still searching for the kittens whose plaintive mews could just barely be heard.

*The floorboards were all up now, and the neatly bundled
cloth, wrapped and folded tight, was fully exposed. It was dirty,
and a sticky bit of cobweb clung to one edge.*

"Let me open it," I said.

"No, me," said Will.

"But I found it," I insisted.

"She's right," James said.

*"I'll let you do it," Will said, "if you promise to share whatever
is inside."*

*"I promise." I lifted the bundle into my arms. It felt too light
to be coins or jewels. And yet it had some heft to it. Some sub-
stance. And it had a sharp, even rank odor, perhaps from having
been under the floorboards, a musty, foul-smelling place. I was
highly conscious of my role as the one who would reveal whatever
might be hidden within the folds, and in that moment I felt
myself to be very important.*

*Carefully, I peeled back the corner of the cloth. Underneath
was a tiny face, with closed eyes and feathery lashes. Beneath
those eyes, a tiny nose and tiny blue-tinged lips. The face was
chalk white and drawn. The dark gold hair on the head was
matted with what looked like dried blood. It was a baby, and it
was dead. That was when I began to scream.*

When Susannah finished typing these pages, it was almost
one o'clock in the morning and she was so pumped she wanted
to go outside and jog around Primrose Pond. But that would totally
wreck her day tomorrow, so she went downstairs, poured milk
and a dollop of maple syrup into a mug and zapped the concoction
in the microwave. Amazingly, it worked and she fell into a deep,
luxurious sleep.

The next morning, she went over what she'd written. She

would need to edit it and revise it, of course; she went through many drafts before arriving at a finished manuscript. Still, this was a good start. She didn't know much about Betsey Pettingill, because there wasn't much to know. She'd done brief online genealogical searches for Betsey's name, both in the historical society in Portsmouth and the state archives in Concord, and neither one was particularly fruitful. There was a Betsey Pettingill born in the mid-nineteenth century—definitely not "her" Betsey—and an Elizabeth Pettingill who lived in the late eighteenth. But what might cause a historian to despair might give a novelist cause to rejoice. The facts about Betsey's life were unknown, so Susannah was free—actually *obliged*—to invent them.

She tapped out an e-mail to Tasha Clurman, her editor in New York, in which she explained her reasons for wanting to defect from the Jane Seymour book, and offered Ruth Blay's story in its stead. Attached to the e-mail was a brief proposal and these new pages, so fresh and immediate that they felt wet.

After hitting send she was too restless to work, so she set out for a walk around the pond. The sun was out, but the temperature was only in the twenties and there was a sharp wind coming off the water. She drew her parka more tightly around herself and kept going. Maybe she would meet Alice again; she actually was hoping that she would. Cally said Alice had wanted to invite her over, and yet so far that hadn't happened. But she'd invited her daughter—more than once. Susannah felt an irritating little pinch of something—was it jealousy?

She stepped up her pace. And look—up ahead was Alice Renfew wearing a fringed red poncho that stood out like a traffic light against the subdued grays, whites, and browns of the landscape. The ever present dog was by her side.

"Hello, neighbor!" she called. And when Susannah was close

enough so that she no longer had to raise her voice, she added, "You have the most charming daughter!"

Do I? Susannah wanted to ask. But all she said was, "She really enjoyed meeting you too."

"Oh, we're way beyond that stage," said Alice cheerfully. "She's been over several times. I find her so bright and engaging. And she's a natural with Jester. You don't see that very often."

"She was horse crazy as a kid and used to take riding lessons. Now she can do it again if she wants; it's so much easier up here." Clearly, Cally was showing Alice a different side of her personality than the one she presented at home.

"She certainly will. I'm going to try her on Jester if she's game. But she's got so many interests. That cape she made—it's extraordinary!"

"Yes, it certainly is." Cape? What *cape*? Susannah realized with a flash of disappointment and jealousy—no use pretending it was anything else—that Cally had shown *Alice* whatever she was sewing up there behind the closed door of her room.

". . . all those interesting colors and patterns together were so original. And the workmanship is quite good considering she's still such a novice. She said she only just got the machine, which is hard to believe. I told her she could borrow pieces from me to use as inspiration. I've got *so* many clothes!"

Susannah just nodded. Where was this extraordinary garment? When would she get to see it?

A squirrel scampered quite close to where Alice stood and Susannah saw the dog look longingly in its direction. Alice noticed too. "Ah, Emma, you are so very, very good! I know how hard this is for you." Alice scanned the ground until she found a good-sized stick. Emma must have known just what was coming; her ears lifted and her snout seemed to quiver in anticipation. As soon as

Alice tossed the stick, she was off. Alice turned to Susannah. "We'll have tea again very soon. And maybe I'll see you at the town council meeting? I'm assuming you got the flyer."

"I did and I was planning on attending."

"Good! It's an important issue and we need to present a united front. Every voice, every body will count." Emma came running back with the stick, which she deposited at Alice's feet. Alice picked it up. "Well, I'm glad I ran into you. Bye for now." She began walking again, the dog keeping pace beside her.

Susannah continued her own walk; she'd grown cold while standing there and made an effort to pump her arms to get the blood flowing. Laced with the jealousy was pride that her daughter had impressed their neighbor. It made the beer-drinking episode seem like an aberration rather than a part of an alarming new pattern.

Cally had seemed subdued and even somewhat chastened these last few days. She had not been drinking—Susannah made a point of sniffing every chance she got—and there had been no evidence of the unsavory Megan either. She had come home alone right after school and spent the late afternoons and evenings doing homework, or working on the "extraordinary" cape that Susannah had yet to see. All right. So she'd warmed pretty quickly to their neighbor and was still giving her mother the cold shoulder. It hurt, but Susannah told herself she was strong enough to take the pain. Then another fierce blast of wind seemed to go right through her parka and all the layers she'd piled underneath. Enough. It was too cold to be out here anymore. She didn't know how Alice did it; she'd have to get her exercise some other way.

Susannah turned around and increased her pace until she saw the back of the house peeking out at her through a tangle of bare bushes. She was home—or at least the imperfect facsimile she had chosen.

FOURTEEN

Nearing the house, Susannah saw the red flag sticking up from the side of the galvanized-steel mailbox. She gathered the letters and let herself inside. The phone was ringing; cell phone service was spotty out here, so she maintained a landline. Leaving the mail—mostly bills, it seemed—on the table, she went to answer it.

"Mrs. Miller?"

"Yes." She didn't bother to correct the mistake. They were still so new in town; maybe it was better to share a name with her children.

"This is Antoinette Benoit. I'm the grade adviser for the junior class at the high school. I'm just wondering if you've been getting my e-mails."

"E-mails? No, I haven't gotten anything from you, but if you can wait a minute, I'll go up to my computer and double-check. It's possible they ended up in the junk folder; I don't look in there as often as I should."

"I understand," said Antoinette. "And I don't mind waiting."

But there were no e-mails from the school in Susannah's junk folder or anywhere else. "Are you sure you have the right address? SJGilmore@gmail.com?"

"That's what I've been using."

"Well, it seems like one of those inexplicable cybermysteries," said Susannah. "I'd certainly like to know why you've been e-mailing me, though. Is Cally having a problem at school?"

"Cally has been cutting school, Mrs. Miller. Over the last three weeks, I can document at least eight unreported absences—"

"Eight! But she's been getting on the bus every morning."

"Well, she might be going to school in the morning," said Antoinette Benoit. "But I can tell you for a fact that she's not staying there. Do you have any idea of where she might be going? That's why I was e-mailing you—I wanted to find out how much you knew."

"And I wasn't getting those e-mails . . ." Could Cally have had something to do with that? Susannah was not computer savvy enough to know if anything had been deleted without her knowledge. "Is she in school now?"

"Yes, I checked before I phoned. And I'm going to talk with her later and tell her we've spoken."

"Good. Then I can speak to her when—"

"I'm afraid there's more," said Ms. Benoit. "She was very rude to Mr. Pearley, the history teacher. She told him his class lecture was so boring it should be bottled and sold as a sleeping aid. I'm sure you can understand how unacceptable that is."

"Of course," murmured Susannah, her mind shooting off in a dozen different directions. Where did Cally go when she cut classes? Was she seeing that girl Megan? Anyone else? What about the drinking? Had she been too lax about it?

". . . I know she's a recent transfer, and that she may be having adjustment issues. And we know about her father—very sorry for your loss, Mrs. Miller—which could also compound the problem. So we are asking—well, insisting really—that she see Ms. Lanigan, the school psychologist."

"Yes, that sounds like it would be a good idea." Would it? Last year, right after Charlie's death, Susannah had suggested Cally see a therapist. "I'm not crazy!" she had shouted. "I'm in mourning, don't you get it? The only thing—and I mean the *only* thing—that would make me feel better is for Dad to be alive. And seeing some stupid shrink isn't going to make that happen, is it?"

At the time Susannah had felt it would be best not to press, but clearly she'd been wrong. In fact, right now she felt she had been wrong about a lot of things, the most significant of which was trusting Cally to sort things out for herself.

"Talk to Calista and then call me back tomorrow," Ms. Benoit was saying. "Then I'll ask you to come in so we can all have a meeting."

After getting off the phone, Susannah fixed herself a sandwich but was too rattled to eat it, so she wrapped it in foil and went upstairs. She was also too rattled to work—and besides, she did not want to return to her fledgling manuscript until she had heard back from Tasha—so she busied herself online, answering e-mail and replying to the occasional reader who contacted her through her Web site. After about forty minutes of digital housekeeping, she was still rattled and thought about trolling the Web for the kind of diverting trivia that the Internet served up so well, like pictures of cosmetic surgery gone horribly wrong or pregnant celebs in bikinis. No—maybe a cute animal site was better: baby bunnies small enough to fit in teacups; puppies snuggling adorably with other puppies, with polar bears, or in one case a monkey.

She got up. This was a colossal waste of time. Even if she couldn't work, she could at least get back to the business of unpacking. Every box she emptied was a small triumph, another step in the direction of making the house on Primrose Pond an actual home. But instead of opening a box, she opened a door—to Cally's room.

She could try to fool herself by pretending there might be a box or two in here she wanted to unpack. That was a big, fat lie. She was snooping, pure and simple. Might as well own up to it. Besides, after the phone call she'd just gotten, she had a right, didn't she? Maybe even an obligation.

The room was very neat—bed made, surfaces uncluttered. Susannah knew that if she looked in the closet, it would be neat too. Cally was an organizer, and she hung her clothes like the spectrum on a rainbow, grouping all the similar hues together. The flower-sprigged wallpaper she remembered from that long-ago summer was covered with pages pulled from the fashion magazines Cally had bought on the drive up here. There was no desk, but there was a table on which the sewing machine sat. The fabric they had brought down from the attic was underneath the table, folded in piles on the floor or in a couple of large baskets that had come from Cally's old room.

Susannah opened the dresser drawers. Socks, underwear, T-shirts all in tidy groupings. No hidden bottles of beer or booze, no evidence of drug paraphernalia either. The most damning thing she found was a pack of Camels, which was upsetting but not a total surprise. She'd smelled smoke on Cally's hair and clothes before, but when she'd asked about it, Cally insisted it was other kids who were smoking—not her. Then she saw it. Hanging on the back of the door was the cape that Cally had made, the one Alice Renfew had been exclaiming about. The one her daughter had not shown her.

Susannah went over to inspect. The cape comprised four different panels, each of a different material—heavy wools, from the look of them, in black, gray, navy, and a surprising golf course green. The inside was similarly constructed, with fabrics of different patterns making up the lining. Some of these had come from the box in the attic; Susannah recognized them. At the neck was a spherical orange button that looked like a gumball, and each of the other four buttons was different: one looked like an Indian-head penny, another was a pearl, a third was made up of glittery red rhinestones, and the last was square and carved from wood.

Susannah had to marvel. Here was Cally's coat of many colors, an apt physical representation of everything her mother believed was inside her. The colors, the patterns, and the careful construction reflected the equally complex construction of her daughter's soul. Susannah felt momentarily overjoyed that *this* was who Cally was—and then, on the heels of that, sorrowful that she was not permitted to see this creative, expansive Cally, only the shut-down, sullen girl.

The phone rang again and Susannah actually jumped. Her first—wholly irrational—thought was that Cally knew she was snooping and was calling to upbraid her. Then she thought it was Antoinette Benoit again, calling to inform her of some new transgression. But when she ran downstairs to pick it up, she was relieved to hear the voice of Polly Schultz, possibly her very best friend from New York.

"I tried your cell but your mailbox was full." Polly was crunching audibly on the other end of the line. They knew each other well enough for this to be acceptable behavior; they called it "eating lunch together."

"I'm sorry; little details like that are just eluding me right now."

"So how's it going? I miss you. We all do."

"I miss all of you too." Susannah had met Polly at Body by Baby, a prenatal exercise class she'd signed up for when pregnant with Cally. She'd formed close friendships with several of the women in the class but always felt a special bond with Polly, who had already had a girl and was expecting twins. The twins turned out to be girls too, and Susannah considered Polly the resident expert on raising daughters.

"It's been hard," she said, and told her about the trip up and the slow, bumpy process of adjustment. But she did not say anything about the note she'd found; she was not ready to share that yet, not even with Polly. Besides, there was so much else to say, especially about Cally. "I just found out that she's been cutting classes."

"Have you talked to her about it?"

"Not yet. I want to do it in person."

"Absolutely." Polly continued to crunch.

"Any advice on how to deal?"

"You know my theory: don't blow up right away, because if you do, there's no dialing it down. See if you can find out why she's cutting—what about the school is bugging her."

"Pretty much everything: the kids, the classes, the physical look of the place. Did I mention the kids?"

"Look, I get it," said Polly. "It's tough to be uprooted in the middle of high school. And she's probably not over Charlie's death—"

"Over it? She'll never be over it! And she blames me for it too."

There was a pause and then Polly said, "Why does she blame *you*?"

"It's the helmet," Susannah said. "He didn't like to wear it so I had to nag him about it. Only that day I didn't nag him. I was working when he left; I was distracted." The tears came suddenly, a fresh flood running down her face.

"Oh, honey," Polly soothed. "You can't be beating yourself up about that forever. You can't. Charlie wasn't some two-year-old you left alone in the bathtub while you ran into the kitchen to fix a cocktail; he was a grown man and he knew what he was doing." Susannah kept crying. "Not that I'm blaming him. Not a bit. But for you to blame yourself—that's flat-out crazy. And you've got to give up that kind of thinking; it's no help to you or your kids."

Polly's defense of her actions just made her cry harder. She had to put the phone down for a second; she was crying too hard to talk. When she picked it up again, Polly was saying, ". . . all that guilt is getting in the way of your moving ahead."

"Maybe." Susannah plucked a tissue from a box on the counter and blew her nose. "But it's been eating at me just the same. So when Cally starts in, it completely undoes me. She won't give it up."

"Cally needs to blame someone. And who's the safest person? You. That's because she knows how much you love her, and no matter what she does, she can't alienate you. Not permanently, anyway."

"You're right. She's trying to push me away, but I won't be pushed." Susannah took another tissue to blot her eyes.

"No, you won't, because you're a good woman and a good mother and you love that girl like nobody's business. And you're going to find out what, if anything, about the school situation you can fix, and if there isn't anything, then you'll find something outside of school that she can relate to. I know you, Susannah. You're resilient. Look at how you took stock when Charlie was killed and came up with a plan for moving your life forward without him; I admire you for that. So do we all."

"There's something else I've been wanting to tell you about," Susannah said. She hadn't told anyone about the note she'd found, and just hearing Polly's warm, reassuring voice made confiding in her absolutely urgent.

"I've got time," said Polly. "What's up?"

The story came out quickly: stumbling upon the note, the hunt for clues, the discovery of the poems, the meeting with two men, one of whom might or might not have been her mother's lover. God, but it felt good to unburden herself. How had she been keeping this in for as long as she had?

Polly listened quietly. "Why are you doing this now?" she asked.

"Because I found that note, and I want—no, I *need*—to know what happened, what it was all about—" She was suddenly frustrated by Polly's response. "What do you mean, why am I doing this? Isn't it obvious?"

"You didn't hear me. I asked, why are you doing this *now*?" Now Susannah was the one who was quiet. "Look, your world has already been turned upside down—Charlie getting killed, moving to a new house, new state, new life. Now you're upending your past too. Your parents are dead; whatever you find out isn't going to change anything. Wouldn't it be better to leave it alone, at least until you're more settled?"

"It doesn't matter if they're dead. *I'm* the one who's going to be changed by all this."

"Sweetie, don't you get it? You already have."

"That's right. I *have*. Which is why I have to pursue it."

"Even if it breaks your heart? You say you need to know what happened. But don't you think what you need to do is heal?"

"Polly, you don't—" Susannah heard the front door open. Jack and his new friend Gilda Mooney had just walked in. "I've got to go," Susannah said.

"To be continued," said Polly. "And empty your mailbox!"

Susannah ended the call as Jack opened the fridge and pawed around inside looking for a snack. She was still rattled but tried to hide it by preparing a cup of tea. Jack closed the fridge, container of milk in one hand, box of donuts in the other.

As Jack and Gilda ate their donuts, gulped their milk, and talked about the upcoming weekend, Susannah sat down at the table and sipped the tea. Was Polly right? Would it be better to leave all this alone and apply herself to the present—her work, trying to make a home here for herself and her kids—rather than dig around in the past? So what if her mother had had an affair? Was it even any of her business?

Susannah turned to the mail. Amid the bills and the mail-order catalogs, there was a large envelope with a hand-addressed label. It was from Todd Rettler. She picked it up but did not open it right away. She knew she could destroy it and put the pieces in the fireplace to burn. Stop this crazy quest of hers right now. Outside, the wind shook the windows in their frames; Jack and Gilda had finished their snack and gone up to his room. She was alone, and the envelope remained unopened in her hands.

Then, all at once, she was tearing at the flap. There was simply no way she could not pursue this. Even if, as Polly had said, she had to break her own stupid heart to do it. Inside, she found a brief article that ran when Claire had been appointed culture editor, a grainy photo of her taken at an office party, a few restaurant receipts, and some lined yellow sheets that contained meeting notes. There was also a brief letter from Todd.

January 26

Dear Susannah,

So nice to have met you last week; you put me in mind of your mother in so many ways. After our lunch, I went digging through some old papers—I'm an incorrigible pack rat—and found a few things I thought you might like to have—just some odds and ends from her time at the paper. Good luck with all; I hope to be seeing you around town.

Warmly,
Todd

P.S. The mystery poet? The name was I. N. Vayne.

Susannah looked through the papers quickly; she would take more time with them when she was alone. His confirmation of I. N. Vayne's name was potentially useful, though she still had not figured out his identity or if he was the same person who'd written to her mother. Then she looked at the note again. The words all had that same right-leaning slant, and they were printed, not formed in cursive.

Even allowing for the degradations of age, there was no way this writing was the same as the writing on the note in the shoe box upstairs, the note whose bold, looping words were now burned into her brain. If she had wanted proof, here it was. Todd Rettler had not written that note to her mother. Polly, had she been here to witness this discovery, might have said it was a lucky break. Todd was not the one; now let it drop. Polly had been right about one thing, at least: Charlie's death had ripped her life apart. She could not rebuild it; she saw that now. All she could do was try to construct some alternate life for herself. And to do that, she had to know who she was, and who, really, were the people who had shaped her. She looked down at the letter again. Todd Rettler had eliminated one possibility. But there were others, and she was going to pursue them.

FIFTEEN

Susannah tucked everything Todd had sent back in the envelope and brought it upstairs. It was after four and Cally still was not home. The conversation with Polly had temporarily pushed the phone call from school out of her mind, but now it had come charging back: something else to worry about.

Jack and Gilda were talking in low voices behind the closed door of his room. Could she be his *girlfriend*? Now the phone call was like a weight, solid and immovable. Where was Cally, anyway? Susannah texted her but there was no reply. Hungry for distraction, she checked her e-mail and there, at the top of the in-box, was something that, for the moment, pushed everything else aside.

TO: Susannah Gilmore
FROM: Tasha Clurman
SUBJECT: Your pages

What you have done here is fresh, interesting, and provocative.
But I am not convinced it's going to work as a novel for Out of

the Past Press, especially since your readers have come to expect something quite different from you. I can tell you are drawn to this material, and I do get why you are not so keen on Jane Seymour. Yet those are not sufficient reasons, in my mind, to jump ship quite so radically.

Look, I know you are going through a bad patch, what with Charlie's death and the move and all. Let me take Jane off your plate; there's a new author named Kitty Redden I'm interested in trying out—I'll bet she would leap at the chance to write her story. You can take a little time off; God knows you deserve it. Cast around for another idea, and if you settle on one, bounce it off me. Or else, if you are really committed to this Ruth Blay project, find a way to convince me that it's going to work.

Tasha Clurman, a crisp, sixtyish Brit with an ink black bob whose battle to quit smoking was waged with long cinnamon sticks on which she perpetually chewed, had first been Susannah's boss, then editor, and eventually friend. Susannah had always trusted her completely. But right now she was determined to prove her wrong. What a day it had been: the school, Polly, the letter, and now this. Yet Betsey Pettingill's voice was clear in her mind. She opened the document and began to type, an act tinged with desperation that felt more like transcription than invention:

I was so startled by the gruesome bundle I held that I dropped it, which made James start to scream as well. Sarah and Patience and Peggs came running over to see what was causing all the commotion. The little ones began to cry when they saw; Patience was the one who took charge. "I must go get Mother," she said. "Wait here." But none of us would do that, not with the baby,

*partially uncovered, lying on the dusty, straw-littered barn floor.
So we all walked silently back up to the house together.*

*My uncle and Mr. Currier were nowhere to be seen, but we
found Mrs. Currier in the kitchen, pounding out a ball of dough
with her fists on a stained and worn cutting board. The sleeves
of her dress were rolled up and her arms were covered in a
fine, floury dust; flour had settled on her face as well. I remember thinking that she looked so pale, like the dead baby out in
the barn.*

*The shrill sound of our voices caused her to say sternly,
"Quiet down! Patience, will you tell me what this is all about?"
So Patience told and Mrs. Currier's expression went from annoy-
ance to controlled but visible horror. "Are you sure?" she asked.
"This isn't one of your pranks, is it? Because if it is, I will be very
angry and—"*

*"No, Mother, it's not a prank," said Patience. "Please come
and see."*

*Mrs. Currier wiped off her face and brushed at her arms;
then she stood, shaking out her apron, which sent the flour dust
everywhere. We all went out the side door and back across the
meadow to the barn. I was petrified when we reached the darkened opening again. Maybe the baby had turned into a ghost
and vanished. But when we stepped inside and went to the spot,
the bundle containing the baby was still there. I had never been
so frightened of something so inert, and I never have been since.*

*Mrs. Currier knelt and took the baby in her arms. "Poor wee
one," she said, and ran the back of her finger across a cold white
cheek. Then she looked up. "Patience, go get your father. He
and Mr. Pettingill are probably down by the stream."*

*Patience sped off and Mrs. Currier set the baby down on a
bale of hay. I noticed that she covered the baby up with the cloth*

and I was grateful for this; the vision of that small, drawn face had been burned into my memory and I did not need or want to see it anymore. Then she asked, "Who found the baby first?" There was a silence during which I wanted to run up to the hayloft and bury myself in the hay. But everyone was looking at me; there was no way to avoid the telling. I explained how the boys and I had been looking for treasure but that I was the one who saw the floorboards and made the discovery.

"Was the baby alive when you found it?"

"No, ma'am," I said. Why would she ask this? Didn't she believe me?

"Betsey, I need you to be very sure when you answer. You said you dropped the baby when you folded back the cloth; maybe the baby was hurt in the fall?"

"No, no!" I cried. "The baby was dead when I found it! Dead!" I was so terrified by this line of questioning that I turned and dashed out of the barn, colliding with my uncle, who had just walked in. Mr. Currier was right beside him.

"What's all this about a dead baby?" He leaned down and scooped me up; sheltered in his strong arms, I felt my trembling subside.

"Come and see." Mrs. Currier led them to the bundle. My uncle peeled the cloth all the way back, revealing the entire baby, which was naked. In that brief instant I saw that it was a girl; then I quickly looked away.

"You think Betsey had something to do with this?" my uncle asked.

"I never said that." Mrs. Currier looked uncomfortable. "But since she was the one who found the babe, I thought it would be wise to inquire about—"

"This child has been dead for days, God rest her soul. Can't you see that?"

"Well, I didn't know exactly and so—"

"If you didn't know, you shouldn't go around laying blame or insinuating that—"

"No need to get angry." Mr. Currier, who had been silent until now, chimed in. "My wife was understandably upset by this horrific discovery, but she meant no harm to the child, did she now, Betsey?" He came close and tried to put a finger under my chin but I pressed my face against my uncle's chest. "What we really need to do is tell the Cloughs—the barn is on their property. And then we need to fetch Philips White. He's one of the justices of the peace around here. He'll know what to do."

My uncle set me down as Mr. Currier saddled up a horse; he would stop at the Cloughs' and then continue on to Justice White's house. Mrs. Currier sent Will, James, and Peggs home; then she told the three of us that we were to come back up to the house. "Can't we play outside?" Sarah wheedled. "Please?"

"All right," said Mrs. Currier. "But you'll have to stay where I can see you."

"What about the baby?" asked Patience in a small voice.

"We should leave her where she is until Justice White gets here." My uncle went over to cover the baby once again. I wondered then if she'd been given a name, and if so, what it was.

Just as we were about to leave the barn, a soft thump caught our attention and we turned. There was the ginger cat, holding one of her kittens by the scruff of its neck. She padded over to the bale of hay on which the baby lay shrouded, twitched the thick rope of her tail, and was gone.

Susannah looked up. The sky was dark now; she ought to be headed downstairs to see about dinner. Scanning what she had written once more, she hit save and set the laptop on sleep. Jack's and Gilda's voices could be heard behind the closed door of his room; maybe Susannah should invite her to dinner? She seemed like a nice girl and Jack was visibly smitten with her.

Cally was walking into the house just as Susannah came down the stairs; they met in the kitchen. There were a dozen questions Susannah wanted to hurl at her daughter: *Why are you cutting classes? Where are you going? Who is this girl you're hanging out with?* But she remembered her conversation with Polly and said only, "How was school today?"

"Fine." Cally walked to the fridge, opened the door, and considered her options.

Don't leave the door open while you make up your mind, was another thing she wanted to say, but again, with great effort, she kept herself in check.

"What's happening with Spanish?" Cally had told her that the high school did not have an advanced French class, so rather than place her in a lower-level—and in their view time-wasting—section, they had placed her in introductory Spanish. This might have been all right had not everyone else in the class been a freshman. *Some of them are Jack's age!* Cally had complained.

"Nothing special. The kids are all jerks. The teacher is okay. He's so short that half the boys tower over him." She emerged from the fridge empty-handed and closed the door.

Susannah put a pot of water up to boil. She was making spaghetti; the meatballs and sauce had been made the day before, so this would be an easy meal. "Do you know Antoinette Benoit?" she asked. "She's the eleventh-grade dean."

"I met her on the first day." Cally looked nervous. Or was this Susannah's projection? "Why?"

"She called me today." Susannah waited, and when Cally didn't answer, she went on. "She told me that you've been cutting classes and that you were disrespectful to the history teacher."

"He's disrespectful to us!" Cally burst out.

Not the answer Susannah would have expected. "In what way?"

"Mom, he is so boring I want to set myself on fire! No one that boring should be allowed to teach anyone else."

She did have a point. "Still, you were rude and you hurt his feelings. Do you think there might have been another way to handle it?" *You see, Polly—I'm trying here!*

"I don't know." Cally pulled out a chair and sank down into it. "I wanted to wake him up."

"And what about the cutting classes? How long has that been going on?"

Cally studied her nails, which were short and painted a vivid iridescent turquoise. "Pretty much from the start." She looked up at her mother imploringly. "Can't I go back to Brooklyn and finish school there? I already talked to Arianna, and she said she would talk to her mom about my living with them. Arianna's room is pretty big and she said we could share it." Arianna was Cally's best friend.

"You talked to Arianna but you didn't talk to me?" Susannah sat down at the table facing her daughter; dinner would wait. "How could you do that?"

"I wanted to see if her mom would agree before I asked you." Cally pinned her with that beseeching gaze. "If she says yes, will you let me, Mom? Please?"

Susannah was quiet. She wanted to acknowledge the desire— that everything could remain the same, that Cally could once more inhabit her old life—before she replied. "I wouldn't get to see you very much," she said finally. "It's a long distance and you don't drive yet."

"I know, but I'm so miserable here! Don't you care about that?"

"Of course I do." Susannah suppressed the urge to reach out and touch Cally's cheek. "But I want to find a way to deal with that while you're still living here, with us." She stopped, unsure if she should reveal any more. "I can't let you go, Cally. I've already lost your father; I can't bear losing you too."

"*You* can't bear it! It's all about you, isn't it? Well, if it hadn't been for you, Daddy would still be alive! It's your fault that he got killed!" Cally stood and pushed her chair roughly from the table. But before she could leave the room, Susannah put a firm, restraining hand on her arm.

"Stop saying that." Her voice was low but fierce. "Stop it right now. You've said it before and I didn't push back. Well, I'm pushing back now. It's untrue, it's cruel, and hearing you say it just tortures me. I loved your father; you know that. But if he was such a big damn fool as to not wear a bike helmet, well, that wasn't my fault. So you can stop blaming me right now." She managed to turn away from Cally before she erupted in loud, gulping sobs. For several seconds, she just surrendered and even luxuriated in it; the strain of keeping things together—for her kids, for herself—was sometimes more than she could tolerate.

"Mom, I'm sorry—I didn't know. I mean, I just miss Daddy so, so much—"

"So do I!" Susannah whirled around and grabbed her daughter in a tight hug. But Cally endured rather than reciprocated the embrace.

"Hey, is everything all right down here?" Jack had walked into the kitchen.

"We're okay." Susannah used her fingers to brush the tears away. And then, "Do you think Gilda would like to stay for dinner? We promise there won't be any more shouting, right?" She looked at Cally, who quickly looked away. So it was to be a détente. Not a peace treaty.

"I can ask her." Jack turned to go back upstairs and Cally went right after him. Susannah remained standing in the kitchen, staring at the place her daughter had occupied just a few minutes before. When was the last time Cally had allowed herself to be hugged? She couldn't even remember.

Then she turned her gaze to the kitchen clock. It was after five—too late to call Ms. Benoit back. But she would call first thing tomorrow and arrange a meeting at school. Maybe today's conversation had opened something up in Cally, forcing her to see beyond her own grief into someone else's. God, she hoped so. Susannah went over to the stove. The water had boiled completely down and there was no longer enough water for the pasta. She refilled the pot and set it on the stove, ready to start again.

SIXTEEN

Since the town hall meeting was being held at the library the surrounding streets were choked with cars. Susannah had to park several blocks away and then pick her way over the snow and icy patches to reach the building. The wreath she had first seen on the door was down now, and the door itself kept opening and closing as more people went inside. It was going to be a full house.

She unzipped her red parka and headed for the stairs along with everyone else. There was Janet Durbin several feet and many bodies away from her; maybe they could sit together. Janet had been so helpful with so many things and Susannah was grateful to her; she hoped that Janet would become a friend, her first in her adopted home.

But when Susannah got upstairs to the space designated for the meeting, she saw that every single wooden folding chair that had been set up was occupied. She recognized the manager from the supermarket, Gilda Mooney's parents, Alice Renfew, and a few other people she'd seen in town. Draping her parka over her arm, she resigned herself to standing. Janet was also standing, though not close enough for Susannah to talk to her. A lectern had been set up by the windows, outside of which the dark night sky could be seen. It was only six thirty, but every last trace of daylight was gone.

"Here, you can take one and pass the rest down." Susannah turned to see a woman handing out stapled packets of material. Taking the one on top, she passed along the rest of the stack and began to read. There was a statement from the Wingate Paper Company claiming the dyes posed no environmental threat, along with statements from a local environmentalist who opposed the dumping. Several xeroxed newspaper articles were also in the packet, and at the end there were photographs of the pond's shore, bright with clusters of foamy pink bubbles.

Susannah looked up. While she'd been reading, more people had filed into the room and were trying to find places to stand. Janet had mentioned that a local politician, Brad Bollender, was scheduled to attend and he was now standing near the lectern, adjusting his tie and speaking rapidly to an assistant. It was twenty to seven now; when would the meeting get started? Jack was at Gilda's, but Cally was home alone. Even though Cally claimed not to mind, Susannah didn't like leaving her alone for too long; she was worried about what trouble she might get into.

Then Corbin Bailey marched over to the lectern, breaking stride only briefly to shake Brad Bollender's hand. Susannah's lips parted involuntarily. Dressed in pressed black jeans, a white shirt, and a moss green sweater vest, he moved like a leader—

swift, sure, and full of purpose. And when he turned his strong blue gaze on the audience, they seemed to feel it too; an appreciative murmur arose from the crowd.

"Thank you all for coming," he began. "It's great to see how many of you turned out tonight, because it confirms my belief"— he looked out at the room—"my deeply held belief that it's the small things, the things closest to our lives and hearts, that are the most important of all. And why? Because they help us to see the bigger issues and connect us not just to people we know, but to people everywhere. Yes, tonight we're here to talk about Primrose Pond, and to tell the folks at Wingate Paper that we don't want their dyes in our water. But Primrose Pond is just the start, and if we can succeed here, we can succeed other places too— Portsmouth, Maine, all over the Eastern seacoast, all over the country and even the world. Water contamination is a *major* issue that ultimately includes the ocean and all the marine life in it— fish, coral reefs, that whole fragile and perilous ecosystem under the surface."

Susannah sat very still watching him. He spoke well, and he seemed to be trying to make eye contact with the audience; when that dark blue gaze locked on hers, she felt a distinct and immediate connection. This was followed instantly by guilt. Yes, she was caught up in the rhetoric of Corbin's words, and she wanted to do what she could to stop Wingate from polluting the tranquil pond she remembered from her youth. But she was also responding to Corbin on some primal, sexual level—she remembered that from her youth too.

Up at the lectern, Corbin had asked for the lights to be dimmed while he showed a PowerPoint presentation that featured images of Wingate's factory spewing indigo-colored waste—if she hadn't known what it was and what it represented, she would have thought it pretty—into a nearby river, a river that ultimately fed into Primrose Pond.

"Excuse me, where did you get those pictures? You weren't authorized to photograph on our property!" A heavyset man with a blond crew cut stood up and began walking toward Corbin. "Turn that thing off. Turn it off right now!"

"Hey, we have a right to see those pictures! It's our pond that you're polluting!" This was shouted out by another man who sat very close to the front.

The blond man turned around. "Not if they were taken without permission. That's trespassing, pure and simple. And it's against the law!"

"If there's anyone breaking the law here, it's you guys. Filling the pond with your industrial waste, your chemical spew. *You're* the lawbreaker here. *You're* the criminal." The man was on his feet now and, though he was not large, he looked menacing—and ready to snap.

"Guys, can we dial it down a notch?" Corbin spoke up, seemingly unfazed, from his place at the lectern. To the blond guy he said, "I have it on good authority that the person who took those pictures was given permission by someone at your company headquarters; if you can wait until we finish here, I can get you the name." And to the man's antagonist he said, "Look, Bob, I know how upset you are over this—we're all upset, or we wouldn't be here. But we can work this out in an amicable way." He paused, looking from one angry man to the other. "Let me finish the presentation. Then we'll be hearing from Brad Bollender and after that from the Wingate representative." He gestured to the blond man, who remained where he stood. "Everybody deserves a say, right? Everybody has a right to be heard."

The man shuffled back to his seat and Bob sat back down. Corbin continued his presentation and was followed by Brad Bollender, then Greg Hartsdale, the representative from Wingate. There was a slew of questions, and a couple of times the tension in the room began to rise again. But every time it did, Corbin managed to defuse it.

At the end of the meeting, Corbin produced a petition that began to circulate. "Let's show our elected officials in Concord how we feel about the dumping," Corbin said. "And let's set an example for the citizens of this state." Susannah watched as the petition made its way from lap to lap, hand to hand. Once they signed, people got up and began moving toward the stairs. When it was her turn, she signed, passed the petition to the person next to her, and joined them. Janet caught up with her when they were both downstairs and standing near the door, now open because the room was so overheated. Susannah stepped outside, savoring the chill of the February night for a few seconds before slipping on her parka.

"Corbin's an effective speaker, isn't he?" Janet said. Susannah nodded, not wanting to say anything that might reveal her own private response to Corbin. "But that may not be enough. The issue may make it all the way to the governor's office, and everyone says that Wingate's CEO has the governor in his pocket."

"So none of this"—Susannah gestured to the people making their way out of the library, heading for their cars or vans—"will make any difference?"

"That remains to be seen," Janet said. Then she turned. "Look, there's Todd Rettler. You remember him from our lunch?"

"Of course." This made Susannah think of the other man at the lunch—she hadn't yet ruled George Martin out as her mother's lover. Had he been here tonight? Susannah had not seen him.

While she was scanning the people still milling around, Corbin came up to them.

"You spoke so well," said Janet. "And I liked the way you handled those two men who faced off—I really thought one of them was going to throw a punch."

"Me too." Corbin brought a hand up to the back of his neck and began to massage it. Susannah noted the gesture; had the tension in the room affected him more than he let on?

"Well, you got them both to settle down and listen."

Susannah agreed; he'd really managed the situation so well. But instead of complimenting him, she stood there fiddling with the zipper on her bag. He made her nervous, that was it. Then Corbin turned to Janet. "Did Susannah tell you that we two go way back? She used to date my brother."

"Really? You and Trevor were an item?" asked Janet.

"It was only that one summer when I was here with my family. I don't think we wrote or ever got in touch again after September rolled around."

"Well, Trevor was crushed when you left. He talked about you all the time."

Susannah felt herself going warm, and no doubt pink, from embarrassment. By the end of that summer, Trevor had become about as interesting to her as a brick. "How is Trevor? He's not still in town, is he?"

"No, he cleared out a long time ago. He went to school in Gainesville and decided to stay in Florida. Said he didn't care if he ever saw snow again in his entire life. He's in real estate now, and he's doing really well."

"Did he get married?" Janet asked. "I thought I heard something about that."

"He did, though it took him a long time to get over Susannah."
Corbin winked. Was he teasing her? If so, she wished he would
stop.

Someone from the meeting came up to him, and they were
joined by another person and then another. She was glad to step
back and watch him. How intently he listened and how patiently
he explained. Clearly these people looked up to him and wanted
more of his time, so Susannah said good night to Janet and headed
for her car.

Then she heard her name and she turned. Corbin walked over.
"A bunch of us are going over to Talley's. Do you want to come?"
She must have looked blank, because he added, "It's a place on
Route 4 that's pretty popular with us locals. You can get a bite to
eat if you're hungry and they've always got something good on tap."

Susannah hated beer but she *was* hungry. "That sounds good,"
she said. "Just let me call my daughter." When Cally picked up,
Susannah could instantly tell she was not alone. She could not
have said how she knew this, but there was something about the
timbre of Cally's voice, an uncharacteristic buoyancy, that let
Susannah know she was with someone. But whom?

"Where are you?" Susannah asked.

"With Alice Renfew. She invited me to dinner. Isn't that the
coolest?"

"She did?" Susannah tried to process this information, but it
was not computing. Cally was having dinner with Alice? How
had this happened?

"Uh-huh. I was over at her barn visiting Jester and she came
out and invited me. She's a fantastic cook, Mom! We had French
onion soup and we're going to have some kind of vegetable dish
and garlic bread too."

Susannah said nothing. Why did this dinner invitation bother her? She ought to feel grateful to her neighbor and glad that Cally was with a responsible older adult instead of some hard-drinking slackers. But instead she was irritated and, yes, jealous. Cally did not seem to notice her silence but chattered on about Alice's house, Alice's clothes—Corbin was still standing there, waiting for her to make up her mind. "Well, that's very nice of her. Be sure to thank her, okay?"

"Okay, Mom. Anyway, I should go now."

Susannah put the phone away in her bag. "It's fine," she said to Corbin.

"Good," he said. "You can follow me in your car."

Talley's was only a few miles away and Susannah liked the place as soon as she walked in. High up on the walls were small windows whose curtains were strewn with pictures of riders, horses, and hounds, and hanging from the ceiling was a chandelier made from a wagon wheel. A popcorn maker sat on the bar's polished wood surface and overflowing bowls of popcorn had been strategically placed along its length. There were enough people to make the bar seem festive, but not enough to make it raucous. And she recognized several faces—people from the meeting and also George Martin. When he caught sight of her, he raised his glass, but Corbin was steering her toward the back, so she just waved. Maybe she'd get to talk to him later.

The back room was smaller, with tables covered in checkered oilcloth and lit by candles in hurricane lamps. Somehow the other people who'd been tagging along melted away and Susannah found herself seated across from Corbin, two plastic-coated menus placed in front of them. She felt awkward, and not entirely sure she wanted to be here. Yes, she was attracted to him. But it was too soon after Charlie, she wasn't ready, and she—

"Listen, I want to apologize to you."

"You want to apologize to me? For what?"

"Teasing you about Trevor. It makes you uncomfortable and I should take a hint. I'm going to cut it out right now." He reached into the bowl on the table for a handful of popcorn. "Forgive me?"

"Forgiven," she said, studying him. "Anyway, it was a long time ago."

"I know. But I'll tell you a secret. I kind of envied him."

"You did?" She was flushing again; the tips of her ears were hot and her face felt singed, as if she'd been standing too close to an oven.

"I mean, I couldn't have done anything about it then. He was my brother and all. But I remember wishing I'd seen you first."

A waitress appeared, sparing her the need to reply. She ordered a slice of quiche and he ordered a burger and a Coke. Then a man who'd been at the meeting came over to talk to Corbin, and Susannah could retreat into herself for a moment. So Corbin Bailey wished he had been dating her that summer. Who knew?

"Sorry about that," he said when the man walked away. "But technically, I'm still on the job." He smiled, gaze steady on her.

"You work hard," she said.

"It's something worth doing. I've lived here a long time—pretty much my whole life, except for the four years I was in Durham, at UNH—and I think the people here are basically good people, people who will do the right thing if they understand what the right thing is."

"What about the people at Wingate? And the governor? Janet says those two are pretty tight." She was glad the subject had been changed—much safer and easier to talk about the present than to delve into the past.

"Dumping that waste may be good for Wingate in the short term. It's easy, it's cheap, and it's what they've always done. But in the long term—no. Public opinion has shifted; people are more critical of companies that pollute and don't give a damn. If they don't clean up their act, they may feel the impact down the road; new contracts won't be offered, and business may dry up." He picked up his glass of Coke and raised it. "To doing the right thing," he said, and touched the rim of the glass to hers. "May it become contagious."

Now Susannah smiled. He made it sound so easy.

"Anyway, apart from community meetings and the environmental impact of the local paper industry, how are you liking your life in town? It's been a long time since you'd been back, hasn't it?"

"I'd never been back," Susannah said. "My parents moved, and then they died. Someone else came in to clear out the house, and a friend of my mother's took care of renting it out."

"I remember your dad," Corbin said. "He was always involved in some project with the house and he'd come into the store to buy stuff. Your mom—not so much. Though there was this one time when I helped him out to the car with his bags and your mom—she was a real beauty, I do remember that—was sitting in the car waiting. She was staring straight ahead, not looking at your dad, not even when he opened the door and got in. I thought she seemed . . . angry."

"She was angry a lot that summer," Susannah said. "Also sad—she was always dissolving into tears." Their food arrived, and again she was grateful for the reprieve; talking with him seemed to lure her to a place that was filled with land mines.

They ate in silence for a few minutes and then Susannah asked, "What about you? Do you like living here? Was this what you planned for yourself?"

"Planned? Not exactly." He contemplated his soda before taking a sip. "I worked my butt off in school; I was really driven,
really committed. I graduated summa cum laude, made the dean's
list, was given departmental honors—you name it. I was accepted
to law school at Emory; they even kicked in with money. But then
the summer after my first year, my dad had a stroke and my mom
needed help to keep the store going."

"What about Trevor? And don't you have a sister?"

He nodded. "Trevor was gone by then and Annemarie was in
Toronto—she married a Canadian guy—so it was up to me. I told
myself it was just temporary; I'd take a leave but go back the next
year. It didn't happen like that, though."

"No?"

"He lingered for almost a year. It was awful. Then he died. My
mom was so broken up I couldn't leave her. Emory was so far. I
figured I'd reapply to other schools closer by. My grades were good.
Some place would have accepted me. But that didn't happen either."

"So you gave up your dream?"

"It wasn't like that. Not really. I found I liked running the store.
And I was good at it too—business has improved since I took
over. Plus, I got to be involved in local causes that matter to me.
Even if it's not the life I planned—or hoped for." He sounded—
disappointed? resigned? Susannah was not sure which. "So what
about you? What kind of work do you do?"

"I'm a writer," she said.

"You write newspaper and magazines articles?" He sounded
interested.

"Novels," she corrected. "Historical, often, though not always,
with a romantic undercurrent."

He nodded. "A blend of fact and fiction, right? What's the
ratio?"

"That depends on the subject." She positioned her fork across her now empty plate.

"Who's your subject now?" asked Corbin.

"Good question. I was working on Jane Seymour—she was the third wife of Henry VIII—only I lost interest along the way. I wanted to do something different, something involving someone local, actually. I'd been researching this Portsmouth woman named Ruth Blay, who was the last woman hanged in New Hampshire, only my editor's not convinced it's going to work."

"Oh, yeah—Alice Renfew mentioned that."

"She did?" This really *was* a small town.

"The other day at the store. My mom was really into her too. She had this thing for local history, and even organized a little group that took day trips and read books together. So I remember hearing about Ruth Blay. Some woman who'd written a book about her came to speak at the library and—"

"Carolyn Marvin. Janet Durbin told me about her."

"Well, my mom hosted the reception afterward. It was all she could talk about for weeks."

"Your mother—she's not still alive, is she?"

Corbin shook his head. "And all those ladies who used to meet with her—they're all gone too. Dead or moved away. But I could help you with your research—drive you to places associated with her. Portsmouth, for one. And I know there must be material at the state archives in Concord."

"That would be great," she said. Did he really need to drive her to Concord? It was less than thirty minutes away. Maybe he was just trying to find a way to see her again. If so, she realized she liked the idea.

"In fact, I have to head over to Concord the day after tomorrow. Do you want to go with me?"

"All right." Had she been right and he was asking her on a date? She wasn't sure.

"How's nine thirty? I'll pick you up."

"Nine thirty is fine."

By the time they ordered dessert—carrot cake for her, cheese-cake for him—the man who'd come over earlier and a few other people from the meeting had wandered by and pulled up chairs. Susannah didn't mind; she was having a good time, better than she'd had in a while. Then the guys started to play a game of darts using a board hung in a corner and Janet joined in, surprising everyone when she scored a bull's-eye.

Susannah turned to Corbin. "You're right," she said. "I do like this place."

"Told you so," he said. "But how about next week you let me take you someplace else? There's a kind of upscale new restaurant in the next town over; I hear the food is terrific, like something you would get in Boston or even New York."

Susannah didn't say anything. That really *was* a date. "I'm not sure," she began, "that is—I—"

He reached out and put his hand over hers; the connection was immediate and electric, just as it had been all those years ago. "I get it. I heard about your husband and I'm really sorry. So forget dinner. Let me take you skating instead. Your kids too—I'll bet they've never skated on a pond before."

"That would be fun," she said. His hand was still covering hers; it was causing little pinpricks of pleasure to needle her skin.

"Great. Maybe Saturday? Or is Sunday better?"

"Can I check with them and let you know?" She doubted Cally would agree, but she would ask anyway; Jack, she knew, would love the idea.

"Sure."

The check came and Corbin insisted on paying it. Susannah got up. It had been a good evening, one of the nicest she'd had in the month she'd been here. Now it was time to go home; Jack would be back from Gilda's, and she hoped Cally would be home from Alice's. She was saying good night to Corbin and Janet in the parking lot when George Martin came over.

"Hello," he said. "I saw you come in and wanted to catch you before you left."

"How are you?"

"Pretty well. I think I might have a couple of letters your mother sent me after she and your father moved away. If I can find them, I'll make sure you get them."

"Thank you, George." Letters! From her mother! "That's really nice of you." Susannah had already ruled out Todd Rettler as the man who might have been her mother's lover. But George Martin was still a possibility, especially if he and her mother had exchanged letters. And then there was Harry Snady.

"By the way, I did find a number for Harry Snady. In Eliot."

"Yes, that's right. I'd heard he'd moved. Did you talk to him?"

"No. The woman who answered the phone wouldn't let me speak to him and she told me not to call again. I was wondering if you might know why."

"That must have been Deedee. His wife."

"Was she always such a bitch?"

"She kept him on a short leash—I remember that."

Susannah wanted to ask more about her, but a man with a trim silver-flecked beard and thin gold-rimmed glasses came up and gently put a hand on George's arm.

"Hate to break up the party," he said, "but I have to be up at the crack of dawn."

"I was just saying good night." George took the man's hand and turned to Susannah. "This is Barry," he said. "My partner."

Partner! Susannah looked from George to Barry and then finally let her gaze linger on George's face, the face of the man who had clearly *not* been her mother's lover.

SEVENTEEN

The morning after the community meeting, Susannah went to the high school and made her way to Antoinette Benoit's office. Cally was already there, seated across from Antoinette wearing what looked like a Catholic school uniform: pleated gray jumper, insignia of some kind on the front, buttons on either shoulder. But paired with the silky fuchsia blouse and lavish cluster of fake pearls, it had transcended its origins. Antoinette said a polite hello to Susannah, who took the other chair in the small office. Then she jumped right in. "Cally, you know why we're here, right?"

"It's Calista."

"Excuse me?"

"My name. It's Calista, not Cally. I don't want to be called Cally anymore. Not ever." She shot Susannah *the look*.

"All right, Calista." Antoinette did not allow herself to get derailed. "We're meeting to talk about your cutting classes—and how that is unacceptable. Do you want to say anything about what's been going on?"

Again, Cally—Calista—looked at Susannah. "I don't belong here," she began. "I don't fit in. The kids here don't get me and I don't get them. My classes are boring, I hate New Hampshire, and I want to go back to New York and live with my best friend, but my mother won't let me." She gripped the arms of her chair tightly, as if she might snap them right off. "I think that about covers it."

"It sure does," said Antoinette, still serene. Not much rattled this woman. "That's quite a list. Let's see if we can unpack those issues one by one." And to Susannah's amazement, Antoinette addressed each of Cally's complaints and laid out a plan that included a move up to a senior history class, a French tutorial to eliminate the dreaded Spanish class, and an independent study in equine management in which Jester, the horse owned by Alice Renfew, had a starring role. There were also to be mandatory meetings with Ms. Lanigan, the school psychologist.

Susannah was largely silent during this conversation. She was grateful for the dean's enlightened attitude about the problem, which was remarkably free from admonishment and threat. It was only toward the end of the conversation that Antoinette hinted at the consequences for Cally if she didn't toe the line. "I've seen your test scores," she said, running her finger over the sheet of paper—presumably the scores—that sat in an open manila folder. "And they are impressive. You'll have many doors open to you." She paused and tucked her neat white pageboy behind her ears. "But they can close just as quickly. That will be up to you, Calista. In the end, it's your decision." She stood and Susannah stood too. "We're going to have a follow-up meeting in a month or so. See where we are then."

"Thank you, Ms. Benoit," Cally said.

Calista, Calista, Susannah had to remind herself. It would take time.

"Back to class with you now."

Cally—no, *Calista*—left the office and Antoinette Benoit turned to Susannah. "I can see it's been a rough transition for her. But let's see if we can get her back on track. I'll talk to Alice later today. I'll bet she'll be tickled by the idea."

"Do you know her well?" Susannah asked.

"Everyone around here knows her; her husband Dave was kind of a local celebrity. Almost every child in town passed through his office at one time or another. And he used to come to senior career day every year; he was just so inspiring. I don't know how many kids he steered toward medicine. A few pediatricians, an oncologist, nurses, X-ray technicians, a radiologist or two."

"That was very generous of him."

"Extremely."

Susannah thanked Antoinette and said good-bye. This meeting had gone well—better than she'd expected, in fact. Calista—there, she was getting it now—had not been too hostile and by the end had even seemed receptive. So why wasn't she more pleased about the outcome?

She was jealous, that was why. Jealous that her daughter seemed to have attached, so effortlessly, to their new neighbor, leaving her own mother outside their charmed circle. Why couldn't Calista find some nice friends her own age to bond with? Someone at the high school? She brooded over this on the drive back. The sky was gray and filled with low, swollen clouds; snow was predicted for tonight and into tomorrow morning. Jealous or not, Susannah wanted to be ready for the storm and she ticked off the list of things she needed: gas, groceries, deicer for the path leading up to the house.

That last item she could pick up at the hardware store, and a trip to the hardware store meant a potential encounter with Corbin Bailey. The thought was like flipping a switch, diverting her foul mood over Alice, and sending an anticipatory buzz right through her. But then she decided, no, she did not actually need to get the deicer; there was enough in the package to get through at least this snowfall. She was going to Concord with him tomorrow—that would be soon enough to see him. And then she'd see him again on Sunday. He was going to come over to Primrose Pond, which was frozen solid, and they were going skating—or at least she and Jack were. Calista, predictably, had already said *No way* to the invitation.

On her way home, she passed Buns of Steel, the exercise studio she had seen when she first drove into town, and, on a whim, parked the car and went inside. Behind a high white desk sat a woman in a tight, cleavage-baring black sweater. A tiny cross glittered on her neck. She was staring at a computer screen but turned to Susannah right away and smiled. "Can I help you?"

"I just wanted to get a schedule and see what kind of classes you were offering."

"Sure." The woman plucked a flyer from a holder on the desk and handed it to Susannah. "We've got a class called Boot Camp at seven a.m. five days a week. Trim and Tone is Monday, Wednesday, and Friday at noon; Tuesday and Thursday is Pilates. Weekends are for spin and yoga. And Jazzercise too. And there's a winter special going on now. If you buy a card of ten classes, you get two free."

As she talked, Susannah kept thinking there was something very familiar about her, although she was having trouble placing her. "Martha Dineen," she said finally.

The woman looked blank and then recognition settled on her

face. "Susannah!" she said. "Susannah Gilmore, right? From that summer, oh, about a hundred years ago?"

"That's me." Susannah and Martha had been close, though their friendship had not survived the distance. Or the time.

"Are you back in town for a visit?"

"Actually, I'm living here, with my kids, in the house that belonged to my parents."

"It's great to see you. I was just about to go out for a break. I close the studio for about an hour. Do you have time for a bite?"

Seated across from Martha in the little soup and sandwich shop down the street, Susannah listened to an abbreviated version of her old friend's life: four years at UNH with a major in chemistry, then training to become a pharmacist. Marriage, three kids. One had Down syndrome. Divorced now, but on good terms with her ex. And living in a committed relationship with a woman. "It wasn't so easy to be openly gay back then. I had to hide—even from myself. Things have gotten so much better."

"Did you marry Andrew Jordan?" Susannah had a sudden vivid memory of the boy Martha had been dating back then—slim, small, with feathery brown hair and a high-pitched, almost hysterical laugh. He'd been the clown of the group, always coming up with one crazy prank after another. They had called him the Joker.

"No, Andy and I broke up after that summer. I married Jim Snady."

"Jim Snady?" Could he be any relation to Harry?

"Yes. We met at UNH. Sweetheart of a guy. If you happen to like guys, that is."

"Is he related to Harry Snady?"

"Yes. Why? Do you know Harry?"

Susannah considered her next words carefully. She didn't want to tell Martha what she suspected about Harry, but she hoped she could ask for her help in reaching him. "No," she said finally. "But my mother did. So I called him and his wife practically hissed and spit. She wouldn't even let him come to the phone."

Martha took a bite of her ham and cheese. "That would be Deedee. In Jim's family, she's . . . legendary."

"I only want to talk to him. Ever since I got back here, my mother has been on my mind. You might even say she's been haunting me." That much was true. "I had hoped Harry could fill in some gaps in the picture. She was a very private person and, though I was her only daughter, I never felt I really knew her."

"I remember your mother." Martha finished the sandwich and patted her lips with her napkin. "So pretty and so . . . worldly. We all thought she seemed different than the women around here. Had a kind of big-city way about her."

"Yet she loved it here. She really did." Susannah glanced at her watch. She ought to be going now; the kids would be home from school soon. But what about Harry Snady? Could Martha engineer a meeting with him? She wasn't even married to Jim anymore. And she'd have to find a way to elude Deedee.

The waitress came with a check, which Susannah insisted on paying.

"You don't have to do that," Martha said. But Susannah knew money was tight: the job at the exercise studio was in addition to her evening shift at an all-night pharmacy in Concord.

"You can treat some other time," Susannah said. "I'll come to a class and we'll have coffee after."

"Sounds like a plan. I want to hear more about what you're up to."

They walked out into the frigid street, and when they got to Susannah's car, Martha gave her a quick hug, the fur on the hood of her coat briefly tickling Susannah's cheek. "So glad we bumped into each other," she said. "I hope we can pick up where we left off."

"So do I." She waited a beat. Should she do it? Was it presuming too much? She thought of that awful woman hanging up on her and told herself, *Be bold.* "There's one more thing. I know it's a lot to ask, especially since we haven't seen each other in decades, but I want to see Harry Snady. Do you think there's any way you could help?"

Martha stepped back. "I think so," she said. "Harry always liked me and I can find a way around Deedee. Besides, he needs to get out more—it will do him a world of good."

"Oh, thank you!" Susannah said and she hugged Martha again. "Thank you so much." She wasn't at all sure that Harry Snady had been her mother's lover. But if she met him face-to-face, at least there was a chance of finding out.

As she was walking back to her car, Martha's voice called after her. "Have you seen Corbin Bailey since you got back to town?"

Susannah turned around. "Why do you ask?"

"I don't know." Martha came closer. "Seeing you got me thinking about that summer. Even though you were going out with Trevor, I always thought there might have been something between you and Corbin."

"He certainly was . . . attractive back then," Susannah said.

"He still is," said Martha. And though Susannah didn't reply, she most certainly agreed.

EIGHTEEN

Driving home, Susannah made a mental list of all the things she wanted to ask Harry when they met. How long had he known her mother? When and where did they meet? Had they stayed in touch when she moved away? He'd directed her mother in several productions; which ones and what roles had she played in them? Susannah and her father had gone to see her mother perform when they lived in New Brunswick. But by that time she was playing older women: Amanda in *The Glass Menagerie*, Juliet's nurse in *Romeo and Juliet*. She had shone in those parts. But before Susannah was born, she'd been young and beautiful; she must have played different kinds of roles. She hoped Harry Snady would be able to tell her about them.

As Susannah's car crunched along the road that went by Alice Renfew's house, her thoughts were abruptly yanked in another direction. Even before a plan had been formalized today, Cally—*Calista*—had been spending quite a bit of time at this house. And soon that time would increase. Susannah's irritation mounted as she drove slowly past the meadow, the barn, and, yes, the horse, leaning his head out of the stall the way he had that first time. She debated stopping and getting out of the car to pat him again, but the gate was closed and, anyway, she wanted to get home.

She parked and let herself into the house. It was too late to start working; her visit with Martha had eaten up the time and now she had to get dinner started. Jack came in first and then Cally—Calista—came in too. Dusk didn't descend until after five today; the days, though still cold, were getting longer. And after the meal was finished and the kitchen cleaned, Susannah felt she could spend some time at her computer. She'd leave the door to her room open so if either of the kids needed her, she'd be available.

She had not given up on the Ruth Blay story; if anything, Tasha's resistance had only made her that much more determined. She would prove her wrong; she *would*. Why she needed to do this was only partially clear to her. Did she hope to expiate her own guilt by wrestling with Betsey's? Because Betsey's guilt was a theme that was pulsing through these pages, a rhythm that Susannah was drawn to and needed to follow. Tasha was giving her a reprieve, and the sale of the Brooklyn house had given her a hefty nest egg. She could afford to indulge herself, at least for a little longer. She gave herself a deadline: the spring. If she couldn't write the pages that would convince Tasha, she'd give up and return to more familiar territory. But it was still early February; spring felt like a long way off.

She sat down at her desk where the computer's screen, left in sleep mode, now bloomed at the touch of a key. Music emanated from Jack's open door; Calista's door, which she had passed on the way in here, was closed. The house was quiet but vibrant; there was energy here—it was humming, it was glowing. It came from their conjoined rhythms, the boy's moody melody, the girl's silent brooding, her own insistent need to shape a story from the very best words she had at her disposal.

She wasn't writing the whole book in sequence yet; these pages were more like impressionistic renderings, placeholders to map out the feelings, the internal psychology of the characters. If she were truly writing this novel, she'd need to flesh out Betsey's life more, as well as the times in which she lived. The religious revival known as the Great Awakening, the renewed war against the French that culminated in the 1745 siege of Fort Louisbourg in Cape Breton, the strict penal codes that were enforced on the local population—all these elements would have to be woven into her fictional account. But she was not there. Not yet.

Once we were at the house, Mrs. Currier told Patience and Sarah to sit down and work on their samplers. Patience was very deft with her needle; the red and blue letters were perfectly stitched and neatly aligned. She had finished them all and was completing a verse from the Scriptures that ran along the bottom. When she saw me looking, she said, a trifle meanly, "You can't read those words, can you?"

"Yes," I said. "I can read them."

"No, you can't," Patience insisted. "You're lying."

I looked at the sampler spread out on her lap. "'Behold the day the Lord hath made; I will rejoice and be glad in it,'" I read. Patience's hand stopped its darting motion, the needle glinting between her fingers.

"How did you know what that said?" she said finally.

"I told you. I know how to read."

"But you're so little," said Sarah. "Littler than me."

"My father taught me."

"Your father!" This seemed even more shocking to Patience than my being able to read at all.

"Yes, my mother wanted me to learn."

"It's not right in a girl so little," muttered Sarah. But I could see she was just jealous. Her sampler was not as nice as her sister's, but it was still better than the one I was working on at home, with all its knots, pulls, and uneven stitches. I'd had to yank out so many that the sampler looked frayed and old even before it was done. My needlework was not as good as my reading, and I was glad no one here could see and judge me for it.

As the girls worked, some of the neighbor ladies came into the kitchen to sit down. The pies Mrs. Currier had been rolling out earlier were baking in the oven at the back wall of the big fireplace; an enticing aroma filled the house. Uncle Benjamin had told me it was too late to go back tonight, so we would be staying with the Curriers, and I was hoping the pie would be served later, after supper.

Mrs. Clough, who owned the barn, said, "What a terrible thing. What will happen to the baby now?"

"I expect she'll be given a Christian burial," said a woman who'd been introduced as Mrs. Brown. "Has anyone called the reverend?"

"I don't know," Mrs. Clough said. "But we should ask. Burying her properly is the least we can do."

"More than her mother did," muttered a woman whose big, puffy bosom made her look like a partridge. "To think she laid her under the floor of a barn—it's indecent."

"That's hardly the worst of it," said a woman as stringy and lined as the other woman was plump. "They're saying she killed the baby."

"Who killed the baby?" I asked. I had been listening to this conversation with growing horror, and even though I knew I was not supposed to interrupt the grown-ups, I could not help myself. I thought of the tiny pale face with its blue-tinged lips. I had known instantly that the baby was dead. But I had never imagined someone might have killed her.

The women stopped talking and stared at me. "Betsey, that's quite enough," scolded Mrs. Currier. "It's very rude to meddle in matters that have nothing to do with you. Girls, take Betsey upstairs, and, Patience, if you can find an extra bit of linen in my sewing basket, give it to Betsey with a needle and thread. Better for her to practice her stitches than to be a busybody." I followed Patience up the steep, narrow stairs to the room above, my face hot with shame. My uncle had gone with Mr. Currier, or else he would have defended me.

"That's Betsey Pettingill, Benjamin's niece. She's the one who actually found the body." Mrs. Currier's voice—condemning yet filled with a strange, gloating joy—was loud enough for me to hear.

Upstairs was a single room with one large bed on one side and two smaller ones on the other; a heavy curtain separated them. Patience went over to the side with the larger bed and knelt to rummage through a covered basket. Then she handed me a scrap of cloth and a needle that had already been threaded. I hunched down on a tiny wooden stool, but before I began I simply had to ask. "What were they talking about? Who killed the baby?"

Patience glanced toward the stairs and then said in a low voice, "I think they mean that woman who came here to stay a while ago. Mother says she's a distant relative of ours, but I don't remember ever hearing about her before. Her name is Ruth. Ruth Blay."

"Why would she kill her baby? I don't understand. Mothers love their babies."

"Not if the baby doesn't have a father," said Patience.

"Of course the baby has a father," I said. "Her father is Mr. Blay."

"Maybe there is no Mr. Blay. Maybe Ruth made that all up," Sarah said.

I looked helplessly from one sister to the other and back again. They seemed to understand something that had utterly eluded me. But I deserved to know; I had found that poor baby after all. I turned to Patience. "Tell me. You have to."

Patience and Sarah exchanged a look. Then Patience began speaking in a low, hurried voice. "Sometimes a woman is sinful and does things that a woman is only supposed to do with her husband. And then she gets a baby in her belly. When the baby comes and there is no husband, everyone knows how wicked she is. So she wants to get rid of the baby—to kill it, even—so no one will know what a bad woman she is or what she did."

"The mama did not kill that baby," I said firmly.

"How would you know?" scoffed Sarah. "You're practically a baby yourself."

I started to cry, and used the scrap of cloth I was still holding to wipe my eyes.

"Be quiet," Patience said. "If you make noise, my mother will come up here and we'll all be punished."

So I stopped, but I set the cloth and needle aside and said, "I want to lie down. Please, can I lie down?"

Patience led me to her bed, where I slipped off my shoes and lay on top of the coverlet. Almost as soon as I did, my eyes closed and I slept—it had been such a long and exhausting day.

When I awoke, the light was waning. Patience and Sarah were gone; they had probably gone downstairs. But I did not *want to go down there. Not yet. I got off the bed, put my shoes back on, and went to the window. What I saw shocked me.*

There was a man—my mother would have called him portly but to me he was just plain fat—with a curled white wig and a waistcoat whose brass buttons barely closed, and he was leading a woman across the meadow. They were heading in the direction of a cart standing by the side of the road; the cart was tethered to a black horse that shook the great column of his neck, scattering the flies.

Mr. and Mrs. Clough stood off at some distance, as did my uncle and the Curriers. Also the ladies who had been at the table, the partridge and the skinny scarecrow woman, as well as the one called Mrs. Brown. I did not like any of them. Patience and Sarah were there too, holding hands. Even from where I stood, I could see how somber they looked. How frightened.

I sped down the stairs, out of the house, and across the meadow to join them. The fat man must have been the bailiff. And the woman he accompanied must have been Ruth Blay. She was slender, and I could see she was well bred. The dark brown hair that showed under her simple linen cap was smooth and shining. Her face was an oval, her eyes dark as her hair, and her lips thin and unsmiling. A spot of color in each cheek made her look feverish. She wore a pewter gray dress and a fresh white apron. When they reached the cart, the bailiff dug into his leather satchel and produced a length of rope; clearly he meant to bind her hands.

"Is that necessary?" she asked, and the bailiff, who could not seem to look her in the eyes, shook his head and put the rope away. Then she stepped up and into the cart, ignoring the hand he held out. He climbed onto the seat and a light touch of the whip on the horse's hindquarters set the animal into dark, fluid motion. Ruth Blay sat upright as the horse trotted off, her back

erect, her face composed. Jump out and run! *I wanted to scream. Go on now—he's so fat he'll never catch you! But she remained still as a statue as the wagon grew smaller and smaller and finally rounded a bend, disappearing altogether.*

That night, my uncle slept downstairs while I slept on some blankets that had been placed on the floor between the beds of Patience and Sarah. Only I did not get much sleep. As Mr. Currier snored loudly behind the curtain, Patience painted a grim picture of poor Ruth's fate. "They'll put her in a jail cell, pitch black and smelly. And filled with rats. Lots and lots of rats."

"Rats!" said Sarah. "I hate rats!"

"And then there will be a trial. She'll have to tell all about the baby—who the father was and where he is now. And if she really did kill it, she'll be condemned to death."

Death! Although the night was warm enough, I felt bone-cold when I heard the word.

"Yes," Patience was saying. "They'll put a rope around her neck and hang her until she's dead. Or burn her at the stake, just like a witch. She'll get so hot her blood will boil and her skin will melt."

I could not speak. How could this be possible? I remained in the makeshift bed, my body curled into the smallest shape I could manage. I wanted my mother then, and just the thought of her gentle brown eyes and kind smile made the tears come again, and they slid silently down my face. I must have slept eventually, but I bolted awake when the first pale light appeared at the window. I put my dress back on and smoothed my hair as best I could with my hands. Then I crept downstairs to find my uncle; I could not wait to leave this place.

To Susannah, it seemed like the house was breathing, in and out, in and out, as she wrote. At some point, Jack stopped playing his music and wandered in to say good night. "Are you still working?" he asked. "Isn't it kind of late?"

"It is, but sometimes the spirit moves me, so I just have to go with it."

"I know what you mean, Mom. That happens to me too, like when I know I should be doing my homework or something but I just have to play a tune. It's like all I can think about and I can't stop thinking about it until it's done."

He was so adorably serious, so seriously adorable, this boy of hers, that she just had to pull him into her arms and kiss his forehead. He didn't seem to mind. She was aware of something faintly acrid in the way he smelled, and it struck her that it was a distinctly male scent—and that it was something new. She had been prepared for all the changes he was going through—the colossal appetite, the growth spurt, and the first suggestions of fuzz on his upper lip and his cheeks, the cracking voice. But this smell—it felt so intimate, so shocking, really. She was a little shaken, and sat still for several minutes after he left, just trying to absorb it.

Then her eyes moved back toward the screen. She'd better go to bed now, or she'd be cranky and sleep deprived tomorrow. Her kids were old enough to get themselves up and out of the house, but she still believed she needed to be up with them in the morning.

So even though she was tempted to look over what she'd written earlier, she knew the trap. *I'll just change one thing here,* she'd tell herself. A word. A line. A paragraph. And pretty soon she'd be not revising but writing again, and then who knew when she'd be able to sleep?

NINETEEN

At nine twenty-five, Susannah saw Corbin's black SUV pull up to the house. She'd been up before seven o'clock and had been ready to go for a while. She was about to step outside, but he got out of the car, walked up to the door, and rang the bell. So he had old-school manners. Nice.

"Good morning," he said. "All set?"

"All set," she said. In the gray morning light, he seemed so vibrant: blue eyes, black-and-silver hair, red parka. He was so attractive, it was actually disconcerting; she hoped she wouldn't have trouble concentrating on her work. She deliberately looked away as she zipped her own parka and followed him outside.

It was a cold day—what else?—and though the light was flat and wan, there were no clouds, and snow was not in the forecast. Corbin had turned on the heat so the car was warm, and as she slid in and buckled her seat belt, he produced two coffees and a bag of blueberry muffins.

"You didn't make these, did you?" she asked.

"No, they're from Johnson's, on Route 4. Do you remember?"

"The place that made bumbleberry pie, right?" But of course she remembered much more than the pie. Watching him swim and dive, that night when he'd touched her . . . Sitting here so close to him now, their legs just inches apart, brought it all back. "And they made ice cream too. It was better than the place in town."

"Way better," he agreed, and then went quiet. Susannah tried to think of something to say. But the proximity of both his body and her memories of it was distracting. Maybe this had not been such a good idea after all.

Finally he said something. "There's been a slight change in plans. My meeting in Concord got switched to the afternoon. So I thought I'd take you up to South Hampton first. That's where Ruth Blay went when she left Portsmouth to have the baby. I remembered that my friend Joe Kayafas lives near there and he has an eighteenth-century barn on his property. I called him and he told me we could go in and poke around."

Susannah was relieved; here was something else to think about besides the line of his thigh or the crisply drawn shape of his profile. She'd already mapped out the discovery-in-the-barn scene, but she could flesh out what she'd written with actual details from the place. It would have been better seeing it in the summer, to correspond with her description. But there was no reason she couldn't come back on her own if she needed to. "Sounds good," she said. "Thanks for thinking of it."

"There's something else I thought of. Look inside the glove compartment and you'll see."

Susannah extracted a sheet of paper, folded in half. She opened it to find "The Ballad of Ruth Blay," a long poem published in

1859, almost one hundred years after Ruth's execution. "This is by that Portsmouth poet Albert Laighton." She'd seen references to the poem but had not yet read it.

"Yep. My mother liked it a lot and so I knew about it from her. I thought I'd look it up to show you."

"'Saw her clothed in silk and satin,'" read Susannah. ". . . 'Dressed as in her wedding garments / Soon the bride of Death to be—' Not too likely. But he's playing up the drama."

"Keep going," Corbin said. "Read the part about the horse."

Susannah scanned the lines and then read them out loud:

Nearer came the sound and louder
Till a steed with panting breath,
From its sides the white foam dripping,
Halted at the scene of death;

And a messenger alighted
Crying to the crowd, "Make way!"
This I bear to Sheriff Packer;
'Tis a pardon for Ruth Blay.

She folded the sheet of paper in half again. "None of that is true, you know. No final pardon came from the governor. And he denied her last request for a reprieve; the execution went ahead as scheduled."

Corbin said nothing. Well, *that* had certainly extinguished any spark she'd been feeling. Then he switched on the radio. But instead of music, he tuned in to listen to a local talk show.

Traffic was light and Susannah looked out the window as they sped along. She had a clear view of snow- and ice-covered fields; the snow would probably not melt until spring. Then Corbin slowed the car before turning into a driveway and bringing it to a halt.

"Why are we stopping?"

"We're here." He turned off the radio.

Susannah looked around. All she saw was a house and, beyond that, a barn. Nothing else.

"South Hampton is a tiny town," he explained. "Eight square miles and under a thousand residents." He got out of the car and casually reached for her hand. The sexual current she'd been feeling earlier switched on again in an instant. "That's Joe's place," he said. "And that's the barn." She followed him across the field where the snow was untouched and deep; their hands remained clasped.

"I didn't realize it was so small," she said. "Is it very old?"

"It was one of the first towns granted by Governor Wentworth after New Hampshire was separated from Massachusetts in 1741."

"So when Ruth Blay was here, the town was almost thirty years old. That would have been considered well established in the colonial period."

"It would," Corbin agreed. "And it was a cultural hub. At one time, there were twelve different religious sects here."

"Is this all information you got from your mother? I'm impressed."

"Well, I did a little brushing up last night. I wanted to be prepared."

"That's very sweet of you."

He smiled and squeezed her hand a little more tightly. "I'm genuinely interested too. I think your project has a lot of potential."

"You do?"

"You seem surprised."

"My editor is not so sure. I'm trying to win her over to the idea."

"I think you will."

They had reached the barn now, a simple structure whose red paint had faded to a warm and mellow coral. A rooster-shaped weather vane sat perched on the roof. Corbin let her hand drop to punch in the code so they could enter; Susannah felt a momentary disappointment when their connection was broken. But she was here to work, wasn't she? Better get to it, then. Inside, the place was filled not with animals, but with three looms of differing sizes and a few large plastic shipping crates filled with various kinds of yarn.

"He's a weaver?" asked Susannah.

"His wife is. She started out as a hobbyist but recently she's started selling. She makes scarves, shawls, blankets—things like that."

Susannah began to wander around the cavernous space. Up in the hayloft, she spied a desk, a computer, and a few chairs—an office area of sorts. The floor seemed to be old wide pine planks the color of ripe apricots whose surface was pitted and scarred from centuries of use—a nice detail, and she made a note of it.

She liked the feeling of being in here. Pale winter light filtered through the barn's high, ice-encrusted windows. The place had a contemplative and even sacred feeling. Churchlike, but in a secular way. She tried to imagine it on a day in June, filled with hay and the pungent smell of animals. She stopped, took some notes, then used her iPhone to snap a few pictures.

"So this is good?" Corbin had come up so quietly she had not even heard him.

"Very good," she said. "Perfect, in fact." He was so close he could have put his arms around her—and she was disappointed when he didn't. They prowled around a little more as she told him about how she envisioned the moment when Betsey Pettingill found the baby.

"I'd like to read it," he said.

"Maybe when it's a little more polished." She wasn't ready to show her work to anyone yet.

Back outside, Susannah took photographs of the exterior and then they walked back across the field to the house, a mustard yellow saltbox with a black door and black trim. She began to circle it, snapping more photographs as she went. Soon she began to get cold and her stomach rumbled; the muffins had little staying power.

"What do you say we stop for lunch before heading to Concord?" He put a hand on her shoulder.

She was instantly aware of the pressure of his fingers right through her parka, sweater, and shirt. "I say that would be great."

They reached the state archive—a squat, bunkerlike brick building—a little after two. Corbin walked her in and said he'd leave her there for a couple of hours. That would be enough time for her to read the documents and absorb whatever resonant details she could. And without the distraction of his presence, she could really focus on what she'd come to find.

Susannah approached the counter behind which several state employees sat. She told the clerk what she was looking for and in a few minutes was handed a thick sheaf of papers contained by a transparent plastic sleeve. "Here you go." She looked down at the material he'd given her, a little surprised by how nonchalant he seemed about it. She'd worked in other places, particularly libraries, where she'd had to fill out forms, show her driver's license, and surrender her iPhone and any pens she might have been carrying. Obviously, the material held by the state archive wasn't considered so rare or valuable.

She sat down with the sheaf of documents and carefully

extracted them from their sleeve. The thin, brittle sheets were covered in ink that may have once been black but had now faded to muddy brown. The governor's wax seal, with its horse and lions, was attached to some of them. On others, it had been lost, the only evidence of its former presence the ghostly tobacco-colored circles that marked the spot.

Here was the indictment, dated June 14, 1768, with its grave accusations: . . . *contrary to our law, Crown and Dignity . . . burial and concealment of her Bastard Child at South Hampton . . .* There was a subpoena, from September 15 of that same year, with the names of the women who'd closed ranks against her—Abigail Cooper, Loveday Brown, Mary Rogers, Olive Clough—and the verdict: *it appears to us of the Jury that the child came to its death by violence.* How could the jury have been so sure that whatever they saw was evidence of intentional violence, and not just the violence of a difficult, solitary birth and the four days during which the body had been hidden away from view? Ruth had written of the bedding and baby clothes she'd made for her child, the work of months. Would she have gone to such trouble for an infant she intended to murder? It made no sense to Susannah. But concealing an illegitimate child carried the same death sentence as murder.

Susannah next came to one of Governor Wentworth's reprieves, in which he postponed Blay's hanging until December 8, *so that she may have better opportunity to prepare for her death . . . expressing a sorrowful, penitent sense of her crime.* Yet she had never confessed, and maintained her innocence until the very end. How easy it would have been to pardon Blay. There was historical precedent; it had been done before.

But Susannah knew that Wentworth, appointed by the British government, was a man standing on the steep, alarming precipice of revolution. And he must have known it too. The unrest that was brewing in the colonies must have terrified him; if British rule crumbled, he'd go down with it. And who knew what kind of chaos that would bring? The law that would hang Ruth Blay was *British* law, and given England's shaky hold in the colonies, Wentworth must have felt an even stronger desire to uphold it. So in a way, Ruth had been sacrificed less for a crime, and more as an example—a sickening thought.

Having already learned that photographs were allowed, Susannah used her iPhone to take pictures of all the documents before putting them back in their transparent holder and returning them to the clerk.

When she stepped outside, she saw Corbin's car pull into the lot, and when he stopped, she opened the door to get in. "How did it go?" he asked. "Find anything groundbreaking?"

Actually, what she'd found was only the evidence of an old, old story. It would be up to her to make it new. She opened her mouth to say this to him, but no words came out. Instead, she was momentarily silenced by the unreasonable happiness she felt at simply being in his company. And all she could think about on the drive back to Eastwood was that, in a few days, she'd be seeing him again.

TWENTY

On Sunday morning, Corbin stood at Susannah's door with a big burlap sack slung across his back. "Skates." He stomped on the mat to shake the snow from his boots before coming inside.

"So many?"

"I didn't know your size." He knelt and opened the sack. Inside were numerous pairs of figure skates, some elegant and pristine, others scuffed and dirty, utilitarian hockey skates and even a pair with double blades.

"Where did you get all these?" asked Susannah.

"I organize a skate swap at the store every year. These are the leftovers. I'll give them to charity eventually, but I thought you and the kids could pick out what you needed first."

"Kid," she said. "Calista won't be joining us."

"Too bad." He sounded genuinely regretful. "I wanted to meet her."

"Maybe another time." Susannah walked to the stairs and called up, "Jack, Corbin's here."

"Coming," called Jack, and in seconds he was clattering down. Had he grown in this past month or even week? He suddenly seemed taller.

"Dude," said Corbin, extending his hand. "Nice to meet you."

"Nice to meet you too." Jack's eyes strayed to the pile of skates. "Did you invite the whole town?"

Corbin smiled. "Just the three of us. I understand your sister can't join in."

"She's busy. Or something." Jack was pawing through the skates. "My friend Gilda was going to come. Only she's sick and her mom said no."

"Bummer." Corbin began going through the pile. "What size are you?" He eyed Jack's feet and then handed him a black pair that had a wide red stripe running diagonally across the side. "How about these?"

"They're cool," said Jack. "Thanks." He unlaced his sneakers so he could try them on. "Hey, they fit!"

Appreciating how he'd found a way to connect with her boy, Susannah reached into the pile to find skates for herself. Here were some made of white leather, with only a small smudge on one toe. She slipped them on and tried to stand. "These work. Now I just have to manage to stay upright."

"I'll stick close," Corbin said. "But if you've skated before, you'll get back into the rhythm of it."

"Do you skate a lot?" Jack asked.

"It's practically a requirement for living in the state," said Corbin.

Skates looped over their shoulders, Susannah, Jack, and Corbin trooped down to the pond. Susannah still wished Calista had come, and she glanced regretfully back at the house. But the day was bright and not too cold, and the surface of the pond, frozen into a slick, cloudy surface, beckoned. So she sat down on a large tree stump to shed her boots and lace up the skates. She had made it clear to Cally—Calista—that she was welcome to join them; there was nothing else she could do.

Susannah was just making her first tentative foray onto the ice when Jack, who'd managed to lace up more quickly, whizzed by. "Hey, Mom!" he called. She watched as he skated in a wide, embracing circle and then glided his way back to her.

"Since when are you such a good skater?" Susannah remembered how tentative Jack had been when she and Charlie had taken the kids skating at the rink in Prospect Park; Calista had been the fearless one.

"I don't know. I just grew up or something. Anyway, it's so much cooler to skate here. The rink was so crowded. And boring. But this"—he spread out his arms to include the wooded shoreline where bare trees, their branches sinuous against the sky, mingled with fragrant pines—"is awesome."

Susannah nodded and then refocused her energy on trying to stay upright. She'd been an adequate skater, but it had been a long time and she was shaky. Too fearful to take the long, swooping strides that Jack and Corbin did, she inched along, hoping her confidence would improve.

"Need an escort?" Susannah turned. There was Corbin, reaching out to her.

"Sure." She took his hand and, even through her mitten, felt the small but perceptible jolt. It was a relief to have his support.

"Did you skate much as a kid?" he asked.

"A little. I was okay—not great, not terrible. But now that I'm living here, I guess I should try to improve my game."

"It'll come back. You'll see." And he gently guided her along until she started feeling more confident and they skated easily together, with Jack weaving around them, along the perimeter of the pond. Jack was right—it was a totally different sensation than that of skating in a rink.

Bolder now, Susannah let go of Corbin's hand and expanded her stride. Soon she was covering the ice in long, swooping arcs, urged on by the unfolding of the shoreline and the shifting perspectives created by the ring of houses and trees that enclosed them. In the house, in town, or driving on the snowbanked roads, the winter felt relentless and oppressive. But out here on the pond, she felt a sense, if not of happiness, at least of possibility. Ahead of her, Jack and Corbin skated around each other or raced. Corbin was a natural on the ice; it figured.

The pond began to fill up and they passed a family with three girls in identical pink parkas, and an older couple who skated sedately, hand in hand. When one of the little girls veered off course and crashed into Corbin, he didn't even seem rattled; he just scooped her up and handed her, dazed but unhurt, to her father.

When they had gotten halfway around, Jack pointed to a brown and yellow house. "That's where Gilda lives," he told Susannah. "Maybe if I yell, she'll come to the window." He raised his voice. "Gilda!"

"Jack, don't—" Susannah tried to stop him, but then Corbin joined in, and after a minute or two Gilda's blond head appeared at the window. She waved frantically, and even from where she stood, Susannah could see the girl's wide smile.

"She's pretty," Corbin said.

"Isn't she?" Jack was waving back. "And she's really nice too." He skated closer to the house and then clomped onto the snowy ground until he was right beneath her. Gilda opened the window enough so that they could talk.

"Young love," Corbin murmured to Susannah. She turned to him. He wore a blue watch cap that covered his hair but brought out the blue of his eyes, and his face was pink from the cold. He looked so . . . alive, and suddenly the thought was like a slap. He was alive, she was alive, and Charlie—Charlie was dead. She turned away, overcome with tears she didn't want Corbin to see. It happened this way sometimes, the grief covert and silent as a stealth bomber, ambushing her when she least expected it.

"You okay?" Corbin was looking down at her, concern and—what, tenderness?—in his expression.

"Yes, I mean—not exactly, but I will be." She sniffed and took off her mitten to grope in her pocket for a tissue; when her hand came up empty, Corbin supplied her with a clean white handker-chief he'd extracted from his back pocket. Their fingers brushed as she took it—he wore no gloves—and again she felt the intense, almost alarming physical reaction she had to this man, a reaction that seemed as if it had never changed, only gone dormant in the years since she'd seen him.

"Is there anything I can do?"

"Why are you being so nice to me?" she blurted out. "What do you want from me anyway?" Now why had she said that? They'd been having such a good time and she'd gone and ruined things.

"I like you," he said simply. "I liked you back when we were kids and I like you now. Does it have to be any more complicated than that?"

"I guess not." She was utterly disarmed; maybe she was over-thinking this. She looked over to see Jack clomping back across the snowy yard; when he reached the spot where Susannah and Corbin stood, he waved to Gilda one last time. Then he turned to Susannah. "I'm getting cold. Maybe we should go back."

"We might as well keep going," Corbin said. "We're more than halfway around already." He skated close to Jack, and Susannah could hear little bits of their conversation—sports, music—eddying around her. She was grateful that he'd let her be for a while; her attraction to him, and the guilt it caused her, was exhausting.

Back at the house, Susannah made them all hot chocolate; she sat across from Corbin with a mug warming her chilled hands. Calista was not home and Jack wanted to bring his cocoa upstairs so he could text Gilda. Before he left, Corbin said, "You're a demon on the ice, dude." Jack grinned and accepted Corbin's high five on his way out of the room. Susannah realized she and Corbin were alone. It was a slightly unsettling thought. "Thanks for doing this with us," she said. "Jack really had a good time."

"How about you?" he asked. "Did you have a good time too?"

"I did." She met his gaze over the rim of her mug.

"You seemed upset out there."

"It passed."

"Can you say what it was?"

She looked down; wisps of melted marshmallow formed a delicate pattern on the surface of the chocolate. "I'd rather not."

He nodded, seeming to accept that. "We're getting some push-back from the people at Wingate. The CEO is pretty chummy with the governor and that could affect the outcome."

"I heard." Susannah was grateful the conversation was moving in a less personal direction.

"You did?" He seemed angry. "Who told you?"

"I don't remember." She remembered quite well—Janet Durbin had mentioned it the night of the meeting—but wasn't sure she should reveal that now.

"Well, it doesn't really matter how you found out." The anger had lifted right off of him. "What matters is what the governor does—or doesn't do."

"Is he going to make a decision soon?"

"That depends." Corbin set his mug down on the table. "First the issue has to get put on the calendar and then—"

The sound of a key turning in the lock distracted them both and then there was Calista, in her zebra-striped coat, standing in the center of the room.

"Here you are." Susannah abruptly stood and walked over to the stove. "I just made us some hot chocolate; can I make you a cup?" Calista was silent and Susannah realized she had not even introduced her daughter to Corbin. "Cally—I mean Calista—this is Corbin Bailey. He owns the hardware store in town and—"

"Hi." Calista barely looked in his direction. To her mother she said, "I've got homework. And you do want me to do my homework, right?" The question was lobbed like a challenge. Ignoring the offer of hot chocolate, Calista marched to the fridge, pulled out an apple, and closed the door with unnecessary force. Then she headed for the stairs, her purple Doc Martens making an accusatory *thump-thump-thump* as she went.

"Ouch," said Corbin when they were alone again. "I guess she's not too keen on my being here with you."

"I'm sorry she was so rude." Susannah had not sat back down again but remained standing, smoothing the front of her apron— made of patchwork calico that Calista had sewn in happier times— over and over again. "I don't know what gets into her." But she did. Of course she did. She could just imagine how the scene looked to her daughter—mom cozying up to a hunky stranger in their own kitchen, a kitchen she hated and wouldn't even be in had her father not been killed. The situation was replete with possibilities for recrimination and blame.

"Well, maybe I'd better be going." Corbin stood and moved toward the bag of skates.

"Let me give you back the ones we wore today." She didn't ask him to stay any longer; the day had been fun but also unsettling, and she wanted time away from him to think it over.

"No, you keep those. And what size are Calista's feet? I can leave a pair for her too."

"She doesn't want to go skating."

"She doesn't want to go skating with *me*," Corbin said. He piled the skates into the sack and pulled the drawstring closed. "But she still might want to go skating."

Susannah stood looking at him. She had always been attracted by his electrifying good looks, but now she realized the aura of calm he projected was equally attractive. She had seen it at the meeting and she was seeing it now. Not that he was retiring—not at all. But he was steady, and so the drama other people created, the foam and churn of it, appeared to just wash right over him.

He straightened up, put on his coat, which she had plucked from the rack by the door, and put his hand on the doorknob. She came to stand next to him, unsure of whether to hug him.

"Remember before when you asked me what I wanted from you?" She nodded, embarrassed to be reminded of her little hissy fit. "Well, it was this." And he leaned down to kiss her.

TWENTY-ONE

The kiss. *The kiss.* Susannah thought about the kiss for the rest of the day, and for the entire evening too. The kiss crowded out everything else; she was still thinking about it when she got into bed that night, and she was thinking about it when she woke up the next morning. It was light, sweet, and tender but had a trace of something more urgent, and more hungering too. A kiss that asked, and a kiss that promised.

The kids noticed her preoccupation—"Mom, are you, like, sleepwalking or something?" asked Jack—and she was so distracted she had to ask him to repeat what he'd just said. Finally they were off to school and she was free to be alone with her thoughts. She had yielded to the kiss as if she'd been waiting for it—and truly, she had—ever since their long-ago encounter on that summer night. It made her replay and analyze other memorable kisses: her first-ever kiss at a ritzy bar mitzvah in Princeton, New Jersey; the first kiss she and Charlie had shared. That kiss had been a surprise—she'd known Charlie for a long time but had never thought of him *that way*—but kissing Corbin was not a surprise at all; it was the fulfillment of a long-banked desire. She had not dwelled on that desire, but clearly it had been there, waiting, and seeing him again brought it all rushing back.

Still the kiss, while delicious, posed a whole new set of problems. First there was the guilt—wasn't it too soon? And then there was Calista's reaction. Her hostility toward Corbin had been so obvious. Susannah was having enough trouble managing her daughter as it was; adding Corbin to her life was going to make that even harder. But there was that pull he exerted, a pull she did not think she would be able to ignore. She had no clue as to how this would unfold.

Feeling restless, she decided to drive over to Buns of Steel for Trim and Tone, which began at noon. That would be a good way to work off her excess mental energy; maybe she would stop thinking about Corbin and that kiss, at least for an hour. Dressed in cropped black leggings and a white T-shirt, Susannah felt at home with the other women in the room, mostly middle-aged mom-ish types like herself, though there was a pretty blonde who looked to be in her twenties and an admirably spry woman who must have been over seventy. When the class was over, she changed and waited for Martha to lock up the studio. Then they walked down the street to the sandwich shop.

"So I did manage to get in touch with Harry," Martha said when they had placed their order and nabbed a table. "And he said he wanted to meet you too. But he can't let Deedee know; she's super jealous."

"Jealous of what? My mother's been dead for years."

"In Deedee's mind, that doesn't matter. Jim told me that Harry had a way with women, especially the ones he directed. Harry once said that he fell a little bit in love with every leading lady. It used to drive Deedee crazy—she'd been one of those leading ladies way back when, so she knew what he was like—and she's tried to keep him away from his old theater friends."

"So that explains why she was so hateful." Susannah picked at her salad; she should have ordered soup or something else warm.

"I guess so. But Harry hasn't been well and, on top of that, she's isolated him. Honestly, he sounded kind of lonely when we talked. I told him about running into you after so many years and he said he remembers your mother quite well. He'd like to meet with you."

"I'd really like to meet with him." So Harry had been "a little bit in love" with all his leading ladies—that meant her mother. Was it possible that his feelings for her had been reciprocated and that he and she had crossed a line?

"What I'm thinking is this: Harry goes for physical therapy in Dover three times a week. Usually Deedee takes him, but I could offer to do it; she and I always got along all right and I think she'd appreciate a break. Once I've picked him up, I could come and get you and the two of you could talk on the drive there and back. I don't think we could stop anywhere, though; Deedee wouldn't like that."

"That all sounds perfect," said Susannah. She pushed aside the salad. Maybe she'd get a cup of tea to warm up. "Just let me know when."

"It will need to be on a Friday. I don't work at the studio on Fridays."

"Say the word," Susannah told her. "And I'll be ready."

When Susannah got home, the red flag on the mailbox was up. Inside she found a large manila envelope from George Martin. The letters he had promised! She tore it open eagerly, extracting both a handwritten note and a typed letter. She read the note first.

*As it turns out I had only a single letter from Claire; I made a
copy for myself and am sending you the original. I feel it belongs
to you more than to me. Your mother was an intelligent and
sensitive woman who shed a special light all those around her
were privileged to see.*

Clearly he thought well of Claire, and he might have been
in love with her. But not in an erotic or romantic way. George
could have been that stock character, the gay male confidant to
a straight woman, but she couldn't remember her mother even
mentioning him. Of course there were a *lot* of things Claire had
not mentioned. Susannah was only beginning to discover some
of them now.

October 29, 1977

My dear George,

*So here I am, plucked from the bucolic loveliness of Primrose
Pond, and plunked down in hopelessly bland and suburban New
Jersey. Yes, the town has that quasi-quaint, college-y feel to it:
an "art" cinema, a couple of galleries, a hand-churned ice cream
shop, and at least three secondhand-book stores. But I pine for
the pond, George. And I pine for you too. You've been a good
friend to me—one of my closest, really—and I appreciate all
you've done for me, especially in these last few months.*

*Our new-old house was found for us by the university and
we got a terrific deal on it. And did I tell you that they paid all
the moving costs and will pick up the taxes for the next five
years? This will mean we can keep the house on the pond. Even
though I don't know when—or if—I'll get back there, I still*

consider the place my spiritual home and it makes me feel good to know that it remains, in a legal sense, mine. I should add that Warren wants nothing to do with it and would be only too glad to sell it. But he is humoring me, you see—now more than ever. What's she getting at? *I can imagine you wondering.* What kind of secret is she hinting at? *Well, I won't keep you in suspense another second.*

I'm pregnant, George. Pregnant and soon to be "great with child." I'm over-the-moon happy but also frightened, anxious, and, if I may be completely candid, more than a little nauseated. Never mind the taste, even the smell *of certain foods is enough to send me bolting from the table, desperate for a bathroom; I should start carrying motion-sickness bags in my purse, just in case. But my doctor assures me that the morning (in my case afternoon and evening as well) sickness is an indication of a high level of hormonal activity—a good thing too because it's the presence of all those hormones that will keep this little lad or lass firmly in place until his or her debut is at hand.*

So now you know. It will be a big change, but I am ready for it. So ready. A new chapter, a whole new book really. Think of me and send news of you when you can. I'll send you pictures as I get bigger and more walrus-like, and if you ever get down this way, you have to stop off and see me. Warren too.

> *Sending you boatloads of love,*
> *Claire*

Susannah set the letter down on the table where she could see it. The white typing paper had yellowed slightly and there were some mold spots dotting the bottom; maybe it had languished in a basement for the last forty years? No envelope either, just the one single-spaced page, and the signature, in surprisingly fresh-looking blue ink. The pregnancy to which Claire referred had culminated in Susannah's birth in the spring of 1978. There was something shockingly intimate about seeing the news delivered in this way, to a friend whom she had known nothing about until recently. And the letter detailed Claire's own reactions, but not her father's. He would have been happy too, wouldn't he? So why did Claire leave him out, other than to say he was "humoring" her?

Reading these two new clues in her ongoing search made Susannah only that much more eager to meet Harry. With George and Todd ruled out, he was looking more and more likely as a candidate. And the fact that he was a director made him a strong contender too. Claire had always gotten so much pleasure from those amateur productions. The stage was a big enough place for the wild sweep of her emotions.

Sitting next to her father in that darkened theater all those years ago, Susannah would watch the woman she knew to be her mother yet did not fully recognize in her public role. Sometimes it had to do with the way she looked: a wig to change her hair color, padding to round her out. But more than that, it had seemed to Susannah that her mother was more alive and more present in her world of make-believe than she often was with them. How could she ever hope to compete with that?

Later that evening, Martha called. She had arranged to take Harry to Dover not this Friday, because Deedee had something planned for them, but the following one. She would pick him up first and then be by around ten in the morning to get Susannah. "Harry says he can't wait to meet you," Martha said.

"Tell him I feel the same way."

When the phone rang again, she thought it was Martha calling to fine-tune their plan in some way. But it turned out to be Corbin.

They had not spoken since their kiss and Susannah felt a kind of adolescent awkwardness overcome her; maybe it was because their connection had been forged when she was still a teenager. And she wasn't sure just how much she wanted to encourage him. But then she just plunged in. "Skating with you was so much fun. I had a wonderful time."

"Me too," he said. "So I was hoping we could follow it up with dinner. Nothing too fancy. Just one of the local spots."

"I'd really like that," she said. "How's Saturday?" Did she want to do this? Yes. But was she ready to do this? That remained to be seen.

"Great. I'll pick you up around seven."

Susannah put the phone down. Saturday night Calista was likely to be out, which meant Susannah would not have to deal with her animosity toward Corbin—at least not then. She'd been spending a lot of time with Alice during the days, but in the evenings she'd been gravitating toward that older crowd. Susannah was not thrilled about either of these developments, but she'd been in touch with Antoinette Benoit and, so far, Calista had been going to school and had even had a couple of sessions with the school psychologist.

Then she had what she considered a brilliant idea. It was so obvious, she couldn't believe she hadn't thought of it before. Before she could change her mind, Susannah tracked down Alice's number and called it. "Alice? This is Susannah Gilmore. I've been meaning to ask you over for tea; how is this Friday?" Her meeting with Harry Snady was not until the following week, so this Friday was wide open. "Terrific. How's four o'clock for you? Great. I'll see you then."

She'd been so obtuse, treating Alice as a competitor when it would have been smarter—much smarter—to enlist her aid as an ally.

TWENTY-TWO

"Thank you so much for inviting me," said Alice as she took off her cherry red coat and handed it to Susannah. "I hope you don't mind, but I've brought Emma. I take her with me everywhere." The dog sat by Alice's feet and looked up at her.

Actually, Susannah did mind; not that she had anything specific against the dog, who seemed unusually well behaved, but she thought Alice should have asked her first. Now she was already on the defensive before she had even uttered a word.

She hung Alice's coat in the closet near the door and brought her guest into the dining room, where the table had been laid for tea. Tea had seemed like just the right meal to offer.

"I love how you've mixed together all these patterns." Alice held up a blue-and-white-flowered plate to admire it. "Charming."

"Thank you." Susannah paused before going into the kitchen to get the water going. "I've been collecting them for years."

"So how are you getting on?" Alice asked when Susannah had

returned with the tea and a plate of scones she'd baked that morning. "Are you settling in all right?"

"It's going to take some time," Susannah said.

There was a silence during which Susannah wished she could think of something interesting, or even tangentially relevant, to say. She just felt so stilted, so ill at ease—and she was in her own home. Alice, seemingly oblivious to her discomfort, was stirring sugar into her tea.

"Do you have raccoons?" There! Susannah was pleased with herself; she had thought of something.

"On occasion," Alice said. "Do you?"

"Yes," said Susannah. "At first I just saw the evidence—cans overturned, garbage all over the yard. But just the other day I saw a pair. And they were so bold, not frightened of me at all. One of them kept on digging through the trash. The other just looked at me, but in a kind of menacing way. He kind of scared me, actually." City girl spooked by a raccoon: she laughed a little, remembering.

"I'll give you the name of the fellow I use to deal with them," said Alice.

"He doesn't kill them, does he?" Susannah didn't want the raccoons in her yard, but she didn't exactly want them dead either.

Alice shook her head as she buttered a scone. "Traps and relocates. Very humane."

"Oh, good." Susannah took a scone. It was a little dry. Did Alice notice?

"I like what you've done with the house. I think your mother would have approved."

"Do you? Did you know her well?" Susannah was instantly engaged. Of course Alice had known her mother; pursuing those three men had made her temporarily forget about an obvious source.

"I did and I liked her. Both of your parents used to come to our Fourth of July party. I can remember seeing your mother standing on the lawn; I might even have a photo somewhere. I bought Dave a camera for Christmas one year and he would not put it down! I used to call him Jimmy Olsen—the photographer in the old Superman comics—to tease him."

"You still miss him a lot, don't you?" She had wanted to ask about the photograph. But this came out instead. Had she overstepped and offended her?

"Naturally." Alice seemed not insulted, but matter-of-fact. "And I'll always miss him. Just like you'll always miss your husband—Charlie, was it?"

"Will I?" Susannah put her teacup down. She didn't want to think that she would always miss Charlie. Or at least not be blindsided with the kind of grief that could still occasionally come over her.

"Of course. But that doesn't mean you won't find a way to be happy. The two emotions can coexist very nicely. Or at least that's what I've observed." Alice reached for the teapot to refill her cup. "Corbin Bailey is a very fine man. I imagine he could make any woman very happy. He's had that drinking problem under control for some time now; I don't think he's in any danger of it coming back again."

Susannah actually felt her mouth opening slightly, a small O of astonishment. "What are you talking about?" She had no reason to hide her connection to Corbin, but she did not like the way Alice had introduced the subject. And though his so-called drinking problem was news, and of considerable interest, to her, she was certainly not going to discuss it with Alice.

"Eastwood has a handful of streets, two churches, one library, one post office, and as much gossip as a town three times its size. Everyone knows everything here; it's awfully hard to keep a secret."

"We just went skating once. It's hardly a secret." How about the kiss? Did Alice know about that? Or their date tomorrow night? She really hoped not.

"Skating together is a lovely thing to do. Like dancing on the ice. Dave and I used to skate."

"You said that your late husband took a picture of my mother. I'd love to see it, if it's not too much trouble."

"I'm sure I can find it. Let me have a look when I go home."

"There's no rush."

The dog, alerted to something outside, lifted her head and uttered a low throaty growl. "Emma!" Alice spoke firmly. "Stop that right now." Emma looked chastened and put her head back down on her paws. "Your father used to come over to our house sometimes to play chess with Dave. And I'd see your mother down at the pond in the summer. She loved to swim, loved the sun."

"Really? I don't remember her swimming much the summer I was here." Susannah had thought it strange at the time.

"Well, this was years ago. I can remember her in a black one-piece bathing suit that fastened around her neck. And big sunglasses. She seemed very fashion forward for Primrose Pond."

Susannah did not recall having seen such a bathing suit. "Did she have any close women friends in town?"

Alice sipped her tea and considered the question. "She knew a lot of people—from the newspaper and the theater. I know Janet over at the library used to special order books for her. And there was another woman, Linda something or other. I can't think of her last name."

"Could it have been Linda Jacobsmeyer?" asked Susannah. Linda was the woman who had cleaned out the house and gotten it ready for the renters, but Susannah had not been in touch with her for some time. She was pretty sure she had lost her contact information.

"Yes, that was it."

"Do you have a number for her? Or an e-mail address?"

Alice shook her head. "She moved away a number of years ago. But it should be easy enough to find her—can't you find anyone on the Internet?"

"I'm sure I could try—"

The door opened and in walked Calista, bringing the chill of the day right in with her. The delighted look on her face when she saw Alice was like something small and sharp puncturing Susannah's heart.

"Dear girl, what a treat to see you!" Alice stood, and, to Susannah's amazement, Calista dropped her backpack and crossed the room quickly to hug her. Emma must have interpreted this as an attack on her mistress; she jumped up and gave a sharp bark. Once again, Alice admonished her, but, this time, when the dog turned in a circle to settle back down, she bumped the table and Alice's blue-and-white teacup sitting near the edge of the table fell to the floor. The cup was empty but it did not survive the drop. "Oh, I am so sorry!" said Alice. "I'll replace it, of course."

"It's no big deal," said Calista, who was already on her knees picking up the pieces. "Mom has, like, a hundred of these." *But that one was my favorite,* Susannah wanted to say. Because it was. "Anyway, you didn't tell me Alice would be here!"

"I was sure I mentioned it." This was not true. She had been hoping that Calista would be off with her friends; that was what she typically did on Friday afternoons.

Calista sat down and helped herself to a scone while Susannah went in the kitchen to throw away the broken cup. Charlie had bought this one for her, at an estate sale on Long Island; she'd had it since before they were married. Then she took out another cup and brought it to the dining room. Calista was now speaking in French, with reasonable fluency; Alice replied smoothly in kind.

Susannah knew a smattering of French, enough to pick her way through letters or diaries when she was writing a novel set in France, but her speaking lagged far behind and she did not attempt to join in. After a few excruciatingly long minutes, Alice finally turned back to her. "She has an exquisite accent!"

Calista beamed and Susannah busied herself with sweeping some crumbs into the cupped palm of her hand. "It sounds like you speak quite well too," she said finally.

"Junior year abroad, a lifetime ago," she said, her fond gaze drifting once more toward Calista. "You should go to France, my dear. Paris."

"Oh, I want to go so much! In college, like you did. Or maybe even a summer program." She glanced at her mother. "If I can earn the money, that is."

"Maybe you can get a job," Susannah said. "You could advertise as a babysitter; I'm sure you'd find work."

"I have a better idea," Alice said. "In the spring, I can start paying you to work with Jester. He truly needs the exercise and I'm just not up to giving it to him."

"But I thought Calista was going to be getting some kind of credit for that at school," Susannah felt obliged to say. "At least that's what Ms. Benoit said."

"I can still pay her, whether or not there's school credit involved." Alice had not finished her scone; so she had noticed. "That way, she could start saving for the summer. We can look up programs together. Antoinette doesn't even need to know."

"I suppose not." Susannah had the urge to pitch all the scones out the window into the yard; she could just imagine the glee of the raccoons. What was *wrong* with her today?

"Really? You would do that? Oh, Aunt Alice, you are the best!" And Calista was up from the table and enveloping their guest in yet another enthusiastic hug.

"Aunt Alice?" Susannah said.

"That's just our little joke." Alice spoke from over the several small braids sprouting from Calista's head. "I don't have any nieces and Calista doesn't have any aunts, so we thought we would just pretend."

Calista straightened up. "You feel like an aunt to me," she said.

Susannah had to turn away; she might actually start to cry.

"And you feel like a niece to me." Alice smiled. There was more talk of Paris programs, and Jester too. Susannah was fairly panting with relief when Alice finally got up to leave. She walked to the door, trailing praise for the scones—a lie if there ever was one—and murmuring about having them all over for dinner *very soon*. Emma followed close behind. Susannah handed her the coat; she did not even want to contemplate such an evening. But the good mood she'd engendered in her daughter lingered after she had gone, and Calista helped clear the table and did the dishes without even being asked. Then she trotted up the stairs to her room; Susannah heard the door close quietly a moment later.

Back in the kitchen, she opened the Tupperware container in which Calista had stored the remaining scones and, with grim satisfaction, deposited them into the trash right on top of the shattered cup. Then she called Polly.

"Of course you're jealous," Polly soothed. "Most natural thing in the world."

"*Aunt* Alice," Susannah fumed. "They barely know each other!"

"It's a girl crush, don't you see? Only the girl is a little older than usual."

"Is that what this is?"

"Absolutely. Just leave it alone and it will play itself out." There was the sound of crunching on the other end of the line; Polly must have been eating an apple.

"You think?"

"I know. Ginny once had one of those on a teacher. I heard about this woman morning, noon, and night and was of course *compared* to this paragon every day for, oh, about nine months, and found inferior in every possible way."

"Didn't it make you angry?" Susannah was sitting at the table, orphaned saucer in her hands. Though most of her tableware was mismatched, that cup and saucer had been from the same set and shared both a pattern and a history.

"Are you kidding? When the parent-teacher conference rolled around, it was all I could do not to pull her hair and slap the bitch!"

Susannah laughed. This was what she loved about Polly—she was so out there.

"But it all simmered down when Ginny found a boyfriend." Another crunch. "Any chance of that happening?"

"I'm not sure." Susannah thought of the crew of boys—young men—she'd glimpsed in the back of the cars that dropped Calista off at the house. "The kids she hangs out with are older, not kids in her class. I'm not sure I like them."

"Do you actually know any of them?"

Polly had her there. "Not really."

"Maybe it would be good to give them a chance?"

Susannah was quiet, not wanting to concede the point. But

she knew Polly was right—it wasn't fair to judge her daughter's friends until she knew them better.

"You still there?" Polly asked.

Susannah looked around the still not entirely familiar room and out the window across from where she sat. White, gray, tan, brown. Snow covered the yard and coated the dark branches of the naked trees; snow, snow, and more snow. God, it was *depress-, ing.* "Yes," she finally said to Polly. "I'm here."

TWENTY-THREE

After dinner, Susannah heard a car pulling up outside the house at the same time Calista must have spied it through the window. "There's Megan." She was already reaching for her coat. "We're hanging out tonight."

"Where?" Susannah tried to see who was in the car, but it was too far away and too dark besides.

"At her house. I won't be late."

"Calista, you know that's too vague."

"We're going to watch a movie." When Susannah did not answer, she went on. "I forgot to tell you—I got a ninety-six on my last English paper—that's a solid A."

Susannah's initial resistance to her daughter's plans melted in the face of this new information; had Calista planned it that way? And anyway, hadn't Polly said she should give these new friends a chance? "An A—I'm proud of you. Well, all right. You can go. Just be back by midnight."

"Okay." Calista put a hand on the doorknob. "Bye, Mom."

A little while later another car pulled up, this one bearing Gilda Mooney's father, who had come to collect her son. With both her kids out for the evening, Susannah was alone. She had a couple of library books she'd ordered through Janet, one on the religious climate of eighteenth-century New England and the other on the evolution of the justice system in colonial America. Both would be useful as background and she wanted to settle in with them.

But after that conversation with Polly, her anger at Alice had subsided and she found herself thinking about the earlier part of her visit, when Alice had talked about her mother. She would contact Linda Jacobsmeyer; she ought to be able to track her down online. But she also had the feeling that the house still held clues, and if she looked hard enough, she would find them.

She had been through the attic and her bedroom pretty carefully. But not the rest of the rooms upstairs. The kids were out, so this was a good time to explore. Susannah opened Calista's door and, after hesitating for a second, went in. She wasn't here to snoop, she told herself. At least not for information about Calista. She found nothing that belonged to anyone other than her daughter.

Jack's room was another story. His clarinet was in its case, but that was the only thing that seemed to be where it belonged. Clothes littered the bed and floor; open textbooks were strewn around. There were sheets of music and random papers; his backpack, gaping open, seemed to have exploded. Susannah picked her way through the mess to the bureau. The bunched-up clothes frothed out of the drawers, but when she poked through them, she saw nothing of interest.

Then she turned to the closet, which was nearly empty. Jack hadn't developed the habit of hanging up his clothes, and very little of what he wore needed hanging anyway. But wedged into the very back of the closet was a narrow three-drawer dresser. It was not visible when she had first opened the closet door and she had not realized it was there.

The top drawer was empty and the middle one crammed, inexplicably, with old phone books—the one on top was from 1975. But it was the bottom drawer—secured by two nails and necessitating a hunt for the right tool to pry them loose—that yielded pay dirt: a menu from Le Chat Noir, a restaurant in Quebec, and a pair of ticket stubs from a theater in that same city. Nestled at the very back were three tiny cakes of soap, each wrapped in a crinkled, yellowing paper.

Had her mother put all these things in here? If she had, it was a gesture in keeping with hiding the makeup bag in the woodshed. Her memory and her powers were slipping, but she still had an instinct to both preserve and hide certain precious artifacts from her past, even if she accomplished both aims rather crudely. The nailed drawer was proof that she still knew, though. And that she still cared. Mabel said she'd made a trip up here alone, without Susannah's father. She could have easily done it then. And the boy who'd driven her up could have helped her nail the drawer shut. Or even done it for her.

Susannah picked up a bar gingerly. SAVON, read the label. And when she turned it over, HOTEL DU LAC, QUEBEC. She set the soap on top of the dresser and looked more closely at the ticket stubs. They were dated August 18, 1994. A small shock of recognition coursed through her. She and her parents had been here, on the pond, in 1994. But they had not gone to Quebec that summer; she was sure of it. That meant that her mother had gone away for a few days—with someone else.

On the front of the menu were the conventional offerings—*coq au vin, blanquette de veau, salade niçoise*—but on the back, she found a poem, or at least the first draft of one; several words and lines had been blotted or scratched out. There was no title.

You were the lyre
I was the hand

You were the ocean
I was the sand

You foamed and you crested
You ebbed and you flowed
In the light of the moon
You sparkled and glowed.

But those days are gone now
They slipped by so fast
Cruel joys and sweet sorrows
All over, all past.

The light it is fading,
And dark fills the room
Soon you'll be the angel who weeps at my tomb.

The tone of this poem was quite different. Not hopeful, not hesitant. Not luxuriating in the aftermath of consummation. No, this poem was a leave-taking: mournful and resigned. Then she looked more closely at the bold, looping writing. Was it the same as the writing in the note? *Was* it? The bits of information Susannah had been gathering began swirling crazily around in her head. The order and significance of each individual element were not clear—not yet. But she believed she was getting closer to some kind of order and, with it, some understanding.

Susannah gathered her contraband, brought it into her room, closed the door, and laid the pieces out like a puzzle. To the array she added the note, the volume of Yeats, the material Todd Rettler had sent, and the letter that came from George. Then she began shifting them around, trying to create a timeline, the way she did with her novels. She had not paid too much attention to the receipts when she'd first gotten them, but now she noticed that written across the bottom of one were the words *Lunch, I. N. Vayne*. So her mother had known the identity of the mystery poet. Had anyone else?

Holding the wrinkled receipt in her hand, she recalled that there had been some kind of camping trip that summer; a bunch of them, including Travis and Corbin, had gone. They had stayed away two or maybe three nights; those could have been the nights her mother was in Quebec. But the dates. She had to know the dates of that trip. Then it hit her. She was seeing Corbin tomorrow night. Maybe he would remember.

Susannah pulled everything she'd assembled out from under the bed and put whatever fit in the shoe box and the rest in a large envelope, then put both on a high shelf in her closet. Then she got ready for bed, where she fully expected she would not be able to sleep—she was so wired from her recent discovery.

But she did fall deeply and quickly asleep; only her dreams—of tumbling, running, and even, in one, skydiving—left her enervated and exhausted the next morning. Would she even be up to her date with Corbin tonight? Maybe she ought to postpone. Then she remembered the kiss and she decided, no, she would not do that. Instead, she would make herself a very strong cup of coffee and try to get her day going.

She pulled her fleecy new bathrobe—she had reluctantly decided to retire Charlie's plaid flannel—over her sweats and thermal top. She'd never needed such nightwear in New York, but now she relied on it. Downstairs, she could see that it was going to be a bright, if cold, day; sunlight splashed on the snow outside and sent its reflected glare back in through the windows. On impulse, she crossed the enclosed porch, opened the back door, and took a few steps through the snow, getting closer to Primrose Pond. This was crazy; it was bone-chillingly cold out here. She should have gotten her down parka, so she turned back to the house, intending to go back and slip it on over the robe.

Then she stopped. Just mere inches away from her was the biggest moose she'd ever seen. Make that the *only* moose she'd ever seen. His fur was a mottled grayish brown, his nostrils gaped large and dark, and his antlers, spanning three feet, looked like bony hands trying to cup the sky. Susannah did not know what to do. She'd read that moose stags could be aggressive and even dangerous; they had been known to charge. So she remained planted where she stood, too scared to move, while the cold stung her hands, nose, and ears.

But as she stood there, heart banging, she had to concede that the moose looked more comical than dangerous, his pliant lips engaged in constant motion. Maybe he was hungry? She thought of Jester eating the peppermint and reached into her pocket. No mints, but a ziplock bag of stale bread that she kept to crumble and feed to the birds. She extracted some of the bigger bits and tossed them onto the snow, as far away as she could. The moose looked but did not move, at least not right away. Then he began to walk toward the bread, lifting one enormous foot after the other.

Keeping her gaze on him, Susannah backed away, slowly at first, and then more quickly. Within seconds, she was in the house, slamming the door. She darted to the window. The moose raised his head, probably in response to the sound. She had enough time to retrieve her phone and take several pictures as he looked around, his antlers bobbing gently. Then he ambled off toward a small copse of pines. Susannah watched him as he went—a stranger hailing from this strange new land.

TWENTY-FOUR

Calista came downstairs just as Susannah was bringing pancakes to the table. She was fully dressed in a pair of black tuxedo pants, fitted black turtleneck, and a knit cardigan that sported ornaments, candy canes, and a fat, full-bearded Santa on the back; it was one of her collection of "ironic Christmas sweaters," of which there were many.

"Where are you going?" As soon as she said it, Susannah realized how much like an interrogation her words sounded; she wished she had spoken more gently.

"To Alice's." Calista helped herself to several pancakes and scrutinized the bottle of maple syrup sitting next to the platter. "Foley Farms," she read. "Megan's last name is Foley; I think this might be someone in her family."

"Her father?" Susannah reached for the butter, imagining a crew of pink-cheeked men with earmuffs, lumberjack coats, and tin buckets—an endearingly wholesome fantasy.

Calista shook her head. "Probably not. Megan says he's in jail."

The fantasy disintegrated. While the kids ate, Susannah pondered the implications of Calista having a friend whose father was in jail. *Don't be so judgmental,* she could hear Polly saying. *You don't know if it's even true, or if it is, what he's in for. Think of all the people wrongfully incarcerated. Or maybe he's a political prisoner.* The maple syrup had an intense, almost burnt taste, and Susannah drizzled a little more on the last bite of her pancake. *What if it were one of your daughters,* she silently argued with Polly. *Wouldn't you be even the teensiest bit worried?*

After breakfast, Susannah was left alone—Jack was off with Liam and Matthew, two new friends from his grade, and Calista, irritatingly, with Alice. But at least that meant time to spend with Betsey Pettingill, and then, tonight, with Corbin Bailey, a prospect laced with equal parts guilt and anticipation. She did not believe in an afterlife, at least not one in which the dead assumed corporeal form and could look down on the doings of those they left behind. Still, she silently addressed her dead husband. *I still love you. I'll always love you. But you're gone, and I'm here without you. And it's lonely. Really lonely. Forgive me, okay?* Then she slipped into the flannel-lined jeans she'd recently ordered from L.L.Bean, and added a sweater and a polar fleece vest; her room could get chilly.

Before she began to work, she did a quick search for Linda Jacobsmeyer; she found five people with that name, but from the details she was able to gather, it was clear none of these Linda Jacobsmeyers was the one she sought. Could she be using another name? Susannah would have to ask around.

But right now, she wanted to return to the manuscript. She pulled out the notes she'd made on her trip with Corbin. A lot of good material here, though she wasn't yet sure how she was going to handle all of it. Right now, she still saw Betsey as a child, and so it was to the child that she returned:

We went on to Salisbury as planned, but the whole time I pined for my mother. She was waiting by the gate for us when we got home. I jumped down from the mare, not caring that I fell and skinned my knees, and went racing toward her. At first I couldn't say anything, but just pressed my face against her apron. Uncle Benjamin came following behind. "Quite a time they had over at the Curriers," he said. "A dead baby was found in the barn—"

"I found it! I found it and I wish I hadn't!" I lifted my face away from my mother's apron and started crying in earnest, letting loose the torrent of tears I'd had to stifle at the Curriers'.

"What's all this?" my mother said. Uncle Benjamin told her the story. I was crying too hard to say much.

"Why, my poor little poppet." My mother knelt and used the hem of her apron to dry my face. "What a fright you had." She looked up at my uncle. "And for the babe found in the barn. Do you think she—that is, would she really . . . ?"

My uncle shook his head. "That's for the jury and the judge to decide," he said. "She's off to Portsmouth now. There'll be a trial."

"She didn't do it—she didn't!" I exclaimed.

My mother did not dismiss me the way Patience and Sarah had. "How do you know?" she asked.

"I just do."

She wrapped me in her arms. "Don't think of it, Betsey. Put it right out of your mind."

She did not have to repeat it. I never wanted to think of it again. And for the rest of the summer, I was able to do just that. It was a lovely season, one long golden day unfolding after another. When it rained—and we did need the rain, for the crops and the garden—it always seemed to rain at night, and in the morning the freshly rinsed sky would be so bright and clear it almost hurt my eyes.

I was my mother's only child; she generally doted on me and was content to let me stay close by her side. I helped her in the vegetable garden or played in the field behind our house. Sometimes we went berry picking and brought home baskets full of dark, tart berries that we turned into crumbles, grunts, and fools. Once we went to a nearby stream and I was allowed to take off my shoes and stockings and wade in; I loved the way the cool, clear water eddied around my feet and ankles. The only place I would not go was the barn. Even though the baby had been found in a different barn, miles away, the commingled smells—of milk, of manure, of hay, of wheat, and of grass, made me think of the other, and the other was what I was resolutely trying not to think of.

It wasn't until late September, when the first scarlet leaves had started to show in the trees, that I thought about the baby and its gruesome discovery again. My uncle had come to visit, and since he'd been in Portsmouth just prior, he shared the news as he sat at our table, drinking the cup of water my mother had fetched him from the well.

"There's been a verdict in the Ruth Blay case," he said.

"What was it?"

"Guilty," said my uncle.

"May God have mercy on her soul," my mother said softly.

"What will happen now?" I had been sitting on the floor, quietly playing with the wooden doll my father had carved for me, and my mother had not realized I was there until I spoke up.

"Betsey!" she said, her surprise evident. "This is not for your ears. Please go upstairs at once."

I picked up the doll. She had a smooth body, rigid arms, and features that had been created by the merest flick of the knife. "What will happen to her? Will she be hanged by the neck until she is dead? Or will she be burned at the stake?"

"Where did you hear such things?" my mother cried. She turned to my uncle. "Who's been filling her head with this evil talk? Was it those nasty biddies down in South Hampton? Benjamin Clough's sisters? Or that wife of his, Olive? Nothing better to do than spread such tales and fill the minds of innocent children with such wickedness?"

"No, it was Patience and Sarah," I said, for though I had not liked those ladies at Mrs. Currier's house, they were not the ones to blame.

"Well, you shouldn't think or talk like that ever again. Mrs. Blay will appeal the decision, won't she?" My mother glanced anxiously at my uncle.

"No, I was told she would not." He looked down at his hands, rough and worn as leather.

"Then you mean—"

"She has asked for a reprieve, though, to ready herself—"

"Not another word," she said sharply and looked at me. "Go upstairs now, Betsey, and take Dolly with you."

I did as she said, cradling the doll in my arms. She had no legs, but the muslin skirt my mother had helped me sew covered up that lack. I looked into her face. Her expression was not smiling, not sad, but calm and comforting. She was the first and only doll I'd ever had and I loved her. But Dolly was not the right name for her. I would call her Ruth instead. I knew better than to say this aloud, though. So I did as my mother bade me and brought her upstairs. Ruth, Ruth, Ruth, I chanted, the name a special, haunting syllable on my tongue, one that I alone would know.

Something else happened around this time. It had nothing to do with Ruth Blay, who languished in a Portsmouth jail, alternately pleading for her life and trying to make peace with relinquishing it. It had nothing to do with those ladies who had turned, as if in one cold, implacable tide, against her. And it most certainly had nothing to do with that June day and the grisly discovery I had made under the floorboards in the Cloughs' barn. But in my childish mind—I had just turned six—it was all jumbled together.

It was October, I think, or early November. There had been a frost, and whatever leaves still remained on the trees were slick and shining with ice. One of our neighbors, Abitha Collins, was big with child that season. This was hardly a remarkable occurrence. She had three older children; the boys were apprenticed out, one to a blacksmith and the other to a cooper, and her eldest, a girl of sixteen, had just gotten married and gone to live in Massachusetts with her husband's family.

Abitha was a small, almost negligible woman, with a weak chin, dusty brown hair, and a wan complexion. I never saw her laugh or smile and rarely heard her speak; her husband, a large, loud man, was considered a bit of a brute and my parents did not seek his company. But my mother felt sorry for her and would often send me over with a loaf of bread or something from her garden. Abitha always thanked me for whatever I'd brought, and one day she gave me a little scrap of lace from her basket. It was so delicate and pretty, I couldn't wait to get home so I could sew it onto my doll's dress.

The next time my mother asked me to go, I started out right away; maybe Abitha Collins would give me another piece of lace and I could make my dolly a cap. The day was gray and chilly but the bread, wrapped in a bit of linen, was still warm, and I held it close to my chest, along with my doll; I took her with me everywhere. When I got to the house, I knocked on the door. There was no answer. I knocked again, harder this time. When there was still no reply, I cautiously pushed the door. It was not locked and I was able to peek inside. At first I saw no one, but then I heard a noise—it sounded like panting. I turned, and there was Abitha, lying in a corner of the room and breathing very hard. The lower portion of her gray-blue dress was wet, and I saw a puddle of clear liquid beneath her on the pine floor.

"Betsey," she said in a low voice. "I'm so glad you've come. Please go and fetch your mother—right away."

"Are you well?" I asked, dismayed by both her prone position and the labored sound of her breathing.

"Yes, yes," she said. "But the child—" She pointed to the hard, round bubble of her midsection. "The child is on the way and I need help. Please go now!"

I had never heard her say so many words at once and, dropping the bread, I turned and ran back across the field that separated our two houses. When I gave my mother the message, she picked up her shawl and together we made the trip again. But once we got to the Collins' house, she said, "You were a good girl in bringing me here. Now you must go home and stay there." I said nothing. My father was away and the house was empty. I did not want to be there by myself. "What are you waiting for?" my mother said. "Go!"

"Please let me stay," I said. "I'm afraid to be alone."

My mother looked at me, as if taking my measure. "Very well. But you have to do exactly as I ask and when I tell you to step outside, you must do that too—do you understand?"

"Yes, ma'am." I nodded, so grateful that I was not to be sent back to the empty house. I set Ruth gently down on the painted sideboard and asked, "Do you need me to fetch Mr. Collins?"

"That won't be necessary," said my mother. "Men are useless at a birth."

What she did ask was that I help her get Abitha onto the bed, where she had first removed the woven coverlet and spread *out several thick white cloths Abitha must have been saving for this purpose. Then my mother lit a fire under the pot of water— fortunately it was full, so I did not have to go to the well—and told me to let her know when it was hot. For the next couple of hours, she soothed and comforted Abitha in her travail, encouraging her to squeeze her hand when the pains came and wiping her brow with a soft cloth that had been dipped into the warmed water. My mother had had only a single child, but she had assisted at the births of many.*

It was only when Abitha's panting and moans turned to actual screams that my mother sent me out. "It won't be long," she said. "The baby will be here soon." I did not want to go outside but I did not want to stay and hear the screaming either, so I took my doll and did as I was told. I set Ruth down on a tree stump and began gathering up things I could use in our games together: acorns that could serve as food, a curving scarlet leaf that could be a plate. To my growing pile I added some pinecones, and more leaves: thin golden blades. While I gathered, I sang to myself, so I would not hear the sounds coming from inside the house. There were birds swooping in and out of the mostly bare trees and rustling from the creatures that lived on the ground—squirrels, chipmunks, and the tiny brown field mice that skittered like shadows.

But why hadn't my mother come to fetch me yet? She had said it would not be long, yet the sun was sinking lower in the sky and the light was fading. The birds quieted and the rustling increased: other animals were coming out now and the sounds I heard might indicate a fox or a skunk.

I looked up to see that a large gray owl had settled on a branch and was looking straight at me. His flat face, ringed with darker feathers, and the fixed orbs of his maize-colored eyes had a hypnotic effect: I could not look away. At the same time I was frightened that he might swoop down and snatch me up. I knew this was foolish; I was too big for him to carry off. But looking at those unblinking eyes, I could almost believe that he possessed otherworldly powers.

Ignoring my mother's words, I grabbed my doll, opened the door, and stepped back into the house. In my fright, I had not registered that the sound of the screaming had stopped. Instead, there was now the muffled sound of weeping. My mother sat on the bloodstained bed, her arm encircling the small, hunched shoulders of Abitha Collins. Across the room, in a woven willow basket, was a still and shrouded bundle. No one had to tell me what had happened. The baby whose passage into the world had caused Abitha Collins to writhe and scream was gone—dead, like that other baby back in June. Only this time I did not scream; indeed I could not have screamed even had I wanted to, because as soon as I saw the bundle, I crumpled to the floor in a faint.

TWENTY-FIVE

$\mathcal{S}$ usannah finished typing the word "faint" and looked up at the clock. Almost five—how had it gotten so late? She had been so immersed in Betsey's world that she'd completely lost track of the time. Glancing at her phone, she saw there was a text from Corbin. The weather report was predicting snow for late this evening, so he wanted to pick her up at six o'clock rather than seven. That way, he could get her home before the snow really started coming down. *Good idea,* she texted back. *Thanks for suggesting it.* Only now she was going to have to rush to get ready.

At least she did not have to factor in the kids. Jack was staying over at Liam's and Calista was having dinner and going to a movie with Alice. And not just any movie showing at the nearby Cineplex; oh, no. They were driving to Dartmouth, in Hanover, to see one of the films being shown in the Truffaut Festival the French department was sponsoring. Though if it was snowing hard, would Alice really want to make the drive? Should she call to discuss it? But that would only make Calista angry; she was going to have to rely on Alice's good sense.

She hit save and turned off the laptop. What was she going to wear? Twenty minutes later, Susannah's bed was a repository of rejected dresses, skirts, blouses, and sweaters. Nothing seemed right. People in New Hampshire dressed down, not up. She did not think she had seen a woman in heels since she'd gotten here. But this date was momentous in its way and she wanted to wear something special, something that said she understood its importance.

Chilly in the bra and panties—peach colored, lace trimmed— she'd changed into, Susannah returned to the closet. Here was something she had not considered: the two-piece number she'd found in the attic when she'd first gotten to the house, still swathed in plastic from the dry cleaners. Extracting the dress from the transparent shroud, she slipped it on, reaching her arms around to her back to get at the zipper. The ivory satin bodice with its black velvet collar made her skin glow, and the black-and-white tweed skirt skimmed her hips in a flattering—and, she thought, subtly sexy—way. And once she put on the matching black velvet jacket, with its jet buttons and tweed cuffs, Susannah felt transformed. She knew she was attractive, but she also knew she wasn't the beauty that her mother had been. Yet in assuming Claire's dress, she seemed to assume something of her allure. It was a heady feeling, and she studied herself in the mirror for several seconds.

Now it was a quarter to six. She rummaged in a drawer for sheer black panty hose; fortunately, she still had a few pairs from her New York life. She didn't know if she could manage the snow with the black patent leather pumps she also unearthed, but she was going to wear them anyway; it was only a few steps to the car and Corbin would just have to take her arm. There was just enough time to brush her teeth and swipe on a little blush, a coat of mascara, and some lipstick. Corbin's car pulled up as she touched a few drops of gardenia-scented perfume to her wrists and the hollow of her throat.

"You look amazing," he said when she opened the door.

"Thank you." She was happy she'd pleased him. Then she took in the black cashmere sweater and white shirt under his coat; his eyes above the white collar seemed even more intensely blue than she'd remembered. He wore dark pinwale corduroy pants, and a quick glance downward revealed good black shoes, well polished, with a buckle on the instep. So he'd dressed up too. She got her coat and, just as in her fantasy, Corbin took her arm on the way to the car.

But once they had gotten on the road, she was suddenly overcome with shyness. Here she was on an honest-to-goodness dinner date, her first in decades. She felt the by now familiar thrum of excitement sitting next to him, and the sight of his taut, well-muscled thigh so close to hers on the seat filled her with a kind of long-dormant longing. Still, this felt wrong, all wrong. Where was Charlie, her best friend, her soul mate, husband and father of her children? Dead, that's where, and for the first time since he had died, Susannah felt a spike not of grief, but of anger. Why had it been left up to *her* to see that he'd worn the bicycle helmet? Wasn't he a grown-up? Didn't he have any responsibility, to himself, and to her and the kids? That's what Polly had said and maybe there was some truth in it. She turned her face to the window; spreading, snow-covered pines rushed close and then receded.

"You're kind of quiet," Corbin observed. "Everything okay?"

"Everything's fine." She turned back to him, willing it to be true.

"I'm looking forward to trying this place," Corbin said. "The reviews have been great."

"So you haven't been there?"

"Not yet. I was just waiting for the right occasion." His eyes were still on the road, but he inclined his head in her direction slightly. "And then you came along."

"Flatterer." But she laughed. He was easy, that's what he was. And God knew, she needed easy right now.

The restaurant, Abundance, was housed in what had once been a barn. The tiny white lights clustered in the bushes and strung around the perimeter of the door allowed Susannah to see the weathered gray boards that made up the structure and the peeling red roof that topped it. Kind of like the barn Corbin had brought her to see. As soon as they walked in, they were greeted by a long farm table covered with artfully arranged bushels of fresh fruits and vegetables: apples were balanced on fluted green-and-gold winter squash; brussels sprouts poured in giddy profusion from a wicker cornucopia. Corbin checked their coats and let Susannah walk ahead as they were led to their table.

It wasn't until they were seated with a basket of fresh bread and crock of herbed butter that she remembered the question she'd wanted to ask. But he might want to know why. Did she want to tell him? She wasn't sure. The appearance of the waiter proffering a wine list gave her a reprieve.

"Can I get you a drink to start?" the waiter asked.

"Ginger ale for me." Corbin slid the wine list over in Susannah's direction.

"And for you?" The pen was poised above his pad.

"I'll start with a glass of the Cabernet," said Susannah. She thought of what Alice had said about his past; was it true? The waiter went to get their drinks, and when he returned, he stood there until she had tasted the wine and nodded her approval.

"Good?" Corbin asked.

"Very." She'd skipped lunch and the wine was going to her

head rather quickly. But it gave her the courage to ask that question that had been goading her. "Do you remember that summer when we all went on a camping trip?"

"I do." He sipped the ginger ale.

"Do you happen to remember the date?" The wine was very good; she needed to slow down until she ordered dinner.

He thought for a moment. "It was in August. Late August, I think."

"But you don't know the exact date?"

"No." She must have looked disappointed, because he added, "Why? Is it really important to know?"

"Yes," she said. "It is."

He didn't ask why and she did not volunteer. What he did say was, "I think I know how I can help you."

"You do?"

"I had a Polaroid back then. Remember those? And I brought it with me. If I can find the pictures I took, they would be dated. That would give you the information you need."

"Yes," she said. "It would."

Just knowing she might have her answer relaxed her, and she began to have a very good time. The food, when it arrived, was delicious. They had ordered seared scallops, filet of beef, salad with slices of caramelized grapefruit, chocolate mousse, mocha cake—and shared it all. Susannah ate everything eagerly, and drank a second glass of wine. She wasn't drunk; she was just feeling good, as if something that had been tightly wound for weeks had loosened in her. Corbin told her about a promising meeting he'd had with the Wingate executives, and asked about her kids and her work. When she showed him the pictures of the moose on her phone, he looked momentarily stern. "You didn't get up close to him, did you?"

"Not very," she said. "Why?"

"They can be really aggressive. Dangerous even. You did the right thing in backing off."

"Jack was sorry he didn't get to see him."

"Jack can see him from inside the house. In fact, I sell motion-sensitive cameras at the store. They're used for security at a lot of places, but birders love them too. I'll set one up at your place if you want."

"That would be great." She took another sip of the wine; oh, but she was feeling good. Very good.

After paying the check, Corbin guided her back to his car just as the first snowflakes were beginning to drift down. "I want to get you home before it really starts snowing," he said as she slid into the seat beside him.

Susannah was quiet. The wine had mellowed her and she was not quite ready to have the evening end. "What about those Polaroids?" she asked. "Do you think you could find them?"

"Tonight?" he asked. The question seemed charged.

"If it's not too much trouble."

"Not too much trouble at all," he said. "But maybe it's not the best idea. The snow and all . . ."

"Let's see if you can find them quickly. If not, we can leave it for another time."

He nodded and they got into the car. The sky was dark now, and the tiny flakes were not registering as white but only as the merest sparkles as they were fleetingly captured by the headlights. She realized she had no idea where Corbin lived, but it was too dark for her to make out any of the few landmarks she had come to know. After a while, he drove up to a neat colonial with a Wedgwood blue door.

"Come on in." He turned on a light and the room bloomed into view: wide-plank pine floors, braided oval rug, a comfortably worn leather sofa and two even more worn armchairs in a floral pattern, a large flat-screen television over the fireplace. Susannah took off her coat, which Corbin hung in a closet by the door. Her excitement at being here was tamped only slightly by her awareness of those photographs. Would he be able to find them tonight? She really hoped so.

"Why don't you sit down?" Corbin said. She sank into the sofa. "I'll go and see if I can find those photos." He turned to leave the room, but before going he said, "I'd offer you a nightcap, but since I've been sober, I never keep the stuff around."

"That's all right." Well, *that* certainly was direct. In his absence, she took in a few more details of the room. There was a floor-to-ceiling bookcase on one side and sliding glass doors on another; the walls, which had been painted a shade of blue lighter than the door, held a couple of concert and sports posters but not a single thing that could be called art. She walked over to inspect the books. History, politics, a whole slew of biographies. No novels or short stories and certainly no poetry.

She went back to the sofa to sit down. A stack of magazines sat on the coffee table and she leafed through current issues of *Sports Illustrated*, *National Geographic*, and *The Home Handyman*. Not a single one held a shred of interest for her. All right, so they wouldn't discuss reading material. They had other things in common.

She checked her phone to see if her kids had texted her and, to her relief, learned that Alice had decided against the movie; the two of them were safe at her house. Then Susannah got up to look outside. A light over the doors illuminated the flurry of flakes and nothing more; beyond that, all was black.

"Found them."

She turned to see Corbin holding a small brown paper shopping bag. "Here you go."

She took the bag. What if the dates corresponded with the dates on the tickets stubs? Then she would have confirmed what until now she could only surmise. God, she was so nervous. She sat down on the sofa and he sat down next to her. But before she could reach into the bag, he put his hand on her wrist. "Look, I'm guessing that what's in there is a potentially huge deal for you. You haven't said what it is and I don't want to pry. But before you look, I want to say something. I really shouldn't have tossed off that last comment so nonchalantly."

"The one about being sober?"

"I should have explained—that is, if you haven't heard already. Eastwood's a small town and things get around, but I'd still rather you hear the story from me."

"Did you have a drinking problem?"

He nodded. "It started after I had to leave law school after my first year. I was disappointed. Angry too. But I was also ashamed. How could I be angry with my dad when he'd sacrificed so much for us? He needed me and it was my turn to be there for him. So I drank to help myself get through all that. I was quiet about it, though. No frat boy stuff for me—I never did Jell-O shots or got so wasted that I woke up the next morning lying in a puddle of puke, my pants gone missing. No, I was a discreet, keep-it-to-yourself kind of drunk. Until I wasn't."

"What happened?"

"My dad had already died, and my mom was actually doing okay. She decided to go visit Trevor, in Florida, and so I was alone in the house. This house, actually—I never moved out. At first I thought I'd just be relieved to be on my own. But I started getting angry all over again, and sorry for myself too. Because of what I told you before—and because of something else."

"Something else?"

"Well, not something. Someone."

Susannah waited, and when he didn't say anything, she prompted, "Who was she?"

"The woman I loved."

"Oh." She didn't like the idea of him loving someone else; she didn't like it one bit and she had to force herself to focus on the rest of what he was saying.

". . . we'd been together for a few years. I wanted to marry her. She was beautiful, smart, ambitious . . . the whole package."

"So what happened?"

"Eastwood, that's what. She wanted to leave town, leave the state, leave the country even. She had this idea about traveling to South America; she thought there would be a lot of business opportunities there."

"And you didn't want to do that."

He looked at his hands, and then at her. "No, I didn't. We fought about it, broke up a couple of times, and got back together a couple of times. My drinking always notched up when we split; it would slow down when she was back. But it was always there, a kind of secret friend. Then she bought a one-way ticket to Mexico City—and just like that, she was gone."

"That must have hurt."

"Hurt doesn't describe it. How about ambushed, gob-smacked, and devastated? I cursed her for leaving me, for not loving me enough, for breaking my heart. Then I cursed myself for not going with her. Or for not going anywhere. I could have picked up where I left off, gone back to law school, and gotten on track again. Only, with her gone, it all seemed too hard, like that train had pulled out of the station for good and I was stuck behind. So I went on a serious bender and landed in the ER, where I got my stomach pumped. Alcohol poisoning. I was damn lucky one of my mom's friends came around that night to bring me a casserole—she found me passed out and called nine-one-one. If she hadn't, well, I wouldn't be here telling you all this."

Susannah sat quietly, trying to absorb it all. "What did you do after you got out of the hospital?"

"I manned up, found myself a twelve-step program in Concord, and made sure I got myself to a meeting at least once a week. That was fifteen years ago and I've been sober ever since."

"Do you still go to meetings?"

"I do, though not every week. And I've been a sponsor to a few people over the years. It feels really good to give back that way." He smiled. "Okay. That's out of the way and we don't have to discuss it again. Unless you want to, of course. But right now I'm sure you're itching to get at those photos."

"I am." But she was torn: his confession, coupled with his near-ness, was pulling her in one direction, the contents of the bag in another. "There's one more question, though . . ."

"Shoot."

"After that woman left you . . . were there any others? Women, I mean."

"A few. But no one who touched me in the way she had. There was one I almost married. Picked out the ring and everything. But in my gut I knew I was settling. It wouldn't have been fair to her— or to me." She didn't know what to say to that. After a beat he added, "Go on and look at the pictures," he said. "You need to do that."

She put a hand on his cheek. How dear he was to say that, even without understanding. How kind. Then she withdrew her hand, reached into the bag, and pulled out several of the photographs. Small, square, and somewhat faded, the photos showed images of her younger self and some of her friends from that summer: Trevor with his arm around her, a grouping of birch trees, the tents they had pitched in the woods. But it was the numbers, tiny, black, and indelible, that leapt out at her: all the pictures she held were dated between August 17 and August 21, 1994—exactly the time her mother was in Quebec with her mystery companion.

"Are you okay?" asked Corbin.

Susannah nodded, not quite ready to speak. So she had been right—while she had been on the trip, hiking through the woods during the day, smoking pot around a campfire and fending off mosquitoes by a campfire at night, her mother had gone to Quebec with her lover. Where had her father been? Had he known what she was doing or had Claire deceived him too? "Can I hold on to these?" she finally asked. "I'll give them back, but I just need them for a little while."

"Sure." He leaned over to brush away the hair that had fallen in her face. That gesture replicated so perfectly the long-ago summer night in which he'd done the exact same thing, the night when she'd wished—how she'd wished!—that she had been his girlfriend, not Trevor's. Without thinking any more, she turned and kissed him. The photos, Quebec, and her mother receded as she felt first his surprise and then his eagerness; he kissed her back, pulling her closer so that she fit snugly against his chest.

When they moved apart, he said, "Thank you."

"Thank you?"

"I've been wanting to do that all night. I figured that coming back here would give me a chance, but then whatever you found in those pictures seemed to derail things."

"No." She put the photos back in the bag. "It didn't. I'll tell you all about them," she said. "Only not now." And she lifted her arms to reach for him.

TWENTY-SIX

They kissed for several minutes, pausing only when Susannah heard a text come in from Jack. She moved out of the embrace so she could read it. *Snowing really hard! So cool! Will text u tomorrow before I come home.*

"Everything all right?" Corbin still had an arm around her.

"Everything's all right." She glanced out the window. The snow was coming down harder now; the flakes, whipped by the wind, skittered and danced. "My son is sleeping elsewhere tonight. So is my daughter."

"So maybe you're not in such a hurry to get home."

"No," she said. "I'm not."

He kissed her again, but this time his hands traveled to the front of her dress, and when he reached under the jacket for her breasts, gently kneading them through the cloth, she gasped, from surprise as much as pleasure. Yes, she wanted him, and yes, she welcomed the caress. But she could not easily separate the *now* from the *then*—for so many years, Charlie had been the only one to touch her; Charlie had been the only one she had wanted. If Charlie had lived, she would have never seen Corbin Bailey again and he would have been relegated to some distant region of her memory. It was because Charlie had been killed, *had let himself get killed*, that she was here at all.

Corbin's hands were still on her breasts, gentle but purposeful, and she felt her desire unspooling to meet his. "Do you want to go in the other room?" he said softly into her ear. She said nothing, but stood and let herself be led into the bedroom.

"Sit." Corbin patted the bed, covered in a cinnamon-colored quilt and punctuated with several pillows. Folded at the foot of the bed was a crocheted afghan of multicolored squares; she wondered if his mother had made it. Corbin was busily lighting candles and then turned off the lamp as he sank down on the bed beside her. His sweater came off easily and then he started to unbutton his shirt, revealing a torso more compact and muscled than Charlie's; Charlie had been reedy and thin. She sat very still, wanting to remove her dress, yet unable to do it.

"Can I help you?" he asked. He was down to his underwear now, white, snugly fitting jockey shorts that were nothing like Charlie's whimsically printed boxers.

"That would be nice." She let him slip the jacket off and unzip the dress. She stood to step out of it, and worried about the panty hose; getting out of them was always awkward. But he seemed riveted by her breasts, partially revealed by the low-cut lace-trimmed bra, a bra she'd bought before Charlie was killed and one he'd never had the chance to see her wear. After he'd died, she had stuffed it away in the drawer for months. Tonight was the first time she had put it on; somewhere in her mind was the possibility that Corbin would see it.

Only when his fingers began to undo the bra's front-closing clasp did everything shut off abruptly; she stood and walked to the window. Snow was still falling and the wind was even stronger now; she could hear it whistling as it whipped through the trees.

Corbin was right behind her. "Where'd you go?"

She turned to face him. "I'm sorry," she said. "I wanted to—I really did. But now that I'm really here and in the middle of it, I just . . . can't."

"There hasn't been anyone since you lost your husband?" She shook her head. "I get it." He put his arms around her. She stiffened until she realized the gesture was intended to comfort, not arouse. "Come on back to bed; it's too cold over here."

She followed him and sat down again. Then she watched while he blew out the candles, one by one. "If you want, you can stay here tonight," he said. "Nothing will happen. Promise." The room was dark.

"All right." She felt tired all of a sudden. So tired. The much anticipated date, the wine, the Polaroids—and now the total flip-flop of her own emotions. "But could you give me something to sleep in?"

"Of course."

Her eyes had adjusted and she could see him walk over to a dresser and pull out a folded pair of flannel pajamas. He handed them to her. "Brand new. They were a Christmas present."

"Thank you."

Clutching the pajamas, she retreated to the bathroom to change. She buttoned the buttons all the way up to the top and tightened the drawstrings on the bottoms. They were too long, so she rolled them up once, and then again. Looking in the mirror, she saw gray reindeer frolicking all over navy blue flannel. Not the least bit sexy—and perfect. When she returned to the bedroom, clothes in her arms, Corbin was already under the covers. She hesitated. Maybe she ought to ask if she could sleep on the sofa.

"There's plenty of room," he said. "You won't even know I'm here."

The comment disarmed her, and, setting the bundle on a chair, she slipped in beside him.

"Sweet dreams," he said.

Was he taunting her? "Good night," she replied. She wanted to add, "I'm sorry" or "Please don't hate me," but really, what was the point? She turned over, away from him, her whole body rigid and unable to relax. But eventually, she heard the deep, steady breathing that signaled he was asleep and she turned over to look at him. He was so sexy and she wished she could rekindle the giddy excitement she'd been feeling earlier. Instead, she turned away again, not believing she would actually sleep, but hoping she could at least close her eyes and retreat from the world for a while.

She awoke disoriented, squinting at the very bright light that was visible through the small spaces between the slats and around the perimeter of the wooden blinds. She remembered that they had been pulled up last night; Corbin must have let them down at some point. But where was he? The quilt was pulled back and the bed beside her empty. Then she heard his voice coming from the other room: he was speaking quietly, but she thought he sounded tense.

She was thirsty and she needed to use the bathroom. And her purse was in the other room too—she wanted to text the kids. But she did not want to disturb him, so she stayed where she was.

". . . he told me he was with us on this," Corbin was saying. "He gave me his word." There was a silence and then he said, "I thought I could trust him. I did." Another silence, this one even longer. "There's nothing you can say to make it right. Nothing. I'm just disgusted, that's all. Betrayed and disgusted." More silence and then the door to the bedroom opened cautiously and she could see him looking in her direction.

"Good morning," she ventured.

"Not so good." He entered the room and she could see, with some relief, that though his chest was bare, he was wearing a pair of gray sweatpants.

"What's wrong?" She sat up and attempted to run her fingers through her hair. She'd gone to bed with her makeup on and she imagined it was smeared all over her face by now.

"Wingate." The word was uttered like a curse. "I had a verbal agreement from the CEO; then the next thing I hear is that that entire alternative we proposed for disposing of the dye—an alternative, I should add, that took months to work out—has been completely abandoned. He's gotten some kind of exemption from the governor, something about the need to 'protect jobs and the local economy.'" He looked over at her. "What a load of crap. If Primrose Pond is ruined, turned to sludge by that damn ink, the town will be ruined along with it. All that waterfront property will go down in value, and when houses lose their value, everything else starts tumbling too."

"I'm sorry," she said.

"Sorry?" For a second, it seemed he might turn on her; then his voice turned remorseful, not angry. "Sorry doesn't even begin to describe it. But for want of a better word, yeah, I'm sorry too."

Susannah got out of bed, went to the bathroom, and then returned to the bedroom to get her things. But when she looked at the folded dress and jacket, the shiny pumps, she wished she had something more appropriate to put on. Corbin must have sensed her discomfort, because he said, "I could lend you a pair of sweats and a sweater for the drive home if you want. Though the drive may have to wait; we had over a foot of snow last night and the roads aren't fully plowed yet."

"Over a foot!" She went to the window and peeked through the blinds. The view outside was dazzling—snow like a layer of whipped cream along the trees and roof of the house next door, snow like marshmallow frosting slathering the trash cans, the wooden fence, the garage. "Does it snow like this all the time?"

"Not all the time." He joined her by the window. "But it's not so unusual either. We're in New Hampshire, remember?"

"Who could forget?"

He smiled, but his eyes looked troubled. He was still brooding over that business with Wingate; well, who could blame him? He got out a pair of black sweatpants and a sweater with a row of angels across the front and handed them to her; like the pajamas, the sweater had a price tag.

"Another Christmas present?"

"Same relative, different Christmas," he said and then added, "She means well."

He left the room to start breakfast while Susannah got dressed—this time she let the too-long pants pool around her ankles—and texted the kids; Jack was ecstatic over the snow and planned to go sledding with Liam, while Calista said she was staying with Alice for the rest of the day. Susannah had a brush and covered elastic in her purse, so she was able to do something with her hair. She also scrubbed the blurred makeup off her face, though there was not much to be done about the sweatpants— loose, baggy, and wholly unbecoming—and the sweater, which was flat-out hideous. Only Calista would have prized it, and added it proudly to her ugly-sweater collection.

Corbin was setting the table when she walked into the dining room. He'd made eggs and bacon and squeezed oranges for juice. They were polite, even formal with each other, and did not discuss what had happened—or failed to happen—the night before. When she asked about Wingate, he said, "I'm not giving up. I'll just have to regroup and come up with a new strategy."

"Like what?"

"I don't know. But there are people in this community who are with me. I'll start the triage today as soon as I get you home."

"When will the roads be cleared?"

"Probably within the hour." Corbin was on his second cup of coffee and had just refilled her mug as well. "Be sure not to forget these when you leave." He reached down and placed the small brown shopping bag on the table in front of her. "I know they're important to you."

The photographs. She had actually *forgotten*. Moving her plate aside, she took them out and laid them on the table. Here was one she hadn't really noticed last night: Corbin was standing shirtless in a small open field while she was on the periphery of the picture, head turned in his direction. Though the image was small, Susannah was sure she was staring.

"It's the dates that are important," she said.

"Confirmation of something you wish you hadn't been able to confirm, right?"

Even without her telling him the details, he understood. He was looking at her and his expression—curious, interested, sympathetic—made it so easy to just tell him. "When I first moved into the house, I found a love letter that had been written to my mother. Only it wasn't from my father—I'm sure of that. It was from someone else."

"Someone you knew?"

Susannah shrugged slightly. "I don't know. But once I found it, I started looking for other clues. Evidence, really. And I found two ticket stubs and a few other things that made me think she was in Quebec that summer, probably with the man who wrote the note. The dates on the photographs correspond to the days she was there—they're the proof I needed."

"Wow," he said quietly. "That's a lot to process." He finished his coffee and put the mug down. "How are you dealing with it?"

"Okay, I guess." She looked down. "I haven't told many people. You're only the second. I told my best friend, but she thinks I should leave it alone, not keep digging." There was a silence during which she was unable to meet his eyes.

"I'm glad you shared this with me," he said finally. "And I get what you're doing. I don't think you should stop until you're ready to stop. You'll know when that is." Susannah looked at him then, at the steady blue gaze that had drawn her all those years ago and that was drawing her now. She got up from the table and went to stand in front of him. He remained very still while she ran her hands lightly along his brow, his face, and finally his lips. Then she leaned down to kiss him; all the uncertainty of the night before was gone, and she wanted him as much as—no, more than—ever.

He stood, scooped her up, and carried her into the bedroom. She pressed her face against his shoulder, arms clasped around his neck. It was only when they'd reached the bed and he set her gently down that he asked, "Is this all right?"

Instead of answering, she shimmied out of the pants and then pulled the sweater up and over her head. Instantly, gooseflesh prickled her naked breasts and belly, but his hands quickly moved to cover her. They were so warm; *he* was so warm. She pulled him down beside her so that they were both stretched out on the mattress. "I've been thinking about you," he said softly. "Dreaming about you, even."

"What did you dream?" she asked.

"About this." He began to kiss the many eager, palpitating places on her skin. "And this, and this, and this."

I had the same dream, she wanted to say. But then the kisses became more insistent and she simply arched her body up to meet him.

TWENTY-SEVEN

Corbin had just turned off the engine when a shiny black Jeep pulled up. A door opened and then shut and suddenly there was Jack, stomping toward them, the crisp, newly fallen snow crunching audibly as he moved.

"Ten inches, Mom!" he crowed. "It snowed ten inches last night. And the drifts are even higher!"

He was right; the mailbox was practically covered and the snow came up to the windows of the shed.

"We sure got hit," Corbin said as he emerged from the car. "But luckily, it was the dry powdery kind. It's the wet clumpy stuff that makes you curse the winter."

"Why?" asked Jack.

"The weight," explained Corbin. "When the snow is wet, it gets heavy—that's when the power lines go down. Or tree branches crack off. Sometimes roofs collapse. Last winter someone was killed when a limb on a hundred-year-old oak snapped and landed on him."

Grim as it was, Susannah was grateful for this exchange; it took the attention away from her. After the last hour she'd spent naked and rolling around in Corbin's bed, there was no way she could hide her exultation, and she didn't want Jack to read it in her face.

"That's terrible." Jack's expression was an equal mix of horror and awe.

"Well, that's not likely to happen again anytime soon. And not from this snowfall. But there sure is a lot of it. Want to help me shovel?"

Months earlier, Susannah had arranged for Mabel Dunfee's husband, Tony, to come by with his plow to clear off her driveway and yard when it snowed, and he'd been here this morning. But the wind had blown the fine snow back over some of the areas he'd cleared.

"Sure thing." Jack picked up a handful of snow and tamped it into a hard white pellet.

"I know you have a shovel, because I sold it to you. Is it in the garage?" Corbin asked Susannah.

"I have two, actually," she said. "After I bought that one, I found another buried behind something in there." She began making her way toward the house, eager to get inside to change before Jack noticed her clothes, all of which belonged to Corbin, including the boots. They were too big, and she was carrying her own clothes and the bag of Polaroids besides, so the going was slow. But Jack was busy talking to Corbin and not paying attention to her.

Unlocking the door, Susannah took off Corbin's jacket, eased her feet out of his boots, and was about to head upstairs when Calista appeared. Damn. She must have come in through the porch door on the other side of the house, so Susannah would not have seen her footprints.

"Mom?" she said, and Susannah could feel her gaze taking in

the baggy sweatpants and the ugly sweater whose price tag still scratched against her neck. "What are you wearing?"

"The sweater? It's pretty awful, I know. But I thought it might fit into your collection—I'm sure Corbin would—"

"That's *Corbin's* sweater? And his sweatpants too? How about *that*?" She pointed to the shiny blue puffer Susannah had left on a chair.

"Well, yes. We went to dinner last night and then when the snow started coming down so hard, it seemed safer to stay over than to drive back." If only she'd gotten up the stairs before Calista had come in.

"You spent the *night* with him? How could you? What would Daddy say?"

Susannah saw her daughter's expression nakedly processing her emotions: incredulity, anger, grief. What should she do? Maintain the fiction and say she'd slept on the couch? But the lie would lead to further and even more bitter recriminations when the truth eventually came out. And it would come out, wouldn't it? It always did. "Daddy would be glad I had met someone who could make me happy. He wouldn't want me to be alone forever. I know he wouldn't."

"A year is hardly forever, Mom." Calista was practically shouting at her. "A year is, like, no time at all."

"A year alone is a long time when you're used to being with someone." She would not raise her voice; she would *not*. "A year is a long time to be lonely." Calista didn't answer, so she went on. "Besides, you don't even know him—you haven't given him a chance. He's a good man. Jack thinks so."

"Jack's not exactly what you call discriminating. And just because he's willing to forget about Daddy when some tool monkey in a down vest shows up doesn't mean that I am. Daddy was an *artist*, Mom! He wasn't just the owner of some backwoods hardware store."

"Who said anything about forgetting Daddy? And what's wrong with a hardware store owner anyway? People need hammers and nails and screwdrivers; your father admired anyone who could do anything with his hands and he would have admired the man who sold them what they needed." She was shouting now too; so much for her good intentions.

"If that's what you want to tell yourself, you do that." Calista was heading toward the porch. Susannah followed her and saw her yank the door open and let it fall shut with a bang. "Cally!" Susannah called, forgetting that she was not supposed to use this nickname. "Cally, come back!" Cally did not answer and she did not turn around.

The light reflecting off the snow was harsh and bright; Susannah had to squint to keep her daughter in sight, her zebra-striped coat easily visible in all that white. Susannah was pretty sure she knew where her daughter was going, but she would not call—at least not now—to confirm her hunch.

Instead, she went back into the house and upstairs, as she had been planning to do. Her hands were shaking, and when she looked in the mirror, her face was splotchy and red. She splashed some cold water on it, stripped off Corbin's clothes, and kicked the resulting heap away. *Damn, damn, damn.* What she had wanted to do was to relive every moment of their time in the bedroom this morning: how avidly he'd kissed her, the solid feel of his chest as he pressed against her, the way he kept his eyes open the whole time. Charlie had been playful and languorous in bed; there was nothing playful about Corbin. He was serious, focused, and passionate—almost feral, really—and even thinking about the sex they'd had made her want it all over again.

Susannah looked down at the heap of clothing still on the bathroom floor. It was not Corbin's fault Cally was being so difficult.

She knelt and retrieved the pile, bringing it into her room to fold. Then she brought everything downstairs to where Corbin was in the kitchen; he had made grilled cheese sandwiches for the three of them and Jack was already wolfing his down.

"I figured you'd be hungry," was all Corbin said, but something in his tone made her feel so—what was it? Seen? Known? Cherished?

Jack looked up from his plate. "We cleared a path to the house, Mom. You can go look when you're done."

"Thank you," Susannah said. "For everything."

"Where's Calista?" Corbin asked.

"Out," said Susannah.

"I'll bet she's over with that horse lady down the road," Jack said. "Alice, right? That's her new BFF."

"I wouldn't say that," Susannah said. She did not want to admit that he might be right.

"Oh, don't be too hard on Alice Renfew. She's probably lonely." Corbin took a bite of his sandwich. "Her husband died over twenty years ago. No kids. She tries to stay busy—she's the president of the garden club and on the board of the historical society and the library. She's active in town, knows a lot of people. But I'm guessing that Calista fills a need in her life."

Hearing Corbin describe it, Susannah almost didn't mind the bond Alice had with her daughter. *Almost.*

"I think it's weird." Jack used his finger to pry up a bit of melted cheese that had stuck to his plate. "I mean, she's, like, *old.*"

"Being different ages doesn't mean two people can't be friends," said Corbin. "Look at us, buddy. I'm a lot older than you are, but we're friends, right?"

"Right!" agreed Jack. "Do you think maybe after lunch we could build a snow fort? My dad and I used to do that . . ."

"Build a snow fort? Hey, I'm, like, the *king* of snow forts—just ask anyone in town."

Corbin and Jack bundled up and went outside to start on the fort while Susannah stayed inside to clean the kitchen. Fort building never had been her thing anyway; she didn't like the cold, which was ironic considering where she had chosen to live. As she worked, she could hear the muted sounds of Jack's high, excited voice. She loved how sweet and totally natural Corbin was with him; nothing forced there. It seemed they would be occupied for a while, so she went upstairs to look at the Polaroids again. Now that she was sure her mother was in Quebec for those few days, it seemed even more essential to find out with whom. She sat down at the computer and sent quick e-mails to Janet, Todd, and George about Linda; she'd let that trail go cold, but she was going to pick it up again. It was entirely possible that Linda would reveal something essential. And Friday Martha was stopping by with Harry Snady. Had he been the man with whom her mother had gone to Quebec? And even if he had, would he actually tell her?

The afternoon light was beginning to wane, casting bluish shadows on the snow outside. She heard the door open as Corbin and Jack came in, and she went downstairs. "Mom, you have to see the fort!" Jack led her to the window; his hand was freezing. "Look how big it is! And it's got a little opening so we can go inside."

Susannah stood looking at the domed structure made of snow and ice. "It's an igloo, isn't it?"

"Yeah. Corbin says the Eskimos are the guys to follow when it comes to snow—they know all about it."

Corbin came up behind her and casually put a hand on her shoulder. Even the light touch set her body humming. Calista would just have to learn to deal with this new development. Where was Calista anyway? If she had gone over to Alice's, it was time for her to come home. She was just about to text her daughter to say this when the phone rang. It was Alice. Susannah moved away from the window and went out to the porch.

"I just wanted you to know Calista's here with me," she said.

"Thanks for letting me know. Can you tell her to be home for dinner? There's a path to the house that Corbin and Jack shoveled, so if she comes around to the front door, it will be easier to get in." She was shivering a little; it was cold out on the porch.

"Actually, I wanted to talk to you about that. Calista's very upset and doesn't want to go home. She wanted to know if she can stay with me for a while."

"Stay with you!" Whatever softening she'd felt toward this woman earlier instantly vaporized. No, she did not want Calista staying with Alice. She did not want that at all. And since Calista was still a minor, she was going to put her foot down right now and insist that her daughter come home. If she didn't, Susannah was prepared to go over and get her.

". . . it wouldn't be any trouble to me; I'm just rattling around by myself in this great big old house anyway. And I think you know how fond I am of her. She'd be so very welcome—"

"You're very kind but that is *not* happening. Calista needs to come back home; this is where she belongs." Susannah looked out at the thick blanket of snow that covered the pond.

"I don't think you understand," Alice said. Did she sound patronizing or was this Susannah's projection? "When she got here, she said she was going to run away. She had it all planned out and it sounded, well, quite plausible."

"Run away? What are you talking about?" Susannah remembered how Calista had wanted to go live with her best friend. Had she actually been putting such a plan into motion? No. She was just being impulsive and dramatic, trying to get a reaction from her mother. Well, it was working.

"She wants to go back to New York. I suggested staying here with me as a compromise. You see, she's really quite unhappy at home right now."

"I'm well aware of that." Susannah knew her tone was frosty if not openly antagonistic. Who was this woman, encroaching on her family, her life? *What chutzpah!* as her grandmother would have said. But underneath her anger was the even more uncomfortable realization that Alice might actually be right—Calista's staying with her was a way of forestalling an even more radical move. She just wished she didn't have to admit it.

". . . know you had words today. Why don't you let her sleep here for a night or two while you both cool down? You can look at the situation again when you're calmer."

I don't need to cool down! Susannah wanted to say. That was not true, though; she had been shouting good and loud when Calista stormed out of the house. "I suppose it would be all right for a day or two," Susannah said stiffly. "But she has to go to all her classes and not miss any schoolwork—"

"I think that's all been taken care of," said Alice. God, but she sounded smug! "There's nothing to worry about on that front."

"All right, then." Susannah tried to be polite. "But I want to stay in touch with you. Daily."

"Of course," said Alice. "That goes without saying."

Susannah got off the phone and went back to the kitchen, where Corbin and Jack were playing pick-up sticks on the table. "I didn't even know they still made those," she said.

"The company is based in Nashua and I like to give a boost to local businesses, so I carry them in the store. There was a box in the glove compartment and I wanted to show them to Jack; he said he'd never seen them before."

Jack was concentrating on the plastic sticks, giving Susannah the chance to gaze openly at Corbin.

"I couldn't help but overhear," he said. "Calista's staying with Alice?" When Susannah nodded, he added, "This doesn't have anything to do with me, does it?"

"Why would it have anything to do with you?" Jack looked up from the game, not noticing that the red stick he held was about to touch another in the pile.

"I don't think your sister likes me very much."

"Why not?"

"Maybe she thinks no one can take your dad's place. And you know what, buddy? No one ever will. But that doesn't mean your mom can't have some company now and then. You too."

"Right." Jack looked back down at the pile of sticks. "I don't understand why she doesn't get that."

Me neither, Susannah wanted to say. But instead, she opened the freezer and took out a Pyrex container of chili. "How about I heat this up and you stay for dinner?" she said to Corbin.

"Sounds like a plan." He and Jack played another round of pick-up sticks, then moved on to checkers; Corbin had unearthed a mold-spotted box in the garage and brought it inside. Susannah was amused at how her son had so quickly taken up these retro amusements; pick-up sticks were already outdated when she was a kid, though she did recall playing checkers, maybe even with that very set.

The meal was easy and relaxed; the only off note was Calista's empty seat, which felt like a reproach. But Susannah tried not to let her daughter's absence ruin her mood, and when Jack went upstairs, Corbin pulled her into his arms for a long, heated kiss.

"Don't worry," he said when he finally let her go. "She'll come around. She just needs some time."

"I hope you're right," Susannah said. "Because I want to keep seeing you."

"And I want to keep seeing *you*. Are you busy on Saturday?" When she shook her head, he said, "Good. I'm going to be tied up with this Wingate thing all week, but we can get together then."

After he'd gone, she went into the kitchen in search of that open bottle of Malbec in the fridge. She hadn't served wine with dinner because she knew Corbin wouldn't be drinking it, but she really wanted a glass. It might help her settle down; otherwise, she was never going to get to sleep tonight. Carrying the wineglass upstairs, she opened her laptop again and found a message from Janet Durbin.

I just heard that Lynda Jacobsmeyer was living in Mexico, but I know she has family in the area and comes back east from time to time.

So it was Lynda, not Linda! It had never occurred to her to check an alternate spelling. Susannah hastily typed the name in and did another search. Lynda Jacobsmeyer popped right up. And even better, this Lynda, her Lynda, was a yoga and natural food enthusiast; she had a blog outlining her yoga practice and posted her vegan recipes. At the very bottom of the page was a contact button. Susannah composed a quick message and then went downstairs to refill her wineglass. Just one more, she told herself. It really had been quite a day.

Jack was still upstairs, so she sat by herself sipping the wine. It was so quiet here at night. So quiet and so still. There was a waning moon and in its cool, distant light she could see the drifts and mounds of snow that surrounded the house. What was visible of the trees faded into the darkness and all that remained glowed white. Was the snow isolating her or protecting her?

She got up from the table and turned off the lights. There was a little bit of wine left and she would finish it while she checked her e-mail one last time. The screen brightened when she opened the laptop, a familiar welcoming presence. And there, in the in-box, the message:

Long time! How many years has it been since your mom died? Eleven? Twelve? I can't remember exactly but I think of her often and I still miss her. She was a very special person. I've thought of you too, and wondered how you are. I wanted to be in touch but a lot has changed in my life this last decade—way too much to go into here. I'll be in Boston around the end of March. We could meet then if you want to drive down.

Did she want to drive down? If only Lynda knew how much. And by the time they met, she would have seen Harry Snady. Susannah did not fool herself into thinking Harry was going to reveal himself too easily to her. But she trusted her own instincts and believed that if he and her mother had been lovers, something in his manner would let her know. And that Lynda would be able to substantiate any hunch she might have.

I'd be happy to meet with you in Boston. Just name the day, typed Susannah. And she felt the rush of possibility as she hit send.

TWENTY-EIGHT

Grabbing her parka and her bag, Susannah headed for the door, which, unlike so many people here, she insisted on locking behind her, and climbed into the Jeep. Martha Dineen was behind the wheel, a torrent of apologies tumbling out of her mouth.

"I am *so* sorry I'm late. There was horrendous traffic on the bridge. And I couldn't even call you because I left my cell phone at home," Martha said.

"That's all right," said Susannah. "I'm just glad you're here now."

"So am I." This was uttered by the man—somewhat frail, but tall and dignified, with still abundant hair combed neatly back from a broad, slightly speckled forehead. "I've been wanting to meet you." Susannah turned to look at him—Harry Snady.

"There's a shopping center on the way and I thought you could drop me there; that way you and Harry can have some time alone."

"Thanks, Martha." Susannah was touched by her thoughtfulness. She climbed in back and Harry extended his hand. A heavy gold ring shone from one finger and his nails were neatly trimmed and buffed. "You're a vision," he said. "The very image of your beautiful mother."

"Thank you." This was the second time since she'd moved here that she had been told she looked like Claire. She had never thought so, but maybe she was wrong. Or maybe Harry just wanted to think so. In any case, he certainly sounded admiring. Even smitten. Was he the one?

"I've never forgotten her," Harry was saying. "She was one of the most talented amateurs I'd ever worked with. I think she could have been a pro if she'd wanted."

"That's what George said."

"Ah, George! How is he?"

"Fine. I think. At least he was the last time I saw him."

"I really should be in touch . . ." Harry turned his face to the window, and the bare, ice-glazed trees rushing by.

"It's Deedee, isn't it?" Martha had been quiet until now. "She doesn't want you to see anyone from the past—isn't that right, Harry?"

He cleared his throat. "Well, she's very protective of me. And I appreciate that. But maybe sometimes she goes overboard."

Martha did not answer, and Susannah didn't feel she ought to offer her own opinion of Deedee, so there was silence in the car. When Martha pulled into the mall's parking lot, she programmed the address of the clinic into her GPS. "You won't be able to call me since I don't have my phone," Martha said. "But I'll be waiting in the Starbucks in about an hour and a half; we can meet there."

Susannah got into the front seat and turned to Harry. "Do you want to join me? It might make it easier for us to talk."

"Good idea," Harry said, easing his way out of the back so he could come around to sit alongside her. Susannah noticed his brown chesterfield coat and scarf. The scarf must have come from Burberry; she recognized the plaid. Even through the scrim of age, vestiges of the handsome, well-put-together man he'd clearly been were still visible. Harry was quiet as Susannah navigated her way out of the lot and back onto Route 4, but once they picked up speed, he began to talk again. "I hope that Deedee wasn't too unfriendly," he began.

"Actually, she hung up on me. And she told me not to call again."

"I'm sorry." He seemed to shrink in his seat. "But she always felt that your mother held too special a place in my heart and it bothered her. So if you mentioned Claire, I can see how that would have set her off."

"Was there any basis for her suspicion?" Susannah was glad to keep her eyes on the road; it spared her from having to look at him as she probed.

"None. I was married to Deedee, and Claire was married to Warren. No, ours was a purely intellectual and artistic connection. We mingled minds, not bodies. Now, if she'd been free, things might have been different, because in all honesty I always was a little bit in love with her. And I like to flatter myself into thinking that maybe she was a little in love with me too."

"She always talked about you with real affection," said Susannah. This was not true; her mother had never mentioned him at all. Yet this could have been a strategic omission on Claire's part, a desire to cover up her true feelings.

"Did she?" His face brightened. "What did she say?"

"She talked about what a sensitive and nuanced director you were, and how you brought out the best in your actors." That sounded plausible, and it seemed to please Harry very much.

"I'm so glad to know she thought of me that way." He ran his hands over his hair, smoothing it back. "I always did try to nurture each actor's own special gift."

"What was my mother's?" Susannah asked.

"She had a great range," he said. "She could be young, lovely, fetching, and seductive. But she wasn't afraid to be unlovely, and that takes a very strong ego. She could do old, she could do shrewish, she could do crazy if she was asked to. And she had a real ear for poetry—she could recite Shakespeare and make it sound so natural, so credible."

Susannah's hands tightened on the wheel. Was this the opening she'd been waiting for? "She developed quite an interest in poetry. Was that something you had in common?"

"Absolutely," said Harry. "We both shared a love of Yeats, among others, and I even directed her in one of his plays. He was a playwright too—did you know that?"

"No." All she could think of was that volume of Yeats, the one in which she had found the note. Had Harry given her the book and tucked the note inside? She gripped the wheel more tightly.

"*The Countess Kathleen.* Fine production it was, too."

Susannah's mind was racing. Had Harry written those poems? Gone to Quebec with her mother? It really did seem possible. She was trying to find a delicate way to continue her probing, but when she glanced over at him, she saw he was dabbing at his eyes with a large white handkerchief.

"Are you all right?" she asked.

"Yes, I'm fine. Don't mind me. I've gotten more emotional with the years. It's just that thinking of your mother, and what we shared, has stirred up a lot of memories."

"Good memories?" Susannah ventured.

"Very good." He blew his nose and gave her a tremulous smile.

I can't ask him any more right now, Susannah thought. *It would be wrong. Cruel.* But even without any more questions, it seemed to her she had her answer.

To pass the time while Harry had his physical therapy, she had brought along a book about the Salem witch trials—she had a hunch that some of the same group hysteria might have been responsible for the condemnation of Ruth Blay—but she found she was unable to concentrate, so she decided to take a walk around Dover while waiting.

It was early March, and still cold, but some of the snow had started to thaw; Susannah had to pick her way through slushy puddles and mud-streaked mounds. There was not much to the town, but she found a thrift shop that yielded a waffle iron still in its original box. Jack would adore freshly made waffles. She bought it for five dollars, and on her way back to the clinic stopped at a bakery for two coffees and a bag of cinnamon rolls. When she got there, Harry was just emerging from his session and accepted the coffee gratefully. "You must have found Ella's," he said.

"I hope you like cinnamon rolls."

"Love them."

On the drive back, Susannah was acutely conscious of her time with him slipping away. "Did you ever have the sense that my mother was unhappy in her marriage?"

"Why do you ask?" Harry was already on his second cinnamon roll. "Did she ever say so?"

"Not explicitly. But I sensed a lot of tension between my parents. Especially the summer we came back here together."

"That was when?" Harry asked. "Sometime in the 1990s, right?"

"1994." So he knew about the visit. He must have seen her while she was in town.

"She called me and we tried to get together. But we didn't manage to make it happen."

"Too bad." How hard should she press? On the way here, her questions had elicited tears. "I know she took a trip to Quebec that summer. My father didn't go with her, though; she went with Lynda Jacobsmeyer." *Or you.*

"Quebec? I didn't know about that. Must have been lovely up there in the summer. Not that I would know—I've never been."

Really? Susannah wanted to ask. But here they were at Starbucks, where Martha was waiting for them. Harry must have gotten tired out from his therapy session; despite the coffee, he dozed the rest of the way back to Eastwood, waking only when they reached her house. When he did, he looked at Susannah with an expression that she could describe only as beatific, and clasped both her hands in his. His ring was heavy and cold against her fingers. "I'm so glad to have seen you, my dear. Thank you for accompanying me in a walk down memory lane. We'll meet again, won't we?"

"Yes, of course." Harry had to be the man who was her mother's lover. He was good looking and cultivated; he and Claire shared many interests. And he'd even said he'd been in love with her. What better proof than that? Yet he had not actually confirmed her suspicions. How could she get him to admit it?

Susannah let herself into the house feeling deeply unsettled. Of course Harry wasn't going to confide in her based on a single meeting. If she wanted an admission, she would need to gain his trust and confidence by cultivating him slowly. And since Deedee was not going to allow that, it would all have to be done on the sly.

She went upstairs and turned on her laptop. It was still early;

Jack wouldn't be home for a few hours. And Calista wouldn't be home at all. She hadn't seen her daughter once since she'd left; Calista had asked Jack to bring over her clothes, schoolbooks, and backpack rather than come and get them herself.

Well, she wasn't going to think about that now. And she wasn't going to think about Harry and her mother. She could channel her agitation into words and onto the page. Use the quiet turmoil to infuse her novel, the one she still hoped to convince Tasha she should write.

She looked over what she had written so far. The symmetry between the two dead babies, Abitha's and Ruth Blay's, was good from a dramatic standpoint. And it underscored the fact that there were so many stillborns in the eighteenth century; it was very likely that Ruth's infant was just one of a very large number.

After the death of Abitha's infant, my mother adopted very strict measures to protect me. She would let no one discuss the deaths of infants or children in front of me, and she made sure to keep any news of Ruth Blay from me as well. "The poor child has been frightened enough," she said. "No need to alarm her any further." It helped too that Abitha's husband died—was killed actually, when a restive horse he'd paid too much for at auction reared up and kicked him cleanly in the temple, splitting his head open—and Abitha moved away to be near one of her older children. Without the reminder, I was gradually able to let these events sift from my mind, like the coarse grains of grit that I rinsed from the squash we grew in the garden.

Seasons passed and years turned. I became a young woman, with a young woman's responsibilities and a young woman's longings. I spent days rolling out pastry dough, kneading bread, mending stockings, and stitching a quilt for my hope chest. I learned to grab a hen by the feet, pin her wings, and slit her throat in the time it took to recite the Lord's Prayer. Then, while the bird was still warm, I would gut and strip it, gathering the feathers to fill a quilt or pillow, and finally place her cleaned, denuded body into the iron pot to cook. That the naked creature's tiny wings and plump thighs resembled the arms and legs of newborn babes was an observation I could tamp down and ignore. "O, that way madness lies; let me shun that; No more of that." Those lines, from King Lear, would guide and instruct me.

When all my work was done and prayers duly said, I would slip out of my dress and into my cambric shift; I would lie very still in my maiden's bed, conjuring the man I might be lucky enough to marry. Would he be dark or fair, young and strong or older and well established? Would he be a blacksmith or a tinker, a baker, butcher, or tailor? A cooper or a candlemaker? Perhaps he'd be a soldier from the militia, one of those brave New Hampshire boys in the smart blue coats who had fought bravely in the Battle of Bennington or the Siege of Boston. The war had been going on for several years by then and we were lucky; New Hampshire did not see the worst of the fighting, though Portsmouth had been in danger from the British ships, and the capital was for a time moved to Exeter.

But the man I married, Joel Eastman, was none of these things. He came from the Eastman family of Salisbury—the very town where I had been headed with my uncle all those years ago. But this was mere chance, I told myself. It had nothing to do with that trip, or the discovery I made while we were on it. And of course Salisbury had changed in the intervening time.

My new husband was a prosperous gentleman farmer with a large herd of Jersey heifers and many acres of rich, fertile land. And he was a fine man too, all I could have hoped for and more.

After we were wedded, in 1785, I bade good-bye to my mother—my father had died some time before this, of the ague—and went with him to his home, a handsome two-story brick house with four chimneys and many windows. Inside, there was a center staircase, a parlor, dining room, six bedrooms, and a big, ample kitchen that became my sovereign domain.

He was gentle with me, Joel was, and the good Lord blessed us with three children in quick succession: Sally, Pettingill, and my namesake, little Betsey. I was a fortunate woman, and I knew it. Yet after the birth of the first, Sally, something strange befell me, something I could not name or explain, but whose grip was no less powerful for that. I was weak, of course. Childbirth, especially for the uninitiated, is torturous work, and my body needed time to heal. But even when it had, my mind did not follow suit.

Day after dismal day, I lay in my room upstairs, cocooned by the feather bed and the counterpane I had stitched for my hope chest. I did not want to see the infant I had brought into the world. Nor did I wish to eat, drink, or have discourse with anyone. One morning, Joel knocked gently and then opened the door. There he stood, twirling his hat on his finger, round and round again. I wished he would just go away. "Dearest, don't you want to get up today? The air is so fine; it would do you good," he said.

"I need to sleep," I said. "I'm still weak."

"But you've slept for so many hours," he said.

"Is it my fault that I'm still so weary from the birth?" I was petulant, wanting only to be left alone in the darkened room whose curtains I permitted no one to part.

"The birth was two months ago," Joel said quietly. "And the child—she needs you."

At first, I had fed little Sally because I had to, but I found the constant tug and pull of her tiny mouth upon my person an assault each time. I remained rigid while she suckled and had to force myself to place my arms around her. Finally Joel had hired a wet nurse from a town nearby, and now when Sally cried I buried my face in the pillow until the wet nurse attended to her and her cries ceased. This went on for several weeks; the child grew and thrived, but I took no joy in it. It seemed I could take no joy in anything.

In the end, it was my mother who saved me. Joel sent for her, and she came. Older she was, and less spry, but her mind was intact and her will strong. She marched over to the curtains and pulled them apart. The sun streamed in, so bright it hurt my eyes. "Close them, please!" I begged.

"Nonsense," she said. "Joel's a fool to humor you the way he does. You're getting up today. Come on, then." When I did not move, she came over to the bed and took my arms, as if to pull me to my feet. "There are only two paths, Betsey," she said. "Toward the light—" She turned slightly, toward the window. "Or toward the dark. And as hard as it is sometimes, we must always go toward the light."

Her words were simple, but somehow they broke through the shell around my heart. I let her ease me from the bed, help me dress, and brush my hair, which, I confess, I had allowed to grow tangled and matted in my despair. Then she poured the water from the ironstone pitcher into the bowl and I rinsed my face. Standing in front of the window, I looked down at the brick path that led up to the house and out at the trees surrounding it: oak, birch, maple. I took a deep breath, and then another. Somewhere, in another part of the house, there was a loud, insistent wail: a baby's cry. My baby.

"Bring her to me," I said to my mother. And she did.

Susannah printed out the pages she'd just written. If she actually got a contract to write this novel, she'd need to flesh out Betsey's marriage a bit more fully, and she made a few notes in the margin. It was only on a second reading that she realized just how much emotional truth she'd invested in that final paragraph. She felt exiled from her own child. So what if Calista was sullen, judgmental, accusatory, and angry? She was still her daughter, her darling girl. Nothing could ever change that.

Susannah got up. Even though she had been calling Alice in the evenings to get the "Calista report," today she just couldn't stand to wait. She picked up the phone and Alice answered almost immediately. "This is getting ridiculous. I want to talk to her." She had kept herself from calling Calista directly; she did not want to run the risk of yet another rejection.

"I can ask," Alice said. Her voice was low; was Calista in the room? "But this isn't a good time to discuss it. Why don't we speak tomorrow, earlier in the day? Better yet—why don't you come here for lunch?"

"Tomorrow is Saturday," said Susannah. "Won't Calista be there?"

"She's planned something with her friends," Alice said. "She won't be back until dinnertime."

Susannah was not at all sure she wanted to have lunch with Alice Renfew; her resentment was still running pretty high. But she squelched the thought. If having lunch with Alice would help her find her way back to her daughter, then lunch was what she would do.

TWENTY-NINE

Remnants of plowed snow were piled high by the side of the road and there were puddles in the ditches. The purity of the landscape was compromised by all the gray slush, but it was a welcome, if messy, harbinger of spring. On the way to Alice's, Susannah passed the barn and made her way up the walk, neatly shoveled to reveal the bricks, laid in a herringbone pattern, below. The door, painted a glossy black, matched the shutters, and lace curtains could be seen through the tall windows.

"Come in, come in," said Alice. She wore a knee-length tunic that appeared to have been made entirely of ribbons—gold, red, embroidered, silver—over black pants and a black turtleneck. As Susannah unzipped and handed over her parka, she felt that her bland gray slacks and ivory sweater were dull by comparison.

"Let's go into the dining room—everything's all ready." Alice turned and Emma turned with her; Susannah followed them both. All the rooms on this floor were painted the same shade of dusty rose; the color set off the white moldings. A rectangular mirror in an elaborate gilt frame hung over a mantel and a large vase of flowers dominated a low marble-topped table. The furniture looked to be antique—or reproduction, Susannah didn't know the difference—and all upholstered in various shades of pink. Needlepoint pillows dotted the sofas—there were two—and chairs, some of which had doilies draped over their rotund arms or backs. The walls were covered with paintings, some in oil, some watercolor, and everywhere, on every available flat surface, were veritable hordes of framed photographs.

Susannah took all this in quickly before sitting down. Alice went into the kitchen and returned with two bowls of corn chowder on a tray. She set them down and took her seat across from Susannah. The table seemed too large for just the two of them, but it had been covered with a floral-patterned cloth and was dense with china, cunningly folded napkins, silver saltcellars, and bud vases so the effect was cozy, not intimidating.

"I know you must feel mistrustful or even resentful of me," Alice said. Susannah had been about to taste the soup—enlivened by bits of red pepper and shrimp—but her spoon-holding hand stopped midway to her mouth. "Still, I think you know I feel a special bond with your daughter and I'm only trying to help."

"I appreciate that," Susannah said, caught off guard by Alice's candor. "But I'm not comfortable leaving this situation so open-ended. I want to set up some kind of timetable here. I want Calista to come home."

"She doesn't want to go home," said Alice. "That's what she's told me."

Susannah had a spoonful of soup to buy herself time; then she had another. It was delicious, and if she had not been having this conversation, she would have really enjoyed it. "This has been brewing for a while," she said finally. "Then Corbin put her over the edge."

"She can't see him replacing her father." Alice began to eat her soup.

"No one is replacing Charlie!" Susannah said. Obviously Alice had been getting her information—or misinformation—from Calista. "I've only gone out with Corbin a couple of times. She's distorting things—"

"Maybe she is," Alice said. "Which is all the more reason to let her stay here with me so she can adjust slowly, without having it rubbed in her face."

To sit here and listen to this woman she hardly even knew analyze her daughter made Susannah want to walk out of the house and never come back. But Alice was a way—the only way, really—to reach Calista. "Well, I want to be able to see her. Or at least speak to her. I don't want to be so totally cut off."

"Of course not," said Alice. "I'd feel the same way if I were in your situation."

But you're not in my situation! Susannah could not decide whether Alice was truly well intentioned or whether she was taking some covert—and perverse—pleasure in making her unhappy. She was trying vainly to frame a tactful reply when the phone rang.

"Please excuse me," said Alice. "I'm expecting a call, and if this is it, I'm going to need to take it." She got up from the table and walked into the kitchen. The dog followed.

Susannah was grateful for the small reprieve. She finished her soup and began to look around the room. Across from her was a low, highly polished wood sideboard on which sat a row of photographs in silver frames. Many of them seemed to be of Alice either alone or with a man she assumed to be her husband. She could hear the murmur of Alice's voice from the kitchen—she'd closed the door behind her—and she got up to take a closer look.

Here was Alice in a dramatic straw hat in front of the Eiffel Tower, and another, in a different hat, in front of the Trevi Fountain. But Susannah was more interested in the legendary Dr. Dave. Tall and broad, he had the body of someone who'd played college football, and a confident, easy smile. In the photos showing the two of them, he was always touching her—arm around her shoulder, pulling her close, holding hands. In one photo, obviously taken decades ago, they were dancing; in another, he was kissing her cheek. The marriage, at least in these pictures, looked like a happy one. And they were well matched in terms of their style: Dave wore elegantly fitting suits, some of them three piece; dramatic hats, like a fedora or a panama; and was partial to bow ties, which he sported with some panache. For a country doctor he was quite the natty dresser.

"So sorry! I had no idea that would take so long." Alice had come back into the room with a platter of small sandwiches. Susannah went back to her seat. Maybe looking at all those photos had softened her, because she no longer felt so resentful of Alice. Corbin had said she was lonely, and seeing the connection she'd had with her husband, Susannah was sure that was true. She knew what it was to lose and mourn a husband, and she wondered whether there had ever been another man in Alice's life after Dave died.

Susannah ate a sandwich—chicken salad, studded with walnuts and dried cranberries—and then the molasses crisps in a different, more accepting frame of mind. Alice was a good-hearted woman, she decided. Calista could have done worse in terms of companions. "Is she making any friends at school?" she asked.

"Not really," said Alice. "I think she finds her peers a bit unsophisticated after what she's been used to. But there are a few young people in town she's been friendly with."

"Yes, I know." Despite what Polly had said, Susannah did not entirely like—or trust—them.

"Oh, you mustn't worry." Alice had picked up on her disapproving tone. "They're a good bunch, really."

"You know them?"

"At one time or another I did; they were all patients of Dave's, and I have a fondness for them. Even the ones who've been struggling a bit. Or maybe especially the ones who are struggling."

Susannah considered this; hadn't Polly said she'd been too quick to judge? "Well, I'd like to meet them, then. Maybe Calista would want to invite them over—she could have a party or something."

"Maybe." Alice got up. "Would you like some tea or coffee? I can't believe I waited so long to ask."

Susannah looked at her watch. "You know, this has been lovely, but I really should be getting back now. We'll do it again soon." And she actually meant it.

The sun had come out, and as Susannah walked home she heard icicles dripping from the trees in audible plops. Jester, Alice's horse, had come to the barn window. Susannah did not cross the field to get closer; the snow was very deep. But she could see him looking at her and she paused for a moment, looking back.

The phone was ringing as she walked into the house, and she hurried to answer it. Martha Dineen was on the other end of the line.

"I've been meaning to call to thank you," Susannah said. "I really appreciate what you did with Harry."

"He really enjoyed it too. And given what's just happened, I'm especially glad he had that chance to talk with you."

"What are you talking about?" Had Deedee found out about their visit?

"It's Harry. You see, he's died."

"Died! When? How?"

"He had a stroke. Last night. It was sudden. And fatal. He was gone by the time the ambulance got there."

Like Charlie, flashed across Susannah's mind. And then, "Oh, no. How very, very sad."

"I know." Martha was weeping; she really had been fond of him. "The funeral is tomorrow. I'd ask you to come, but there's still Deedee to consider . . ."

"Of course," said Susannah. "I don't think she'd want to see me."

"No, I suppose not." Martha sniffed. "Anyway, I just thought you'd want to know."

"Yes," Susannah said. "I did. Thank you—for everything."

She said good-bye and stood motionless in her kitchen. *Was he or wasn't he?*

Whatever the answer, he would not be able to tell her. This realization left her feeling cheated and resentful. After all her relentless, even obsessive searching, this was all she was going to get? Had the story been a novel, she would have put it down in disgust. No satisfying arc, no closure. But she was a novelist, and she knew better than most people just how seldom life yielded the cohesion of art.

THIRTY

Susannah was still in the kitchen brooding about Harry when Calista phoned. She knew it must have been at Alice's prompting, but she didn't care. "I miss you," she blurted out. "I wish you would come home."

"I know you do, Mom. But I'm really happy here. Alice and I are having the best time. She's teaching me to cook all these really cool French dishes and she's got the most amazing collection of vintage clothes; I've been making patterns using her pieces."

"That's another reason to come back—your sewing machine is here."

There was a short pause. "Actually, it's not. I came over and got it. Along with all that fabric and stuff. Jack helped me."

"He did?" First the clothes and books; now the sewing machine? Was Calista moving in with her? "When?" Susannah felt vaguely betrayed; Jack had not even *mentioned* it.

"Yesterday. Jack said you had gone to the supermarket."

"I see." She felt as if she was going to cry, and she did not want Calista to hear.

"Listen, Mom, I know you're upset. But I guess you're doing what you have to do—I mean with Corbin. And I'm doing what I have to do. Can't we leave it like that, at least for now?"

No, we can't! Susannah wanted to wail. Hearing Calista sound so mature and reasonable was making her feel even worse; she was the adolescent here, and Calista the adult. "I still wish you would give him a chance. I can invite him over for dinner. You can get to know him."

"Not yet," said Calista. "I'm just not ready."

What could Susannah say to that? They talked for a few more minutes about school, and then said good-bye. Susannah did not ask if and when they would speak again; she was not sure she wanted to hear the answer. When the phone rang a minute later, she pounced. Maybe Calista was calling back to say she'd changed her mind or—

But it was not Calista calling; it was Corbin. "I'm going to have to postpone dinner tonight," he said. "I've got a big meeting with the people at Wingate first thing on Monday morning and I'll need the whole weekend to prepare. But let's get together Monday night. Either we'll have something to celebrate or you can help me drown my sorrows."

"All right." She was disappointed but maybe just a little relieved too. How was she going to manage to have a relationship that drove her daughter from the house? And it had been such a crazy day besides; Monday would be calmer—she hoped.

Jack came downstairs and flopped on the couch. "Can we make a fire? We haven't made one in a while. Maybe we could even toast marshmallows. Or make s'mores."

"Of course we could!" Susannah jumped up. She still had one child under her roof; she should make the most of any time he wanted to spend with her. But she saw that the basket holding the wood was empty.

"No fire?" Jack sounded disappointed.

"We can still have a fire. I just have to go out to the shed to get some wood."

"I'll go," he said, so ready to be the man.

"Are you done with your homework?" she asked.

"Not exactly . . ."

"Something tells me that means no."

Jack sighed. "It means no."

"Tell you what. Finish your work while I get the logs and start the fire. When you're down, we'll make the s'mores."

"Can we play checkers too?"

"Checkers too." Imagine that a kid with a whole arsenal of electronic entertainment at his disposal would want to play checkers; that was Corbin's doing. See, Jack liked him. Why couldn't Calista?

Susannah put a flashlight into the pocket of her parka and zipped up her boots. Then she ventured out. The lock on the shed door would not yield at first, but after a couple of frustrating, curse-inducing attempts, she was finally able to get it open.

Inside the shed it was cold and pitch dark; she flipped the flashlight on. Better. The wood was arranged in neat stacks, the pale ends of the cut logs facing out. In the far corner, she saw a faded blanket, speckled with wood shavings, covering up something that might or might not have been more logs.

Harry Snady's death should have curbed her desire to investigate further. But it didn't, and she went over to inspect. After all, she might yet find something that confirmed Harry's identity as her mother's secret lover.

Whatever it was she saw could not be reached easily, and she had to climb—or crawl, really—over some of the logs to get to the blanket. When she pulled it away, she found a very beaten-up-looking overnight case. The pattern was instantly recognizable—it was part of a set that her mother had owned. The case was covered in dust and the sticky residue of spiderwebs. And it was locked—of course.

Using the blanket, she wiped it down as best she could and looped the strap over her shoulder. Then she picked up two of the most accessible logs and brought everything inside. Jack was waiting by the door.

"I was getting worried," he said. "You were gone so long."

"Was I?" Susannah put the overnight case down; she hoped he wouldn't ask about it.

"And you're, like, all dirty. What were you doing out there, Mom?"

"Welcome to country life." She tried, lamely, to make a joke of it. "Woodsheds are funky places. Anyway, I've got the logs. Want to bring them over to the fireplace?"

Jack took them while Susannah stuffed the overnight bag in the pantry behind several rolls of paper towels; she would deal with it later. That didn't happen, though; first they made the s'mores and, with them, a pleasant, chocolaty mess that required cleaning up. Then Jack wanted her to quiz him for a history test he had the next day, and by the time they were done, she was tired and a little achy too; in climbing over those logs she had bruised her knees. She needed a hot bath and bed. Besides, she didn't want Jack coming in and asking what she was up to. The overnight case would wait until the morning, when he'd gone off to band practice.

But in the morning her plans were derailed again. Jack over-slept and missed the ride that would have taken him to practice, so Susannah had to drive him.

When she got home, she discovered that something had broken or burst in the washing machine—it had been nothing but trouble since she'd moved in—and now two inches of sudsy water was qui-etly pooling on the basement floor. After a few frantic calls to wash-ing machine repairmen, she managed to get one of them to come right over—and pay him double time for coming on a weekend.

As she opened the door to let him in, she saw that the raccoons had struck again: the garbage cans were lying on their sides and a trail of eggshells, coffee grounds, apple cores, and orange peels was littered festively around the yard, the red and orange bright against the snow. Alice had given her the name of someone who could deal with the animals, but she had never gotten around to calling him.

What else could go wrong? It almost didn't matter; she just had to inspect that bag. Jack was still out, so, leaving the mess in the yard for later, she hauled the overnight case out of the closet and took it into the kitchen. The lock was rusty and would not budge, but after she whacked at it with a hammer a few times, it popped open with an emphatic little *thwock*; now she could finally unzip the damn thing and look inside.

The bag was not very full. A little digging yielded a very sheer white nightgown, yellowed now, with a big ruffle around the neck-line and a long, bedraggled satin bow. Underneath was a pair of white satin bedroom slippers with marabou trim at the toes. The feathers were matted and a bit damp; they smelled faintly of mold.

Although this had certainly been her mother's bag, Susannah did not recognize either of these items, neither of which looked like anything her mother would have worn; she had to wonder whether

Claire had loaned the bag to someone else. Then, at the very bottom, she found a tiny bottle of Chanel No. 5, the once gold liquid now turned to the color of burnt sugar. But Chanel No. 5 had been Claire's signature scent; it was the only fragrance she wore, and Susannah recalled the numerous birthdays and Mother's Days when she or her father would present Claire with that iconic white box whose unadorned black lettering seemed the epitome of elegance.

Susannah set the nightgown and slippers on the table and regarded the flacon of perfume. If it *had* belonged to her mother, it was likely that the nightgown and slippers had been hers too. Maybe she had used this overnight case when she went to Quebec with her lover, the nightgown and slippers worn only when she was with him, a different woman leading a different—and secret—life.

Finally, she put the bottle down too. Was there anything she had overlooked? The case seemed empty, but there could have been something else at the very bottom. Susannah reached her hand in once more. There *was* something down there, some scrap of fabric, maybe a pair of underpants or a slip. What she pulled out, however, was a red silk bow tie, quite creased, with a subtle pattern woven into the silk. A *bow tie.* Why was it in here, with the nightgown and the slippers? Because it was another precious artifact, worn by her mother's lover when they were together? She knew that he was a poet, that he was married, and that he might or might not have been Harry Snady. And now she knew that he wore a bow tie.

Just, she realized with a thudding shock, *like Dr. Dave.*

THIRTY-ONE

Susannah sat down on a kitchen chair. Was it really possible that Dr. Dave, David Renfew, Alice's adored husband, had been her mother's lover? She suddenly, urgently wanted it to have been Harry, especially now that he was no longer alive. Dave was dead too, but Alice was very much alive—Alice, who had infiltrated her family and alienated her daughter.

Abruptly, Susannah got up and brought everything to her room. This new revelation was so startling, so disruptive, she didn't know what to do; she had to talk to someone. Corbin. He'd know just what to say. But he didn't pick up, so she left a message saying only to call her back as soon as he could. She knew he was busy preparing for his big meeting the next day. Still, she hoped he'd find the time to get back to her sooner than that.

She was almost grateful for the mess in both the basement and the yard; she had something to do with her restless energy, some problem she could attack—and solve. The water from the ruined washing machine—she was having a new one installed next week—was gone, but there were still plenty of gummy or soap-slick spots that needed scrubbing. Then the raccoon-generated debris in the yard took half an hour to clean up.

Around dinnertime, Jack called to ask if he could spend the night with a boy in his grade named Grant.

"It's a school night," Susannah pointed out.

"I know, but his mom says it's okay and we'll take the bus together tomorrow. He lives closer than we do, so I can sleep a little later." When he sensed her wavering, he added, "Please, Mom? I really want to." It was the first time he had mentioned Grant, and Susannah was glad his circle of friends was widening. She said yes.

That meant Susannah was alone. Alone and quietly frantic. She didn't know what to do with herself. She didn't even feel she could call Alice to check in on Calista; she didn't trust herself to talk to her.

Too agitated to read or write, Susannah turned on the television and found a good station out of Boston that played old movies; tonight's offering was one of her favorites, *All About Eve*. With pillows behind her and an afghan over her legs, she tried to settle down to watch the film. It was working, sort of, and she thought that it would have been nice to have some company, even of the nonhuman variety; for the first time since she'd gotten here, she considered the idea of a pet. Alice had the ever elegant Emma. And Polly had recently acquired a sleek Siamese cat with ash-tipped paws and tail. Still, a pet was a major responsibility; she'd have to mull it over some more. But at least she was thinking about something besides her mother and the two men she might have been involved with.

Bette Davis had just told her guests to fasten their seat belts when Susannah heard the noise outside. It sounded like something scratching or shuffling, and her first thought was, *Those damn raccoons.* Good thing the guy Alice had recommended would be here next week too, along with the brand-new Maytag.

The noise got closer and whatever it was out there sounded, well, bigger than a raccoon. Could it be a moose? Or a bear? Since Corbin had put in that motion-sensitive camera, she and Jack had seen pictures of several deer, an owl, a fox, and a moose that may or may not have been the one she'd already seen. Then she heard a loud thump and a very distinct word: *Shit.* It wasn't an animal out there. It was a *person.*

Petrified, she muted the television. Then she unmuted it again; she didn't want him—because it was almost certainly a man—to know she was on to him. Was he a burglar, a rapist, a *murderer*? Her phone was in the kitchen, charging; she could creep over, get it, and call nine-one-one. In a few silent, terrified seconds, she managed to reach the kitchen; then something smacked hard against the window and, in her terror, her hand shot up and the phone flew out of it and across the room like a missile. She screamed.

"Susannah! Don't yell! It's me—Corbin!" The voice was muffled, but she could still hear it.

"Corbin!" She ran over to see and, sure enough, Corbin was standing outside, head and shoulders caked with snow. But what was he doing here? Quickly, she went to the door and unlocked it.

"You scared me—" she began.

"I'm sorry—I'm so sorry—I just—" He came into the house stumbling a little.

"Why didn't you ring the bell or call me to let me know you were coming?"

"Sorry," he repeated. "Sorry, sorry, sorry." Flopping down on the couch, he unzipped his jacket and sent a little spray of snow flying. Then he leaned over and put his head to his knees. Anne

Baxter had just given a brilliant audition and Bette Davis was in a lather; Susannah clicked the television off and stared at Corbin.

He was drunk, that's what he was. Now that she stood closer, she could even smell the liquor on him. "Corbin," she said, sitting down next to him. "Corbin, what's happened?"

"Wingate," he mumbled into his knees. "The meeting. Monday."

"Yes, I know," she said. "You've been getting ready. Preparing."

"Oh, I'm ready." His head shot up. "Ready, willing, and able."

"So then why are you . . . drunk?"

"Drunk? Who said I was drunk?" He looked around the room for his accuser, ready to take him on. "I'm not drunk. No way, José. Nyet."

"Darling." She took a different tack, her voice gentle and low, her hand on his knee. "Won't you tell me what happened?"

"The meeting," he moaned more than said.

"I already know about that." They were back to square one; getting information from someone this wasted was not easy.

"No," he said. "No, you don't. Yeah, there's going to be a meeting. But I'm not invited."

"What are you talking about?" Was this more drunken rambling? He did sound more coherent, though.

"Wingate. That snake. That *bastard*." He started breathing heavily. "He wanted me off the committee. Out. Done. Finito."

"But why?" She had seen him at the town hall meeting, remembered how everyone looked up to him, admired him.

"I scare him."

"What do you mean, you scare him? Did you threaten him?"

"No!" He looked insulted. "You know me better than that."

"So then what—"

"Wingate needs a puppet—someone he can control. That's not

me." He leaned his head back on the couch, closed his eyes, and pressed his fingers to the bridge of his nose. "I'm tired . . ." he said. "Really tired. All that work I've put in on the case. Two of my employees down at the store just up and quit—no warning, no explanation. And those applications just sitting on my desk— it's like they're sneering at me."

"Applications? What applications?"

"To law school."

"I didn't know you were reapplying to law school."

"I didn't want to tell anyone unless I got in. But I figured if you could come here and reinvent your life, I ought to be able to do it too. Especially since I don't have to move to another state and I don't have kids depending on me."

"Where?" She thought he would make an excellent lawyer.

"Boston College. New England Law. Places where I can go at night, so I won't have to give up the store. It'll take longer. But I think it will be worth it."

"I think you're right." She reached out to touch the side of his face and his hand moved up to cover hers.

"Can I sleep here, Susannah?" he asked. "Please? I won't be any trouble . . ."

"Of course you can." Then it hit her. "Corbin, how did you get here?" She withdrew her hand from under his.

"I think you know the answer to that," he said. "Unless you want me to tell you that little story about the stork."

"No, I mean, how did you get to my house tonight? Did you drive?"

He nodded and made a vague gesture with his arm. "Car's out there somewhere. I left it on the driveway. I wanted to surprise you." He smiled, a smile that was as inviting and sexy as ever.

Susannah did not smile back. Bad enough that he fell off the wagon and got drunk. But *driving* drunk? That was a whole other level of self-destructiveness. What if he'd gotten into an accident and hurt himself—or someone else? She would not look at his face as she helped him off with his boots and fetched a pillow and blanket. Then she brought him a tall glass of water, and a bottle of Tylenol for the hangover that was waiting in the wings, and sat with him until he fell asleep.

After that, she went up to bed, where she remained awake for a long time. Part of her still wanted him with her in bed. The gentle weight of him on top of her. The feel of him as their bodies curled together in sleep. Yet she did not get up to invite him to join her. Corbin Bailey may have been the sexiest man in the entire state. Or the entire country. But he came with way more baggage than she had first realized—and, really, didn't she already have enough baggage of her own?

THIRTY-TWO

"Jesus, am I sorry." Corbin was sitting in her kitchen very early the next morning; a mug of strong black coffee sat steaming in front of him. "I haven't had a drink in more than fifteen years. But that thing with Wingate—it was a kick in the teeth. A punch in the gut. Or both. It threw me—it really did. So I told myself I would just have one. One couldn't hurt."

"But it wasn't just one." Susannah stirred milk into her own coffee.

"It never is." Corbin said. "At least not for me." He picked up the mug and took a sip.

"Is there anyone to appeal to? Any way to get Wingate to change his mind?"

"He says he won't negotiate at all if I'm involved. So for the sake of the pond, I should just bow out without making a major issue of it. It's the pond that's important—not my ego."

"And you think he'll do the right thing?"

"That prick? No. But he'll make a show of considering it—that

way, it looks like he's a reasonable guy. When in fact he's manip-
ulating the situation to serve his own agenda—he doesn't care at
all about the pond or the people who love it."

Susannah got up. "I'm making oatmeal; would you like some?"
She almost hoped he'd say no, but he didn't, so she went over to
the stove to prepare it. A few minutes later, she brought over the
bowls and sat down to eat. Maybe he sensed her discomfort,
because he finished the oatmeal quickly and stood up to leave.
"Look, I wanted to tell you again how sorry I am—"

"It's all right. I'm just glad you weren't hurt. Driving over here
when you were drunk was *not* smart."

"—and that I wanted to make it up to you somehow." When
Susannah didn't answer, he added, "We're still on for tonight,
right?"

"About that . . ." she began.

"If you can't make it, we could do it another night . . ." He
studied her face. "Or not."

"I'm not sure what I want." There, she'd said it. "I'm very attracted
to you. And I like you—a lot. But what happened last night—"

"Will never happen again."

"Can you say that for sure?"

"Who can say anything's for sure?" He sounded wounded. Also
angry. "But if it makes you feel any better, I'm going to go to a meeting today." When she said nothing, he elaborated. "A twelve-step
meeting."

"I knew what you meant," she said. "But this isn't about me
feeling better. It's about you. You say you fell off the wagon because
you were stressed, disappointed, and angry. Well, life is filled with
stress, disappointment, and anger; how are you going to handle
yours? With a drink? Or four?"

"Hey, no need to get nasty." His expression hardened. "I know what I've done and I know what I'm going to do. But if you don't trust me—"

"Trust is something you have to earn—"

"And I haven't earned yours." He stood and zipped up his jacket. "Yeah, I get it. I really do."

Susannah followed him to the door. Was she doing the right thing? Maybe she was being too judgmental. Too harsh. "Will you be okay getting home? I can drive you if you want."

"That," he said, "won't be necessary." Then he left. She stood there in the wake of his departure, not sure whether she felt relieved or gutted. She realized she hadn't told him about Dave Renfew and the bow tie.

Susannah gathered up the dishes and put them in the sink to wash. If she took a break from seeing Corbin, would that mean Calista would come home? That was the first even remotely positive thought she'd had since she'd opened her eyes. She immediately picked up her phone to call her.

"I can't really talk. I'm getting ready for school." Calista didn't even bother with *Hello*.

"I'll make it fast." Susannah knew she should wait, but she so badly wanted her girl back under her roof again.

"So you're not going to see him because of me?" Calista asked.

"That's part of the reason, but there are other reasons too." No need to go into them, though. "Maybe I was moving a little too fast." There was a silence. "So you can come back home, okay? Now that you won't have to deal with Corbin—"

"But I like living with Alice. Even if Corbin isn't around, I don't want to come home. I want to stay with her."

"You don't get to decide. You're still a minor and I'm not giving my consent, Calista. You have to come home."

"Try to make me!" Calista flared. And then hung up.

Her anger was strangely comforting to Susannah; it made her feel adult again. Adult and in control. It also made her own anger justified—at her daughter, and at Alice too, for acting as a wedge between them. Under the guise of concern for Calista, she was alienating her from her own family—

The phone rang again. It was Alice. "Susannah, I have to tell you that I heard that last conversation. Or at least Calista's side of it. And I'm sure you're very upset—"

"I'm not upset," Susannah said. "I'm furious and I—"

"I know, I know. But I have a suggestion. Why don't you come for dinner tomorrow? The three of us, though you can bring Jack too if you think it's a good idea. We can talk things over sensibly."

Susannah said nothing. She felt so condescended to, so *patronized* by this woman—but what other choice did she have? "I'll be there," she said finally. "What time?"

"Come at six," Alice said. "We have a lot to discuss."

We have a lot to discuss, Susannah mimicked in her head. *We? Who's we? You're nobody to us. You're nobody to me.*

The phone was still in her hand and she quickly called Polly; why had she waited so long to confide in her? Luckily, Polly picked up right away. Curling up on the couch under the afghan, Susannah spilled the whole improbable story.

"I don't even know where to start," Polly said. "Your mom? Calista? Or Corbin?"

"Take your pick," Susannah said. "I'm drowning and you're the life raft."

"You're not drowning, honey," Polly said. "But you are flailing. First things first. You go to that dinner tomorrow night and you keep an open mind. Very open. Calista is acting out like crazy—just be glad she picked a classy septuagenarian and not a bunch of coke-snorting stoners to do it with."

"I think there are a few of those in the picture too." Susannah thought of those indistinct figures she'd seen in the cars that had come to pick Calista up.

"All the more reason to have a counterweight." Polly took a breath, as if just gearing up. And after forty-five minutes of her advice, sympathy, and occasional burst of wit, Susannah felt better—and then she immediately felt worse. She had not worked for days; she'd better get some writing time in today. She hoisted herself off the couch. The dishes were drying, the counters wiped, and the floor swept. She'd put her house in order and she was ready to begin. Somehow the agitation was working for, and not against, her and she was able to enter the story easily.

We had been living in Salisbury for about three or four years when I met Prudence Dunne. She was a good decade older than I was and she had come from Portsmouth, where her husband had been the jailor. She told me she had not liked being the jailor's wife and even when she knew those imprisoned belonged behind bars—the man who'd killed his wife and three children as they slept, another who'd burned down his neighbor's house and barn—she still felt pity for their wretched state. "And then there were the women," she said. "I remember that poor Ruth Blay, plain as day, locked up for killing her newborn babe. I used to see her sometimes when I went down to the jailhouse to meet my William. She had such a fine manner, even in jail. Always "please" and "thank you" and "would you be so kind." I never believed the things they said about her."

Prudence and I were in her kitchen, and she had just poured the tea from a blue-and-white-flowered pot. Just hearing that name again was like a spike pressing into my hand. But I did not tell Prudence about my unfortunate connection to Miss

Blay. I had not even told Joel; there had seemed to be no reason to dredge all that up again. "I heard about her." I worked to keep my voice even. "It was all such a long time ago." I did not want to talk about it. Not then. Not ever.

Then Sally and Pettingill came bursting into the room, along with Prudence's two youngest boys. They were all flushed with excitement. "We want to go down to the creek," said John, the older of the two. "Please say yes, Mother."

Prudence seemed to be thinking it over as she sipped her tea. My two were fairly dancing with anticipation, Sally hopping back and forth from one foot to the other, Pettingill tugging on her hand. It was a warm day in June, much like that other day, I realized. That day I did not allow myself to remember, except when the memory came unbidden, late at night as I slid down into sleep, or at dawn when I wrested myself from it again.

"You children may go," she said at last, and a muted whooping arose from the four of them. "But, John, I am placing you in charge. No one is to go in any higher than his or her knee, and you're to stay in the cove at all times."

"Yes, Mother. Thank you, Mother," said John, ushering the others out of the room. "I'll watch them."

Prudence was about to say something when little Betsey started fussing in her wooden cradle nearby, and I went to pick her up. Even this slight noise caused my breasts, already so taut and full, to leak and I did not need to look down to know that the front of my dress was wet. I quickly unbuttoned and put the baby to my exposed breast to suckle. She latched on and greedily began to drink. She had a good appetite, this one, and she would grow healthy and strong. "There, my little poppet," I said softly, using the term of endearment my own mother had so often used. "Drink your fill."

I did not look up but I could feel Prudence watching me. Still cradling the child, I stood. "I think I need to lie down for a bit," I said. "Won't you please excuse me?" I did not want this moment, fleeting as I knew it was, to be marred by anything else she might choose to say. I remembered the darkness that had enveloped me when my firstborn came into the world. I had rallied, and I had never been afflicted that way again. But the memory stayed with me, and gave the infancy of each successive child an almost aching sweetness. I knew how quickly the time raced by, and how soon the nurslings began to teeth, tumble, walk, and talk. I would surrender this babe to the world soon enough; best I should keep her close and tend lovingly to her as long as I was able.

The next weeks were especially busy and I did not have a chance to visit with Prudence again. But in early July she called on me, and it was my turn to pour the tea, from a pot that was not blue but pink and silver lusterware with a border of tiny flowers across the rim. Joel had ordered a whole set all the way from London as an anniversary gift and I cherished the shimmering pieces, proudly displaying them along with my pewter and silver plate on the Chippendale lowboy I kept oiled and polished in my dining room.

"May I offer you a scone?" I asked Prudence. My scones, buttery and flaky, were a point of pride, and this batch had come from the oven only a scant hour ago; they were still warm.

"Yes, thank you." She took the scone and spread it liberally with apple jelly.

The children were off riding with Joel, except for Betsey, asleep in her cradle. She was just beginning to crawl and I had my hands full keeping up with her; I was glad for the short reprieve.

"I remembered something else about Ruth Blay." Prudence seemed to devour the scone in a mere bite and she helped herself to another. No wonder she was so stout, with chubby hands and little ripples of flesh wreathing her chin.

I was silent. Though it had happened years ago, I had never forgotten the sight of that proud, pale woman being taken away in the cart. And I'd never forgotten my own unwitting role in bringing that about.

"It was about the father of the child. She never named him, you know." She eyed the plate of scones but did not take a second one. *"They said it was because he was married."*

How could Ruth Blay go to her grave without revealing the identity of the man who'd brought her to the gallows? *"Could it be that, despite all, she had loved him and perhaps even wanted his child? Because there are ways . . ."*

"If you mean pennyroyal and the like, I don't blame her for not daring to try it. The devil's weed is what it should be called—women have died from it." Temptation got the better of her and she helped herself to another scone.

"But she died anyway." I glanced down into my empty cup where the dregs made a lacy pattern at the bottom.

"There was a man whose name was spoken in connection with hers . . ." Her eyes seemed almost to glitter. *"John Page."* I must have looked blank, because she continued, *"Reverend John Page. From Hawke. She'd been teaching there for a time and he was the one to oversee her work."*

"A man of the cloth!" Poor Ruth.

"A very learned man," continued Prudence. *"He got his training at Harvard and he was married, with children of his own. But he might have taken a fancy to her—they say he liked his*

liquor and he liked the ladies. And she had a way about her, she did. Even being in jail couldn't dull her light."

I considered Ruth's decision to keep silent. Even if she had named Page—or another man—there was no certainty that she would have been believed. And such a revelation would have ruined her reputation as well as his. They would have lost their positions and been subject to a cruel and public whipping. So it was little wonder that she had stolen off to South Hampton to have the baby alone.

"Do you truly think she killed it?" I asked. Maybe she planned to give it to a childless couple. I wanted to believe that about her; I wanted it very badly.

Prudence shook her head. "No, I don't. She was so very remorseful. And having a baby, and a first baby at that, all by herself? No midwife or other women to help; no groaning beer or groaning cake to make it a little easier? Even with all the help, babies die—why, I lost two of my own. No, the birth could have gone wrong in so many ways. It's just that this baby was hidden away. And then found . . ."

"That was very unfortunate for her." I could scarcely get these words out; it was as if guilt had clamped a hot, heavy hand across my mouth.

"I heard it was a bunch of children playing in the barn," Prudence said. "They pried up some boards and there was the babe, stiff and still as wax. I can imagine such a sight would haunt you forever."

"Forever . . ." Suddenly I stood. The guilt I had been feeling turned to bile, bitter and choking, and I had to step quickly outside and go behind the lilac bush, where I emptied the contents of my stomach. I stood gasping and panting for a few seconds before walking somewhat unsteadily to the well. I drew

a bucket and used the cool water to rinse out my mouth and wash my damp, sticky face. Then, feeling somewhat restored, I returned to the house. My guest was standing in the back doorway, looking at me with an expression of great concern. "Are you unwell?" asked Prudence.

"Yes and no," I said. Now that I was calmer, I understood the true meaning of what had just transpired. It had not been simply the awful burden of my guilt rising up inside me; I was once again with child.

THIRTY-THREE

The next afternoon, Susannah knocked on Jack's door to tell him about the dinner at Alice's and ask if he wanted to come along. His clarinet was out; he must have been about to start practicing.

"There's going to be yelling, isn't there?" he asked.

"Why do you say that?"

"Because I know you're mad that Cally won't come home."

"I'm hurt by her behavior," Susannah said carefully. "And yes, I suppose angry too."

"See?" Jack looked at her imploringly. "Yelling. Don't make me go, Mom. I really don't want to."

"You don't have to. Will you be all right here by yourself?" She knew he still didn't like to be left alone.

"Sure." And after a pause, "Maybe Corbin could come over for a while. You know—we could hang out."

"He's busy today." She wanted to get off the topic. Jack had clearly bonded with Corbin and was going to miss him. So, she had to admit, was she. In fact, she missed him already and more than once had replayed the night they'd spent together in minute and lacerating detail. But then she thought about him stumbling around drunk outside her house and, even worse, driving in that condition, and decided she could move beyond those memories.

"I'll be okay." He picked up the clarinet. "I'm going to practice for a while. And later I have a science project I should be working on."

"Okay, but if you change your mind, you can always walk over." She lingered in the doorway for a moment, but he picked up his instrument. She'd been dismissed.

When Susannah arrived at Alice's, she found her as gracious as ever, ushering her into the living room and offering her a drink, which Susannah accepted. A good glass of wine might take the edge off the conversation that loomed. When Calista came tripping downstairs—even her tread seemed so much lighter here— Susannah stood. Her daughter was wearing a gray knit jumpsuit with silver buttons the size of bottle caps running down the front; her narrow waist was cinched by a claret-colored suede belt. Susannah did not recognize the garment and wondered if it had come from Alice.

"Doesn't she look marvelous?" Alice said. "Geoffrey Beene, late 1970s. It was too big—of course—but Calista was able to take it in herself."

Susannah's intuition had been correct. "It's great," she said. Calista's own quirky sense of style was definitely being honed and polished by spending time with Alice. She took another sip of the wine.

As they sat down in Alice's dining room—she had changed

the tablecloth to a blue and white paisley and added several tall white candles in crystal holders—Susannah tried not to look at the framed pictures of Dave. What if one of those photographs showed him wearing the red bow tie? She would not be able to concentrate on anything else.

While Alice served the salad and passed the bread, Calista had been dispatched to the kitchen and brought in a bowl of ratatouille, which she set on the table. Emma looked up briefly but then settled her long, tapered snout back on her paws again.

"We made it together," she said. "But she really did most of the work." Alice looked fondly at Calista. "I think your daughter has the makings of a superb cook; soon she'll be as skilled in the kitchen as she is with the sewing machine."

"That's because you're such a good teacher." Calista sat down and shook out her napkin before placing it on her lap. "Mom, can I serve you?"

Susannah nodded. This display of mutual admiration had sucked the words clean out of her and she bent over her plate, trying to concentrate on the food. The delicately seasoned meal might have been lumps of papier-mâché for all the enjoyment she had putting it in her mouth, but she tried to feign an appropriate response.

"It's been wonderful having Calista here with me," Alice said as she dipped a bit of bread into the sauce. "I hadn't realized how little I liked being alone—until I wasn't any longer."

"And I love being here, Mom. It's like being in a museum or something. Alice has the most amazing collections—she's been teaching me all about them. Crystal, paintings, porcelain, silver . . ."

Alice laughed. "Nothing here is museum quality, not by a long shot. But Dave and I did a lot of traveling and I was always picking up something in a flea market or an out-of-the-way little shop.

We did have fun . . ." She paused. "And it's so nice to have someone to share it with again. In the summer, I often drive to estate
sales—not that I need anything, but I still take delight in the hunt.
I'm hoping I can take Calista with me sometimes. Maybe we'd
even get to do a Paris trip, though summer is not an ideal time to
be in Paris. I'm thinking the countryside would be better—
Provence, or the Loire Valley."

Susannah put her fork down and looked from one besotted
face to another. Cooking, sewing, trips to France. What a charming little lovefest was going on here. What an absolute *blast*. "I
can see how you're enjoying this interlude together. But I think
you're forgetting that it really is an interlude."

"Does it have to be?" asked Alice.

"Yes. Calista is my daughter and I want her to come home—
sooner rather than later." Did she really not get it? Or was she
taunting her? Susannah truly could not tell. She turned to her
daughter. "I know you were upset about Corbin. But you won't be
seeing him much. You might not be seeing him at all."

"Oh, I heard about the other night . . ." murmured Alice.

"What did you hear?" Susannah was aware of how harsh she
sounded, but really, Alice's comments were so inappropriate, so
invasive.

"That he'd had too much to drink and foolishly drove over to
your house. He's very lucky he wasn't hurt."

"That's not the point." Susannah was sorry she'd even brought
him up. "I just know Calista was upset by seeing him and I want
to let her know that isn't going to be an issue—at least not now."

"But I still want to stay here," said Calista. "It's not even about
Corbin anymore."

"Calista, I'm still your mother; you belong at home with me."

Susannah saw a look that passed between Alice and Calista, a look that excluded her with all the finality of a door slamming in her face. She averted her gaze, which settled on a picture of Dave. She was *not* going to focus on that now.

"Of course you're her mother—no one is disputing that," Alice said. "But it's also fair to say that Calista and I share a special bond, a bond that might even be equal to—or surpass—the biological one."

"If you had any children, you wouldn't say that—you'd know better." The comment, flung like a grenade, created a short, stunned silence. Then both Alice and Calista started talking at once.

"I'm sorry if I offended you—"

"Mom, you're being so *mean*—"

"Your mother doesn't intend to be mean," Alice said. "This is all so new to her; she doesn't really know how to respond. Sometimes it takes someone outside the nuclear family circle, someone with greater objectivity who can—"

"Just stop!" Susannah pushed her wineglass away; it toppled, but fortunately it was empty and merely rolled across the table. She righted it and stood up. "I'm fed up with your acting so enlightened and superior—"

"I don't feel superior. Far from it." Alice remained seated. And calm, which made Susannah even angrier. "I'm just saying that an outsider might be able to see what an insider is blind to, that's all. It's a matter of perspective."

Instead of answering, Susannah went over to where the photographs were grouped. Red, red, where was the damned red one? She did not see a single photograph in which Dave was wearing a red bow tie; could she have been wrong? But there were other photos in this house, scads of them, and she marched into the other room, scanning the framed snapshots on the end tables, credenza, and mantelpiece.

"Mom, what are you *doing?* Are you *crazy?*" Calista's voice came from the other room.

Susannah ignored her and just when she thought she really was crazy and had invented the whole thing, she saw it. Dr. Dave, in a crisp white shirt, dark blue blazer, and vivid red bow tie. The photograph was eight by ten, considerably larger than many of the others, and when she snatched the thing up from the shelf, she could even see the suggestion of the pattern woven into the silk—just like the tie she had found in her mother's overnight case.

When she turned around to go back into the dining room, she saw that Calista, Alice, and even Emma had followed; they were clearly confused and waiting to see what she would do next. "You think you know everything," Susannah said. "That you've been blessed with such extraordinary vision. But did you know—did you even have a clue—that your husband, your beloved, sainted Dr. Dave, was having an *affair?*"

"What on earth are you talking about?" Finally Alice seemed flustered and Susannah took a spiteful, even savage pleasure in having pierced her infuriatingly intact armor. "That is pure and unadulterated nonsense. He adored me; we adored each other. What other woman could have turned his head?"

"My mother, that's who!" spat Susannah. "Your husband was having an affair with my mother. I don't know for how long, and I don't know why or when it ended. But I know it happened."

"I'm sorry to say this, especially in front of Calista, but I do think you've gone off the deep end, Susannah. Maybe it's your anger at me, your grief over your husband, or your disappointment over Corbin, but you're totally unhinged. Dave and your mother? Not possible. Simply not possible."

"Does the name Le Chat Noir mean anything to you?" Somewhere inside was a voice telling her not to reveal what she'd learned in front of Calista, but her fury—and her hurt—were so much louder; together, they drowned the voice out entirely.

Alice looked confused. "No. Should it?"

"Le Chat Noir is a restaurant in Quebec. I've got proof that my mother was there with a man, and that man was your husband."

Alice looked blank and then suddenly her face went ashen and her mouth dropped open slightly; for a second, Susannah thought she might have caused her to have a stroke. Then she seemed to recover, at least enough to speak. "Calista, darling, I am going to have to ask you to go back home with your mother now."

"Why?" cried Calista. "Please don't make me go with her! She's crazy—you even said so!"

"No, I'm afraid I was mistaken. Deeply mistaken. You can come back again tomorrow. But tonight I need to be alone."

Calista whirled around to face her mother. "Why were you saying all that stuff about her husband? You didn't even know him."

"I'll explain later." Gently, Susannah set the photograph back down. "Right now, you need to come with me."

"I won't!"

Alice crossed the room and put her arm on Calista's shoulder. "Please, dear. Do it for me."

Calista's eyes searched the older woman's face. "All right," she said finally. "But you have to promise I can come back tomorrow. Do you promise?"

"I promise. Tomorrow." Emma trotted obediently behind her while she got their coats and walked them to the door. Susannah could not even look at her and walked out of the house without saying good-bye. The night was black and still, and the only sound she heard was the *crunch-crunch-crunch* of Calista's purple Doc Martens as she followed silently behind.

Once they were back at the house, Calista marched up the

stairs to her room, where she slammed the door loudly. No point
in engaging with her now; Susannah decided to call Polly instead.
Maybe there was some wildly entertaining morsel of gossip happening back in Brooklyn that would take her mind off the mess
of her own life.

But Polly had no juicy gossip with which to distract her. And
after commiserating about the high drama involved in raising
teenage girls in general and Calista in particular, she asked, "Are
you still pursuing this thing with your mother?"

"Yes." She waited, and when Polly didn't say anything, she
added, "I know you told me to let it go—"

"But you can't."

"No," said Susannah. "You're probably right—this crazy hunt
is filling some void left by Charlie's death. But knowing does
nothing to change how I feel. It's like a mission."

"I hope it's not a suicide mission," said Polly. "You're dragging
other people into it now—you think your mother was having an
affair with Alice's husband?"

"I *know* she was."

"And you felt compelled to tell her because . . . ?"

"Because I wanted to hurt her," Susannah said. "And I did."
The admission made her feel ugly and small.

"Well, I get *that*," said Polly. "But still, maybe this whole thing
is a distraction—so you don't have to think about Corbin."

"That's over."

"Over! What are you talking about? I thought you told me the
night you spent with him changed your life. That it was like some
do-over from that summer."

"It did, but it's still over. Polly, he's an alcoholic. Or recovering
one. He showed up here falling-down drunk. He'd actually gotten
in his car and driven. I just can't deal with that."

"Maybe it would be better to deal with a guy who's battling with his demons—and loses sometimes—than with some dead guy who may or may not have slept with your mother." Susannah didn't say anything, so Polly kept talking. "You said you're sure this doctor, this pediatrician, was the one. Can't you let it go?"

"No," Susannah said. "I can't. There's one more person I have to talk to. Then maybe I can back off."

"Maybe?"

"Maybe is the best you're going to get from me." There was no point lying to Polly. Or to herself. She had come this far in her search and she wasn't about to abandon it now.

THIRTY-FOUR

As soon as the door closed, Alice walked over to the liquor cabinet to pour a drink. In recent years she had been partial to wine, but tonight she needed something stronger. She made herself a vodka martini, which had been Dave's favorite drink. How he'd loved to mix a pitcher of martinis and bring it out to where they'd set up the chairs. "Here's to summer," he'd say, lifting his glass to the last of the evening light. "Here's to you, darling, still the most beautiful girl in the world." He'd meant it too. She knew he had. So then what to make of Susannah Gilmore's astonishing—and preposterous—revelation? Except that somewhere Alice knew that, although the revelation may have astonished her, it really shouldn't have. There were clues. More than one. But she had steadfastly chosen not to see them.

She got up. The drink needed an olive—Dave had always insisted upon olives—and, to her amazement, there was a nearly empty jar of cocktail olives buried deep in the recesses of the fridge. When she had deposited the olive into her glass, she took a couple of dog biscuits from the jar; Emma deserved a treat as well.

Leaving the unfinished meal and all the dishes on the table, Alice took her drink into the den, lit a fire, and settled on the love seat to watch the flames crackle and spark. Emma had followed her and after looking up to ascertain that, yes, this was where they were sitting, gracefully tucked her long limbs under her body and went to sleep.

Alice supposed she had in some way deserved Susannah's venom; Susannah would have seen her as a competitor for her daughter's love, and she understood that even if she didn't agree. And it would have been easy to dismiss her, and ascribe the intended barb of her words to anger and a desire to wound in return. But Alice knew there was something else there, something that once in a great while nipped at the edges of her consciousness. Generally, she pushed it away, out of her mind, out of existence. Tonight she could not.

Alice had met Dave in the summer after her junior year at Smith; he was a few years older, and had just started medical school. It had been love at first sight for both of them, and it was only her mother's begging that had kept her in Northampton for her senior year; she was that ready to walk away from college and her diploma to become Mrs. Renfew forever and ever. As it was, they married two weeks after her graduation and had a whirlwind honeymoon after which she embarked on the life of a doctor's wife, throwing herself into the decoration and maintenance of their house in Eastwood, where Dave had taken over the practice of a pediatrician who was retiring.

They'd been happy here; he was loved by everyone, not just in town, but in several neighboring towns as well. She helped out at the office when he needed her, got involved in charity work, and when her parents died and left her a sizable inheritance, indulged her love for fine clothes and went abroad for vacations—it was a charmed existence and lacked only one thing to make it perfect: a child. And when Lucy Delvaux had shown up, it seemed like that dream was finally within her reach. They would have their baby, with his penny bright hair. They would love each other always and bask in their love for him. Except it had not worked out that way.

The months after Lucy left had been terrible ones. By mutual agreement, she and Dave did not try to adopt a child again; she did not feel she could face another disappointment. Dave was ever tender with her, ever solicitous. That was when he had surprised her with her first horse—Touchstone—since she'd loved riding while in college and had participated in several shows. He thought it would cheer her up, take her mind off the baby. It had helped, in a superficial sort of way. And he was very dear to have tried so hard.

But maybe all that *trying* had tamped their passion. Because things had changed between them, and though their affection was as steady and strong as ever, they were less like lovers and more like brother and sister. They went from a couple that made love often to one who made love occasionally, then rarely, and eventually almost not at all.

The fire had died down and Alice's glass was empty. She wasn't going to have another drink; she wouldn't let herself. So she went into the dining room where the remains of the meal still sat on the table. She knew she ought to eat something, but she wasn't hungry. She was tempted to throw all the leftover food down the garbage disposal, but that was wasteful, so instead she ladled it out into small plastic containers that she stowed in the freezer.

With the dining room tidied, Alice went back into the study, where she kept leather-bound albums of photographs; the photos she kept displayed throughout the house were only a small fraction of her collection. They were organized according to year, so it was easy enough to find what she was looking for. She had told Susannah that she had a photo of her mother, but she had not gotten around to finding it. Now it was imperative that she did. She flipped through one of the albums from the mid-1970s, and then another.

It was in 1976 that she found the photograph she'd remembered. It was one of several taken at their annual Fourth of July party, and since that was the bicentennial year, the party was even more crowded—and memorable—than usual, the house and lawn overflowing with their friends, family, neighbors, and patients. There had been three cakes decorated with blueberries, strawberries, and Cool Whip to look like flags—here was the photograph that documented them—and in many of the photos she could see the dazzle of the sparklers Dave had bought and freely handed out.

But there were no sparklers in the photograph of Claire Gilmore; she was dazzling enough without them. The camera caught her with a drink in hand, pressed close to her chest. Black curls massed from her head, and her dress, with its pale blue flowers, revealed the lines of a slender, youthful body. She was looking at someone with great interest and great animation; that someone, as Alice recalled, had been Dave. She knew because she'd taken the photograph; she'd borrowed the camera that night and had gaily wandered through the party, snapping as she went.

Taking the photograph from its sleeve, Alice walked into the kitchen and then through a door in the kitchen that she rarely used anymore. The original house was built in the late eighteenth century and there had been two additions over the years; one of these, right off the kitchen, had been used for Dave's office.

Alice turned on the light. Years ago she'd donated any usable medical equipment to a local clinic, but everything else she'd left pretty much intact. Here was the small waiting room where she'd hung reproductions of Norman Rockwell prints featuring children on the walls and set up a wooden dollhouse in the corner; there was the reception desk with its glass jar of lollipops. Beyond the waiting area were two small examination rooms and Dave's office. It was toward that room that she walked now.

Dave's desk, an antique she'd found at auction, was still here, along with the blotter and the banker's lamp with the green glass shade that came from her own parents' house. Behind the desk stood his oak rolling chair. She slid it out and sat down.

On the floor beside the desk was a shredder, an incongruent element in this room but one Dave had deemed necessary. After he'd received the diagnosis of the illness that would kill him but before he fully succumbed to it, he'd systematically gone through his files and shredded almost everything. It was only later, after he'd died, that she'd found a stray folder wedged in the back of a deep drawer in the desk, a folder whose contents she'd examined, puzzled over, and then returned to the top desk drawer. It was still there and she pulled it out now.

There was only a single sheet of paper inside, on which was written these lines:

The pale blue flowers on your dress
So small, so shy
Did they say yes?

I heard your voice
I watched you dance
I made you mine with just a glance

Though I would never dare to press
Still I hoped you would say yes.

Your lilting laugh
Your sidelong glance
I held you when you came to prance.
We spun and twirled; no more, no less
And yet it seemed you might say yes.

Your ink black curls cascading down
Your doelike eyes, so warm, so brown
Your easy smile, so wide and free
All these, did they say yes to me?

There was no signature, and nothing identifying other than a dropped letter—the *h*—that she recognized as the defective key on the typewriter belonging to her husband. Could he have written this? She'd never known him to read poetry, much less write it. Still, he could have typed it. But why? She had not known—or wanted to know—the answer then. But she understood it now. She set the photograph next to the poem—it was all here: the dress, the hair. Dave had written it and Claire Gilmore had been its subject.

Alice sat staring at the poem and the photograph for a long time. Then she got up, turned off the lights, and went back to the liquor cabinet. "You think it's all right if I have another," she said to the dog. "You understand, don't you?"

As she poured the vodka into the glass, she thought of Dave's final night on earth. The morphine drip had eased the pain but made him ramble; his mind reeled and wandered all over the place. *Le chat noir*, he'd kept saying. *Le chat noir*. At the time, Alice had thought these were random words, plucked from the rudiments of French he knew; he'd always admired—and envied—her fluency in the language. But now she understood that those words had been anything but random; they were specific and intentional, his last, vain attempt to remember—and commune with—a woman he had loved. A woman who was not Alice.

THIRTY-FIVE

Calista was gone before Susannah was even out of bed; she must have left the house in the dark. There was a text message—*At Alice's*—and nothing else. But since she was up so early, Susannah had time to make Jack scrambled eggs with cheese and an English muffin for breakfast.

"Why aren't you having anything, Mom?" He spread jam on his muffin.

"I'm not very hungry," she said, looking down at her cup. The coffee was black, not her usual milky infusion, but she needed it. "I'll eat later."

"You're upset about Calista."

"Why do you say that?"

"She was here last night. Now she's gone." He swallowed a bite of the muffin and followed it with a swig of orange juice. "Is she ever coming back, Mom?"

This was exactly what Susannah had been wondering. "Do you want her to?"

Jack seemed to consider the question seriously. "Yes, but only if she could be the way she used to be. She's so mean to me, Mom. I think she hates me or something."

No, she hates me, Susannah wanted to say. "She's just so angry now. So angry about so many things."

"She said you were saying bad stuff about Grandma. Not that I really remember her, but still. Cally does. And that whatever you said got Alice really upset."

Susannah heard the school bus wheezing up the hill. "You'd better go," she said, "or you'll miss the bus. We can talk about this later." When Jack had gone, Susannah looked at the breakfast dishes and decided to leave them. She was roiled, she was churning, and she had a sudden urge to talk to Corbin. Apart from that one lapse, she had always found him to be so steady. So accepting and free of all judgment. But she couldn't call him—she'd put an end to that. Better to distract herself with work.

She made herself a second cup of coffee—a mistake, but, oh, how she craved it—which she brought upstairs. Just as she sat down and flipped open the laptop, the phone rang. "I haven't heard a peep from you in ages." Susannah recognized Tasha's British accent as well as her habit of dispensing entirely with greetings; she always dove into any conversation headfirst.

"I've just been very busy getting settled and all."

"I know, I know. But I wanted to check in just the same. See how it's going."

"By 'it' you mean the writing?"

"Well, yes. Are you still working on that New England lady?"

"She's not exactly a lady in the strict sense," Susannah said. "But yes, I am."

"And?"

"I think it's going pretty well," Susannah said. "I think. You'll have to be the judge of that."

"Why do you think you're so drawn to this? It's a real departure for you. What's the hook?"

"I'm not entirely sure," she said. "But I know I'm fascinated by the issue of guilt—what Betsey Pettingill did, and the unintended consequences it had. I just can't stop thinking about that—how a random, entirely forgettable act could have such an effect. On Ruth Blay, of course. But on Betsey too."

"Are you telling Betsey's story? Or Ruth's?" asked Tasha.

"Both." And in that moment Susannah realized it was true. "The two stories are so intertwined; one shapes and directs the other. Of course there's not a lot known about Betsey's story, so I'm going to have to invent parts of it. I'll stick as close to the facts as I can, though."

Tasha was uncharacteristically quiet. "All right, then. You keep at it. I've got Kitty Redden doing Jane Seymour and I think she's going to work out. When do you think you can get me another batch of pages? I'm going to need more in order to make up my mind."

"April. Or early May at the latest."

"Brilliant," said Tasha. "I'll look forward to seeing them. And if you have any questions, anything you want to hammer out over the phone, you know you can call me, Susie. Anytime."

"Thanks, Tasha. I appreciate that." The only other person who ever called her Susie had been Charlie. She said good-bye and hung up the phone.

Susannah looked at the clock in the corner of her computer screen; it was almost ten o'clock and she'd been up since six. That second cup of coffee—black and even stronger than the first—was making her jumpy. She'd better have something now before she started feeling light-headed. But before she went back down to the kitchen, she did a quick check of her e-mail and found a message from Lynda Jacobsmeyer.

I moved my trip up and will be in Boston on March 14. Can you
drive down to meet me?

Susannah immediately wrote back and asked Lynda to suggest
both a time and place; she was totally flexible and would accom-
modate herself to Lynda's schedule. Then she turned to her black
leather Moleskin planner and used a red Sharpie to circle the
date. But she didn't really need to; she'd already committed it to
memory.

There was snow coming down the day Susannah drove to meet
Lynda, tiny, dizzy flakes that clung briefly to the windshield before
the wipers dispersed them. In Susannah's view, it was a negligible,
almost inconsequential snowfall. Only a blizzard would have kept
her from this meeting, and maybe not even that. The knowledge
about her mother and Dave Renfew was throbbing inside her like
a pulse; she just prayed Lynda would be able to confirm it. Or by
some unimaginable miracle, deny it.

There weren't many cars on the road driving down to Massachusetts, but as she neared Boston, traffic grew heavier. Still,
it wasn't a long drive and she thought that, later in the spring, she
might bring the kids—or kid, if Calista was still giving her the
cold shoulder—to the Museum of Fine Arts, which was where
she was now headed. Lynda had suggested it, actually. There was
a show of Japanese woodcuts she had wanted to see in the morning, and she told Susannah to meet her in the coffee shop at noon.
"I hope you don't mind," she'd said. "But I had to cut my trip short
and this was the only time available."

Traffic notwithstanding, Susannah arrived at the museum
early; she had given herself more than enough time for the trip.

After she sprang for the valet parking near the Huntington Avenue entrance, she went inside. Lynda was somewhere in this building, no doubt looking at images of kimono-clad geishas and water lilies floating in ponds, but even in her eagerness she did not want to intrude. Besides, she didn't want Lynda to be distracted when they talked.

So she decided to walk around the museum by herself for a bit; she had never been here. And when she scanned the museum's map, she knew exactly where she wanted to go: the eighteenth-century American galleries. Her laptop was at home but her Moleskine was in her bag; this could be an impromptu research trip.

She started with the paintings, the stiff, mannered portraits that aspired to the ease and fluency of their European counterparts but somehow failed. Pausing in front of an image of Mrs. Henry Bromfield, she took in the inexpertly rendered blue satin gown, the obviously fake landscape behind her, and the tiny flower the sitter held between her thumb and index finger. Susannah leaned closer to read the label. The artist was John Greenwood, one of the first native-born American painters; he'd been trained by Thomas Johnston, a Bostonian heraldic painter and engraver. Next was a family portrait by Greenwood, with several women seated around a small table and the men standing behind them. This one was marginally more engaging, chiefly because of the basket of needlework and the flame stitch canvas work displayed on the table. There was something observed and specific about those humble objects; the artist wasn't just relying on tired conventions like the grand vista or the flower.

Susannah left the painting gallery and found her way to examples of furniture, pottery, and needlework. Like her mother, Ruth Blay had been an excellent seamstress; she would have appreciated the tight quilting and tufting on these blankets, the careful stitches in an embroidered table runner. She made some notes before moving on. Here were more artifacts to enliven the fictional world she was creating: a brass-trimmed dressing table made, the wall label said, of San Domingo mahogany, yellow poplar, and cedar. And what about this side table out of whose exquisitely carved leg a human face emerged? These were the things in which she could see and feel Betsey and Ruth and Prudence; these objects still held a whiff of the times they had lived in and through. She found herself so entranced that the pinging of her phone, letting her know there was a text, actually came as a surprise.

I'm in the Garden Café, waiting. Should I order you a coffee?

Lynda! Susannah immediately left the gallery and found her way to the café. Seated alone at a table was a slim, deeply tanned woman with a loose gray-blond braid hanging down her back. She rose when she saw Susannah approach and they hugged.

"It's good to see you," Lynda said when they were sitting down again. "Really good." Her face, close up, was lined and spotted with sun damage, but in the burnt sienna landscape of her face, her green eyes were bright and intelligent.

"Thank you for making time for me," Susannah said. "I know you've had to pack a lot into this trip."

"I don't get here very often," Lynda said. "Tulum is pretty far from New England."

"In every way possible," said Susannah. "Do you like living there?"

"What's not to like?" said Lynda. "I call it Paradise Regained." She sipped her coffee and nudged a container in Susannah's direction. "I ordered it black so you can add milk and sugar if you want."

Susannah put her hand on the container but did not pick it

up. How to begin? She'd been thinking about this meeting for so long, but now that she was actually here, she found herself strangely silent, at least about what mattered most. Fortunately, Lynda was still talking.

". . . so you didn't come to the New Hampshire house after your mother died, did you? I was trying to remember the last time I saw you."

"It was at the funeral. I never got to New Hampshire. Jack was a baby and Charlie had broken his wrist, so he was pretty much out of commission. Dealing with the house in New Jersey was all I could handle. You did everything in New Hampshire and I'm very grateful to you for it."

"I know you are, sweetie. And I was so glad you didn't sell the place. Your mother loved it so."

"She did, didn't she?" Susannah saw her opening; she just had to be brave to walk through it. "I've been talking to people that knew her, and they all say that."

"Whom have you been talking to?" Lynda looked interested.

"Janet Durbin, for one."

"Janet! Don't tell me she's still at the library?"

"She is. Also Todd Rettler and George Martin."

"I can't believe it! George was her good buddy when she lived on the pond. And Todd was her boss but a friend too. So he's still alive?"

"He is, and he's doing fine. Not like poor Harry Snady."

"Don't tell me you saw Snady." Lynda's green eyes opened very wide.

"I did. And then just a day later, he died."

Lynda seemed to be taking this in. "That's a shame. But I can't believe that wife of his let you near him. She was wildly jealous of your mother, you know. Harry had a thing for her and it made Deedee nuts."

"Did my mother 'have a thing' for him?" Susannah said quietly.

"Harry?" Lynda seemed to be studying her. "No. Not possible."

"Why not?" asked Susannah.

"Because she would have told me." Lynda said.

"Then he wasn't my mother's lover?" Susannah now found herself wishing it *had* been Harry; it would have made things so much less . . . complicated.

"What makes you think your mother had a lover?"

Susannah looked straight into those clear green eyes. "Evidence, that's what. A note, poems, ticket stubs, a menu. And a red silk bow tie that belonged to Dave Renfew."

Lynda's gaze did not waver. "So you know." She knotted her bony, tanned fingers together.

"Then it's true."

"She confided in me, yes."

"But how could she? What about my father? And what about *me*?"

"They never wanted to hurt anyone." Lynda reached out to put her hand on Susannah's. "Though I think your father knew anyway. That's why she left the pond, and the house. She moved to New Jersey with you and your father; she never saw Dave again."

"Except that one summer. The summer we came up here together and she went with him to Quebec."

"How in the world did you find out about that? She thought she covered her tracks so well."

"Not well enough," Susannah said.

"Try to see it from their point of view. He was dying and he knew it. They wanted to be together that one last time."

Susannah looked down at her coffee. "Can you tell me how it started?" she asked.

"He first met her at one of their parties—the big Fourth of July party, I think. Then he began writing these love poems and sending them to her at the paper. He signed them I. N. Vayne. Obvious. But touching too. She didn't know who had written them—at least not at first. Then she remembered talking to him at the party and she put it all together. She was flattered. But of course she was not available for anything other than friendship. So she called him from her office, to invite him to lunch to tell him, all very proper and professional."

"So what happened?" She withdrew her hand from where it rested under Lynda's.

"She found herself very drawn to him. As he was to her. He kept calling, and they would run into each other around town. One night his wife was away visiting a cousin somewhere, and your father was at a conference in Boston. Dave invited her to dinner. She knew it was a bad idea, but she told herself she could rein it in and that nothing would happen."

"I guess she was wrong." Susannah could hear the bitterness in her tone.

"Don't judge her too harshly," Lynda said. "She loved your father. She just never counted on meeting someone like Dave. They were soul mates, those two. And as dear a man as your father was, I think you know that wasn't a way to describe what he was to your mother."

Susannah said nothing. She had been seeking this confirmation ever since she'd returned to the house in January; now that she had it, why was she so angry? And it still didn't add up. If Dave had been her 'soul mate'—a mawkish, sentimental term that really should have been stricken from the language—then why had she up and left him? She didn't buy that it was because of her father; if Claire had been thinking about her father, she never would have embarked on the affair in the first place.

Lynda glanced at the watch on her caramel-colored wrist. "Look at the time! I'm sorry, but I've got to get going. It's after one and my plane leaves at quarter to four." She stood and started gathering her things—a fuzzy black capelike garment, an embroidered fabric bag covered in tiny winking mirrors.

"You still haven't told me when it started," Susannah said.

"1976? 1977?" Lynda slipped into the cape and added a white hat with a black tassel at the top. "I think. I can't be too sure—it was so long ago." She came around the table to stand close to Susannah. "Don't blame the messenger, sweetie. You came here looking for this. That's why you were so eager to see me. So it's not fair to be angry at me for giving you what you wanted, is it?"

"Nothing's fair," said Susannah. "Did you just figure that out?" She was being hateful but she didn't care. She was shaking as she went in search of her car, paid, and got in, shaking despite her parka, her own hat—*sans* tassel; she left that sort of thing to her daughter—and her scarf. She had wanted to know, hadn't she? Well, now she did. And did she feel any better, any closer to the elusive, beautiful mother she had never quite understood, or to the steadfast but perpetually perplexed man who had been her father? No, she did not.

Navigating her way through the unfamiliar Boston streets with the help of the minivan's GPS, Susannah tried not only to make some sense of what she'd learned, but also of what her life would be like going forward. Not that any of this would change the externals—kids, writing, little brown house on the pond. But inside—inside everything was rearranged like in a kaleidoscope: the pieces the same, the configuration entirely new.

As she threaded her way back to the highway, the minivan's pistons firing, its wheels turning, her mind stayed stubbornly stuck in its own muddy rut. The dates—something about the dates was off. Lynda had not known exactly when her mother and Dave Renfew had first been together. But Susannah had been born in 1978 and she suspected that her mother's connection to Dave might have started *before* her birth; the poems she'd found were from the late 1970s.

Then it became clear to her, and the menacing, shadowy thing that had been only dimly apprehended moved right into the glare. It was the date, the date that was out of step with the sequence she had been so carefully establishing. Her birthday was in April; nine months earlier, in August, her father had been away, invited to some economics convention at Oxford. She knew because it had been one of the high points of his professional life and he talked about it often. Her mother had not gone with him. "Spend a month with all those economists? Really?" she had said when the subject had come up. "One is quite enough." And she'd plant a little kiss on her father's head, if he was sitting, or his hand if he was not. It was a joke, harmless and lighthearted. Except that it was not. That month when Warren was gone was the month she had been conceived. Only he had not been the one who had been responsible. She'd always heard the story about her being born several weeks in advance of her due date. But she had been a big baby, over eight pounds. What preemie was eight pounds? No, she wasn't premature. She was full term—and the illegitimate daughter of another man.

So focused was Susannah on this even more startling revelation that she did not see the car ahead slowing down until she was practically on top of it; she slammed on the brakes only seconds before she would have hit the bumper. The car behind her screeched to a stop and various heads popped out of various car windows.

"What the hell—?"

"Where do you think—?"

"What in God's name are you—?"

Sorry, sorry, sorry, she muttered to everyone, to no one, to herself. *Lynda.* Lynda would know. Susannah looked at the clock on the dashboard. It was two o'clock. Lynda's flight left at three forty-five. Would she have time to get to Logan before Lynda boarded the plane? She didn't know, but she sure as hell was going to try.

Her fingers felt clumsy and inept as she punched a new destination into the GPS. Thank God for that soothing, robotic voice; nothing human could have calmed her as well. Soon she'd turned away from the center of the city, in the direction of the airport. She drove as fast as the speed limit allowed, tempted to exceed it but not daring, because if she was pulled over, that would only squander precious minutes.

It was twenty-five to three when she reached Logan. But she hadn't counted on the fact that there were several terminals; how would she know which was the right one? She scanned the names of the airlines on the sign overhead: Air China, Adria Airways, Aegean, Aer Lingus, Aeroflot, Aerolíneas Argentinas, Aeroméxico. Lynda was returning to Tulum. Aeroméxico would be the logical place to start. After a couple of wasted loops, Susannah located the parking lot and sprinted toward what she hoped was the correct terminal, nearly slipping on a patch of ice and righting herself only at the very last second.

Inside was the busy hive of people embarked on their journeys—backpacks and suitcases, dogs in carriers, rolling carts piled high with luggage. The families, the babies, the lovers, the businessmen, the frail old ladies with walkers, the men in wheelchairs—they were all here, all with somewhere to go, somewhere to be.

Susannah saw the long line of people waiting to have their bags opened and IDs inspected. Lynda would have been on that line and passed through security by now. Susannah realized that without a ticket, she would not be allowed to follow her beyond the gate. God, but she was an idiot—she was so desperate to talk to her again that hadn't thought of that until this very minute. Panic and disappointment churned inside her. Still, she had to try. Pulling out her phone, she called Lynda. "I have to see you," she said.

"What are you talking about?" Lynda said. "Where *are* you?"

"I'm at the airport. Are you flying Aeroméxico?"

"Yes, but what does that have to do with anything?"

Thank God she'd gotten at least *that* right. "I'm in the terminal. But I can't get past security—I don't have a ticket."

"Susannah, you're not making any sense. Are you sure you're okay?" She sounded a little annoyed. "Why did you come here?"

"You know why I'm here." There was a silence, so she went on. "I don't want to do this on the phone. Please come back out and talk to me."

"But I'll have to go through security all over again. There isn't enough time."

"He was my father, wasn't he?" Susannah blurted out. "Dave Renfew was my father." When Lynda didn't respond, she added, "Please tell me. I deserve to know."

"He was," Lynda said finally. "And you do deserve to know." The annoyance was gone from her voice, replaced by something softer and kinder. "Your mother was never able to get pregnant when she was married to Warren. It didn't bother her all that much; she wasn't sure she wanted children. Then she found out she was carrying Dave's child and it changed everything. She might have even left your father at that point. But she knew Dave would never leave Alice. If she had his child, though, she would know that a piece of him would be with her—always."

"His child—you mean me," Susannah said.

"Yes, you," said Lynda. "But she couldn't raise you with him so nearby; it would have been too painful for her. It was just dumb luck that the offer from Rutgers came when it did. Your mother urged your father to take it. And he did."

"Did he know?" She didn't even know that she'd started crying; she registered the wetness on her face as having come from some other source.

"Your mother never told him. Whether he guessed . . ."

No, Susannah thought. *He believed I was his—I know he did.* "Why didn't you tell me back at the museum?" She was aware that someone was looking her strangely, and she moved away to avoid the scrutiny.

Lynda sighed audibly into the phone. "I saw no reason to volunteer the information. I didn't want to violate your mother's confidence. Or to hurt you. But now that you've asked, I can't lie."

"Dave Renfew—did he know?"

"Not until that summer in the 1990s when you came back. Your mother told him when they went away together."

"I barely remember meeting him that summer. It was only in passing."

"He remembered," Lynda said. "And he told your mother that nothing could have made him happier."

Maybe one day that thought would be a comfort to her. But

today was not that day. "I guess that's it," Susannah said. She couldn't bring herself to add *Thank you*, so she simply said good-bye. Then she left the terminal, found her car, and began the drive home.

Daddy, you loved me, didn't you? I know I loved you. And she did. Dozens of memories began a ferocious clamoring for her attention: Warren patiently teaching her to dive off the board at the municipal pool where he'd also taught her to swim. The pancakes he'd made, with faces composed of whipped cream, raisins, and sliced bananas. The way he'd always keep a bag of M&M's or a Heath bar—her two favorites—in his pockets for her to find. She thought too of all those books of his she'd found in the attic. She hadn't so much as looked at them, but she would look at them as soon as she got back—she'd take out every single one, caress the covers and the spines, kiss the pages that he'd touched and read—

Her phone was ringing; she could hear it from inside her purse. But she was driving, so she let it go to voice mail. The ringing stopped; good. She would see who called later. But then it started again, and once again she did not pick up. The traffic had gotten worse, slowing to a crawl. There must be something clogging things up—construction or an accident. She crept along, made more and more anxious by the delay. Then the traffic just stopped. After twenty or so extremely tense minutes during which she went absolutely nowhere, she saw several policemen threading their way through the cars. One was speaking through a megaphone, so she opened her window to hear him.

". . . three-car pileup a thousand yards ahead . . . making every effort to reroute traffic . . ."

A three-car pileup could mean a serious delay; it might be hours before she got home again. She reached for her phone to play the messages:

Hello, Mom? Are you there? It's me, Jack. Mom, something terrible is happening! There's a fire at Alice's house. Cally is there. So are a bunch of her friends. Someone called the fire department and I can hear the sirens. I want to go over there but I'm really scared. Are you there, Mom? If you're there, please, please, please pick up.

THIRTY-SIX

Susannah saw the smoke before she even got to Eastwood. The dark gray coils hung heavily in the sky, stubbornly refusing to dissipate or disperse. Although she would have liked to floor it and speed along these curving country roads at 110 miles per hour—or even better, teleport to her destination—she drove only as fast as seemed sane until she was turning up the road that led to Alice's house. A shiny red truck with the words EASTWOOD AUXILIARY FIREFIGHTERS blocked her access, so she stopped the car, flung the seat belt aside, and rushed the rest of the way on foot.

The side of the house closest to the road seemed intact, mint green paint fresh as ever, but as she drew closer she saw the devastation wrought by the fire—the other side was blackened and blistered and the windows ravaged, their panes reduced to mounds of shards that glittered in the soot-covered snow. Fortunately, the fire had not spread beyond the house; across the meadow, the barn that housed Jester was untouched. Someone should go check on him, she thought. Make sure he was okay.

A knot of firemen, faces smeared and grimy, was standing nearby. One of them turned to her. "You can't go any further, ma'am. It's not safe."

"My daughter." Those were not words she spoke; they were prayers. "She was inside."

"No one's left inside," he said. "We got everyone out. Alive."

"Are you sure?" He nodded and something in her gave way; she sank down to the blackened snow.

"Hey, are you all right?"

Susannah allowed him to pick her up, and once she was on her feet again, she leaned on his arm for support. "Was anyone hurt?"

"Not seriously. The kids are all at the hospital now—being treated for smoke inhalation, I guess. Mrs. Renfew fell and broke something, I think. We got her out of here on a stretcher. But she'll be fine."

"Oh," said Susannah. The relief rocked over her in waves. *Not seriously, not seriously, not seriously.* Then the rest of his words sank in. Mrs. Renfew. Alice. What had she broken? Who was with her? She should go to her. But she had to find her children first. Where were they?

Before she could ask, she saw someone come out of the house, yellow suit bright against his blackened face. In his arms, he carried the limp body of a dog—Emma! Susannah broke away from the fireman she was still leaning on. Maybe the dog could still be saved. She walked up to the fireman who was now setting Emma gently down, and when he turned to face her, she recognized the blue eyes shining out from all that grime. They belonged to Corbin Bailey. Corbin had been in there, with the smoke and the flames. He could have been hurt. Killed. The thought was intolerable to her.

"What are you—?"

"Did you see—?"

They spoke over each other and then both stopped. "You first," he said, and set the dog down at his feet.

"What are you doing here?"

"I'm part of the auxiliary fire force. I've been doing it for about ten years."

"He"—Susannah pointed to the fireman she had first approached—"said that everyone got out and everyone is okay."

"That's true—all accounted for. Your kids are fine—I made sure of that."

"If everyone was okay, why did you go back in?"

"Alice was frantic about the horse and the dog. The horse is fine. But the dog . . . I went back in to look for her. I found her in a closet upstairs."

"Is she . . . ?" Susannah couldn't bring herself to say it.

He inclined his head, the slightest of nods. "The smoke got her."

"You put yourself in danger to save her." Again, Susannah felt sickened at the thought of his entering a burning building; she put her hand to her mouth until the urge to retch had passed.

"That's what I signed on for," he said. "I just wish I had found her sooner."

Kneeling, Susannah stroked the animal's head. Even in death, she looked dignified.

And what about Alice? She didn't know yet. Who would be the one to tell her?

Susannah stood up, suddenly propelled by anxiety. Her palm was smeared with black and she tried vainly to wipe it off. Her phone was still somewhere in the car, along with her bag. But calling was no good anyway. She had to find them—Alice, Jack, Calista—and see for herself that they were still alive, still breathing. She turned to the dog one last time—and then she crumpled in on herself, sobbing. Emma. Charlie. Her mother's secret, her father's sadness. No, not her father. Her father had been Dave Renfew. The sobbing intensified.

"Hey." Corbin was right behind her. He pivoted her body around so that her face rested on his chest as she cried. "It's all right. Everyone's all right."

"Not Emma!" she wailed. "Not Charlie!" *And not me,* she wanted to say. *I'm not all right. I don't even know who I am anymore.*

"No. Not Emma. Not Charlie. But you're okay. And your kids—they're okay too. I'll take you to see them. You'll feel better."

"But what about Alice? Who's going to tell her about Emma?"

"I can do that if you want me to."

She stopped to consider this, her sobs quieting. That last conversation, the things she'd said, the way she'd *wanted* to hurt her. Alice would not welcome her; why should she? "That would be a great help to me. Thank you."

"Okay," he said. "We'll go now. Just give me a minute." He took off his helmet and went over to one of the other firefighters, gesturing to the dog while Susannah wiped her wet face with her hands, forgetting how dirty one of them still was.

Then they got in her car, but she let him drive; she was too shaky to do it herself. On the way to the hospital, she was quiet. She had tried calling both her kids, but neither one had picked up. She would see them soon, though. The fire had driven the new knowledge about her parentage right out of her head, but now it was creeping back. Then she realized she didn't even know how the fire had started; thinking about her parents would have to wait. "What happened at Alice's?" she asked Corbin.

"Your daughter told me she'd invited some friends over—Alice knew all the kids and said it was okay. They were upstairs smoking weed. Someone got careless with one of the joints and set it down somewhere. It fell on the floor and started to smolder in the rug. By that time, the kids were high and not paying attention. Then the rug burst into flames and the flames spread to one of the curtains. The kids were all screaming and colliding with each other, trying to escape. But Calista was calm enough to call nine-one-one. We got there before the fire blazed totally out of control."

"I heard Alice was hurt."

"She fell and broke something. Hip maybe. But we got her out before there was any serious damage from the smoke."

"Thank you," she said quietly.

"You're welcome." Then, "And you would be thanking me for . . . ?"

"Making sure my children stayed safe. Saving Alice. Trying to save Emma." She paused. "Just being you. I would have felt terrible if anything had happened to you in there."

"That's a nice thing to hear." He kept his eyes on the road. "Really nice. I know we were new to each other, but I've missed you, Susannah."

"I missed you too." And she had. It was getting dark now, so she couldn't read his expression. But she imagined what it might reveal: Gratitude. Surprise. Forgiveness. Just like hers.

They turned onto Pleasant Street and Corbin pulled into the parking lot of the Concord Hospital. He turned off the ignition, shifted in his seat, and took her hands. She was desperate to see her children, yet she remained where she was, hands encased in his. His drunken lapse seemed less important now. He would deal with his problem; it wouldn't define him. She leaned toward him ever so slightly, but it was enough. He let go of her hands and pulled her into his arms.

"We'll talk," he said against her cheek. "We should talk. But not now."

He got out of the car and Susannah followed him into the hospital. Calista and Jack were sitting in the waiting room of the ER. Calista's face and clothes were soot-smeared; there was a gray blanket wrapped around her shoulders. As soon as they saw her, they jumped up and came running over.

"Where were you?" Jack asked. "I was calling and calling!"

"Mom, I am so sorry. I never meant for that to happen—never!"

"Okay," she said, gathering them both in her arms. "Okay." She closed her eyes and let herself take them in. Jack's newly muscled, rapidly growing body; Calista's delicate spine. The burnt smell in their hair and clothes. The tears—because they were both crying now—that ran in cloudy rivulets down Calista's grimy cheeks.

"Is Alice going to be okay? Corbin brought her out and he told me she'd be all right. Will she, Mom? I wanted to go and see her, but they said not yet." Calista wiped her eyes with her sleeve.

"She will and you can," said Susannah. "But let's sit down now. Let's sit down and talk." She saw Corbin standing at some distance from them. "You too," she said. "You come too."

"It's all my fault," Calista said. "All of it. If I hadn't been such a brat, none of this would have happened. Can you ever forgive me, Mom? Can you?"

"Corbin told me how the fire started," Susannah said. "And he told me that you were the one who kept your head and called nine-one-one. I am so proud of you for doing that."

"When we saw the flames, everyone just panicked and tried to get out. I wanted to get out too, but I was worried about what would happen to Alice. So I called nine-one-one. I knew they would send firemen. And they did." She looked at Corbin. "They sent you and you went inside and saved her. You're, like, a hero."

"She's going to be just fine," Corbin said. "We can all go see her later."

"I wish we could bring Emma," Calista said. "That would really cheer her up."

Susannah's expression must have revealed everything. "Did something happen to her?" Calista asked. "Please tell me that she'll be okay."

"The horse is fine. But Emma didn't make it," Corbin said, and when Calista started to cry, it was Corbin who put his arm around her. To Susannah's astonishment, she seemed to accept the comfort, and cried into his chest just where Susannah had.

"I used to see them walking together," Jack said. "Alice is going to be so sad." Then he began to cry too. They sat like that for a few minutes, the kids crying, the adults murmuring consoling words, until Corbin found a vending machine and brought them all cups of tepid, overly sweet hot chocolate, which they guzzled as if it was the most delicious thing they had ever tasted.

"Do we tell her tonight?" Susannah asked when the last, grainy drops had been downed.

"I don't think so," Corbin said. "Anyway, she may not even be awake yet. We haven't checked in a while."

"Let's check now," Calista said. "Please?"

So together they rode the elevator to Alice's room on the fourth floor. "She's fine," said the nurse. "She broke a hip, but it didn't need replacing. Her bones are pretty strong for someone her age."

"We wondered if we could see her," Susannah said.

The nurse looked at their raggedy little group, still dirty, still disheveled. "Are you Emma and Calista?"

"I'm Calista." Her daughter stepped forward.

"She's been very anxious about you, and about someone named Emma. She kept asking." She looked at Calista. "Do you know who Emma is and if she's all right? Everyone we saw here tonight was okay."

"Emma was her dog. She died in the fire," Susannah said.

"Oh," said the nurse. "That's going to be bad."

"I can tell her," said Corbin. "If she's worried and keeps asking, she ought to be told, right?"

The nurse hesitated. "I guess so. But try to be gentle."

"Got it," said Corbin. "We'll just be a few minutes."

Susannah gave Calista's hand a small squeeze; to her surprise, Calista squeezed back. God, but she was grateful to Corbin for offering to break the news to Alice. She could not have done it. "We'll be in the lounge," she said.

"Are you okay?" she said to Jack when they were alone.

"I am now," he said. "But I was really scared when I called you, Mom."

"How did you find out?"

"There was all this smoke. When I looked outside, it was like the whole world had turned to black fog. I ran out to see what was going on and I heard the fire trucks. I followed them to Alice's house."

"I'm sorry I didn't pick up right away," she said, putting an arm around him and drawing him close. "I was driving." *And I just found out that the man I thought was my father was not my father.*

"I know." He put his head on her shoulder. "And it's okay now."

Is it? She wanted to stop thinking about this, but then she would have to think about Corbin and Alice. What was he saying to her? And how was she taking it? She was sorry for how she'd hurled those words. Truly, deeply sorry. Was there any way to make things right? And then she saw how.

"I'll be right back," she told Jack. She walked over to the nurses' station. "How long will Mrs. Renfew be in the hospital?" she asked.

"That depends on her recovery," said the nurse. "It could be as short as a few days or it could be as long as a couple of weeks."

"What about when she gets out? Will she be able to go home?"

"Not right away. They'll send her to rehab first."

"She lives alone. She might need some help even when rehab is over, right?"

"Oh, definitely," said the nurse. "Does she have any children? Anyone who can stay with her?"

"Maybe," said Susannah. An idea was just forming in her mind, a very good idea. Even if she had someone, Alice's house would not be habitable for quite some time. "Maybe instead of someone staying with her, she can stay with someone else."

"As long as it's not too far away," said the nurse. "The surgeon will want to do follow-up visits."

"Oh, it's not far at all," Susannah said. "In fact, it's just a little way down the road from where she lives now." Because she had already decided that, no matter what Alice said about it, she was going to insist that she come and live with her.

THIRTY-SEVEN

"How did she take it?" Susannah asked. They had just left the hospital and were driving back to Primrose Pond; Corbin was at the wheel.

"Not too well."

"It was awful, Mom!" Calista added from the backseat. "She cried *so* hard. But when I told her how sorry I was and that it was all my fault, she stopped crying and hugged me."

"Really?"

"Uh-huh. And she said that if it was my fault, it was hers too because she'd told me it was okay to invite those guys over. It wasn't like I was doing it behind her back."

"That's a very . . . evolved . . . response." Susannah wondered whether Alice would be so tolerant when she delivered her own bombshell, the one that was ticking madly inside her.

Corbin made a turn onto their road. There was Alice's mutilated house. The damage was less visible in the dark, but the heavy, even putrid smell of smoke still hung in the air and made its way into the car. She was glad when they were past it, but the smell lingered. She felt she might be sick.

When they reached the house on Primrose Pond, though, the feeling passed. She touched Corbin's arm. "Come eat with us. I'll bet you're starving."

"If you're sure it's okay . . ."

Susannah leaned forward and caught Calista's gaze in the rearview mirror. "It's more than okay," she said. "We insist."

While Corbin took the first shower, Susannah boiled water for spaghetti and opened a jar of tomato sauce she had in the cupboard. Calista was with her, setting the table.

"All the other kids—are they all right too?" Susannah asked.

"Everyone is fine, if a little freaked out. No one remembers who left the joint around, but I'm sure it wasn't me."

"I didn't ask you if it was," Susannah said.

"I know. But I wanted you to know. Alice too. I tried to tell her, but I don't think she got it."

"You can try again."

Calista finished setting the table and came over to where Susannah stood in the kitchen. "What's going to happen to the house?"

"She has insurance, I'm sure. That will pay for the repairs."

"Too bad they can't repair Emma." She started to cry again, and Susannah put her arms around her. "Alice loved her so much. And I love Alice."

"I know you do, sweetheart."

"But I love you too, Mom. Even if I've been a bitch lately." She hugged Susannah tightly; her bones felt as light as a lark's.

Susannah's own eyes filled with tears at the admission. "If you can't be a bitch with your mom, who can you be a bitch with?"

Then Jack came into the kitchen holding Corbin's uniform and the clothes he'd been wearing underneath. "Corbin says this stuff smells really bad and he was wondering if you could wash it."

"I'll do it," Calista volunteered, and took the whole armload down to the new washing machine in the basement.

While Corbin waited for the clothes to be ready, he put on the sweatpants and sweater he'd given to Susannah the night she had stayed over. If Calista remembered that Susannah had worn them, she did not bring it up. But Calista was a different girl tonight. Or more accurately, the girl she used to be, before her father was killed.

Once they all had showered, they ate the spaghetti and a loaf of garlic bread that Susannah had found in the freezer. Corbin didn't have his car and Susannah didn't feel up to driving him, so she invited him to stay over.

"I can sleep on the couch down here," he said.

"No, you can't. I need to be with you," she said.

Susannah went into Jack's room, and then Calista's, to say good night. Then she went into her room, where Corbin, grime-free and hair still damp from the shower, awaited her. He wore the sweatpants but no shirt, and for several minutes she lay in the warm circle of his arms, listening to his heart beating steadily in his chest. *Alive,* she thought. *Alive, alive.*

"Thank you for telling her," she said. "I really couldn't face it."

"I know this whole thing shook you up."

"It did. But there's more. We had a conversation that was pretty upsetting a few nights ago. I'm not even sure she'd want to see me after what I said."

"What did you say?" he asked quietly.

"That her husband had had an affair with my mother."

Corbin was silent for a few seconds. Then he said, "Are you sure?"

"If I weren't, I wouldn't have told her." And then she filled him in on how she'd come to her conclusion, leaving out only the last, most shattering bit.

"Wow," he said. "That's some story."

And there's more. But she wasn't quite ready to tell it. "So what's going to happen? With Emma, I mean." The question had just occurred to her.

"Alice asked me to call Dr. D'Arco—he's a vet in Manchester. She said he'd take care of it."

"Where *is* the dog anyway?"

"I told the guys to cover her up and bring her to the basement. I figured it would be cold enough down there. I just didn't want to leave her outside for any other animals to find."

"I'm glad you thought of that." She snuggled closer. "I'm glad you thought of a lot of things." She would tell him what else she learned about Dave, but she couldn't do it now; the adrenaline that had been coursing through her veins had suddenly and totally emptied out.

"Me too." He kissed her hair. "Me too."

By tacit understanding, they did not make love that night. But she was deeply grateful for his presence, and when she saw him lying next to her in the morning, she thought, yes, this was where he belonged.

Susannah gave the kids the option to stay home from school; yesterday had been pretty traumatic for both of them. But they both wanted to go. "I can see Alice later, can't I?" Calista asked.

"Of course. One of us will drive you." It was time for Calista to get her driver's license—another thing to take care of. Once the kids were gone, she offered to drive Corbin back to the firehouse.

"Do you know how to get there?"

"Not really."

She let him program the GPS and said nothing else for the duration of the drive; the only voice in the car was Siri's. It was only when they had pulled into the driveway and she'd stopped the car that she blurted out, "There's something else I have to tell Alice. Something even worse than telling her that her dog died."

"She loved that dog like a kid," said Corbin. "What could be worse than that?"

"Just wait until you hear this," Susannah said. And then she told him the story.

"I wouldn't even know where to start," he said when she had finished.

"Well, it will be my job to figure it out."

After they said good-bye, Susannah was unmoored and spinning. It had been a relief to unburden herself. Now that she had, though, she was even more restless and agitated. The information was not content to remain static; it required action on her part— but what?

She began driving with no particular plan or destination. Resuming anything resembling her former life was not an option. Because that's what it was: former. From now on, there would be a sharp split bifurcating the way she understood herself, her past, her family—everything. And it would all boil down to that one moment: Before she knew. And after.

She found herself on Route 4, heading in the direction of Concord. She knew where she was going now, drawn by a pull too strong to ignore. She stopped in a Hannaford on the way, where she bought a box of Earl Grey tea and some flowers, a predictable mix of roses, carnations, and baby's breath but the best the supermarket had to offer.

The parking lot was pretty full, but, strangely enough, the spot where they had parked the night before, right under a streetlamp, was vacant, almost as if someone had been saving it for her. She parked the car and went inside.

Alice was sitting up in bed when Susannah arrived. Her hair was down around her shoulders, making her seem vulnerable and, despite her lined face, almost childlike. This was not going to be easy. "Hello," Susannah said. "How are you today?"

"As well as can be expected." Her voice was cool but not too hostile—or at least that was what Susannah wanted to believe. She warmed a little when she saw the gifts. "Earl Grey—you remembered," she said. "The tea here is wretched. And flowers too—so pretty."

They weren't, actually, but Susannah was grateful for the small reprieve granted by locating a vase, filling it with water, and setting it on the windowsill. Then she sat down on the chair near the bed. "Alice, there's something I want to say to you. It's about that last conversation we had when I was at your house. The one about your husband—and my mother."

"I remember," Alice said. "I remember every word."

"I'm sorry I said it that way. And sorry I hurt you. I was feeling hurt, though. Not that that's an excuse. Just an explanation."

"I understand," Alice said stiffly. "Or I tried to. Maybe I overstepped with Calista and let my own needs blind me to yours. But I was so taken with her, you see. I wasn't being very sensitive." She sat quietly for a few seconds, looking down at the package of tea she still held in her hands. "But the other part—the part about Dave and your mother. Well, that was true. I didn't want to believe it, but it all makes sense now. Those irksome little details I tried to push away for so long? They were all bits of a puzzle I could never solve. But you did."

"What details?" Susannah moved closer to the bed.

"Dave's last words were *Le chat noir*. He repeated them several times and I thought he was rambling. He'd always wished he'd spoken French. Once he even bought some language tapes and another time he enrolled in an adult ed class. But it didn't last long—he had no mind for languages. So at the end I thought he was remembering some random phrase he'd learned. I was wrong. He was remembering—your mother."

"And that trip. But the affair must have started years earlier, don't you think?"

"I do," said Alice. "Because here's another thing: after he died, I found a poem about a woman in a flowered dress in his desk—"

"Pale blue flowers?" Susannah asked. It must have been the same poem she had found!

"Yes, pale blue flowers. And then I found that picture I'd told you about. It was of your mother, in that very dress. And it was taken in 1976, at our Fourth of July party. Maybe that's where it started for them."

"But not where it ended."

"No, the Canada trip—that was the end. Though I'm not sure how much there was in between. Your parents moved away."

"Quebec wasn't the end either." Susannah was dreading what she would have to say next. "There was one more thing. My mother knew about it, though for a long time your husband didn't."

"Knew about what?" Alice put down the box of tea.

"Me."

"What are you talking about?"

"My mother got pregnant with Dave's child. Dave was my biological father."

"That can't be!" Two vivid streaks of color appeared on Alice's face.

"That's what I thought at first," Susannah said. "But Lynda Jacobsmeyer confirmed it."

"You saw her?"

Susannah nodded. "In Boston. I suspected and I asked her outright. She said it was true, and that my mother had told her."

"Oh," said Alice. "Oh, oh, oh." Her eyes shone brightly but no tears fell.

"If I'm Dave's biological daughter, then that means Calista and Jack are his grandchildren. So we are a family—kind of. Which is why I am going to ask that when you get out of the hospital—or rehab if you have to go to rehab—you come to stay with us."

"But I could never—I mean, I couldn't impose—"

"Where will you go? How will you manage? Your house won't be livable for months; you'll need help. Let us help you." Susannah's face was wet. "Please."

"I don't know . . ." Alice looked down at the box of tea that sat on top of the blanket, and then back at Susannah. "Maybe we can try it," she said. "Try it and see how it goes."

THIRTY-EIGHT

Susannah parked on South Street in Portsmouth and got out of the car. Flanking the house on the corner was a bright blaze of forsythia; it was a sunny day in April and the yellow flowers seemed even brighter when seen against the cool blue sky.

"Do you have everything?" Corbin asked.

Susannah checked her bag again; everything, including her much thumbed copy of *Hanging Ruth Blay* by Carolyn Marvin, was there. "Good to go," she said.

They walked into the cemetery together. This was the execution site where Ruth—she was never Blay in Susannah's mind—had been brought, and Susannah felt compelled to see it. She didn't know exactly where the gallows had been erected, but Marvin's book showed a photograph of the spot; Corbin had wanted to come along to help her find it.

Last week he had gone with her to the historical society, where the curator, Sarah Rux, had laid out a blue linsey-woolsey on a bed for their inspection. Its provenance was uncertain, so Susannah knew the quilted blue cloth with its many holes may or may not have belonged to Ruth, but she had wanted to see it anyway. They had been planning to go to the cemetery too, but it was raining hard and so they'd postponed it until today. This was the final stop—for Ruth, and for her.

"Let me see the photo again," Corbin said. She obliged. "Do you think that it's over there?" He pointed to a monument similar to the one in the picture, but when they got closer to inspect, the names didn't match. They kept walking, though, hand in hand, except for when Susannah stopped to take notes or photograph an old headstone or arresting statue. Angels with their wings open or folded, heads gazing heavenward or down in sorrow. Babies with lambs. Crosses, representations of Jesus and of Mary—all the myriad expressions of mourning or grief. She'd had Charlie cremated—he'd always said he wanted that—and had scattered his ashes, again heeding his wishes. But there was something to be said for a final resting spot, a place to localize the swell of sadness that still rose up from time to time.

"Was she buried here? Ruth Blay?" Corbin asked. He'd taken off his jacket and carried it under his free arm.

"She was, but there's no marker."

"So it's all about the spot."

"All about the spot," she agreed. "Wait, what about that?" She dropped his hand and hurried over to another monument. "No, that's not right either. The name we're looking for is Sise."

They kept walking until Susannah began to feel hungry—and the need to use a bathroom. She knew they could go and get lunch—and find a ladies' room—and come back, but she wanted to look one more time and began to walk the paths again. And here, on the north side of a reed-ringed pond, was the monument she sought. "Look!" she called to Corbin. "Here it is." The name, Sise, was the same as the one in the photo. He walked over to join her.

Without the trees, which would not have been so tall and mature, and the headstones, the view would have been pretty much as Ruth had seen it, her last sight before all sight was gone. The place was not a cemetery back then. The land, owned by the South Church, had been a pasture and was often used as a military training ground. Samuel Hall, a farmer, owned land adjacent to the field, and he was furious that the crowd—it had been a large one—had damaged his stone walls in an effort to get closer. Susannah had seen the documents in which he'd demanded recompense.

The scaffold would have been built on the highest point, overlooking the pond. Ruth would have been brought by a cart that carried the plain wooden coffin she'd be buried in; Susannah knew that was common practice. And then, when her hands and feet were bound and she'd uttered whatever last prayers she had in her to utter, the noose was placed around her neck and the order given to send off the cart. Unless her neck had been broken by the fall, she would have dangled there, left to die of slow strangulation.

Susannah let the images, no less harrowing for being imagined, seep through and into her. She wanted to feel them so she could write them. And she needed to write them, to write them as vividly, respectfully, and humanely as she could.

"Horrible," she said finally. "Let's go." She took his hand and they walked off.

They went to Gino's, on the waterfront, for lunch, where they ate lobster bisque and lobster rolls; the granddaughter of the original owner, Concetta, knew Corbin and came over to say hello.

"I heard you're giving old Wingate a run for his money up there in Eastwood," she said.

"I'm doing my best," he said. Corbin was back on the Wingate crusade again. The committee members had told Mr. Wingate that they refused to negotiate with anyone other than Corbin as their leader, and someone got the governor's ear too. Susannah was so glad; she knew how much it meant to him.

The air had turned a little cooler by the time they got in the car to drive back. Spring was coming, but it was coming slowly.

"Will I see you later?" Susannah asked when Corbin dropped her off.

"I've got a meeting, but I could come over later if you want." Since that drunken night at her house, he'd been attending AA meetings again. Extra insurance, he'd said.

"I want." She leaned in to kiss him. Actually, she was looking forward to a little time on her own this evening; she wanted to begin the process that would transmute the facts of her field trip into fiction.

"Susannah, is that you?" Alice called out when Susannah walked into the house.

"It's me," Susannah answered. She went into the kitchen and found Alice seated at the table drinking a cup of tea. No one else appeared to be at home. "Did you do that all by yourself?" she asked.

"I did," Alice said. "The occupational therapist was here supervising me, but she said I was coming along splendidly. Just splendidly."

"That's great." Susannah hung up her coat and began putting her things away.

"And I spoke to the contractor; things are coming along at my house too. Soon I'll be out of your hair."

"You know I don't feel that way." Susannah sat down across from Alice and took the older woman's hand. "I don't feel that way at all."

"I know you don't, dear. But as grateful as I am to you—all of you—I'm eager to get back home again. I'm redoing the living room, you know. I'm fed up with all that pink."

Susannah smiled. She wasn't lying when she said that having Alice here wasn't any trouble. It was different, to be sure, but it was a good kind of different. Alice's presence had helped her adjust to this new self, the one whose father was not her father. She'd had so many questions about Dave: What was he like? Had he wanted children? Had they ever tried to have any together? Alice told her a story about a near adoption of a little redheaded baby boy; was that part of her attraction to Calista? Lynda had told her he'd been happy when he found out. Did Alice think that would have been true?

These questions had not been easy for Alice at first; she too had to readjust her version of her past and rewrite the story of her marriage in her own mind. Dave's infidelity had hurt her terribly, just as Claire's had hurt Warren. But here they were, each with an unexpected connection to the other—unexpected, and sometimes touched with grace. She had decided not to tell her children what she'd learned just yet; she wanted to get used to it herself first. Maybe in the summer, when they could be out on the pond, the long, cold winter well behind them.

Susannah got up from the table to start preparing dinner. Alice insisted on washing her own cup, spoon, and saucer—"See, I'm getting more self-sufficient every day"—and then went to lie down for a while. She couldn't manage the stairs, so with the help of a pair of folding screens she'd found at one of the antique stores on Route 4 and a rented hospital bed, Susannah had partitioned the living room and created a space for her. Fortunately, there was a bathroom downstairs too; Corbin had added safety grips to the shower stall so she could get in and out by herself.

Calista came in and then Jack and Liam; the kids pitched in with dinner prep and they had an easy, relaxed meal. Calista even volunteered to clean up, with Alice keeping her company and helping when she could. The boys disappeared to Jack's room, and Susannah was able to go upstairs with her laptop and her Moleskine; the notes she had taken earlier were all there.

Tasha had asked her why she was so attached to this story; she had told her it had something to do with guilt. Guilt—her own, Betsey's—that was the animating force, the guilt that linked them, and the guilt that pushed her ahead. She had not given Betsey a real chance at expiation because she sensed it was not time yet. Before expiation, there had to be confession, and her character would need to unburden herself. But there was this piece of the story, the most grim, the most awful, that she still had to tell. And having been to the cemetery in Portsmouth, the last place where Ruth Blay had walked and lived and breathed, she felt she was finally ready to try.

THIRTY-NINE

I'd been thrice blessed, and carried easily with the first three, but this pregnancy was a hard one. I was sick all the time and often it was not only the taste but the mere smell of certain foods, like the lamb stew Joel liked so much or shepherd's pie, that turned my poor stomach inside out. And of course I was so very tired. Nursing my little Betsey and keeping up with the other two at the same time stretched me thin and taut as a thread. Prudence was a godsend during those months, always offering to take the older children to play with hers, even keeping them overnight sometimes. She brought me loaves of her light, airy bread—one of the few things I could keep down—and honey from the bees her husband tended.

One evening, we sat together in my kitchen. It was September, but the air still held the warmth of summer. The children were all asleep and Joel was off to Boston on some business. So it was just the two of us. I was about to prepare a pot of tea, but Prudence laid her hand on my wrist. "I have something else I *think you'll like better," and from the capacious folds of her skirt she produced a small bottle filled with a dark liquid. "Elderberry wine," she explained. "I brewed it myself last spring when the fruit was in season. It's just the thing to calm your nerves and settle your stomach."*

I looked at the bottle. While Joel liked to partake of beer or ale and, when he could get it, wine, I tended to abstain. Spirits made me feel both silly and sleepy, and as a mother, I did not want to encourage these qualities in myself. But maybe Prudence had a point. I was in need of calming, both body and mind, and I did not see how a small tipple would harm me. Fetching two small glasses from a shelf, I brought them to the table and let Prudence pour.

The first taste was sweet, with a hint of spice. Then came the slight burn, but it was subtle, starting in my chest and radiating out to my arms and fingers, legs, and even toes. I had another sip. "Delicious," I declared. To my surprise, the glass was now empty. Without asking, Prudence refilled it along with her own. Then we touched our two glasses together gently.

"I've got a couple more bottles in my pantry," she said. "So I can leave this one here with you."

"Oh, no, you shouldn't." But I was secretly glad she had made the offer. The wine was making me feel so peaceful, so tranquil. I might be moved to take a small nip every night; it would no doubt make bedtimes that much easier. "Could I give some to the baby? When she's teething?"

"You certainly can," said Prudence. "Rub it on her gums. It will quiet her right down."

"You never did tell me the rest of the story about Ruth Blay." I surprised myself with these words; I had not intended to bring up the subject again. Prudence did not know that I was the child

who had discovered the dead baby, and even though I was desperate to know the particulars, I feared that talking about it might somehow lead the finger of blame to point at me. But alcohol loosened my tongue and let down my guard. The words were out now; I could not take them back.

"I didn't? Well, I can tell you now. She went to jail and there was a trial straightaway."

"Yes, I remember that part; you told me."

"Did I tell you about the indictment, then? How it was filled with the names of all those women who sought to single her out and smear her name?"

"Women?"

Prudence nodded and wiped her mouth with the back of her hand. "Oh, yes—there were several of them. It was long ago but I remember them still. Abigail Cooper was one. Loveday Brown another. And Mary Rogers and Olive Clough."

That last name pierced my hazy spirit-created bubble. I remembered Olive. I most certainly did. And maybe some of the others who had been at the table, so ready to accuse and judge. "They were against her, then?"

"Every last one. She was arraigned in August, but the trial was adjourned until September 21—I still remember the day because it was my good mother's birthday. It lasted only a single day and then the jury thrashed it out for several hours—all night long, I was told. They came back with a guilty verdict. I'm sure those women"—and she stopped to wrinkle her face in disgust—"had poisoned the well."

"But she asked for a reprieve?" This I vaguely recalled from my childhood.

"Twice asked, twice granted. But the third time . . ."

"Denied." I knew the ending, if not the details.

We sat quietly for a few minutes and the ensuing silence was filled up with the sounds of the night outside: moths that beat against the lighted window, the scuffle of small animals, the soft but menacing hoot of an owl. "Were you there?" I asked finally. "At the end?"

Prudence nodded. She may have filled her glass yet a third time; I was no longer paying such strict attention. But I could see her eyes had widened and gone glassy with tears. "It took place in Portsmouth. The morning was cold but there was quite a crowd, for it had been on everyone's tongue for weeks. She came in a cart, she did. They must have gone down Middle Road to Cow Lane and entered the field on South Street. Her hands were tied and her skirts too. I saw her right close up as she passed. Pale, straight, and silent. She was not looking at anything visible; she was looking, I could swear, into Eternity." She stopped for a moment to take another sip.

"There was a little rise and that's where they erected the gallows; Gallows Hill, it was called. That's where the cart stopped. When they put the noose round her neck, a little cry went up—there were many who believed her innocent, you see—and people kept turning toward Governor Wentworth's grand house on Pleasant Street. He'd granted her reprieves twice before. But not that day.

"There was a minister there too—I don't recall his name— and together they said a short prayer. She looked worn to the bone, the poor girl did. But like a bone, she had been scoured and bleached, everything stripped away. She was a walking spirit. Then there was a moment when she seemed to revive, like she was waking from a horrible dream. The color came into her face and she looked around her wildly and began begging for a few more moments to live. The minister laid his hand on

her shoulder and shook his head. The order was given and the
cart took off." Prudence's face was wet with tears. As was my
own. "Her eyes closed, and then opened, which is how they
stayed. I wish I could say it was quick. But it was not." She
sniffed loudly and used the corner of her apron to wipe her nose.
"There was no justice on that day," she said. "No justice at all."

Susannah looked at the clock. It was nine thirty. Corbin would
be here in an hour or so. She could have stopped typing and looked
over what she'd done, made some preliminary edits as she read;
that was how she usually worked. But not tonight. She was on fire
and she had to keep going, just to get it down. She'd edit later.

After that conversation, the past came rushing back at me with
the force of a stallion gone wild. I started having nightmares
again, the kind I had not had for years, and I'd bolt awake, sweat
beading my face, heart like a wagon wheel racing down a hill.

"What is it?" Joel would ask, drawing me into the safe circle
of his loving arms. "You were moaning in your sleep."

"Nothing," I always told him. "Night fancies."

"Night terrors, from the sound of it." But he'd settle back into
slumber, and when he was breathing steadily again, I'd slip from
his arms and out of bed. I'd wander the house—a different and
less welcoming place in dead of night—and check on my two
older children. Betsey was in the cradle near our bed, so I already
knew she was safe. Then I would go downstairs and into the
kitchen, where I'd tucked the little bottle of Prudence's elder-
berry wine on a shelf behind some of my earthenware bowls. I
was the only one who used them, so I knew my secret was safe.

I poured a little of the wine in a small cup—if Joel should
happen to wake, I did not want to be seen drinking a glass of

wine—and sipped it slowly. The bottle was nearly empty. I would have to ask Prudence for more. Or try to make it myself, once the fruit was in season again. After finishing my cup, I was calm enough to sleep again, so I crept back into bed, beside my lightly snoring husband. He would not have to wonder or ask where I'd gone.

I cannot say why I did not tell him my story. We were frank with each other about most things, and he had a tolerant and forgiving nature. But this secret was too heinous to reveal. All of the terrible events Prudence had recounted? I had helped set each and every one of them in motion. I had not meant to, and I certainly had not wanted to. But I had done it just the same. God did not judge us by our intentions, but by our actions. This much I knew.

If only we had not stopped at the Curriers' on that day. Or if it had been raining, which would have kept us from the meadow and the barn. Or if it had been one of the other girls who had found the baby. Or one of those boys. But no. It had been me, only me. And nothing would ever change that.

A couple of weeks later—it had already turned sharply colder and the leaves dropped from the trees as if all on cue—Prudence stopped by my house carrying one of her breads, a jar of honey, and a bundle. I thanked her for the bread and honey; though my appetite was better now, I still had a special hankering for the loaves she brought. She said nothing about the bundle and left it by her feet as we sat and visited. While we sipped our tea, we chatted of the usual things: a neighbor's cow had died, Prudence's youngest boy had an earache, there was to be a new minister at the church come spring. But when we had exhausted all these topics, she drew the bundle onto her lap and opened it.

"This belonged to her," she said. "It was there when my Josiah went to clean out the cell."

I looked down at the dark blue linsey-woolsey Prudence held. It was expertly crafted, with tightly rendered quilting in a lovely looping pattern. "Did she make it herself?"

"Yes." *Prudence nodded.* "I remember when her mother brought it to her; it may have helped keep her warm in that cell."

"Her mother didn't want it—after?" *I asked.*

"She never came for it. Josiah said I might keep it, but of course if she had ever asked for it back, I would have gladly given it to her. She'd been a sempstress, you know. And she'd taught her daughter well." *We both looked admiringly at Ruth's cunning handiwork.* "I just thought you might want to see it," *Prudence said.* "Given what we talked about and all."

"Thank you for showing it to me." *I reached over the increasing swell of my middle to touch the fabric and in that moment remembered the woman I'd seen sitting in the cart and being taken away. I had not believed her guilty then. I did not believe it now. Then I asked Prudence if she would like some more tea, and when she said yes, I rose, with some difficulty, to pour it.*

"Let me," *she said, and she refilled my cup as well. I thanked her and sank back down. I was carrying low, and the weight of the child inside me seemed always to be pulling me toward the ground. I would be glad when my time came around.*

We had a mild winter that year, not much snow at all. The woods around the house were alive with rabbits and deer; Joel went hunting with our son sometimes, and though the bloody carcasses they hauled home pained me, I was grateful for the food they put in my pot and on our table. I had now entered that phase of constant and ravening hunger, and could be found up late at night not tippling but consuming whole meals: chunks of cold stew eaten with my fingers straight from the pot, or the legs of fowl that I chewed on like an animal, my face greasy, my lips slick. Morsels of Prudence's bread that I did not slice but tore, scones or jam tarts I had made for the children, the sweetness cramming my mouth, making me want more, more, more. Joel was amused by my insatiable appetite. "You're carrying a giant," he'd say, fondling my taut belly, my ripe breasts, "or maybe a pair of giants." And then he'd pull me close for a kiss.

It was late December and I was home when my water gave way, soaking my dress, wetting the new Turkey carpet Joel had bought me as a Christmas gift. But I was not alarmed; I had been through this before and knew what to expect. I sent Pettingill over to get Prudence and she brought the other women to help prepare the groaning cake and beer for my lying in.

The labor was swift and fierce. I thrashed, I screamed, and once or twice I even cursed. Prudence kept the children and Joel away and she ministered to me herself, as tender as any mother. Finally, the baby came in a great, hot rush of blood and wet and pain. Not the pair of giants that Joel had teased about. Not even one giant. Only a tiny, dark-eyed girl who did not even cry when she came forth. "Her name is Ruth," I said when she had been wiped, wrapped, and placed at my breast. I saw Prudence look over at me sharply, but I did not hesitate. "Ruth Blay Eastman."

"Betsey, are you sure—?" Prudence began.

"Very sure," I said. "I've never been more sure of anything in my life."

I was tired then. So tired from travail. So after suckling little Ruth for a bit, I handed her to Prudence and went to sleep. When I awoke, perhaps an hour or two later, little Ruth was asleep in her cradle and everyone else but Prudence was gone. I could tell from her steady look that it was no coincidence that she was still there: she was waiting for me. And when she opened her mouth to speak, I knew I was right.

"Why?" she said.

"I had to." I did not pretend not to know what she meant; it would have been an insult to her memory to have done that.

"Why give her that burden? What if someone remembers? What will they think? And what if it brings her bad luck? Did you ever think of that?"

"It doesn't matter." My eyes strayed to the tiny infant in her swaddling. "I owed it to Ruth, because I am responsible for her death."

"What are you talking about? Have you gone mad? I'd say you'd been drinking too much of that elderberry wine, but I've been here the whole time, so I know you haven't."

"I haven't gone mad, and no, I'm not drunk. I know what I know. And though I have never spoken of this since my parents died—not to Joel, not to anyone—I will tell you because I think you deserve to know. And when you do, you will understand." I told her then, the story unspooling from my lips just the way it did here, in these pages. The day in June, the barn, the floorboards—and what I found beneath them. "If I hadn't come upon that infant, Ruth Blay never would have been indicted, tried, or convicted. So I'm the one responsible for her death, just as sure as if I'd tied the noose myself."

"Don't ever say such a thing! Don't even think it!" The sharp sound of Prudence's words woke little Ruth and she hurried over to rock the cradle. When the child slept again, she turned to me. "You couldn't have known. No one could. The Lord works in mysterious ways that we'll never understand. But He guided you into that barn and He was there when you lifted the floorboards. It's not our place to question why."

I had not thought about it in this way before, but it brought me no comfort, no peace. This was not a Divine plan, because

*if it were, I could have no business with the Lord ever again.
No, this was the Devil's work, pure and simple. "You may be
right," I said finally, "though I cannot for the life of me see how.
But at the very least I will name my child for her, the one I
wronged, albeit unwittingly. For I believe to this day that she
was more sinned against than sinning. And I'll believe that until
the day I die."*

Susannah actually let out a sigh when she typed those words,
a long, audible exhalation. There, she had done it, what she'd set
out to do. Now she could only hope that Tasha would respond
enthusiastically and allow her to fill in the blanks. She saved the
document and turned off the laptop. Outside the room where she
sat, the sun shone on Primrose Pond and the trees that encircled
it had started to come into leaf: tentative, shiny, green. The long
winter was finally over.

When she had started delving into Ruth's story, Susannah had
no idea that her mother had also given birth to a child who was
technically illegitimate. But the differences in the two narratives
outweighed any superficial similarities.

Claire had had the protection of her husband, and hid the secret
of Susannah's parentage quite well. Even if her husband had known,
he seemed to have been willing to maintain the fiction. And if that
fiction had been exposed, Claire's options would have been far from
bleak. Had Warren left her, she could have raised her daughter on
her own. Or Dave Renfew might have acknowledged paternity. So
many things would have been possible.

Yet despite all that, Susannah could not help but see the two
stories as linked, at least in the winking constellation that made
up her firmament. Was Claire frightened when she first learned
she was pregnant? Did she ever consider having an abortion? Or

telling Warren? And was it hard to pretend that the child she carried belonged to the man she had betrayed? Susannah knew that she would never have answers to these questions. But they would never stop circling, round and round, in her mind.

She heard a car pull up and stop, then a door slam. Corbin. She'd given him a key, to let himself in. Suddenly she couldn't wait to see him. She hurried down the stairs so she could meet him halfway.

FORTY

Loaded down with wallpaper and fabric samples, Susannah followed Alice into her house. It was May, and the woods around the house were raucous with twittering birds; in the last week or so, Susannah had seen mushrooms dotting the damp earth under the trees, gray rabbits and tawny chipmunks scurrying by, and this morning she saw a deep blue butterfly with a thin white border around its wings hovering right outside the kitchen window. Spring had finally come to Primrose Pond.

Alice glanced around the room, nodding. "It looks very good, don't you think?" The contractors had finished the repair work and she was moving back home. The samples Susannah toted were to be used in Alice's ever expanding redecoration scheme; she now planned to redo the entire first floor.

"Very good," Susannah said. She actually felt a little sad that Alice was leaving. She'd gotten used to having her there, and both of the kids loved her—a kind of grandmotherly figure, if not an actual grandmother. For Susannah, she was not a mother, though. But she was the connection to Dave. Her father. The words still did not quite gel.

"Here, let me take all that." Alice set the swatches of material and rolls of patterned paper on a marble-topped table near the door. "There's something I want to show you." She led Susannah through the kitchen to a door; beyond that door was what looked like a waiting room. Dr. Dave's office. "After he died, I never could bring myself to touch any of this," she said.

Susannah looked around at the small sofa, basket of toys, and Norman Rockwell prints, all featuring children, hanging on the walls. A wooden dollhouse sat on a low table in one corner. There was a short hallway with two open doorways and she walked toward them—examination rooms, she supposed, though they seemed pretty empty now.

"His office was back here," said Alice. Susannah followed her toward the end of the hallway. The door was shut, but Alice opened it and led her inside. Susannah began to hear a small whirring or even roaring in her ears. Dr. Dave's space. Her father's space. Dave Renfew was not her father in any sense of the word that truly mattered. Except that he was. She took in the oak desk and swivel chair, the medical tomes that lined one wall, the diplomas that hung on the other. There were photos too, lots of them. In one of them he wore that red bow tie. Notes and drawings, presumably from his young patients, were on that wall as well, an outpouring of affection and gratitude, rendered in brightly colored Crayolas.

She walked over to the chair. "May I?" she asked. Alice nodded and she sat down. A brass holder held several sharpened pencils and a couple of black pens.

A leather-trimmed blotter, a bulging Rolodex, and a prescription pad whose edges had curled and browned. Nothing had been moved or changed. Susannah reached out to touch the swirling, jewel-like colors of a glass paperweight. It seemed to be lit from within.

"I bought him that in Venice one year. All the children loved it," Alice said. "He'd let them hold it while he was talking to their parents."

"I imagine it was very soothing."

"That desk—that's where I found the poem."

"Were there any more?"

"Not that I found. Before he died, he shredded most everything, I think. Somehow he missed that."

"Do you think he wanted you to find it?"

Alice looked like she was considering the question. "I don't know," she said finally. "He loved me, I do know that. And he wouldn't have wanted to hurt me."

"No, he didn't. I'm sure of that." Susannah thought of the note that had been tucked into the pages of the book that she had happened upon back in January. "Because I found something he wrote to my mother that said as much. He loved you, Alice. And my mother loved my father."

Alice bowed her head and clasped her hands. Then she looked up. "Is it possible to love two people at the same time?"

Now it was Susannah who paused. What if she'd met Corbin again while Charlie was still alive? Would she have succumbed to her feelings for him? "I'm not sure," she said finally. "I've never been tested that way." She wanted to open a drawer, but that didn't feel right, so she picked up the prescription pad. There was something written on it, and she realized that she recognized the writing, the same writing that she'd seen in the note. Seeing it was another small shock, but one that helped confirm her new understanding. "What are you planning to do with this space?"

"I thought I would just leave it," she said. "I've got plenty of room in the house, and I don't need it. But now I've changed my mind. Time to let it go."

"Or transform it," said Susannah. "Turn it into something new."

Alice was nodding. "Yes, that's a better way to look at it."

"I think so too." Susannah's hand returned to the paperweight. "I'm wondering . . . maybe you'd let me have something that was his . . . a keepsake of some kind."

"I'll give you some photos," Alice said. "And take the paperweight. I can see that you like it."

"I like it very much." She ran a finger over the wavy pattern. "But you gave it to him."

"And now I'm giving it to you."

Susannah picked it up, the smooth weight of it pleasing in her hand. "I'm going to tell them about you. About us, really. I just need to find the right time."

"You'll know when it's right." Alice did not ask what she meant; she seemed to understand right away. "There's no rush."

Susannah was ready to leave the office when Alice put a hand on her arm. "There is one more thing I think I should say to you."

"What's that?"

"I'm sorry."

"Sorry?" Susannah was confused.

"For how I behaved with Calista. I was wrong to step in between the two of you. I told myself it was because I wanted what was best for her. And that wasn't untrue. It just wasn't the whole story."

"And what was the whole story?"

"That I was doing it for me. To fill some loneliness I'd been harboring for years. An emptiness. An ache."

"You really wanted a child."

"I really did. But that didn't give me the right to try to take yours."

Susannah put her arms around Alice, and for a few seconds held her very tight.

FORTY-ONE

Susannah walked back to her own house slowly, stopping to pick some wildflowers—tall pinks, purples, and blues whose names she had yet to learn—for her kitchen table. As she arranged the flowers in an old glass milk bottle, she thought about Alice's apology. She had not realized how much she had needed it until it was offered. Maybe the two of them would become, if not friends, then something else, something they had yet to invent.

Susannah spent the rest of the morning getting her living room back in order. She repositioned chairs and moved the bed and folded up the screen near the door. Corbin would help her bring them to store in the garage; he would be over tonight. Maybe later in the month she would have a yard sale—everyone around here seemed to do that. Alice could join her if she wanted. She suspected that there would be many things Alice was ready to let go of now.

After finishing in the living room, Susannah went upstairs to her laptop. The week before, she had thought she was ready to

send the material she'd been working on all these months to
Tasha. In addition to the sample pages—she had about fifty in
all—she had assembled a timeline of the events she'd narrated.
She hoped it would help Tasha see the scope of the story. Then
she had realized there was something missing, a postscript, as it
were. And so she wrote a coda, purely fictional, but in her mind
satisfying. There was no evidence whatsoever that Betsey's life
had unfolded in this way. But it was Susannah's need for
symmetry—and to give some modicum of peace to her character—
that impelled her to write it as she did.

*About a year after little Ruth's birth, Prudence took sick and
died. With her death, so died my secret. I had told no one else
and I never would. But once I had Ruth's namesake in my
life—a serious, dark-haired child whose needlework was uncom-
monly fine—I began to think of her, the other, more often than
I had in recent years. I felt the need to atone for my sin against
her. Yet it was not clear how I might do this. Then the path
opened before me; why had I not seen it before?*

*I had, as I said, many children, and so I was well versed in
what to expect from the process of bringing them forth, and I
had assisted in many births in the area, as was the custom. I
noticed that the other women present began to defer to my judgment and seek my advice; I became, for all practical purposes,
a midwife, skilled in delivering newborns and easing hardship
for their laboring mothers. Sometimes a child died, or a mother,
but more often than not the babes I delivered and their mothers
lived and thrived. So I developed something of a reputation in
these parts.*

*I began to experiment with herbal remedies of my own devis-
ing to mute the pain, and also with implements to aid in the*

deliveries, first trying silver serving spoons or tongs to help grab on to a babe that would not slide easily down the narrow passage. What would my Sunday dinner guests have thought had they known! Later, I went to the village coppersmith and had him make me larger versions of both, with slight alterations I had requested. When he asked what my purpose with these implements was, I demurred. Though no witches had been burned in New England for a long while, I still thought it was best to be circumspect. A woman who knew too much—about the birthing process or anything else—was considered suspicious.

The girl came to me one stifling evening in August, when nightfall did nothing to cool the air and the insects hummed and buzzed urgently in the dark. I had never seen her before; she was not from around here. Short and slight, from the back she resembled a child. But when viewed from the front, the roundness straining against her gown was clear for all to see. She told me she had a husband, and that he was away. This was a lie, of course. I knew that she had no husband—and yet here she was, belly as big as the moon. Poor poppet!

"What's your name, child?" I asked.

"Anne Smith," she said. Another lie. "I was told you could help me," she said. "The pains have started and I think my time is near."

"The water—has that broken yet?"

She nodded, and her eyes held the glazed terror of a rabbit caught in the jaws of a fox.

"Well, let's get you settled and see what's what."

By this time, Joel had built a guest cottage set a little ways from the house, and it was sometimes used when our home overflowed with company. But when it was empty, I delivered the babies there. There was a back room that I claimed, with a *clean, soft bed, plenty of fresh linens, and a little fireplace where I could heat the water. I kept my copper implements in that room, in a locked trunk and well hidden from prying eyes.*

I had the girl Anne—if that's what she told me, I would not challenge her—lie down and loosen her garments so I could see how far along she was. To my surprise, she was nearly ready to start the pushing, so I had her disrobe and slip into one of the cambric shifts I kept folded and stacked for just this purpose. I might have asked one of the other women I knew to help, but I sensed she would not want this and so I did not. Besides, it looked as if it were going to be an easy birth. I was confident I could manage it on my own.

I was right. The birthing went swiftly, and she did not cry out, only twisted her head against the pillow and contorted her mouth terribly from the pain. Strands of her brown hair had come loose and stuck to her forehead; I smoothed them away and pressed a cool cloth to the spot.

"You are so kind—" She stopped, clearly gripped by the convulsion. But it was all over quickly and once I had washed and swaddled the babe—a fine rosy boy, bald as an egg—I placed him in her arms. It was then that she started to weep, great torrents of tears splashing down and leaving dark spots on the cambric.

"What is it?" I said, though I knew. "It's all done now—you have your boy, and he's a nice big one too. Who would have thought a little wisp of a girl like you would have such a strapping baby?"

She cried harder and I brought another cool compress for her wet, mottled face. "I lied." She hiccupped. "He has no father. At least no father who will claim him."

"Ah," I said. "I see." And of course I did. It was an old story. The oldest. Men will play, women must pay.

"I don't know what to do! My father sent me away and my mother would not go against him. I have nowhere to go, no one to help me—"

"You're wrong," I said. "You have me."

"You?"

"I will help you. And it will be our secret. It was dark when you came, wasn't it? No one saw you."

"No one," she said.

"Good," I said. "That's important."

"What will you do?"

I looked straight at her. "The less you know, the better." Then I got her cleaned up and helped her stand. She held the infant— quite tenderly, I thought—while I stripped and changed the bedding. Then I brought her some supper and tucked the two of them in. "Don't light the fire or a candle, or make any noise at all. I'll be back soon."

"Is there anything I can do?" she asked.

"Feed your son," I told her. "And then kiss him good-bye."

While she was eating, I went out and saddled Harley, the gentle gelding that Joel had bought for me. As it happened, Joel was away on business in Concord and was spending the night there with one of our sons. Good. What I planned to do was best known by as few as possible.

The horse was unused to seeing me here at night and pressed his muzzle into my hand, looking for an apple. "Not now," I told him. "Later." It was pitch dark but I had a lantern and the horse knew the way out of the barn, across the meadow, and to the pebbled road that led toward Jaffrey. We rode along quietly, and when we got to the house I tied up the horse to the iron hitching post and knocked softly on the door.

The man who opened it had broad shoulders and heavyset arms. His face, in the humid night, was slightly flushed and I could see the dark stubble on his unshaven cheeks. "Betsey!" he said. He was surprised to see me. But not unhappy. "Are you here because—?"

"I am," I said. "And you'd better hurry. I want it all done before morning."

He ushered me inside and called out, "Mary, it's Betsey Eastman! Betsey's come!"

A woman hurried to the doorway, a few just-starting-to-gray curls escaping from her linen cap. "May the Lord be praised," she said softly when she saw me. "We'll be there as soon as we can."

"I'll be ready." Then I turned and went back out to Harley, who had been waiting patiently for me. I had an apple concealed in my dress pocket, but I did not want to tarry; I would give it to him when we were at the barn again.

The Wainwrights—that was their name—arrived soon after, and Anne handed over the boy to them. Through the years, I'd delivered five or six—I had lost count—of Mary Wainwright's babes, all of them born dead, save one, and he'd lived less than an hour. I'd told Mary that if there were ever a babe in need of a mother, I would call on her. Now that time had come.

They took the child with a reverence that was truly touching to see, and stole away quietly, using the dark to cloak their journey. I kept Anne hidden in my birthing room all the next day, and at dusk the following evening I took her to the home of friends in Somerset, with whom she had secured a ride to Portsmouth. She hugged me good-bye, and I insisted she take a small parcel of food and another dress—she had almost nothing with her—and she promised to repay me when she could.

"That won't be necessary," I told her. "You have already repaid me, more than you can ever know." Because it was that other one I was thinking of, the one who'd come to Salisbury alone and friendless and found not comfort, not kindness, but— because of me—sorrow and death.

Some years later—it might have been three, it might have been four—I got a letter from that girl. She had indeed gone to Portsmouth and found work in a tavern. This might have led to a life of moral degradation and ruin. Instead, she caught the fancy of an older gentleman, a widower who owned a fleet of whaling vessels, and he married her. He set her up in a very fine house, with maidservants and a butler, while he trolled the high seas in search of the whales and their precious oil. She had a daughter the first year of their marriage, and then a son. All this she put forth in her letter, and included were some bills whose value far exceeded that of a loaf of bread, a slab of ham, and an oft-mended old dress.

Of course there had been curiosity about the Wainwrights' new baby—and speculation, both of which were followed by a brief formal inquiry. I told the magistrate that the child, a foundling, had been left in a basket at my doorstep, probably because of my reputation as a midwife, and though there was no witness to confirm my story, there was none to deny it either. After a while the talk died down. The girl who had given him up had shed her old identity. No one knew her or where she had come from, and until her letter arrived, no one knew where she had gone either. After reading it twice, I destroyed it, ripping it into smaller and smaller pieces and then burning those in the hearth until only ash remained. The child slid seamlessly into his new life and became known as Will, the Wainwrights' darling boy, cynosure of their lives. That was all anyone ever needed to know. My part in the story was never revealed. Until now.

Susannah attached the timeline and the sample pages to the e-mail she had composed to Tasha.

Here it is. You said I had to decide if I was telling Ruth's story or Betsey's. I think the answer is that I'm telling both. In my mind, the two are bound together, braided as tightly as wires. Betsey's actions had fatal consequences for Ruth, and Ruth's tragic death shaped Betsey's life; they truly can't be separated.

What you're seeing here is just the rudimentary mapping out of the story. I'll need to add more—about Betsey, about Ruth, and the times in which each woman lived. Ruth's life has a clear and tragic arc. But this is not true of Betsey and Betsey needs her story too. And in the absence of the factual material, I plan to fill in from my imagination. I've already written a scene in which Betsey has a small role in the birth of a neighbor's child, and another in which her work as a midwife is explained and described.

Thanks for your vote of confidence, and for letting me pursue this unfamiliar path; I think it will take me to a place we both want to go.

Then she hit send. The answer, which Susannah read while sitting at the desk in her bedroom, took only a few days to arrive. Tasha wasn't one to let things linger.

I think you've nailed it, Susannah. Or in any case, you've convinced me that this story, Ruth's and Betsey's, is worth telling and that you're the woman to do it. I think it's going to be a very strong book—maybe your very best. I'll get the contracts department to draw up the paperwork. What do you think about a deadline of January 7? Let me know; excited to be a part of your new journey.

Yes. Tasha said yes! Susannah would get to write her book. She hadn't realized how happy this would make her until the possibility had become a reality. She reread the e-mail. January 7. That would be just a little over a year since she had first moved back here, to this town, this house, this new and surprising life.

Her eyes strayed out the window to the pond, which was swollen from all the snow this past winter; the water lapped high along the shoreline.

Last January, she could not have imagined Corbin or Alice or Dave, and yet all three had become so important, even vital to her. She could not have imagined Ruth or Betsey either; had she not come here, to Primrose Pond, their stories would not have ever been known to her. Sometimes, she still felt that rough blade of grief over Charlie's death hack through her—that would never entirely go away. But now she had, if not everything, then so much: love where she had not expected to find it, work she truly and deeply wanted to complete. Her children were thriving. And it was finally spring—the air was mild, and clusters of tulips and late daffodils had cropped up around the house. Susannah reached out to stroke the glass paperweight Alice had given her, the convex surface smooth under her fingers, the swirled, shining colors a tiny counterpoint to the glittering surface just beyond the window's frame.

EPILOGUE

~~~~~~

Susannah dips first her foot and then her ankle into the placid water of Primrose Pond. Although it's early August, the water is cool. No matter—to her, it's perfect, and she wades out until she's waist deep before diving in. Then she propels herself under the surface for a few seconds before emerging again. The water is very clear. Even at this depth, she can see her legs, and even her toes, beneath her. Scanning the horizon, she can make out the houses across the pond. They are mostly hidden by the trees' lush growth; last winter's heavy snow has created dense canopies all around. The birch trees stand out, white and slender, amid the green, and pockets of cattails cluster along the banks.

Laughter erupts from the wooden raft a few yards away. There's Calista, red hair a shock in the sun. While her friends—there are three, all girls—are clad in skimpy bikinis, Calista wears a discreetly dotted one-piece from the 1940s that she and Alice found in a thrift shop in Maine; it makes the other girls' choices seem cheap and obvious. When Calista catches sight of her, her arm shoots up and she waves. The deep freeze of the winter is over, and although there are still moments of friction, by and large her prodigal daughter has returned.

Jack is on the raft too, with a couple of his friends, including Gilda, the pretty blonde from across the pond. He's grown even more these last months, and his face is losing the soft curves of boyhood so quickly that Susannah fears she won't even be able to remember what they were like.

Pushing her soaked, mink brown hair out of her face, Susannah swims over to the raft to join them. She hoists herself up and the kids shift over to make room for her. "Look, Mom—there's Alice. And she brought Panda with her!" Calista starts to swim toward the elderly figure walking down the path. Alice wears a long white caftan covered in tiny embroidered flowers, a large straw hat, and large, dark glasses. In her arms is a small brindle Pomeranian: Panda. Calista reaches the dock and pulls herself out of the water so she can hurry up the path to meet Alice.

Although Alice and Susannah have moved tentatively toward each other, Susannah has to accept that their relationship will always have an undercurrent of—what, tension? Resentment? Alice still has to live with the knowledge of Dave's betrayal, and Susannah is the concrete proof of it. Explaining the story to Calista and Jack had brought all that up again. And Susannah cannot entirely forget those months when Alice seemed almost her enemy, intent on wooing her child away from her. But the kids seem oblivious to these undercurrents, and effortlessly cast Alice in the role of grandmother; Susannah can see how their easy acceptance and affection have helped to soften the spiky edges.

The dog starts squirming when she sees Calista, and Alice hands her over. After Emma's death in the fire, Susannah had combed the region looking for a rescue poodle for Alice. And she'd

376 YONA ZELDIS McDONOUGH

found what she thought was the perfect one: a year-old apricot standard owned by a family in Newington whose youngest child developed a severe allergy to the supposedly hypoallergenic dog. But to her surprise, Alice declined. "Emma was the poodle to define all poodles," she said. "I couldn't ever have another." And instead, she found Panda—the anti-poodle.

As Calista stands cooing over the fluffy little dog, Polly Schultz, who is visiting for the week, walks down the path, flip-flops smacking loudly. She has a big striped towel under one arm and a paperback under the other. "Are you coming in?" Susannah calls out to her.

"Not yet," Polly calls back. "Later."

The kids jump back in the water to splash and play. Susannah is alone on the raft, whose gray, peeling paint is enlivened by velvety green pelts of moss. The sun, steadily beating down, is warm on her skin and she closes her eyes.

"Want to go for a ride?"

She opens them again to see Corbin, paddling straight toward her in a canoe.

He is shirtless and deeply tanned; he holds the paddle with a confident grip. "Let's swim instead," she says. So he brings the canoe in, ties it securely to the dock, and swims back out to the raft. Then he waits, treading water, as she jackknifes in. Once again, she is embraced and enveloped by the cool ripples.

When she surfaces, she is looking right into his face, his blue eyes bright—oh, so bright—in the late summer sun. He's not Charlie, and he can never take Charlie's place. But she loves him and he loves her. They've even talked about moving in together, though for now, shuttling between the two houses seems to be working just fine. She leans in, their foreheads so close they are touching. Then they begin to swim in tandem, parallel to the grassy banks of the pond. To Susannah, it seems like they could keep on swimming forever.

ACKNOWLEDGMENTS

I would like to thank Jennie Fields and Sally Schloss for their early reading of this manuscript, Sarah Rux at the Portsmouth Historical Society for sharing with me the one item that may have belonged to Ruth Blay, and Carolyn Marvin, whose excellent and informative book, *Hanging Ruth Blay: An Eighteenth-Century New Hampshire Tragedy*, ignited my interest in the subject. Also special thanks to my sister-in-law, Roni Brown, for walking with me in Blay's footsteps, and for not leaving the cemetery in Portsmouth until we had found the grim spot where Ruth was hanged.

Tracy Bernstein is a perfect dream of an editor with whom I have now been privileged to work a fourth time, and Judith Ehrlich, my stellar agent and trusted friend, always pushes me a little further than I think I can go. Finally, I offer unending gratitude to my husband, Paul McDonough, New Hampshire native, Portsmouth son; it is because of him that I have come to cherish the place, and its stories, as my own.

THE

HOUSE

ON

PRIMROSE

POND

Yona Zeldis McDonough

This Conversation Guide is intended to enrich the
individual reading experience, as well as encourage us
to explore these topics together—because books,
and life, are meant for sharing.

A CONVERSATION WITH
YONA ZELDIS McDONOUGH

Q. Your past novels have been set in or near New York City; why did you make the leap to New Hampshire?

A. New York was always my default setting. With the exception of four years in college and a year abroad, I've lived in New York my whole life. So it was easy to set my books there, especially around Park Slope, Brooklyn, where I have lived since 1992. But lately I began to feel restless in the 'hood and sought to move beyond it. The question was: where? A writer needs to have sufficient familiarity with a place to make it come alive on the page. And that takes more than Google research. So I gravitated to New Hampshire, my husband's home state. We have spent many happy summers there in a cottage on a lake, which inspired the setting of *The House on Primrose Pond*. I love the spot dearly and felt I could write about it with the necessary authenticity and passion.

Q. How did you come to write about Ruth Blay?

A. The characters of Susannah and Alice came to me quickly, as did as their respective backstories. Yet I had an urge to make the story bigger than them. I looked to New Hampshire history (this is where Google is very effective!) for inspiration. I was thinking of something on a grand scale—a fire or a flood. Instead I stumbled on Ruth Blay, and once I did, I was hooked. The story felt to me so shocking yet, in another way, so familiar. The man who got Blay pregnant was never even named, yet she went to her death for her "crime." Chilling. But not surprising.

Q. How closely did you stick to the facts when writing her story?

A. I tried to keep to the facts of Blay's life as best I could, though not a lot is known about her. I was able to see and examine actual documents pertaining to the trial housed in the state archives in Concord, New Hampshire, and I visited the cemetery in Portsmouth where she was hanged. I also saw the tattered remains of a garment that is thought to have been hers.

Q. What about Betsey Pettingill?

A. Even less is known about Betsey Pettingill's life, which gave me more room to invent and imagine it. I chose to make Betsey the narrator of the novel-within-the-novel, which meant I had to conjure what she might have thought and felt, as well as create fictional events to round out her very long life. I do know that she expressed remorse for her role, however inadvertent, in Blay's death, and I used that information to shape her character.

Q. Can you talk about the poetry in the novel? Was that a challenge to write?

A. I hold with Wallace Stevens, who said, "Poetry is the supreme fiction." How I wish I could really write it! But since the poet in the novel is an amateur, I felt liberated from having to write verse that had real merit on its own. Instead, the poems I wrote formed a little synopsis of the romance he and Claire Gilmore had. The first poem is a kind of seduction, a plea. The second is an exultation and celebration. The final one is a lament. Even though I felt I was far outside my comfort zone, I really did enjoy writing the poems.

Q. The novel contains several letters, e-mails, texts, et cetera. Why did you choose to include those things?

A. This is a quest novel, and as such, it includes many clues. These clues were often in a written format, like the poems that Susannah finds and the unsigned love note intended for her mother. I wanted to include these things to add to the texture of the novel and to layer it with that kind of quotidian yet essential detail. Our lives are filled with these bits and pieces, and I felt they would have a place in the story.

Q. Apart from two chapters, the novel is told from Susannah's point of view; why did you make those exceptions?

A. I knew that this was Susannah's story from early on. But Alice has a pivotal role, and often her behavior can seem puzzling, inappropriate, or even bizarre. I felt I needed a couple of chapters from her point of view so that her particular history could be explored and understood. Even though she makes some inadvisable choices, those choices are in part determined by her disappointments, longings, and regrets. I wanted the reader to know her better, and judge her less.

Q. You have not written anything historical before. Is this a new direction you'll be following in the future?

A. I found this foray into the eighteenth and nineteenth centuries kind of thrilling, and, yes, I am eager to try my hand at historical fiction again. I am working on a novel set in 1947 now, and I have an idea for a novel set in New Orleans, around 1917. I'm eager to dig in!

QUESTIONS FOR DISCUSSION

1. Susannah feels she is indirectly responsible for her husband's death; do you agree or disagree?

2. What do you think drives Susannah's burning need to find out about her mother's secret life? What would you do in her situation?

3. Do you feel Alice's behavior toward Calista is justifiable, or is she seriously overstepping?

4. Susannah might easily have kept to herself what she found out about Dr. Dave. Do you think she is right or wrong to share it with Alice?

5. In what ways do you identify with Calista's need to separate herself from her mother or with Susannah's pain at the separation?

6. What is the connection between Susannah's story and Betsey's?

7. After some pretty bad behavior, Susannah gives Corbin another chance; what would you have done?

8. Do you imagine it's likely they will stay together? Why or why not?

Yona Zeldis McDonough is the author of the novels *You Were Meant for Me, Two of a Kind, A Wedding in Great Neck, Breaking the Bank, In Dahlia's Wake,* and *The Four Temperaments,* as well as twenty-six books for children. She is also the editor of two essay collections and the fiction editor at *Lilith* magazine. Her short fiction, articles, and essays have been published in anthologies and in numerous magazines and newspapers. She lives in Brooklyn, New York, with her husband and two children.

CONNECT ONLINE

yonazeldismcdonough.com